## *Praise for* Next To Last Chance

Louisa Dixon tackles sexism, racism, and corrupt politics in a fast-paced debut that is sure to signal a long run for this talented newcomer.

*—Ft. Lauderdale Sun Sentinel*

By the time you finish this tale of Southern greed and evil, you'll probably look forward to the next book on Laura Owen's continuing job as Safety Commissioner, but won't wonder at all why Louisa Dixon has long since left that position.

*—Independent Publisher*

Written by a former commissioner of the Mississippi Highway Patrol, [*Next To Last Chance*] has an insider's special knowledge working for it as the main character, a woman not unlike the author, finds herself in the midst of drug wars and political murders for a fast-paced story worth reading.

*—Bookviews*

In a genuine, easy going style ... Louisa Dixon bares her soul through Laura Owen: wife, mom, and den mother to nearly 500 of the toughest men to patrol the highways.

*—Clarion Ledger*

ALSO BY LOUISA DIXON

*Next To Last Chance*

# OUTSIDE CHANCE

# OUTSIDE CHANCE

*Louisa Dixon*

GENESIS PRESS

Genesis Press, Inc.
315 Third Avenue North
Columbus, Mississippi 39701

Outside Chance

ISBN 1-885478-63-1

Printed in the United States of America

FIRST EDITION

*For Jerry and Ben*

*And for those men and women of the Department of Public Safety who imagined what could be and never quit trying to achieve it.*

# OUTSIDE CHANCE

# ONE

Master Sergeant Trey Turner, a criminal investigator for the State Patrol, left the barn doors wide open to watch for the woman's car leaving the main house. He was butchering a buck that had been hanging, aging, in the refrigerated meat locker. The predawn sky over Saragossa, thirty miles from the mercury-vapor glow of Jackson, Mississippi, was still a star-studded black.

Trey figured it wouldn't be much longer—little Miss Junior Executive never allowed herself to be late for the office, even when she spent the night with his neighbor and friend, Brent Wexler. She was a pert little thing, often lounging around in her skin-tight exercise outfit and perfect makeup, and always smiling, showing off her blindingly white teeth. The woman was obviously betting Brent would dump his estranged wife, Grace, for her, because whenever Brent so much as crooked his finger, she obediently trotted out to the farm to share his bed.

What a little fool.

Trey turned back to the deer carcass, a huge animal, killed right there at the farm. Since the cattle had been moved off the lower hundred acres in preparation for planting pine trees, the deer had begun to graze more freely. Though Brent and Trey did most of their hunting in Second Creek, when they'd heard this fellow snorting in the woods at the edge of the pasture, they hadn't been able to resist the urge. The afternoon set aside to tear down fencing was lost to the frenzy of the chase, as they wildly pursued the animal through the woods until they trapped him. He was twelve points—a big sucker.

Car noises broke the silence. Trey looked up from the stainless steel drain table to see her silver Honda practically fly past. She must be late.

At least she was gone.

The freezer was filled with neatly stacked white packages of steaks and filets when Brent appeared an hour and a half later, looking distinctly reinvigorated and ready for the corporate battlefield.

"Mornin'," Trey called out as Brent Wexler carefully stepped closer, guarding his polished tassel loafers from the bits of flesh that littered the floor. Brent was over six feet, a shade taller than Trey, but ten years older. Though not nearly as muscular as Trey, Brent was in terrific shape for a man of fifty-six. He was the founder and president of Wexler, Inc., an extremely successful road, bridge, and foundation construction company. He was also Governor Gibbs Carver's closest advisor and in charge of all fund raising for Carver's political campaigns.

"And a good morning to you," Brent replied, sickeningly chipper.

"Got that buck in the freezer this morning. It'll be some fine dining."

"Perfect timing. I'll be needing a good bit of it this weekend."

"Something happening?"

"We've got guests at the camp—Reed Morgan."

Trey knew the Western District Highway Commissioner all too well. He held back a sneer.

"He invited himself," Brent apologized. "Probably wants

something from me."

"More money, I'll bet," Trey said sourly.

"And not wanting to be stuck with him alone, I invited some other people."

Trey just nodded. His second job, and the one he vastly preferred, was working for Brent, either helping out at the farm, or overseeing the Red Crown Hunt Club in Second Creek, Mississippi. In the latter, he'd had substantial practice hiding his disdain for some of the members and guests.

"Got to keep up relationships," Brent offered as explanation.

"Yeah, but at the club?"

"Didn't have a diplomatic way out of it. By the way, are you available Tuesday next to set up a little barbecue at the office?"

"Sure."

"No problem getting the time off?"

"I've got so much vacation time built up, I could take off next year and still have some left over."

"Good. The Governor and I want to feed a few legislators, but I don't want to bring them out here. Got to do it before my snorkeling trip to Roatan."

"When do you leave exactly?"

"Last of the month. Can't wait."

■ ■ ■ ■

"Hurry up, Will," called Laura Owen, Commissioner of Public Safety and head of the State Patrol for Mississippi, to her six-year-old son. "Get Ranger's gate up and put your rain jacket on."

"Ohhh, Momma," Will whined.

"All right," Laura conceded. "Just take it with you."

She chose the shorter of two trench coats and pulled it on over her straight wool skirt and black sweater. Barely five-foot-three in heels with her curly hair fluffed up, the longer coat made her look like she was standing in a hole.

"I wanna open the garage door myself," called Will as he raced past her, stuffing a jacket into his backpack.

"Do you have your library books?"

"Yes, ma'am."

Laura locked the house to the rattle of the garage door opening. It reached the top of the garage ceiling and stopped as she was depositing her briefcase behind the seat of her state car, a navy blue Ford Crown Vic. Then it started to close again.

"Will Owen!" she said, with more anger in her voice than the transgression deserved.

"I didn't mean to," said Will. "Honest." The door stopped and then began opening again.

"Look me square in the eyes, young man, and tell me that again," Laura said, cranking the engine. Two police band radios came to life, emitting their normal morning jabber. The corners of her son's mouth began to curl into a smile. "Do that once more, and I'll take the door control away for good," she warned, backing the car out. "Seat belts."

"Can I get the newspaper?" Will asked as Laura drove down the drive.

"Nope, it's on my side today." Laura pulled up next to a plastic bag on the edge of the driveway, opened her door, and scooped up the newspaper, handing it to Will.

"See if you can read me the headlines, please."

Will unwrapped the paper and stared at the front page, searching for words that he knew. Laura glanced over and pointed to a photograph of Gibbs Carver. "There's the Governor."

"I can't read anything, Momma, the words are too big," said Will, discouraged.

"That's okay. Try sounding out the words under that picture. You can always spell what you don't know."

"Car..."

"Carver," Laura supplied.

"Will," he said. "There's my name!"

"It's not your name. It's the word *will*, as in 'Carver will.' Keep going."

"I don't know this next word."

"Spell it."

"V-E-T-O."

"Carver will veto," said Laura. "Great," she muttered.

"What does "veto" mean?"

"It means he'll stop it from happening, or try to."

"P-A-Y," Will spelled.

"Carver will veto pay. I bet the next word is R-A-I-S-E."

"How'd you know that?"

"Figured it out. You'll be able to do that one day."

Will looked at his mother's gloomy face. "Is that bad, Momma?"

"It's not good."

"Want me to try another one?"

"No, Sweetheart," Laura said frowning. "That was more than enough."

"What's wrong?"

"Just office stuff. Nothing you need to worry about."

Will pulled out the second section, featuring a huge diamondback rattlesnake.

"Cool," he said, admiringly. "Look at this snake."

"I'd rather not."

■ ■ ■ ■

Neither the House of Representatives nor the State Senate was reconvening until after two in the afternoon, so only a few cars were in the Capitol parking lot when Laura pulled in just before eight. She parked under the portico in the spot reserved for official vehicles and the Governor's car, and hurried inside, moving so fast her raincoat billowed out behind her like a cape.

"Good morning, Commissioner," said one of the two capitol guards seated inside the glass-walled office.

"Good morning, gentlemen," Laura answered curtly, preoccupied with rehearsing her remarks. Her words were barely heard above the quick thrumming of her low heels on the marble floors, which reverberated down the long hallways. She noticed one guard's quick smile at his companion and the thump of his big finger on the newspaper's front page. As he looked away, Laura slowed down to hear him say, "A buck says she's angry about this."

Laura was a complete enigma to many in the law enforcement community of the state and she knew it. They didn't know what to make of her, and most retreated to hostility in their confusion. But the Capitol Police and the State Patrol—the two groups who saw how hard she was working—were more charitable; some even harbored a grudging admiration.

She took some comfort in the second guard's response. "I'm betting on her and I hope we get to ride the Patrol's coat tails." The man stood and called out to her, "Hang in there, Commissioner."

"I'm doing my best," she replied.

Laura let herself in the side door to the Governor's warren of offices, and took the broom-closet-sized elevator up to the third floor. When she stepped out, Vic Regis, the Governor's chief of staff, was pouring himself a cup of coffee at the tiny kitchenette tucked into a corner. His tall, thin frame filled the enclosure.

"Good morning," said Vic, his smile warm. "This is an unexpectedly delightful beginning to the day. Did I forget a meeting?"

"No," said Laura, swallowing her anger for a moment and returning his smile. "I took a chance you'd be here."

Vic was the brains behind Governor Gibbs Carver, having plotted the successful transformation of Carver, the businessman with no political experience, into Carver, the governor. He had then shepherded his boss through a turbulent but productive first term in office, and a contentious but ultimately successful reelection effort.

He was also an old friend and champion of Laura's. They'd known each other since high school, and had been classmates at both Ole Miss and the University of Virginia law school. In fact, Vic was the one who'd proposed her appointment to Carver. Though they'd gone head-to-head many a time on policy issues, somehow the debates had never altered their friendship.

"What's up?"

"Tell me one good reason for the Governor to announce he was limiting pay raises to two hundred dollars per employee," Laura asked, her anger seeping back into her voice.

"It's not what I suggested," Vic said, shaking his head, "but it's the way it came out. A reporter backed him into a corner last night."

"Did he think about what it means to take such a hard line this early in the game?"

"Not at that particular moment, no," Vic said. "Mostly he was getting harassed about funding for his programs."

"Well, I can't guarantee what the troopers will do...."

"What do you mean?" Vic asked.

"The rumors have been flying—everything from unionizing to a slowdown, to blue flu. We've been telling them we'd keep working for the maximum raise we could afford, but with this, I don't know."

"You've got to make them understand there's a limit to what we can do. We can't raise their salaries and not raise the other state employees'."

"Why not?" Laura said. "You did it for the teachers."

"That was different."

"No, it wasn't—same song, second verse. Take half that revenue I suggested to fund the crime bill and give the troopers a pay increase."

"Selective raises cause more trouble than they..."

"For whom?" Laura countered. "Certainly not for the troopers."

Vic stared at her, clearly impatient. "Carver doesn't want a selective raise ever again, and we can't afford an across-the-board pay raise."

Laura forged ahead, undaunted. "For the past four years, Carver's been saying there wasn't any extra money...."

"You've gotten more out of him than any other department head," Vic cut in. "New troopers, no budget cuts."

"But that doesn't put more money in their pockets," Laura protested. "Casino revenue is rolling in and it's time to make good on the promises. We've got the lowest wages in the country."

Vic took off his wire rim glasses and rubbed his eyes.

"My big accomplishment," Laura said, "has been making it easier for troopers to have a second job. Have you thought about what that means, for christsake? They get to work double time to make ends meet."

Vic started to say something but Laura pressed on. "We make the job as interesting as we can, create incentives, make promotions fair, but all that's smoke and mirrors if some real money doesn't appear pretty damn soon."

"I'll keep trying, but I'm just the messenger. We're on the same side on this one."

"Meaning what?"

"Meaning I agree with you—the troopers ought to get their raise, an even bigger one than you've proposed, if it were possible. Beyond the obvious equity of it, raising their pay can work as well as any crime bill for boosting Carver's law enforcement image."

"Then why is he so against it?"

"Do you want the real reason?"

"Yes."

"Number one, he's stubborn. Number two, he's running for Barksdale's Senate seat and he's got specific things he wants in place as the campaign heats up."

"Like what?"

"A few education programs, several health care issues, the criminal justice reform bill, the modest increase for all state employees, and a long overdue capital improvements bill."

"Oh, I see. He wants his name on a few more brass plaques. It's becoming clearer to me."

Vic didn't reply.

"So you're saying I ought to suck it up and help him get elected so I can lose my job?"

"You won't lose your job."

"Get real, Vic."

"You're the one department head the Lieutenant Governor

would keep."

"How do you know that?"

"Trust me, " Vic said. "You've got to make sure the troopers know that a slowdown or forming a union will cost them. They won't get an ounce of sympathy from anyone if they use those sorts of tactics."

"Maybe, maybe not. Just don't be surprised at what they do, and don't blame me when they do it."

"Laura," Vic said, reaching for her arm before she could leave, "try very, very hard not to let it happen."

Laura looked deeply into Vic's eyes. The sharper tone and message were unexpected. "Is that some sort of threat?"

"No more than what you just said," Vic replied calmly. "It's just a warning. I know Carver, and he's feeling more and more like he's out on a very shaky limb with you in office."

"A limb of his own making," Laura snapped back. "He only wanted me so he could score some points with women."

"I won't deny that...."

"And you also can't deny I've helped beef up his law enforcement report card, which," Laura added, "was in miserable shape a year ago."

"Another point well taken," Vic said. "But it's a tossup whether you'd help or hurt in a state-wide race. He won't hesitate to act in his own interests, and you could be history. He'll say something about lack of leadership qualities."

"What's his problem with me?"

"He can't control you the way he does all the other agency heads."

"But aren't I supposed to be the patrol's advocate?"

"Yes, but..."

"Or just your emissary to them?"

"Don't say 'your.' I'm trying to tell you, Carver and I are not one and the same person."

"Whatever..."

"No, it's important to me that you know the difference," Vic said. "There are lots of times I adamantly disagree with what he insists on doing. But once I've made my pitch and he's taken a different course, I can't say anything."

Laura seethed. "Maybe you ought to."

"It would cost me my job, and right now, this is what I want to do and where I want to live."

"Sounds like a tricky place to be."

"It is, particularly when it involves you."

"How so?"

"Because you've found your niche at the Patrol," said Vic, looking her straight in the eyes.

"Maybe."

"No maybe about it. I've never seen you fight as hard for anything or anyone. Professionally, I mean. And that makes it all the more difficult to be the bearer of bad news from the Governor."

Laura looked away, always uncomfortable when a conversation focused directly on her.

"Kinda like my situation with you is difficult," Vic added, his voice softer.

"In what way?"

"This is my niche—being the mover behind the scenes, keeping the trains running, laying track, figuring out new routes. I hand out orders on the Governor's behalf all day long, without a second thought. I never want to jeopardize our relationship."

"Sorry if I jumped on you," Laura said, contrite.

"I would have been surprised if you hadn't. I'm usually prepared for it."

She stood up to leave. He reached for her arm again and she turned toward him. "Will you be able to put on your game face for the Governor's surprise birthday party?"

"Why was I invited in the first place?" she asked, mystified. "Will he really want to see me there?"

"First of all, it's not a surprise party—not really. He wants you to mix and mingle with your detractors, allay some of their fears."

"Was that your idea or his?"

Vic smiled.

"Yours. I knew it."

"But he agreed, readily. The Governor's trying to give you every chance to make it work."

"Black tie?" Laura asked.

Vic nodded.

"I'll see what I can find to wear. Would a dress uniform be appropriate? I could have one made up special."

"You wouldn't, would you?" asked Vic, and Laura knew he was wondering if she might do something that outrageous.

"Pink with gold braid," she added. "And those gold scrambled eggs that generals have on their visors."

■ ■ ■ ■

Colonel Blake Coleman, a career criminal investigator for the State Patrol, appointed chief by Laura when she became Commissioner, looked out his office window at the bustling headquarters parking lot and the massive communications center and garage on the far side. Once, the chief's office had been on the opposite corner of the fifth floor with a view of downtown and a private bath, but Blake preferred this vantage point on comings and goings. He had an elephantine memory and an insatiable interest in what was happening around him, which is why he'd swiftly become one of the patrol's best investigators.

Down below, Coleman saw five men—one in plain clothes and four uniformed troopers—talking to Lieutenant Colonel Robert Stone, Director of Criminal Investigations. Robert was not only a sharp investigator but Blake's most trusted friend and ally. The highest ranking black officer in the Patrol, Robert was known by all as a reasonable, level-headed man, a reputation which made the younger troopers comfortable telling him what was on their minds. He'd become the single best back-channel to the commissioner and the chief.

Three of the troopers had their backs turned so Blake couldn't identify them, but he could tell all were black and was fairly certain one was a representative of the Troopers' Federation. Robert started moving away from the group. At 46, he was in great shape, not muscle-bound like some of the weight lifters, but lithe and powerful. With a parting comment and a wave, he walked briskly toward the main building, jamming his hands in the pockets of his wool sports jacket to keep warm. The group continued talking after he'd left, and from their hand gestures, no one seemed very happy.

The phone rang and Blake swiveled around to answer it, punching the button as if he wanted to jam it permanently out of commission. "Coleman," he said. His jaw was tight, chiseling the lines of his long face.

"Got a minute?" Robert said.

"You in the lobby?"

"Yeah, how'd you know that?"

"Saw you in the parking lot."

"That's what I want to talk to you about. I'll be right up."

Blake was still watching the group amble toward the shop, arguing, when Robert arrived.

"What's the word?" Blake said, jerking his thumb toward the window.

"They're pissed off about the Governor, just like everyone else in the state. I was trying to convince them a slowdown was a bad idea."

Blake stared out at the parking lot, watching the activity as if he were in an air traffic control tower. "They're figuring," Robert said, walking toward the window, "that the Commissioner won't be able to change the Governor's mind."

"She's down there right now."

"What do you think?"

"I think Carver doesn't give a damn about state employees," said Blake, running his hand through his gray hair. "He's looking down the road to Washington. Did you tell 'em the Legislators don't go home until the end of April this year, and it ain't over till then?"

"I did. The problem is the rank and file don't understand how it works, and when the Governor said no more than $200 per employee, they think it's all over unless they do something drastic."

"We ought to have field trips to the Capitol, let these guys see what goes on."

"That's not a bad idea," replied Robert, stretching his arms in the air and bringing his hands to rest behind his head. He was a handsome man with a generous mouth that broke into an easy smile, just the right contrast to Blake's tight lipped seriousness when they teamed up to work cases. "And at the same time, we ought to show the Legislators what they do."

"We lost Jessup to the feds this morning," Blake said. "He starts at fifteen thousand more than he's making with us."

"I doubt if he's the last."

"Hardly. We train 'em, they swipe 'em."

"You can't blame the guys, though."

"I don't," said Blake. "I just wish we could get something for them this year. It might give us a chance to hold on to the really good ones."

"Just how much would a 5 percent raise cost?"

"For just the Patrol, a million and a half. An 8 percent raise would cost 2.4 mil. But if we get more, everyone else will be screaming for their share. Someone's ox has to be gored pretty good to come up with that much extra change."

"It's more than the money, you know. They're testing her," Robert said.

Blake nodded, "I know."

■ ■ ■ ■

The elevator opened onto the fifth floor of State Patrol headquarters and Laura stepped out, still steamed about Carver. She waved at her secretary and turned the corner toward her office without a word.

"Commissioner," Deborah called after her. "There's someone here to see you."

Laura spun around to see Everett Passage, an energetic CPA and Director of Investigations for the State Auditor's office, stand up, smiling. He was of medium height and slight, with straight blond hair—closer to Laura's size, an ounce of comfort for a small person so often surrounded by much taller men.

"Everett," said Laura, the strain on her face lifting for the first time since she'd dropped Will off at school. Everett had been Laura's strong right hand when she'd had his position, and he'd assumed the director's chair when Governor Carver appointed Laura to head the State Patrol. "What are you doing here?"

"In the neighborhood, so I stopped by and got lucky," Everett answered. "Do you have a moment?"

"Absolutely. Did you get some coffee?"

He nodded, lifting a styrofoam cup.

"Well, let me get mine and you can tell me what's going on. I've begun my yearly sentence of hard labor with the Legislature so I need all the distraction I can get to stay sane."

For twenty minutes, they sat on her couch and caught up. Everett regaled her with the latest details of misspent public funds. It was a welcome change from the tedium of budgets and pay raises.

"This guy actually got reimbursed for the catering costs of his wife's surprise 40th birthday party. They had coded it 'training expenses' and attached a list of employees who attended the 'session.'"

"When will they learn?" Laura muttered, not surprised at any of Everett's tales. She'd encountered plenty in her tenure as director, and before that when she was practicing criminal law. If there was a way to cheat, there was always a will, regardless of any get-tough talk by ardent politicians.

As his stories ran out, Laura watched his easy manner dissolve into self-consciousness. She liked Everett immensely— he was hard-working and candid—and they'd made a great team. "So, do you need some help with a case, or did you just stop by for old-time's sake?"

"I'm hoping you'll be able to find a place for me out here."

Laura perked up. "And leave the Auditor's office?"

"I gave three weeks notice about an hour ago."

"Just like that?" Laura said, astonished at Everett's impetuousness.

Everett nodded. "The auditor's not the same guy anymore. I've seen it coming over the last several months."

"How so?"

"He's running for governor, and it must be making him cautious."

"That's a mistake. He ought to be out there making more headlines, not less."

Everett nodded. "And I think he's already started making deals."

"Like what?"

"I talked to him just over a month ago about Reed Morgan—Western Transportation Commissioner. Something may be rotten in his district, though I don't know what yet."

"Payoffs?"

"I don't know, except the IRS is auditing him..."

"How do you know that?"

"A guy came to me looking for information."

"Did he say what he suspected?"

"Those guys never tell you anything," said Everett. "Anyway, I looked at the numbers and the per mile costs seemed higher in the Western District, but just slightly. I thought we ought to look into it, so I went to the Auditor to talk about it. He said full speed ahead—and that's what I did. I started nosing around and asked for a few contract files."

"And?"

"And then a few days later, he told me to drop it."

"Did he give you a reason?"

"No, just that I was behind on a bunch of other stuff and everything else needed to be finalized before anything new was started—particularly something based on nothing more than a hunch."

"Baloney."

"My sentiments exactly. That's why I quit."

"Now I understand," Laura said. "It's too bad though. There was so much you could have done—we'd only scratched the surface when I left."

"I hated to do it, too, but I can't be part of that. So, don't you need a financial investigator?"

"Always, but I certainly don't have a job that pays as much as you're making. I took a salary cut when I became Commissioner, you'd take an even bigger hit."

"Money's not the issue."

Laura knew that. Over the past eight years, Everett had quadrupled a substantial inheritance playing the stock market, and now, what the state paid him was pocket change.

"Just let me get my teeth into something, that's all I ask."

She walked behind her cluttered desk and pulled a computer list from her drawer, talking as she flipped through it. "We've got an Accountant/Auditor II slot that we haven't been able to fill because the salary's so pitiful."

"I'll take it."

"Are you sure? It's probably less than half of what you're making."

"Absolutely."

"The accounting department needs this person badly, I know that for sure. They're always scrambling."

"I can do that job, too."

"You don't know what the job is yet."

"Whatever it is, I can do it in half the time and spend the rest of the day on investigations."

"I see your self-assurance hasn't dimmed in the least."

Everett blushed.

"We need help tracing dopers' assets to drug profits," Laura said, "so we can petition the courts to forfeit the assets to us. It's a great whack at the dopers, and it helps my budget at the same time."

"I'm game," Everett said. "When can I start?"

"Do you know our comptroller?"

"I do—good man."

"He's the one who has to say yes—it's his slot. You'll have to talk him into letting you split your time. I could order him to do it, but I don't think that's the best way to approach it."

"I can handle him."

"And then you need to talk to Blake Coleman, the Chief.

Have you ever met him?"

Everett shook his head hesitantly.

"Tall, straight gray hair, fifty-something, dark eyes that see right through you?"

"I think I've talked to him on the phone. Mostly I've dealt with Robert Stone, on a case up north a few years back. One of those supervisors we went after. And I've talked to him recently about another case."

"Blake's a nice guy. He and Robert go way back. They worked as a team in the field. Blake gets right to the point, doesn't screw around. You'll like him."

She dialed Blake's secretary and asked her to find Robert Stone and have the two of them come to her office in half an hour.

"Let's go see what plans I'll be interrupting by hiring you into this position. I'm sure the comptroller already has someone in mind."

They headed out of her office and down the rarely used interior stairwell to the fourth floor, pausing before she pushed open the fire door.

"Now, don't forget two things. You'll be threatening to everyone in the office because you've got the credentials to be the comptroller and..." she pointed a finger to emphasize the next, "you'll be labeled as my pet, which can make things sticky when it comes to day-to-day relationships."

"Don't worry," Everett said.

The comptroller was behind his desk, staring at his computer screen while the fingers of his right hand flew over the keypad, punching in numbers.

"Busy?" Laura asked.

"Just one minute," the man said, not taking his eyes off the monitor, "and I'll be through. Have a seat."

When the comptroller looked up to see Everett standing there, he stood up and stuck out his hand to greet him. "Howdy, stranger," he said with a big grin. "Is this a social call or are we targets?"

"Never a target in my book," Everett smiled.

"Everett has his eye on your Accountant II slot," Laura said.

"You're kidding me."

"Totally serious."

"The job's yours," the man said to Everett.

"There's a hitch," cautioned Laura. "I want him to split his time with Investigations so he can work on asset forfeitures."

"That's no problem," the comptroller answered. "You can do my stuff before lunch."

Everett smiled at Laura.

"I'll leave you two," Laura said. "Come back up in a few minutes, okay?"

"Thank you, Commissioner," the comptroller said.

"It's my pleasure, I assure you," she replied.

Robert and Blake arrived from different directions about the same time and Laura waved for them both to come in while she finished up a phone call.

"Heard anything new?" Robert said quietly.

Blake shook his head. "You?"

"Nothing."

Laura hung up, and looked at both of them. "This has been one helluva morning. I go to the Governor's office to suggest that a hard line on the pay raise issue isn't such a hot idea, and Vic tells me to watch it—if the patrol gets out of control, I'll lose my job."

"That's not going to happen, Commissioner," Blake said, his deep voice unwavering. "It's the main topic at Friday's Captains and Majors meeting. I've asked the Troopers Federation representatives to be there, too."

"Glad you're so certain about it," Laura replied. She pawed through the jumble of paper on her desk, found Everett's resume, and handed it to Blake. "Anyway, just when it's looking very bleak, a tiny ray of hope appears. Do you remember Everett Passage, Robert?"

"Sure, I talked to him just a few weeks ago about some case he had going."

"Is this the guy who took your old job?" asked Blake.

Laura nodded. "He quit this morning. Wants to move out here with us."

She knew Blake didn't know Everett, but was pleased with Robert's interested, "Hmmm." Laura wanted to bring Blake around quickly. "How would you like a CPA to pick apart a doper's finances to get a forfeiture?"

"Aren't you treading on the Feds' territory?"

"Have you seen money coming in besides what we find on a guy?" Laura asked.

Blake shook his head.

"I rest my case."

"Why'd he quit?" asked Blake.

"The Auditor told him to back off Reed Morgan."

"Western District Transportation Commissioner?"

"The same."

"What's Morgan done?" Robert asked.

"Everett didn't get that far. He first found out that the IRS is auditing Morgan, then he started nosing around. He mentioned his plans to the Auditor who initially said to have at it, and then a couple of days later, the Auditor tells him to shut it down."

"And he quit because of that?" Blake asked.

"He can afford to, twice over," said Laura. "He's made a killing in the stock market."

"It would be nice to have money to invest," Blake said. "He can't be an investigator...."

"He'll be hired into one of the accountant slots open in the comptroller's office."

"Is that okay with the comptroller?" Blake asked.

"It's a done deal, if you agree to it."

Laura watched Blake read the resumé slowly, knowing he wouldn't miss a word.

"I need our drug interdiction efforts to be a success," Laura said after a few moments. "A big success—the value of my stock down at the Governor's office is dwindling."

"And you think he can do the job?" Blake asked.

"I know he can," said Laura. "What do you think, Robert?"

"From what little contact I've had, he seems real smart," Robert said, "and as decent as they come."

By the time Everett reappeared, Laura had Robert on board but knew that Blake remained skeptical. Blake spent fifteen minutes grilling the accountant for information, his quiz revealing more about Everett than even Laura knew.

"I hope you won't be offended if I run a background check and put you on the polygraph," Blake said. "We do it on all the officers. Though you won't be sworn, you'll be right up in there with them, and we can't afford to take any chances."

"Just tell me where and when to report," Everett said with a smile. "I really appreciate this, Laura."

She saw Blake bristle at Everett's use of her first name—he never called her anything but Commissioner and never allowed anyone else to do so. He'd shared his reasons the first day she was in office when she'd suggested he call her Laura. Her size and youthful appearance were sufficient impediments to her authority that an attitude of familiarity on the part of Patrol personnel would only serve to undermine her further.

"We'll be glad to have you with us, we need all the help we can get. Anyone the Commissioner..." Laura heard Blake stress her title just enough for Everett to take notice, "trusts as much as she trusts you, is welcome here."

"I appreciate the vote of confidence," Everett replied, pausing himself before adding, "Colonel."

"Now tell us what's been happening with Reed Morgan," Blake said.

# Two

Will had every piece of wooden train track out and was busy creating an extensive railroad system on the living room floor with the help of his third favorite sitter, Anna. Neither of the neighbor boys had been available, and boys were always preferable to girls as far as Will was concerned. His puppy, Ranger, was inching closer to a red wooden engine, now slightly frayed at the edges from her gnawing little teeth.

"I won't be too late," Laura said as she picked her way carefully through the construction, heading for her son. When a black suede shoe landed right next to him, Will looked up.

"How come you're all dressed up, Momma?"

"I'm going to a birthday party," Laura said as she knelt down to kiss him.

"Like that?" Will asked, shocked.

"It's a grown-up party."

"Do I have to get dressed up for my birthday?"

"No, Sweetheart." Laura looked at Anna. "I'll call if I'll be later than 9:30. Will can have a snack before he goes to bed and a glass of milk, but make certain he brushes his teeth."

"Do I have to go to bed?"

"At least be in bed by 9:15. You can look at books, if you want."

Vic was at the reception desk talking with Captain Sandy Quinn, the man in charge of the Governor's security, when Laura arrived at the side door of the Mansion.

"Good evening, Gentlemen," Laura said, lifting the hem of her long dress as she mounted the stairs. She was wearing black crepe with a fairly daring neckline, accented with a silver thread embroidery that was repeated at the cuffs, a gleaming silver choker, and diamond drop earrings. The straight lines and high heels gave her an extra inch of lean height. Laura hadn't worn anything designed to be so enticing since her late husband, Semmes Owen, had died the previous year.

Vic bowed slightly. "Good evening," he said, smiling broadly. "I see you decided against a dress uniform."

Sandy just stared at her.

"Everything going fine, Sandy?" Laura asked.

"Yes, ma'am," he stammered.

"Shall we?" Vic said, motioning toward the historic portion of the Mansion and the party. As he reached for the door handles, Laura stopped him and straightened his bow tie.

"You look perfectly beautiful," Vic whispered.

She blushed. "Thank you. You're looking pretty spiffy yourself."

As they stepped into an already crowded room, Laura checked for a face, not just familiar, but friendly, and saw a woman in dark blue in the adjoining room. She was tall with dark brown hair and very fit.

Laura leaned toward Vic. "Do you know that woman across the Back Rose Parlor? In the blue dress."

"Next to the guy in the red tie?"

"That's the one."

"I do, and so do you. That's your old friend Naomi Skipper from the University of Virginia. The guy is one of the pollsters, and he's trying to impress her, or so he told me. Plans to ask her to marry him."

Two men, who'd just collected their drinks at the bar, approached Vic. Laura stood beside him long enough to not seem rude, then took her leave with a gentle squeeze of his hand, and headed for Naomi.

"Laura Hemeter?" the woman said when she saw her.

"Naomi?"

"My God, what are you doing here?"

"I'm Laura Owen now and I'm..."

"So you're the pistol-packin' momma? Madame Commissioner of Public Safety?"

Laura smiled. "You haven't changed a bit—you still cut right through it. But how did you know about me?"

"I didn't know it was you, I just saw the name Laura Owen in the polling data."

"Oh, Lord, I wonder what those results look like."

"It wasn't all bad, if I remember correctly. But I wasn't paying that much attention. I will now, though."

"You're working for the pollster?"

"No, I'm still stuck practicing law in DC. But I was looking over the numbers on the plane down here with John." She motioned toward the man with the red tie who was deeply involved in a conversation with several men. "I think this Magnolia tour is designed to soften me up for the kill."

"Are you finally admitting marriage is a possibility?"

Naomi rolled her eyes. "I'm getting to that 'now or never' stage, don't you think? I wish the patter of little feet didn't scare the wits out of me."

"What kind of law are you practicing?"

"Corporate stuff, telecommunications regulations."

"Long hours, big salary?"

"You got it. What about you? How'd you get this job?"

"Vic Regis."

"He's so humbly handsome," Naomi said, gesturing over the sea of heads at Vic, still trapped at the door by a group of contributors. She leaned a little closer so she wouldn't be overheard. "Behind those wire rims lurks one terrific lay, let me tell you."

Laura couldn't stop herself from blushing. "I wouldn't know about that."

"That's right. You're married, aren't you?"

"Was married. My husband died about a year ago."

"I'm so sorry," Naomi said, bringing her arm around Laura's shoulder. "I didn't mean to be so flip. I've been totally out of touch and hadn't heard. That's terrible."

"Thank you. He died in a car accident, so it was kind of sudden. Now it's just my son and me."

"How old is he?"

"Will's six, going on seven next month. I wish you could meet him. How long will you be here?"

"Just tonight. We've got reservations in New Orleans tomorrow at the Windsor Court and then some place in Dallas—Turtle Creek Hotel or something like that."

Laura whistled in awe. "The Mansion on Turtle Creek. If that doesn't soften you up, nothing will."

"Of course, it's half pleasure, half forced-march. John's seeing another client tomorrow in Metairie, so I get to loll around the hotel."

"Or wander the quarter."

A man approached the two of them, clearly interested in talking with Laura. She glanced his way and smiled, signaling him to wait a moment.

"I wish we had more time," Naomi moaned.

Laura drew closer to speak quietly. "The citizens can never be kept waiting."

"What about e-mail? Are you on line?"

"Yup."

"Let me write down your address." Naomi whispered in John's ear and he handed her a pen and business card without interrupting his conversation.

From his customary corner of the room, Brent Wexler watched as Governor Gibbs Carver feigned surprise when he entered to shouts of "Happy Birthday" from the two hundred friends and supporters. The event had been Sarah Carver's idea, but Brent capitalized on the opportunity, adding the "big givers" to the list. A small combo sent dance music wafting through the air, and delicious aromas lured the guests to the buffet tables.

During Gibbs Carver's five years in the Mansion, Brent had encouraged the Governor's natural affinity for the limelight and public accolades. The driving force had become his personal success and all it brought with it. But success and ambition required lots of cash and that's where Brent had come in, delivering the modern mother's milk of politics day after day.

Grace Wexler, Brent's elegant wife, stood with him at the Carvers' side near the receiving line in the spacious Foyer as they greeted guests. He'd married her over twenty years before in part for her highly developed social skills. With discreet ease, either Brent or Grace intervened at the strategic moment to avoid Gibbs' or Sarah's fumbling with a name or the particulars about a contributor. It was another flawless performance and Brent knew not a soul ever recognized the two-step they were dancing.

Over the past six years, every person present, as well as hundreds of others, had been approached personally by Brent for campaign contributions, debt retirement contributions, and contributions for every pet project of Carver's. Brent had cultivated his ability to make each donor feel that his or her concerns were being heard, loudly and clearly, by the Governor himself, a talent that had paid off very well, time and time again. Soon he would be asking for a lot more money. The Governor's run for the U.S. Senate would be expensive, and this soireé was both a thank you for past largesse and the first stroking of many to come as they pulled and prodded away the hundreds of thousands of dollars they would need.

After nearly two straight hours of greeting and smiling, Brent leaned Grace's way. "Gibbs and I are running down to his office for a break. Handle the door with Sarah, and remember who leaves so we can follow up later if need be."

Brent started past her, Grace's gracious smile beaming at someone across the room. She caught his coat sleeve, but Brent ignored the tug—he didn't plan to stop. Then Grace grabbed his wrist, drawing him back.

"What the hell is the matter?" he said, his teeth clenched behind his broad smile as he nodded to a guest.

Grace didn't immediately respond but looked down at the shiny Rolex watch he was sporting. "New?"

"A late Christmas present to myself. Surprised you haven't noticed it before."

"Look, Brent, this isn't my party," Grace said. "My feet are killing me. You stay here, and Sarah and I will take the break." In the midst of their argument, they turned together to nod and smile at the most recent arrivals who were headed for Gibbs and Sarah.

"What did you say?" Brent asked, never breaking his smile.

"I said, 'this isn't my party.' You handle the door, I'll take the break."

"That's what I thought you said." He surveyed the room over her head as he spoke quietly but caustically, looking down only as he gently patted her cheek. "Be a good wife and do me this favor. Make it an early anniversary present—something small for the man they all think has everything. I don't ask much really—nothing, in fact, except a few public appearances."

"I don't know why I put up with your arrogance."

Brent patted her cheek one more time and walked away toward Carver. It took several minutes for the two men to make their way to the double doors of the office section of the Mansion but finally, they slipped out and hurried down the wide hallway to Carver's office. They hadn't talked in three days, an unusually long time for the two to be out of touch.

Carver poured them each a bourbon and they settled into the over-sized easy chairs, comfortable for their long frames.

"Your little Commissioner is looking quite fine tonight," Wexler said.

"I planned it as a bit of rehabilitation, but I was expecting her to wear some frumpy little suit."

"That neckline hardly counts for frumpy. I'd say she's doing quite well. And Vic looks smitten."

"They're just old friends."

"Old friends can become new friends," Wexler said.

Carver raised his glass in a toast. "To the most important thing—lots of money." The Governor took his first sip. "This evening is already going remarkably well in the fund-raising area." He handed Brent a check from one of the guests for $10,000. "Here's a start."

Brent looked at the payee—Gibbs Carver Campaign Fund—and the signature. "You'll have to give this back, I'm afraid. An individual can't give this much to a federal campaign."

"I know that, but I assumed you could find a way to handle it," Gibbs said.

Brent shook his head. "I've been talking to various people about the Federal Election Commission auditors. Those guys are serious—we can't play fast and loose anymore. No one's been watching until now."

Carver grunted, disgusted. "What's that going to mean?"

Brent swirled the bourbon around in his glass. "I don't know how it will play out, frankly. Three or four people out there tonight would write checks for $25,000 each if I asked, but it's too risky. Officially, they can't give more than a thousand, two thousand with their spouses."

"Can't you do what you did with corporations? Get them to spread the money around to family and friends?"

"Theoretically, but a lot of these people don't want anything to do with the tawdry mechanics of avoiding contribution limits. Some are downright offended if you suggest it to them. They consider that our problem, and in the past, I've always solved it for them. There'll have to be a lot more fancy steppin' this time."

"What about businesses?"

"No corporate contributions at all—just political action committees, but even those are limited to five thousand dollars. And no cash over $200. Only $100 can be anonymous."

"Goddamn regulations." Carver paused for a moment, sipping his drink. "Could I keep this as a gift and then contribute it to my own campaign?"

"Possibly..." Brent turned over Carver's idea. "Possibly, but I'll have to check on the tax consequences. There's no limit to how much you can give your own campaign. But to be safer," he handed the check back to Carver, "it needs to be made out to you personally. Remember, if the FEC ever does an audit, a check like that floating around could place you directly in the middle of campaign fraud, a death sentence. I think it'll get down to how well we can convince everyone to go the extra mile, either spreading their cash around or finding lots of new contributors."

"If we get the capital improvements bill through, that ought to open a few spigots," Carver said. "It's guaranteed full employment for the construction trades."

"How does that look?"

"Pretty good. It originated in the House so Holden Bowser on Appropriations is handling it. He and I have always been able to talk straight."

"Did Harry Curlett's project at Ole Miss make it into the bill?"

"It did."

"Good, because he called me this morning," Brent said. "Left a message that he couldn't be here tonight and asked the status on the project. Now there's someone who will go the extra mile for you. But it's strictly I'll scratch your back, you scratch mine with Harry."

"So you think we can do it?" Gibbs asked.

"Absolutely." Brent gave Carver a final toast before tossing back the last of his bourbon. "I'm looking forward to the next installment of the Gibbs Carver Show: Carver Goes to Washington. I'll find a little townhouse in Georgetown and we'll carry on."

Carver smiled and finished his own drink. Brent knew he'd lifted Carver's momentary gloom over raising money, replacing it with fantasies about the nation's capitol.

As Carver and Wexler ambled down the hallway to return to the party, the doors from the formal rooms slid open and Vic and Laura stepped through.

"So there you are," Vic said.

"Took a little breather," Carver said to Vic. He smiled approvingly at Laura, then turned to Wexler. "Brent, have you met Laura Owen, our Commissioner of Public Safety?"

"Only in passing at some legislative function," Brent said, extending his hand to Laura. "And you certainly weren't dressed like this."

Laura smiled. "Nice to meet you Mr. Wexler. I've heard so much about you and your phenomenal ability to raise money. I'm in awe."

"No, I'm in awe. You seem undaunted by the job of controlling all those troopers."

"It's not always easy, but I assure you, it's never boring."

"Are you leaving so soon?" Carver asked.

"It's a school night and I've got a babysitter whose time is almost up," said Laura. "By the way, Happy Birthday, Governor."

"Thank you, though I'd rather not remember how fast time is flying by." He turned to Wexler. "We'd better rescue our wives."


Vic walked Laura out to her car, his hand resting gently on her back as they made their way across the parking area. City lights obliterated the night sky, but the fresh air was a welcome relief from the smoke and noise of the party.

"Did I pass tonight's little test?" Laura asked.

"With flying colors," Vic responded.

"If I'd had my druthers, Naomi and I would have slipped out to talk. But I stayed, like a good little girl."

"Duly noted."

"Let's hope it helps."

Vic leaned toward her and quickly but softly kissed her cheek. "It helped me immensely, I know that for certain."

His touch was electric. Laura was certain her face was absolutely crimson and the only thing that saved her was the darkness.

"Good night, Vic," she whispered, almost stammering with excitement.

She backed her car out, waving good-bye. But in her nervousness, she didn't go far enough to safely swing past the car next to her and had to do it again.

Vic was still standing there on the edge of the drive, watching. Laura waved again, knowing she looked like a ditzy schoolgirl. Her stomach was still doing back-flips.

■ ■ ■ ■

Blake cleared the table and was washing the dishes after dinner while Sally attended to her mother. When a car pulled into the driveway, he dropped his scouring pad and rinsed off his hands, picking up a dish towel as he moved toward the carport. As soon as the driver's door opened, a burst of police radio traffic filled the air. The trooper slid back in to turn off the radios, and when Blake finally saw his face, he recognized Master Sergeant Levi Davis. The leather of Levi's Sam Brown belt crinkled as he straightened up and approached Blake.

"Levi," Blake said, hurriedly drying his hands and extending one in greeting, "this is a surprise."

"Hey, Blake," Levi said. "Or do I have to call you Chief?"

"No chief stuff after hours."

"Am I disturbing anything?" Levi asked with the awkward politeness of an old but neglected friend.

"No. Just finishing up the dishes while Sally gets her mother in bed."

"She lives with you?"

Blake pointed to the rooms off the carport. "Built her an apartment a few years back when she couldn't live alone anymore." He motioned toward the back door, "Can you stay a minute?"

"Sure. I was hoping I'd find you home."

"What brings you up here?"

"Deidre had to do some shopping so I dropped her at the

Mall."

"Want a beer?" Blake asked as he held the door open for Levi.

"No, I've got too much driving to do."

"Coffee then?"

The two big men filled the small kitchen. "Nah, that would be too much trouble."

"No trouble. Sally made some with dinner," Blake said, motioning toward the breakfast nook for Levi to take a seat, then opening a cabinet for a mug.

"Then I'll have a cup. Cream and sugar." Levi looked at a family photograph that hung near the table. "How are the boys?" he asked.

"Grown, one graduated, both gone for all practical purposes," Blake said, handing Levi his coffee and a spoon, pointing toward the sugar bowl. He swung open the refrigerator and retrieved a carton of milk, then returned to the sink and his scouring.

"I can't believe it's been that long," Levi said.

"They were gone before I knew it," Blake said. "Where are the twins now?"

"San Francisco."

"Both of them?"

"Molly and Emily finished nursing school a couple of years ago, specializing in emergency medicine. They work in a trauma unit out there. They've got an apartment, they're paying off their school loans, and seeing the world."

"Together, I presume," Blake said.

"Always. And the boys?"

"Not quite so settled, but at least they're able to cover their college loans most of the time. Brooks is playing around programming computers—he's got his own little business and pays all his bills. Paul runs the locker room at a country club in Phoenix while he finishes up school."

"You should be proud," Levi said.

"I am."

"At least they didn't want to be cops."

"Sally would have died a thousand deaths. What's new down your way?"

"The usual, nothing much."

Blake glanced at Levi sipping his coffee, then added the pan to the precarious tower of dishes in the drying rack, wondering what had really brought Levi by the house. They'd been classmates in patrol school—their wives had their babies about the same time. But when Levi transferred home so Deidre would have help with the twins and Blake switched to investigations, their paths hadn't crossed as often and they hadn't kept up the way they should have.

"How's the air on the fifth floor?" Levi asked. "Enough oxygen up that high?"

"I sometimes wonder if I made a mistake taking the job. I make more money but I've got no job security—first time in my life. I don't like the feeling."

Levi took another sip of his coffee. "Those of us at the bottom of the ladder never think about it that way. Is it worrying you?"

"Some days more than others. Commissioner Owen's great to work with," Blake said, lapsing into his standard sales pitch on Laura. "She doesn't try to run things day to day, but..."

"But she's still a woman, right?"

Blake regretted sounding so equivocal. "No, not that. It's just that everyone's waiting for her to trip."

"And if she goes, you go?"

"That's usually the way," Blake said, "if history's a teacher."

"We don't need that to happen."

"No, I certainly don't," Blake agreed. "I've got two mortgages on this place, and then there's Sally's mother."

"That's why I stopped by. Thought you ought to know the scuttlebutt."

Blake's jaw tightened, making his long face taught and stern. "Tell me."

"The talk about a slowdown is getting serious," Levi said.

"Jeez Louise. I don't have time for crap like this."

"I doubt you do. Some of them have decided to wage their

own private war over this pay raise business."

"Who's behind it?"

"Billy Cook, for one."

"Trooper Federation rep?"

Levi nodded.

"I don't know him except to see him," Blake said. "I'd heard he was pretty sharp. What's his deal?"

"He is smart, but he needs more money," said Levi. "Like all of us do."

"Where does he live?"

"Claytonia, Carver's hometown."

"Maybe's he's related to the governor."

"I doubt Cook is any relation—he was assigned there, bought some land, and stayed."

"Too bad," Blake said. "We need someone with an inside track."

Levi nodded. "I'm working on it."

"Are the men listening to Cook?"

"Some are, some aren't," Levi said. "I thought I could reason with him but I'm not getting through. He's not a bad guy, he's just desperate for a solution."

"Has anything started yet?"

"Not that I know of."

■ ■ ■ ■

The enormous conference room on the fifth floor of headquarters, built to Pentagon dimensions, was filled with patrol officers, all captains or above, plus the thirteen Trooper Federation representatives. All the men were in uniform except four plain clothes officers from criminal investigations, Blake, and Robert.

The conversations came to an abrupt halt when Laura entered, closing the door behind her. She walked to the empty seat between Blake and Robert at the top of the huge conference table. The troopers had quit jumping to attention when she appeared, a custom that had made her uncomfortable from the very first day, but their undivided attention and its pregnant silence, was just as unnerving.

"Good morning, gentlemen," Laura said as she sat down, placing her coffee cup and a single sheet of paper in front of her. She looked from face to face, all the way around the table, a practice that brought her racing heart under control as well as to make contact with every single person in the room.

"I appreciate everyone being here this morning. I won't take much of your time. I want to talk about pay raises, blue flu, and slowdowns."

Two men at the far end of the room, leaned away from the table, bringing their beefy arms across their chests, and settling their eyes on Laura.

"We've all got our jobs in this organization and part of mine is to prepare a budget and lobby it through the legislature. I asked for at least a five percent across the board pay raise with realignment. And I'm working on it—every day. But," Laura punctuated her delivery with a pause, "I need your help."

A few men loosened up with Laura's conciliatory tone but most of the trooper federation representatives remained impassive.

"As I understand the state budget, while there might be enough money to raise the Patrol's salaries five percent, there's not enough to cover the other 22,000 state employees. And that's the problem.

"The Governor has never liked singling out special groups and he doesn't want to do it again. When he gave the teachers a special raise, he caught holy hell for it. And though he took a pretty hard line in the paper, the game is far from over because there's more than just the governor in this discussion, as you know.

"However, while all this is under consideration, it's been made crystal clear to me that any work disruption will not be tolerated. Slowdowns and strikes by other government employees might be disruptive, but if the Patrol slows down, it's flat out dangerous. The direct correlation between enforcement and fatalities means that if you stop working, someone dies. That cannot happen—we'd never recover from it.

"Tickets have been up for the past year and fatalities have fallen to an all-time low. But the driving public has a short memory, as you all know, and it won't take much to reverse the trend. That's your job, and if you don't do it, there won't be a reason for a raise."

Laura paused, looking from face to face again, measuring her impact. In that moment came a tentative voice from the far end of the table. "Commissioner?"

Billy Cook, with his ruddy freckled face and strawberry hair, sat straighter in his chair. Laura nodded his way. "I don't mean to be disrespectful, ma'am, but if you're saying we should be good little troopers and do our jobs, and it'll all turn out okay, you're mistaken. We've been working our hearts out, and we've still got troopers on food stamps."

Laura was shaking her head before he'd finished. "I'm not saying that. I'm saying we need to fight for this with every weapon we've got—with the exception of slowdowns or walk-offs. You can talk to every legislator you come across, call in every chit you've got, sic your mothers on them—I'm sure you have tricks up your sleeves that I'd never think of," Laura said. "But don't slow down. Something bad'll happen just as sure as I'm sitting here, and it'll be all over."

Laura looked around the room one last time at the men staring back at her, all waiting for the revolutionary bit of wisdom she didn't have to offer. The sometimes intoxicating sense of power that came with her position rushed out of her, and she felt distinctly out of place. Blake and Robert were the only ones not watching her—they'd been surveying the assembly.

"And one more thing. If you pull a legislator over, I wouldn't write a ticket unless you have absolutely no other choice. We've got to do this without getting back into the trap of fixing their tickets."

A few men chuckled.

"If there aren't any more questions, I'll turn this over to Colonel Coleman," Laura said. "He's always full of good ideas."

Blake sat forward in his chair, looking past Laura to lock stares with Robert. "As the Commissioner said," Blake began, shifting his eyes quickly from Robert to Laura and back to Robert again, "we have to fight this one with all the ammunition we've got, and we're going to need every possible vote. I presume that if we put our minds to it, we'll find we have a line to every legislator or we know someone who does."

Robert leaned toward Laura and whispered, "If I were you, I'd leave now."

A flash of puzzlement crossed her face, then she pushed back her chair. "You're right. Plausible deniability."

"Whatever you want to call it."

Blake stopped when Laura stood up.

"Excuse me, gentlemen," Laura said, "but I've got an appointment downtown."

"We understand," Blake said, nodding at Robert.

# THREE

Second Creek, once a thriving little burg just east of the mighty Mississippi, lay abandoned, strangled in the sinewy kudzu vines. But it still boasted prime deer and turkey hunting. Brent Wexler had bought up every parcel that came on the market until he'd amassed a three-thousand-acre tract that he'd turned into an exclusive hunt club for his friends. He was there nearly every weekend, often hosting clients and politicians.

February weather had been terrific—crisp, clear, lacking only the flair of autumn colors. Barren browns and the winter-worn green of pine trees predominated, though here and there tiny bright green shoots were tentatively peeking out. Small game and quail were the only things in season, but the big animals never lost their skittishness, vanishing instantly at any approach.

At other times of the year the land was overrun with hunt club members, but with so little to hunt, by late Sunday evening Brent and his last guest, Reed Morgan, were the only ones left. Morgan, in his sixth term as Commissioner for the Western Transportation District of Mississippi, was a big man grown soft and florid with years of wining and dining. He'd stuck to hunting all day, but as he and Brent ambled toward the house, Morgan finally turned the subject to business, his voice thick with regret.

"I should have quit while I was ahead," Morgan said slowly and deliberately.

"What do you mean?" asked Brent, eyeing the man with immediate suspicion. Half a head taller than Morgan, his taut, muscular body made Morgan's appear even more rotund.

"The goddamn Internal Revenue's been auditing me since December."

"Why didn't you say something?" Brent said. "I know people over there. I might have been able to help."

"I doubt you could have done anything with the IRS, but anyway, I thought it was routine. Figured they were only looking at the write-off for the Appaloosas. But they've got questions about every damn thing I've bought and where I got the money. I'm not sure what to do about it. I don't want them investigating any deeper than they are...." Morgan paused a moment. "And neither do you."

"What are they looking into?" Brent asked as casually as possible.

"Cars, jewelry, the horses, of course."

"But I fixed it so all your money came from the real estate developments. What's the big deal?"

Morgan trudged on without a word.

Brent grabbed at Morgan's elbow and spun him around. "What have you been doing that I don't know about?"

"There's been lots of cash from different people."

"From who?"

"I never reveal names—that was our deal."

"Bullshit. That was our deal about me. You owe me the truth, I made you what you are."

"You got that all wrong. It took two...." Morgan waved a couple of stubby fingers in Brent's face, "two, and I ran all the risks."

"Don't flatter yourself."

Brent started walking again, hoping to ease the tension and loosen Morgan up. "How much are you talking about?"

"A hundred thousand over the last three years."

"Jesus. How goddamn greedy are you?" said Brent. "Who'd you get the money from?"

"Suppliers."

"Like who?"

"You know, suppliers."

"No, I don't know. What kind of suppliers?"

"Asphalt, culverts."

The ruddy color from two days outdoors drained out of Brent's face. "How close is the IRS?"

"Closer than I'd like," Morgan mumbled. "They haven't found all of it—maybe half. I'm saying it was gifts from my family."

"Is that possible?" Brent asked, clearly skeptical.

"Theoretically. I have an aunt and uncle who never had any children and who died within two weeks of each other last summer."

"And why are you telling me this now?" Brent's eyes seared into Morgan's. "Are you about to trade me in?"

"No, I wouldn't do that," Morgan said, turning away to avoid looking at Brent.

Approaching the last bend, the smell of venison on the grill made Morgan pick up his pace. After the screen door slammed, Morgan caught sight of Trey, turning the meat with a long fork.

"Trey's phenomenal," Morgan said, trying to change the subject. "Why isn't he more than a master sergeant at the Patrol after all these years?"

Brent, preoccupied with Morgan's confession, took a moment to reply. "The responsibility doesn't interest him, I guess, and the extra money definitely can't match what he makes being free enough to work for me in his off-hours."

"What all does he do for you?"

"He runs this place for me, and helps out at the farm." Then a thin smile crept across Brent's broad lips, and he added, "Whatever needs to be done."

■ ■ ■ ■

Life had been good to Brent Wexler. He'd been on a roll since he'd catapulted Reed Morgan into the Western District Transportation Commissioner's position. Morgan had been a small-time businessman and party regular when the previous commissioner announced his retirement twenty years before. Brent, then a young comer in the road-building trade, instantly recognized the possibilities and convinced Morgan to run, anonymously financing the campaign. With Morgan in place during the next four years, Brent had skimmed thousands off the top of state road contracts through nonexistent cost over-runs, paying Morgan for his part with shares in slam-dunk real estate ventures and other investments.

It was clever and virtually undetectable. And they'd had the sense to quit before in-depth auditing practices had been insti-tuted. Meanwhile, Morgan had been delivering what the peo-ple wanted—better roads and near immediate attention to pot-holes, busted or missing signs, and every other petty problem that was called into his hotline—making him invulnerable at the polls.

But Brent had long since tired of Morgan. He was small potatoes, the kind of politician who actually liked spending the morning on the front porch of a store, shooting the breeze with the locals, or speaking at the county tobacco-spittin' contest. Once Morgan was firmly ensconced, Brent had set his aim higher, spending every spare moment of the last seven years maneuvering his close friend, Gibbs Carver, into the Governor's Mansion and then keeping him there. Morgan had been relegated to a distant backseat in his life, but Brent now suspected ignoring his old crony had been a mistake.

"I'm going on, Brent," said Morgan, pushing back from the table, not looking either Brent or Trey in the eye for more than a micro-second. "Great meal, Trey. Thanks for everything this weekend."

Morgan had eaten with dispatch, ignoring the savory flavor

of the meat and salad, and passing entirely on the red wine. Now that he'd made his admission, he wasn't interested in the inevitable third degree he had coming from Brent.

Trey watched Morgan move toward the sink with his plate. "Sure you won't stay the night and leave early in the morning?"

"No, got to be at work first thing," Morgan said. "Best to get the driving behind me tonight. Thanks anyway."

"Need help packing up your gear?" Trey asked.

Morgan shook his head. "No thanks."

Brent tossed his napkin down and stood up. "I'll walk you to your car."

"Don't bother."

"No bother at all," said Brent, rising from his place.

In the wide center hallway, Morgan stopped at the gun case and picked up his rifle and the .22 automatic Colt Woodsman he always carried with him for snakes and small animals.

A full moon lit the way through the twisted shadows of the oaks lining the drive.

"What else haven't you told me?" Brent demanded.

Morgan popped open the trunk of his silver Mercury Marquis to put his rifle away. "There's a guy from the auditor's office who started snooping around."

"Who?"

"The one who runs investigations now, after Carver moved that woman out to the Patrol."

"What's he interested in?"

"Western District contracts, but only recent ones. Don't worry, I squelched it."

"How?"

"The auditor and I arrived at one of his famous understandings." With the relief of getting it all out, Morgan's bravado was returning and he looked Brent square in the eye for the first time. "He wants to be governor, and I want to stay right where I am, so we worked it out."

Brent returned his look with a glare. "How much will it cost me?"

After maneuvering his big body behind the wheel, Morgan

leaned over and put the .22 in the glovebox. Starting up the engine, he rolled down the window. "I've agreed to help him raise money for his campaign."

"And that was enough?"

"He's hungry. He knows what I..." Morgan faltered, then corrected himself, "excuse me, what *we* have done in the past." Hurrying to get away, he nodded back toward the house. "My thanks again to both you and Trey."

Brent stepped forward, hand on the rearview mirror. "Not so quick, Morgan. How fast is all this coming down?"

"My accountant said I've got some time—early summer maybe. We're still producing documents."

Brent leaned on the door, looking straight into Morgan's eyes. "I want to know more about all of this."

"Don't worry, I can handle it—just like I always have." A distinctly sickly grin spread across his face.

Brent backed up and crossed his arms over his chest. "You'd better." Brent's stare never left Morgan. "And keep me updated."

Clearly uncomfortable, Morgan nodded, then turned around in the drive. As the taillights disappeared down the lane to the main road, Trey left his spot on the porch and walked over to Brent. "You don't trust him anymore, do you?"

"Can't," Brent replied. "That joker's gonna do me in."

"Come on," said Trey, turning toward the house. "Your dinner's getting cold. No need to neglect a fine piece of meat because of a lard-ass like Morgan."

After a few more moments staring at the darkened lane, Brent followed in silence. When he reached the kitchen, Trey was zapping his plate in the microwave.

Brent finished his food, sipping his vintage wine slowly, lost in the implications of what Morgan had told him. He helped clear the table while Trey loaded the dishwasher and then, wine glass and bottle in hand, he ambled down the dark wide hallway to the terrace. "Bring a glass along if you like," he called back.

Outside in the chilly air, Brent closed his eyes, concentrating on the chirps and croaks that erupted into the night.

How could my world be crumbling so suddenly? thought Brent. Is it really happening or is my resolve just deteriorating? He pictured Morgan, his flabby mind and body, his greedy hands grasping for more.

No, it's real, and I, Brent Wexler, kingmaker, will be left holding the bag. The whole goddamn bag. What a fool I've been.

When he opened his eyes, he was startled: Trey had slipped silently into the chair next to him. "It's downright scary how quietly you move," Brent said.

"Practice. Years of practice," Trey said, pouring himself some wine and looking Brent's way.

Brent had always envied Trey's raw physical power—so distant from the verbal financial jousting Brent engaged in everyday. Muscular, tanned to bronze from outdoor work, Trey was a quiet man, often underestimated. He was skilled with every sort of weapon, utterly patient but deeply aggressive, never faltering in the face of any agony—human or animal.

During the fifteen years he'd worked for Brent, Trey had risen from employee to trusted friend. Familiar with a host of things Brent had been unacquainted with—the woods, weapons, the lower rungs of government—Trey had expanded Brent's horizons. Once on Brent's payroll, he was never more than a stone's throw away. As for Trey, he seemed utterly comfortable with Brent, never forcing or trying to dominate him.

"I can take care of Morgan if you need me to," Trey said, as dispassionately as if he were talking about cleaning fish. "I could make it look like a suicide, accident, whichever would be best."

Brent closed his eyes again. What were the odds he'd survive unscathed? Probably not too bad. But what if, just what if he lost the bet? He couldn't shoot craps on his reputation. He absolutely couldn't tolerate the indignity of failure.

He took a deep breath. "The timing on something like that wouldn't be so hot—they're looking at him right now." Brent poured himself another glass of wine, enjoying the rich mellow taste despite his anxieties. "He's going to talk, or he already has. Otherwise, he wouldn't have mentioned it. I guess I should be thankful that somewhere in that greedy, twisted mind, he still felt duty bound to warn me. That, or he figures I can use my connections to stop the IRS."

"Couldn't you?"

"Maybe, maybe not. The IRS is one thing, but it's the other one I'm really worried about."

"Other who?

"Morgan told me tonight that the auditor's investigator—some new guy—has been asking about contracts in his district. He's says he's nipped it in the bud, but I don't believe him."

Brent took another swallow, leaned back, and closed his eyes again. Trey waited silently, certain the rest of the story would emerge in good time.

"It used to be one-stop shopping. You could fix something with a single visit to the United States Attorney. But that was before everyone got on this anticorruption bandwagon. Now they all sit around watching each other, waiting for a tasty tidbit to drop—like a bunch of vultures."

The noisy night chorus suddenly stopped for a moment. It was one of those inexplicable lulls after all the caterwauling that makes the quiet so remarkable humans lower their voices, too.

"I could probably handle an IRS audit," Brent said. "Those guys rarely go back as far as my dealings with Morgan. But the auditor's office might dig deeper and give the IRS the ammunition they're looking for."

"You're giving them more credit than they deserve, don't you think?" Trey asked.

"I wish I were," Brent said, his voice trailing off.

They sat, sipping their wine for several minutes until Brent spoke again. "I can't bear the thought of disgrace. It's worse than losing my money, my friends, my life. Back when Morgan and I hatched this scheme, I was younger. I could stomach the game, the tension. But even then, I hated always wondering if someone would discover what we'd done. I had it all set—out of state bank accounts, everything—I was ready to flee at a moment's notice."

"And it never happened, did it?" said Trey confidently.

"No, not even a whisper of a tax audit. But I've got a different feeling this time."

"You're overestimating them."

"Don't think so. I've got to get out of here somehow while I still can."

"Why you?" Trey asked. "Why not him? I told you I could make it look like suicide. Or homicide—one of his jealous girlfriends could have knocked him off."

Brent smiled. "That bastard's blown a fortune on one bimbo after another."

Trey grunted, disgusted.

"No, I can't run the risk that he's already talked or that he'd leave something incriminating behind," Brent said. "Prison's not an option, and I refuse to spend my time and money avoiding it."

"I thought you always told me there weren't any traces," Trey said.

"There weren't really—nothing except the contracts themselves. I paid Morgan off with investments in land development deals. And I still buy him a new wardrobe every year or so."

"So what do you have to worry about?"

"Morgan told me tonight that he's taken payoffs from suppliers—recently."

"That's his problem."

"No, it's still mine. I've always assumed I'd made him enough money so he wouldn't take anything from anyone else. But if the IRS has some leverage on him and he rats on those guys, he may rat on me. Once they start looking closer, there'll be enough to get me."

"Beyond a reasonable doubt?"

Brent nodded. "Probably. I made good money back then, very good money—the foundation for everything I've got now."

"You really think they'd go back that far?"

"I don't want to be here to find out."

"You ought to let me take care of Morgan and you take your chances. If..." Trey jabbed his finger toward Brent, "and that's a big if, he left anything behind that pointed toward you, we could deal with that when the time comes."

"That's exactly what I don't want to do," growled Brent. "I don't want to run away when they're after me. And as close as I am to Carver, the press would be all over the two of us. What might have been negotiable, would become a bloodbath. Just for the trophy. Can't you see it?" Brent framed the words with his hands. "'Governor's fund-raiser and best friend indicted for fraud. And then the columnists would start in. How far does this go? Inside the Capitol? Inside the Mansion?' He'd lose the Senate seat before the race even began."

"He's decided to run for sure?"

"Yessir. It's too good an opportunity to pass up."

"Then don't be a fool and miss out on that. Why don't you sleep on it? There have to be other ways."

"Maybe you're right," Brent said, shaking his head. "I'll sleep on it, and you do the same."

Brent didn't sleep though. He lay there most of the night, thinking, calculating. Over and over he came back to the question of whether he could ride out the storm and survive it, and always the answer was no.

By three in the morning, he was convinced he had to get away. But how the hell could he do it? How could he get out of this mess without a pack of bloodhounds on his heels?

Living, once he got away, wasn't the problem. It wasn't the first time he'd started over. He hadn't been born Brent Wexler and orphaned like he'd told everyone. He'd grown up in Arkansas and left home for the Navy. His people had been poor and ignorant and he'd never wanted to be like them. After he'd done his hitch, he'd enrolled at Ole Miss, in Oxford, took a new name, starred on the football team, married Grace, and let her father introduce him to businessmen. A new life. He'd never returned to his real home in nearly forty years. He had no idea what had become of his parents or siblings.

Brent didn't expect it to be as easy this time. But suicide—real suicide—would be better than what would happen if he had to stay and face the music. He'd always been ready to make a getaway—ready since the day he hatched the plan with Morgan. He had a second passport in his real name and money in international bank accounts in both his names. But he'd never planned the actual escape.

How to leave without anyone looking for him?

While he was in Roatan on his annual snorkeling trip, he could rent a boat, head out alone with an inflatable life boat to get back to shore, capsize the boat, and they'd think he'd drowned.

Brent turned the possibilities over and over in his head. Wouldn't work. The island was small. Too many people might see him.

How then?

Trey could do it. That sort of thing was his bailiwick. He'd think of something. He'd just have to get Trey to do it. For enough money, Brent thought. That's the answer: Trey.

He shifted in his bed, settling into a position to sleep and closed his eyes. A moment later, he was alert again.

No, not just money. For the promise of joining him. For that, Trey would do what he wanted.

That was it. The promise of joining him.

And Trey wouldn't make mistakes.

■ ■ ■ ■

Long before dawn, Trey was in the kitchen again. On an occasion when they had to drive to Jackson, breakfast was usually a quick affair, but Trey fixed a full meal this morning, wanting to draw Brent out about this business with Morgan, hoping Brent would let him handle it his way. French toast, sausage, orange juice, and coffee were ready when a ragged Brent appeared.

"Mornin'," said Trey. "Doesn't look like you got much

sleep."

"I didn't. How about you?"

"A little," Trey lied. He'd slept like a baby, as he always did.

Lack of sleep had not diminished Brent's appetite, however. He dug into the food as though he hadn't eaten in days.

"Any new thoughts?"

"All I've decided for certain is that I don't want to sit around waiting for the other shoe to drop. I want to disappear somehow in a way that no one will look for me."

"And I can't talk you out of it?"

"No. This is the only chance I've got."

Trey smothered his French toast in syrup, then sliced through the entire plateful. He speared a piece, and ate, hungrily. But his face was grim. "Then you'll have to die."

"Die?"

"Well, dying as far as the world thinks. Then you disappear to this new life you seem so hell-bent on starting. I'll figure out how to do it while you decide how you're going to live once you're dead. Probably a car wreck that catches on fire. The body would be destroyed—like that city commissioner tried to do several years back. Only you won't get caught like he did."

"Will you join me when I get settled?"

Trey looked at him and smiled.

"I have enough for both of us to live well, very well," Brent said. He could see that Trey was pleased. "Like we do here."

"Is that a firm offer?"

"Yes."

"Then, I'll do it," said Trey.

■ ■ ■ ■

Trey didn't waste any time—two days later he was in New Orleans. He'd planned on an quick hit, but a sudden cold snap and unusually chilly temperatures were dampening his spirits. He scanned Jackson Square for prospects and saw none.

Trey had watched the populations of panhandlers, street entertainers, and homeless people who worked the French

Quarter swell over the past twenty years—half parasitic, half symbiotic with the ever-growing crowds of shop-till-you-drop tourists that pulsed through Canal Place and Jackson Brewery. But not very many people of any stripe were out this day. Most of the tables at the Cafe du Monde were empty, an almost certain gauge of the tourist traffic. He drove up and down several streets, and then decided to leave his truck on North Peters, walk back toward Jackson Square, and give it a try anyway. If he wasn't successful, he'd come back later in the week.

He moved from one perch to another along Decatur, hovering around the steps of Washington Artillery Park, watching the few lonely horses and carriages which patiently waited for fares. None of the men trolling for spare change from passersby were tall enough. He'd been at it for nearly three hours when finally, looking across at St. Louis Cathedral and the Lucky Dog wienie wagon parked on the curb, he saw a potential match for Brent coming toward him. The man appeared to be tall enough but was slightly hunched over. Many layers of clothing concealed his actual build.

Trey looked at his watch. It was 4:00 P.M. and growing colder. He figured the fellow would be on the streets for at least another hour, and then at dark might head toward the Rampart Mission or some other stewpot for a free meal. He stood up as the man approached him to make sure he was tall enough. The man's stench almost made Trey gag, and for a moment, he reconsidered his plan, but given what Trey needed, the filth and odor were probably unavoidable.

Quickly crossing the street, Trey turned up along the park, weaving through the sidewalk artists and vendors who'd braved the cold. He raced around the block, slowing as he reached Decatur to get his breathing back in pace. His man was crossing the street from the edge of the Brewery, headed toward him. By the time he shuffled the intervening block, Trey was leaning casually against a window, right in the guy's path, pondering how to survive with this dead-beat beside him for the hour it would take before he could safely dump him into the back of the truck.

As the panhandler approached, Trey pulled out a crumpled pack of cigarettes and popped one up toward his mouth, stretching his leg into the sidewalk to dig into his pants pocket for a lighter. The last move caught the man's attention.

The drifter eyed the cigarette longingly. "Got a smoke?" he said, coughing out the words.

Trey shook his head, expressionless. "Only a couple left...." He paused looking into the man's forlorn face, then relented. "You look worse off than me. Here."

He pushed a cigarette toward him and leaned forward to offer a light. The man's odor was repulsive but Trey intentionally delayed giving him a flame, holding him there as long as he could, hoping to engage him in conversation. "Jesus, it's cold tonight."

The guy grunted a combination assent and thanks after the cigarette finally caught. Trey watched him shuffle a couple of steps, then called to him. "Know where I can get a free meal?"

The drifter turned and looked Trey over before he answered. "A few blocks down on Rampart, if you're not too picky."

"Thanks."

The drifter moved on.

Trey hoped the man would walk toward the truck but he stayed on Decatur, heading toward Canal Street. Trey ambled along a block behind him, then left his prey's trail. Snatching up the parking ticket sticking out from under the wiper of his truck, he climbed in, filed the ticket above the visor in a rat's nest of receipts and gas tickets, and cranked the engine. He turned the heater on full blast.

Pulling around onto Bienville, he slowed down at the Decatur intersection. His quarry had stopped to say something to a fireman waiting outside the station. Trey pulled around the corner and slid up to the curb in front of the House of Blues and watched the man move toward Canal Street where, at the corner, he turned west and disappeared from view.

Trey pulled out and moved up to the intersection, partially blocking the crosswalk, looking down the block and finding the guy working patrons coming and going from the Marriott.

When the light changed, Trey stayed right where he was, rolling down the window to signal the car behind him to go around, ignoring the couple of inconvenienced citizens who felt duty-bound to bang on the camper shell to lodge their protest.

From his vantage point he could see the man make his slow progress, speeded only by a uniformed hotel guard who hustled him on. Trey waited where he was, sitting through a second light, until he saw the guy turn in on Chartres, walking with the one-way traffic, back into the Quarter. With a quiet "Yes," Trey pulled out and moved up the street, now impatient for the light to change so that he could get the guy in view again.

After the faster traffic moved by, he drove down Chartres acting like a lost tourist, passing the guy, then stopping when he appeared in the rearview mirror. He leaned over to roll down the window.

"Hey," Trey called loudly to him. "Where's Rampart from here?"

The guy looked over, not recognizing him or the truck.

"It's me—'Smokes,'" Trey called.

The guy was still confused but stepped closer.

"Where's Rampart from here?" Trey repeated.

A glimmer of recognition spread across the guy's face and he approached the door. "You got wheels?" he said, incredulous.

Trey sighed with relief, then grimaced for the guy's benefit. "That's all I got. I sleep in the back."

"More than me," the man grumbled.

"And I can't waste gas chatting," Trey said curtly. "Where's this place to eat?" Trey turned down the heater to listen but warmth still wafted from the cab of the truck though the open window, licking the man's face.

"Turn up there," said the guy, waving his arm toward some location down the street, "and go all the way to the next big street—several blocks, don't know how many."

"Thanks." As Trey pulled away, the guy checked out the battered truck and shell. Trey rolled a yard or two and stopped again, close to the curb so that a car could pass on the driver's side. "Wanna ride?"

The man hesitated, taking a moment to peer in the grimy rectangular window of the old camper shell where Trey had stashed a box of junk, an old suitcase, a ratty moth-eaten blanket, and a filthy pillow. He grabbed the door handle. "Yeah."

Trey's pulse and breathing quickened. He was going to be able to do this. He could give Brent his way to escape.

Though the warmth made the man's stench even stronger, Trey stifled his reaction and cranked up the heater to seal the deal. "Roll up the window. You'll get warm, I promise you."

Trey checked the rearview mirrors. The empty wall of the Marriott parking garage was on the passenger side of the truck. There was no one on the street ahead or to the other side. And the camper shell obscured the view from behind.

Trey breathed in deeply, the repugnant smell of the man suddenly filling his whole head. He reached toward the radio dial, exhaling. At 870 AM, WWL, Trey stopped tuning, drew in another full, foul, breath, smiled at the man, then let loose with a lightning swift blow smashing the man's Adam's apple with the outside edge of his right hand. It was a move he'd practiced for years on the empty seat of his patrol car for just the occasion when a prisoner got out of hand. Then Trey grabbed the stunned man before he could react and brought his arm completely around the drifter's neck in a sleeper hold, squeezing as tight as possible to shut off the carotid arteries in the vice of his fore and upper arms. The man clawed at Trey's arms a few times, then passed out. Trey kept the pressure up, his eyes shifting from the rearview mirror to the street ahead of him. It was a full minute before anyone appeared, and by then, the man was nearly dead.

A low sports car approached from behind. Trey turned toward the drifter's limp body, hiding what was happening from the passengers. The car passed, never even slowing down.

He pulled his arm in tighter and increased the pressure for the final few seconds. The man was dead. Trey grunted, a deep throaty rattle, as an orgasmic shiver swept through his body. He took another deep breath and exhaled. Then he reached past the body and locked the door. He pushed the dead mass down so it was lodged below the heater and glovebox and couldn't be seen from passing cars. He yanked a blanket he'd stuffed behind the seat and covered the body. Then he shut off the heater and cracked open his own window a bit.

Trey left the Quarter, drove out Poydras to I-10, and headed toward Mississippi. At Manchac he pulled off the interstate, turned north up a rarely traveled road he'd scouted earlier, and stopped at a deserted rest area. He backed the truck into the north corner so that on the outside chance anyone passed by from either direction, they wouldn't see his movements clearly.

Trey pulled out the corpse and draped it around his shoulders like he was walking with a drunk. He pushed it into the camper, straightening out the legs and arms as best he could. Rigor mortis would be setting in by the time he finally reached the farm, and it would be easier to get a long straight body into the cooler than a curled up one.

Despite the dropping temperatures, he kept the windows down the entire ride. Freezing seemed preferable to the stench.

■ ■ ■ ■

Trey was in the barn when Brent drove in from the office.

"So what have you come up with?" Brent asked. Trey watched him button his camel hair coat against the cold.

"A car wreck's the best solution."

"You can do it? I mean, so no one knows?"

"Yeah."

"How?"

"I'd find a body to put in your car, set up the wreck, and have it all burn to a crisp, including the corpse."

"Where would you get the body?"

"That's not a problem." Trey stepped toward the meat locker and swung the door open. The naked body of the homeless guy was hanging from a hook, suspended by a web harness about his torso. His skin was a chalky, grayish color.

"Jesus Christ." Brent recoiled, moving toward the outside to retch. "Close that."

Trey shut the door.

"Who is he?"

"You don't need to know, but rest assured, no one cares that he's gone, and there aren't any traces. I picked him because he's your height."

"You must be pretty sure you can pull this off."

"They don't autopsy wreck victims when there's no suspicion of foul play. I can handle that, no question."

"Man, you are one cold-blooded dude." Brent moved to his car. "Come up to the house and let's talk about it," he said.

Trey gave Brent a half hour to change out of his clothes before he pulled up to the main house.

"Beer?"

"Sure."

They settled in the living room where the national news was on the big screen television with the sound muted.

"I'm slitting my own throat, if I do this for you," Trey said.

"How so?"

"I'm making it easy for you to go on the chance that I can follow later. When you go, I lose everything—no more hunt club, no more outside income, no more house at the farm...."

"You own that."

"But you're my neighbor. With you gone, I'd be living next to the bitch..." Trey's voice turned bitter, "excuse me, Grace, or whoever she sold it to."

"She'll sell it," Brent said. "She's hardly set foot on the place in years. Too many bad memories."

"Whatever—that's gonna be the end of my privacy," Trey said.

"I'm not asking you to do this for free. I know what you're taking on and I owe you. Jesus, I almost puked down there."

Trey shrugged his shoulders.

"I'll leave you two hundred fifty thousand up front," Brent continued, "and send more each year until you can join me. I can't guarantee what will happen with the farm, but I took care of the hunt club years ago."

"How so?"

"I executed an option clause that gave you right of first refusal to buy the house and as much land as you wanted if anything ever happened to me."

"Why'd you do that?"

"If I ever lost this place, for whatever reason, I wanted you to have a chance to get it, free and clear, figuring you'd let me visit every once in a while."

"Is it valid?"

"Sure," Brent said. "You paid me quite well for it...."

"I did?"

"Yeah, you did. My accounts show you paid me five thousand dollars for the option. Happened to be the same amount you repaid after you'd borrowed some money. But since I never wrote down that loan, I called your payment consideration for the option. Look at the memo line on your check to me. There's a copy of the deed in my safe deposit box."

Trey shook his head. "I'm amazed." He had fleeting thoughts about what he could do with a quarter million, but his pleasure faded quickly. The prospect of losing Brent's companionship was deeply disturbing. Brent was father, brother, and friend—Brent completed him, anchored him, and over the years, he'd discarded nearly all other relationships. He did his assignments for the State Patrol, sometimes with notable ability, but his pleasure, the time when he was most at ease, was with Brent, whether it was at the farm or the hunting camp. Now, all that would end.

"And you still don't see any alternatives?"

"No," said Brent. "I want to walk away—before anything starts with Morgan—take up a new life with no one looking for me. I can work with a clean slate. I can't live with this."

"But if you leave and then Morgan talks, they might look at the wreck."

"Your job is to make it look so good they don't investigate," Brent said.

"I'd rather not take the chance of him talking," Trey said.

"Not now, while I'm here, and not any time soon, when my death is still fresh in their minds. It's better just to let him be. He's not stable."

"Is there something more than this Morgan business?" Trey said. "Something else I don't know about?"

Trey, his investigative instincts alert, noticed that Brent didn't respond immediately.

"Morgan was my only mistake—but a very big one. It's all financial stuff, nothing more."

"State or federal?"

"What?"

"Are they state or federal violations?"

"They'd come after me on taxes, but maybe theft, too—so both."

"Too bad," Trey said. "Federal time you could handle."

"No," Brent said, shaking his head. "I can't, and won't risk being publicly humiliated and destroyed."

"Does Grace know about any of this?" Trey asked, pronouncing her name as though the very act of saying it was distasteful. Trey'd never had much success with women—not with his mother who'd raised him single-handed, nor his wife who'd left him after five years, nor his daughters who, as babies, screamed at his touch. He'd rarely seen any of them since the girls were toddlers.

"Hardly," Brent said. "You know we don't see each other except when there's entertaining. It's been years since she paid any attention to what I do. She takes her allotment and that's it."

"Are you sure?"

"She'll be glad when I'm gone, I doubt she'll ever look back. She'll get the insurance money and a lot of real estate. Everything except the option I'm leaving you."

Trey grunted again. "How much time do we have?"

"Not much. The sooner it happens, the less the chance someone will associate my death with Morgan, if he should make a move."

Trey nodded, not saying a word.

"We can arrange it around my trip to Roatan. I'm leaving on Thursday, and I'll be back one week later."

"Good, that'll give you several days to change your mind," Trey said. "I can always bury the guy in the cooler somewhere." Then he added, "Do you know that the majority of people who disappear can't stand it and come back?"

"I'm not the majority."

"That's what everyone says," Trey replied. "It's not as easy as you think. You'll need a new identity. Have you worked that out?"

"I have."

"How?"

"I think it's better if you don't know those details, don't you?"

Trey looked at Brent, edgy about being denied a crucial piece of information. "Maybe."

"You'd be able to pass a lie detector if it comes to that."

"But it won't."

Brent smiled. "I figure that's true, but I don't want to take any chances."

"And you trust me to do this?"

"I trust you more than anyone I've ever known. You've been a loyal friend for a long time. And though money can't repay you entirely, there'll be plenty so you can get along, no matter what."

Trey's thin lips barely curled upward. "Late night return from New Orleans after the trip. Fell asleep at the wheel."

"Sounds perfect."

"If it doesn't work, we can claim the car was stolen." Trey let it sink in. "But I want one other thing."

"Yes?"

"We close the camp for a day—no one's out there anyway—and hunt like we used to, before the club, before all of this. One more trophy buck and a set of antlers for the wall. Maybe it'll clear your head."

"Deal." Brent smiled. "But right now I want some food and brandy. Join me?"

"Sure thing." All this could be handled by taking care of Morgan, Trey thought. But a more bullheaded bastard than Brent Wexler had never been born. It always had to be done his way.

■ ■ ■ ■

Brent closeted himself at Saragossa for the next two days, keeping in touch with the office over the phone while he went through boxes of papers, culling the incriminating pieces, but keeping enough so that it didn't look like he'd pitched everything. He separated the business documents from the fund-raising and campaign materials and organized it all in the file cabinet.

Every paper, every topic brought memories flooding through him, feeding his anger over Morgan's stupidity.

There he was, right on the verge of real power, and he had to give it up because of that fat bastard.

When he left for Second Creek and the hunt club, he was ready to explode, but grateful that he'd be occupied the next day. Hunting was still the one certain, ecstatic release in his life.

Hunting hadn't always been so satisfying for Brent. He'd started years before, like every other busy man turned weekend killer, driving to the camp on Friday, getting up before dawn, gearing up, heading out to a deer stand, slaughtering an animal, bringing it back in, eating a hearty dinner, drinking late into the night, doing it again on Sunday, then leaving.

All that changed when Trey had started working for him and went along one morning. Brent killed a ten-point buck with a shotgun—it took both of them to load the animal into a truck. Back at camp, Trey, with his usual relish, immediately set to work skinning and dressing. Brent was watching his rapid, skillful maneuvers, when Trey, who rarely spoke when absorbed in a task, said, "This was too easy."

"What was?"

"Killing this buck, it was too easy."

"How so?"

"We had all the advantages."

"What are you suggesting?"

"That we switch to bows, don't use any stands, that we really hunt."

Trey had caught him at a moment when Brent had more spare time than usual. The idea intrigued him and over the next several months, Brent, under Trey's tutelage, mastered the compound bow. But then they changed again to more primitive models, always seeking to level the playing field with the animals. Trey taught Brent all the hunting techniques he'd learned in the Marines. They ran through the woods, increasingly swiftly and silently.

With each outing, their obsession had grown. Brent put off for another year starting up the hunting club he'd promised several friends, not willing to share the land and its pleasures with anyone other than Trey. Whenever the two had several days they could set aside, Brent disappeared immediately to Second Creek. Their weekends had evolved to challenges, issued the first night—the challenger decided what weapons and supplies each could take and how long they could hunt. They'd split the property in half, giving each fifteen hundred acres, and the score was kept in pelts, skins, or gobblers brought in. The competition was keen, but that wasn't the real attraction—it was the abandon, the killing, by knives, if possible—that aroused them both. After the club was opened, they had fewer opportunities for the challenges, one of Brent's greatest regrets.

This time, both acutely aware that it was their last hunt together, they didn't separate. They set out well before dawn, carrying bows, a few arrows, Bowie knives, and matches. They moved down the dark trails with ease, not stopping for small game even though they were growing hungrier with the passing hours. The sun was nearly up when they found quarry fit for a last hunt—as big a buck as they'd ever seen on the place, two hundred and fifty pounds easily—feeding quietly near the opening of a deep ravine, the walls of which were too steep to provide an escape.

As the animal wandered into its trap, grazing along the way, Trey and Brent separated to close in on it from opposite directions, shutting off both exits. Every nerve tingled, every muscle tensed. The buck never interrupted its meal until Trey's arm, moving to pull an arrow from his quiver, caught its eye. It looked up, utterly motionless, then in the next instant, turned from Trey and headed toward Brent, who stood blocking the narrow north exit. The desperate animal struggled to mount the embankment, but failing, charged Brent, his antlers down. Trey shot an arrow into the buck's hind quarter at the last moment. The animal raised its head and bolted past Brent who'd scrambled out of danger.

The buck stumbled but regained its balance, heading out of the clearing. Trey was beside Brent in a moment and they took off in pursuit, following the trail for hundreds of yards through thick underbrush and wet bottoms until they had the creature in sight again, moving ever more slowly, disoriented by his wound.

The two men bolted ahead, wildly lunging at the animal, ignoring its obvious inability to either fight or flee. In an instant, Trey sliced across its throat and Brent slashed deep into its side, finishing it. Trey pushed Brent away for more, opening the belly with another flash of an incision, exposing warm flesh, the organs still pulsing.

Both men paced around the dead animal, reeling from their triumph, inspecting their prey, then dropping to the ground, spent.

Without a word, Brent set about collecting wood for a fire and Trey carved away enough meat for them to satisfy their now intense hunger.

■ ■ ■ ■

Trey was up at five, as usual. The near freezing temperatures overnight had glazed the roads with an icy frosting that made his seven-mile run on the Saragossa cut-off treacherous. When he returned to his house, he switched on the small television in the kitchen to catch the morning news shows. The programs were filled with bulletins about the weather system gripping the entire eastern half of the country in an icy hand. At a piece on soup kitchens in Boston, Trey started talking back to the TV.

"Leeches," he muttered, "nothing but goddamn leeches" as the camera focused on a homeless person. Trey turned away to crack several eggs to scramble them and when he looked up, the reporter was interviewing a well-dressed, well-fed teenager who had been serving food.

"And you," Trey called, waving his fork in the direction of the television, "you are a damned sucker, if I've ever seen one. Your parents must be crazy." The topic switched to a cease-fire in one of the many bloody international disputes and Trey poured his eggs in the pan, a relative calm returning.

Brent drove the less valuable of his two Mercedes, a vintage 1964 230 SL, through the open doorway of the barn a half hour later. By the time he'd loaded his bags into the back of the old Ford farm truck, which had recently been outfitted with a new camper shell, Trey had appeared from his house, ready to go.

"Mornin'," Trey said. He locked the barn door and then slipped behind the wheel.

"The keys are in the ignition," said Brent. "I left luggage in the trunk and a loaded briefcase behind the front seat. The clothes, shoes, watch, rings, and cufflinks are on the passenger seat."

Trey nodded, cranked the pickup engine and rolled out of the drive, stopping to lock the gate behind him.

"What's that weird smell?" Brent asked.

"Your double."

"He was in here?"

"I killed him when he was sitting right where you are now."

"Jesus."

"Gotta do whatcha gotta do."

All through Mississippi, they made small talk about the hunting camp and the farm, as if avoiding a painful topic. Past Hammond, Louisiana, the road rose to an uninterrupted elevated ribbon of concrete above the swamp, teeming with life in the summer but inhospitable in the cold of winter. Brent finally turned the conversation to what they needed to discuss.

"There's $250,000 in cash in the safe for you," Brent said. "It should be plenty to exercise the option on the hunting camp house. I'm betting Grace'll unload it. She never liked the place. But Grace's no fool, and she's not one of your fans, so she'll drive a hard bargain."

"I don't like doing that. It'll look suspicious. There's no way I could have money like that."

"I leave it up to you how to play it out, but I think it would be good to have control of some or all of that land."

"How soon do you think all this'll take place?"

"They'll file an accounting of my estate within ninety days of my..." Brent paused, choosing his word, "demise...and there's really no reason that the court won't let her sell assets right away."

"What about the farm?"

"I've been thinking about it. I doubt she'll want that either. Too much trouble and too many difficult memories."

"I hope so. I'd hate to pass her on the road every morning. What do you think she could get for it?"

"If a developer picked it up..."

"You're shittin' me, aren't you?"

"No. People are looking for country land. There would be sixty ten-acre parcels, one with the main house on it. That could fetch well over a million—probably two, depending on how it was marketed."

Trey shook his head. "There goes the best setup I've ever had."

"That's where the option on the camphouse comes in. Get the club to build their own house on the other end of the Red Crown Road. You'll have complete privacy—sell the farmhouse and ten acres for fifty thousand if you want. The camp is more remote, probably better in the long run, anyway."

"It's farther from Jackson," Trey retorted.

"Not that much."

The silence was thick. "We'll see," said Trey. "You know, you can call this off—right up until the last minute."

"I know that. You can back out too."

"I'm not the one who's got to live through this. No one will ever prove anything against me. You make the decision."

"I'll be out of the country by the time it's happened."

Trey shook his head. "I'm telling you, you don't need to do this."

"And I'm telling you, it's my one clear chance."

The roadway broke out of the swamp into the causeway across the Lake Ponchartrain inlet, funneling cars into the city. Oil refinery stacks rose in the distance, and beyond that, New Orleans. The end of their many years together was at hand. Trey didn't want to talk about it, but he couldn't forget it either. As he pulled up to the Delta Airlines entrance, Trey hopped out to help with Brent's gear.

"I can handle it. You get on with what you have to do. I'll check in with you when I fly back in next week."

"I'll be at the house. If I'm not, though, bump my pager."

There was an awkward silence as they stood there, each confident of the other's friendship and loyalty, but still uneasy. Brent laid his hand firmly on Trey's shoulder. "Thanks for all you've done. I'll let you know where I am as soon as possible. Be paying attention for a signal, I just don't know what it will be yet."

"I will."

Brent stuck out his hand and Trey took it. Brent was holding on very firmly, and Trey looked away, almost embarrassed.

"No matter what happens," said Trey quietly, "I owe you—you've set me up for life. That's more than anyone could ever ask for."

"No, I owe you. You're giving me a new life."

Trey's eyes bored into Brent's.

"You're giving us a new life," said Brent, quickly correcting himself.

Trey's smile returned. With nothing further to say, he climbed in the truck, filled with regret. As he cranked the engine, he reached over and rolled down the window, shouting to Brent who was heading toward the terminal.

"Hey, have a good time in Roatan. I'll wait for your call." Trey waved his index finger in a friendly salute.

Brent nodded, and Trey pulled away from the curb.

# FOUR

Laura stood in front of the open refrigerator staring into the abyss, clueless about lunch the next day for Will. Already in his pajamas and teeth brushed, her son was drawing spindly dragons at the kitchen counter, impatient for Laura to finish cleaning up so she could read to him. Some days he followed her around like a shadow, never letting her out of his sight and this was one of them. Laura wasn't certain if the clinging was normal for a six-year-old or a function of losing his father. Probably a little of both.

"Do you want a hot lunch tomorrow, Sweetheart?" she asked.

"What is it?" Will said, never taking his marker off his paper.

Laura closed the door and consulted the school lunch menu which was stuck to the front with a magnet. "Chicken noodle soup and a grilled cheese."

"What's for dessert?"

"Cake."

"Okay!" said Will enthusiastically.

"Are you going to eat the soup and sandwich or do you just

want cake?" Laura asked.

"I'll eat the sandwich," Will promised.

"Good, solves that for another day," Laura muttered.

"Are you finished yet?"

"Yes," Laura said, closing the dishwasher and spinning the dial to "on." The machine immediately began its ominous rattle, an annoying noise but not so bothersome that she'd considered taking a morning off for a repair man to come.

Will jumped down and raced across the main room to the extra large overstuffed chair, big enough so he could sit beside Laura comfortably. Her late husband Semmes, an architect, had designed their simple house with a large, airy main room. Three bedrooms and an office were off the hallway to the side. A fireplace dominated the main room, with the couch and reading chairs in front of it. The huge chair had been Semmes', but since his death, Will had staked it out as his favorite spot.

She began to read and had only read three pages of *The Indian in the Cupboard* before Will began to doze against her shoulder. Laura had gently extricated herself to get his bed ready when the phone rang. For a moment she considered not answering and listening to the message later, but then she raced to pick it up in time.

"I just got a call from the newspaper," Vic said. "They wanted a comment from the governor on a story they'll run tomorrow about troopers on welfare. Did you know about this?"

"No. No one's called me."

"Apparently, one of your boys—in uniform—was seen standing in line to get food stamps," Vic said, clearly irritated.

"Are you surprised?"

"Well..."

"Hasn't anything I've said gotten through?" Laura asked. "There are three issues for troopers: money, money, and money."

"And I've told you why we can't do it this year."

"Then at least the Governor could stop insulting everyone by acting as though they don't need a raise."

"Where do we get the money to pay for it?"

"I've already told you—cut back on the crime bill and take half the revenue."

"Did you arrange this?" Vic asked, ignoring her answer.

"Nope. But it was only a matter of time until it happened. Without seeing the story, I'll bet I know who the trooper is."

"Why?"

"We've got a real go-getter, trained in smuggling interdiction," Laura answered. "But he's also got four kids, so he's eligible for assistance. What did you say to the reporter?"

"I told her 'no comment.'"

"That's safe."

"Just pray there isn't a picture, Laura," Vic said.

"Did they say they had one?"

"I didn't have the courage to ask." He sounded weary to the bone. "If you hear anything let me know."

"Will do," Laura said.

"And if they call you, I hope you'll have no comment."

"I'll do my best."

Will was sound asleep by the time Laura hung up, curled up in the chair with his head on the armrest. She roused him enough to guide him to his room—she couldn't carry his sixty-five pounds more than a few steps safely, a change she both welcomed and regretted. His tight hugs around her neck had always felt so good, so reassuring. Now his hugs were the only ones in her busy life, save a rare, but always less tenacious embrace from an old friend or a family member. Although Will mumbled something about her reading to him some more, once his head touched the pillow he was out again.

Whatever jump she'd had on drifting off to sleep early had been lost with Vic's phone call. Laura was now wide awake without a book that really grabbed her, no new videos to watch, nothing worth seeing on television, and too distracted to work on taxes. She tuned in the classical music station and filled the main room with something she was fairly certain was Mozart, then got the mountain of accumulated clean laundry and folded clothes in front of the fire.

The monotony of folding didn't do the trick either, so once everything had been put away, she made herself lemon tea with honey and a shot of bourbon, turned off all the lights, and settled back into Semmes' chair to stare at the flames.

Laura wasn't entirely beyond weeping over her husband's death, but tears seemed to sprout at the oddest times—no longer evoked by talking about him or remembering things they'd done together. Now it was those cloying, poignant telephone company commercials or cozy Christmas beer ads with a smiling couple snuggling in a horse-drawn sleigh on a snowy night that brought an instant melancholy. The initial desperation and anger had given way to a dull confusion about her future. When Semmes had been alive, she'd fantasized about the years ahead, about places they'd visit, and projects they'd undertake—large and small—but she'd lost her ability to imagine a future.

Now she was only certain of two things: Will loved her absolutely, and she needed to hold on to her job. The State Patrol, for better or worse, was a road taken. Where to, she was never entirely certain, but it never failed to captivate her, which was exactly what she needed most.

But what's going to happen if the Governor wins the election? she wondered.

And what about Vic? He was all business when there was business to tend to, but how nice it was to get one of his smiles, not to mention the sweet kisses.

She closed her eyes, too confused to even think about the possibilities.

After a moment, Laura picked up her mug and went to her office, turning on the computer and settling back in the upholstered swivel chair, her feet up on the desk. When the computer finished powering up, she clicked on the icon to connect to the Internet. The computer beeped. She had e-mail waiting: a message from her service provider about the monthly billing, a news service, and a message from "Naomiskip" that had been sent early that morning.

**LAURA:**

IT WAS GREAT TO SEE YOU IN JACKSON. I'M SORRY I'VE TAKEN SO LONG TO SEND YOU A NOTE, BUT A FEW DAYS OFF ALWAYS PUTS ME WAY BEHIND AND I'VE GOT A TRIAL COMING UP. I DON'T KNOW IF YOU'RE AS HOOKED ON E-MAIL AS I AM, BUT IT SEEMS LIKE IT'S THE ONLY WAY I COMMUNICATE ANY MORE.

BIG NEWS: JOHN POPPED THE QUESTION. (MY GOD, DALLAS IS A TRIP. THEY DO IT BIGGER AND FLASHIER AND THEY'RE ABSOLUTELY CERTAIN IT'S BETTER. THAT RESORT WAS NO EXCEPTION.) AND I ACCEPTED! HE GAVE ME THIS UNBELIEVABLE EMERALD-CUT DIAMOND RING THE SIZE OF DELAWARE. SAID IT HAD BEEN HIS GRANDMOTHER'S—SHE MUST HAVE HAD GREAT BICEPS DEFINITION AS A RESULT. EVERYONE NOTICES THE RING, WHICH MEANS NOW I'VE GOT TO STOP CHEWING MY FINGERNAILS. ANOTHER VICE BITES THE DUST.

WE DIDN'T SET A DATE, AND OF COURSE, I'M HAVING SECOND THOUGHTS. TELL ME WHAT I SHOULD DO. YOU WERE ALWAYS BETTER AT CONTRACTS THAN I WAS.

CIAO, NAOMI

Laura hit the reply button and immediately began typing.

**NAOMI,**

GREAT TO HEAR FROM YOU AND JUST WHAT I NEEDED. WILL'S ASLEEP AND I WAS FEELING LONELY AND SORRY FOR MYSELF.

CONGRATULATIONS! IF YOU LOVE JOHN, IF HE MAKES YOU FEEL CALM AND SAFE, THEN I SAY GO FOR IT. THERE'S NOTHING LIKE IT. I KNOW.

ONE REASON I'M SORT OF BLUE IS VIC JUST CALLED ME WITH THE NEWS THAT I'VE GOTTEN MYSELF IN ANOTHER JAM. THE TROOPERS WANT AND DESERVE BETTER PAY, BUT UNFORTUNATELY IT ISN'T ON CARVER'S MASTER PLAN. TOMORROW THERE'S GOING TO BE A FRONT PAGE STORY ABOUT TROOPERS ON FOOD STAMPS. AND I'M GONNA GET IT FROM CARVER, I CAN ALREADY FEEL IT COMING. CAUGHT BETWEEN ANOTHER ROCK AND A HARD PLACE. AND IT'S ALL EVEN MORE COMPLICATED BECAUSE OF VIC. NOT SURE WHERE MY RELATIONSHIP WITH HIM IS GOING, BUT THERE MAY BE SOMETHING THERE. AND I LIKE IT. A WHOLE LOT.

NEED ANY EXPERIENCED ATTORNEYS? I MAY BE LOOKING FOR A NEW JOB.

LATER, LAURA

P.S. SEEMS AS THOUGH WE'VE PICKED UP MID-SENTENCE.

■ ■ ■ ■

Dr. Rachel Stone, division chief of pediatric anaesthesiology at University Hospital, was standing on her hands, her lithe body propped against the far wall next to the fireplace, when Lt. Col. Robert Stone trotted into the huge country kitchen and family room from his five mile morning run, sweat gleaming on the dark, well-toned muscles of his arms and shoulders.

"Man, it's muggy out there," he said, pulling a dish towel from the drawer to wipe his face. He dropped the newspaper, still in its rubber band, onto the counter and looked across the family room at his wife. "Only in Mississippi can you freeze your ass off one day, and sweat it off the next. What's on your schedule today, Sugar?"

Rachel brought her legs down and forward, and then slowly stood up. "A pretty tricky procedure on a three-month old to replace a heart valve, then some routine cases this afternoon."

Robert filled a huge blue tumbler with water and immediately gulped down half of it. He refilled it and moved toward the fish tank at the end of the counter, watching a blue angelfish wander around the rocks he'd piled in the center. He opened the lid to feed them.

"Your father just called," Rachel said. "I let him talk to the answering machine but you probably ought to call him back."

"Something wrong?"

"Sounds like your nephews got in a little trouble again last night. I think there was a fight in a juke joint from what I could gather."

"What were they doing out on a school night?"

"Your father mentioned that, too."

"I hope no one bailed them out."

"He didn't say," she answered. "I probably should have picked up and talked to Daddy, but this wasn't the day to start with one of his speeches about your worthless brother letting those boys run wild."

"Don't apologize," Robert said. "It's my family, Baby, not yours." Robert took another big swig of water. "I have to say, this is one of the rare times I'm thankful we don't have children."

Rachel didn't reply. It wasn't a matter of choice or lack of trying—she had never been able to conceive. They'd finally given up on all the fancy new drugs and techniques, mainly out of fear of an unhealthy multiple birth. She opened up the paper and glanced at the headlines. "You'll have a big day today, my love."

"Why do you say that?" Robert asked, moving closer to look over her shoulder.

Above the fold on the front page was a photo of people waiting in front of a counter clearly marked 'Food Stamps' with the headline, "Troopers on Welfare." The last two in line were an unidentified trooper and a sheriff's deputy. She handed the front section to Robert and kept the second section, checking the financial page first and then the obituaries. Robert read the story intently, then looked up at his wife, smiling.

"Aren't you surprised?" Rachel asked.

"Nope."

"You planted this?"

"No comment," Robert said, kissing her on her forehead. "But I think I'd better get a shower and head in."

■ ■ ■ ■

The elevator to the private quarters of the Mansion banged open and Carver strode out, swatting his hand with a rolled up newspaper. Captain Sandy Quinn jumped up from behind the front desk.

"Good morning, sir," Sandy said.

"Morning," Carver growled, never slowing down. "Get Owen on the phone."

"Yes, sir," said Sandy, picking up the phone and punching in some numbers. "She may be en route to the office right about now, though."

"Whatever," Carver said. "Just find her."

Sandy tried her office but when Laura didn't answer, the call flipped over to Deborah, Laura's secretary. "She hasn't arrived yet," Deborah said. "Do you want to talk to the chief?"

"Sure," Sandy answered.

"Blake Coleman," came a deep voice a moment later.

"Chief, this is Quinn. The Governor wants to talk to the Commissioner. Know where she is?"

"She should be here shortly," Blake said. "Robert and I are scheduled to meet with her at nine. Is there a problem?"

"I'd say. The man's so pissed he can hardly see straight."

"Bet that picture on the front page hit a nerve."

Sandy looked down at the morning paper spread out on his desk and the back of a trooper's distinctive gray and blue uniform. "I think that's a fair assumption."

"We'll get her to call ASAP," Blake said.

As he hung up, Blake heard a knock on his door and looked up to see Robert.

"I see that hint you dropped worked like a charm," Robert said, sliding onto the sofa.

"The Commissioner's going to catch hell for it though. Quinn says Carver's hopping mad."

■ ■ ■ ■

"Just what did you intend to accomplish with this stunt, young lady?" Governor Carver asked over the phone.

"Sir, I had nothing to do with this story," said Laura, barely controlling her glee. "If I'd known about it, I would have stopped it."

"Sure," said Carver sarcastically. There was a quiet knock on her door and Blake looked in with Robert behind him. Laura waved them forward, then put her finger to her lips for silence.

"I'm serious, Governor. That trooper works narcotics interdiction. He routinely relieves drug couriers of thousands of dollars—I wouldn't want to cast any aspersions on his motives or veracity."

Carver didn't have an immediate comeback. "Obviously, I'm not privy to that kind of information."

"Most troopers have second jobs and some even have third jobs to make ends meet," Laura said, rolling her eyes in exasperation. "The men have families to feed."

"I've heard this before—you've made your point quite well on that score, Ms. Owen," Carver said, still aggravated. "I expect you to keep a lid on this sort of thing in the future."

"I don't know if I can, sir," Laura said.

"Do your dead-level best," Carver said and hung up.

Laura picked up her copy of the morning paper and flashed it at Blake and Robert. "This was brilliant, gentlemen."

"Sounds like the Governor doesn't think so," Blake said, running his hand through his gray hair, smoothing it away from his forehead.

"He's not a happy camper." She pointed to the paper. "Kinda wish I'd thought of it myself."

"We'd like to take credit for the idea but..." Robert began.

"But of course you can't," Laura interrupted before either could make any admissions. "Neither of you had anything to do with this, at least not directly. Correct?"

"Nothing whatsoever," said Blake, smiling enough to show the beginnings of deep dimples. He unbuttoned the collar of his shirt and loosened his tie as if he'd been suffering in it for a whole day instead of an hour.

"From what I hear," Robert chimed in, "that news reporter just happened to be at the Welfare Office with a camera."

"Wonder how a deputy sheriff happened to be there, too?" Laura asked. "Incredible coincidence."

"You're right about that," Blake said. "Amazing."

■ ■ ■ ■

"Come in, Madame Commissioner," said Holden Bowser, Chairman of the House Appropriations Committee. "Do I understand correctly that you're in kind of a pickle?"

"That's one word for it," Laura said, taking one of the two seats in the small office created when the Capitol was renovated.

"Since it was a trooper's picture in the paper, the Governor's furious at me. On the other hand, the troopers don't think I have much sway with the Governor or he wouldn't be opposing the pay raise. Damned if I do and damned if I don't—as usual."

Bowser leaned back from his work and smiled. Although a diminutive man—only three inches taller than Laura—he had an incredible memory for figures, the perfect attribute for his position. He'd watched her struggle with the senators and representatives who didn't 'cotton' to the notion of a woman in the commissioner's chair. But he liked Laura's pluck—it was admirable as well as entertaining. "Ahhh, yes, the ecstasy of leadership. Not exactly what you had in mind when you took the job, I expect."

"Hardly," Laura said. "If I had known then what I know now, I doubt I would have agreed."

"I bet you would have," Bowser said. "You impress me as someone who likes a challenge."

"Yes, but I usually prefer better odds."

"You know it went out over the wire," Bowser said, "and got picked up by half the newspapers across the country."

"Yes, I know," Laura said, shaking her head. "We've seen some of the copy."

"'Lowest-paid police in the nation,' I think the headline was in the *Atlanta Journal-Constitution*—bottom of the barrel again," Bowser said. "Puts me in quite a jam. If we were only talking about law enforcement, I'd be home free—I can always find a million or two here or there. But the other employees are in just as bad shape, and that's a much bigger nut to crack."

"What can I do?"

"Find a funding source for starters," Bowser said.

"The crime bill has several new fees in it. I think it'd perfectly appropriate to use half those funds to pay the troopers. And it would all be under the guise of getting tough on crime."

"Now that's a interesting trade-off. Wouldn't it gut the bill?"

"Not entirely. You can hold off on implementing some of it for another year."

"But what about the rest of the state employees?"

"They aren't my problem."

"They are now, if you want your men to get their raises."

"I'll work on it," Laura said, regretting her snappy answer. "But I don't know why there can't be a larger raise just for cops, like you did for teachers."

"That may be where we end up, but it won't be an easy thing to sell to all the members. Particularly not when you've got the

Governor on the same side of the issue as Senator Gabriel Collel. He's spending every waking moment trying to discredit you. What did you do to him?"

"All I did was ask him to document some travel expenses when I was in the State Auditor's office. And he couldn't, so I asked him to repay the money."

Bowser looked at her askance.

"That's all," Laura said. "I swear."

Bowser studied her. "You know the Governor is driving a hard bargain on this one."

"I know. If his agenda passes in total, then he'll consider the pay raise."

"So I have my work cut out for me. I sent the Governor a request for comparisons on pay scales between us and the rest of the Southeast," Bowser said. "One of the agencies we asked for was the Patrol so he knows we're interested."

"I think we've already collected most of it."

"Good. Get it to me as fast as possible. And work on this revenue issue."

"I will."

"If we pass this, they'll expect something in return, you know," Bowser said.

"Who will?"

"The legislators."

"They'll be getting better law enforcement."

"I think they're thinking a little less grandiose and a little more personal," Bowser said.

"Like what?"

"Let's just say, now would not be a good time for a legislator to get a ticket. You're going to need every vote you can find. If it came up today, I doubt you'd get your majority in the House."

"Well," she said with a deep, tired sigh, "discretion is our motto." As Bowser settled back his chair, she added, "If there's room for it, of course."

"Of course."

Brent landed at New Orleans International Airport in the late afternoon, hurrying down the concourse until he checked the flight departures on a near-by teleprompter and discovered that the 8:00 P.M. flight to LaGuardia was delayed until 10:00 that night.

With his tennis racket case over one shoulder, a hanging bag over the other, and a leather briefcase and dark blue gym bag in his left hand, he lumbered from the baggage claim area to Delta's Crown Room and settled into the thick quiet of the spacious phone booths to make calls. Five days' growth covered his chin and jaw, a thin but promising gray beard, the first time in many years he hadn't shaved his Roatan stubble before coming home. In his white shorts, polo shirt, and holiday tan, he was the picture of driven prosperity. He punched in the number for the Northwoods house—his wife's domain.

"Grace, how are you?"

"Fine," she said, sounding unusually perky. "My little theater trip to New York was great, I have garden dirt under my fingernails, and I'm watching a terrific Geographic special on the Outer Hebrides while I drink a cup of tea. How was Roatan?"

"Cooler than usual. I think I'm getting too old for diving."

"Why so?"

"It wore me out this time. We dove and snorkeled everyday, but I was too tired to eat dinner half the nights."

"Maybe you should have a checkup?"

"Probably so. Missed the last one and never rescheduled."

Brent waited for a response but only an awkward silence followed. He picked up the thread of the conversation. "I'm taking a client out for dinner then I'll head to the farm."

"You don't need to give me an itinerary, we're long past that."

"Probably so, probably so." Brent let out an audible sigh. "I'm sorry about that actually."

"Sorry about what?"

"About not needing to give you an itinerary."

"Why so melancholy?"

"Don't know, really. Chalk it up to the reflections of an aging man."

"Cut back on coffee, it might cure your malaise," she said with her usual efficiency.

"Maybe we could go out one night this week."

"We need to—Sarah Carver told me last night that quite a string of events are lined up—almost as bad as during the campaign."

"You were at the Mansion?"

"No, they were here for dinner with the Prescotts, but everyone called it quits by 9:30. All old fogies...like you."

Brent bristled slightly, not knowing how to respond. Silence descended again which Brent finally broke. "Well, let me go. I'll call you in the next day or so."

"Drive carefully, Brent. Stay over if you've had too much to drink or it gets too late—the roads have been awfully slick with this cold weather."

"I will." Brent intentionally sounded forlorn, something he rarely displayed for Grace.

"Would you like to come here instead?" she asked, hesitantly.

"What a nice invitation, Grace. I never dreamed I'd hear that again."

"Is that a 'yes'?"

He could almost hear her flinching as she waited for his response. "I'd be awfully late. I think I'd better not."

"Well, be careful," Grace said.

Brent wondered which one of them was more relieved.

■ ■ ■ ■

Trey Turner had dropped the chilly arm of the dead man to answer the phone in the unheated barn, drawing out the long extension cord that allowed him to talk from practically any corner of the immense work area without resorting to a portable phone. He preferred solid land line phones, so people couldn't listen in. He was glad to hear Brent's voice again.

"Just hung up from talking with Grace. I told her my schedule."

Trey's thermal underwear kept his body warm, but for all the fine hand movements, he was wearing latex rather than lined leather gloves, and his hands were freezing. The farm equipment had been moved aside and Brent's Mercedes was parked, headed in, wheels straight, directly in front of the overhead doors. The hood was up, and a mechanic's dolly was on the floor nearby.

With the phone cradled between his ear and shoulder, he went back to the huge stainless steel drain table. It was normally used to skin and dress out beef, deer, and game. The corpse lay there half dressed. Scrubbed, shaved, shorn, manicured, and bedecked with Brent's watch and ring, Trey had transformed the derelict into a skinny version of his friend. All the grimy detritus of the man's former life had been burned, the ash heap reignited twice for safety's sake.

Trey resumed buttoning the sleeves of the white dress shirt as he talked, carefully phrasing each bit of information, becoming almost cryptic at times—a consequence of his history of wiretapping so many unsuspecting people.

"And what *is* your schedule?"

"I'm having dinner with a client and then driving up. Supposed to meet him at eight this evening. I'd better get going or I'll be late."

"Well, allow plenty of time and drive carefully, particularly if you take the cut-off. It's been really cold and the roads get slick as the devil after midnight."

Trey knew Brent would pick up the real message: he'd scheduled the wreck for right at midnight.

"Thanks for the warning."

"I'll see you tomorrow maybe."

Brent hung up, reassured by Trey's all-business tone that every-thing was moving according to schedule, but unsettled by his own lack of control. He'd always been in on the kill—whether it was schmoozing with the client, or hammering out the details of a deal. He liked—indeed, he demanded—that feeling of domination as he maneuvered something to closure. This time he wasn't involved, couldn't be, and it bothered him.

He headed toward the Crown Room's bathroom to change his clothes and take off his wig but at the door, decided the risks of being recognized there were too high. He left in search of a spacious handicapped-access public restroom where he could spread out his stuff. He found one far enough from the gates so it wouldn't be crowded with the surges of men as planes unloaded.

His hanging bag dangled from the back of the door, filled with clothes, shoes, toiletries, and half of his $12,000 in cash. He'd organized carefully in Roatan so that everything he need-ed was in that one bag. After removing his new hairpiece, he leaned over the toilet and carefully shaved away his already thinned eyebrows with an electric razor, the small bits of hair barely disturbing the surface of the water as they landed. He shook the remaining hairs from his undershirt, then stripped to his underwear and changed into a new wool jacket with suede elbow patches, a white shirt with gold cufflinks, dark pants, cot-ton tie, and loafers. He filled the now-empty hanger of the hanging bag with a set of sweatpants and sweatshirt from his gym bag and stuffed his running shoes into the bottom of the suit compartment. As a final touch, he popped out his contacts and donned Coke bottle-thick prescription glasses.

The gym bag and tennis racket, stripped of their identifying tags, remained in the corner beside the toilet as Brent stepped cautiously out of safety with his toiletry kit and briefcase in one hand and the hanging bag in the other. The restroom was empty again, the noisy fellow who'd been reading a paper in another stall had left. He draped the bag on a door and turned to the mirror. Naked mounds where bushy eyebrows had once been, framed his deep-set eyes. The effect was devastating, and

Brent, who once delighted in staring at his own image or striking a pose in whatever mirrored surface presented itself, turned away, intensely uncomfortable.

Brent searched his kit for skin lotion, and as the initial shock passed, he studied his image more carefully. He cleaned the reddish spots on his smooth scalp where the tape had held his hairpiece in place, and by the time he'd rubbed moisturizing lotion over his whole head and into his naked eyebrows, he was content to stare at himself again. He wadded the hairpiece into a towel and stuffed it deep in the trash barrel.

Shortly after seven o'clock, he walked tentatively out onto the concourse. As he made his way to the ticket counters to check in, he nervously scanned the waves of people who approached him, looking for familiar faces to avoid. Frustrated travelers were lined up trying to make new arrangements because of the delay in the 8 P.M. flight. Realizing he would have to wait among them, he stepped up to a newsstand to buy a paper, searching for Jackson's ever-thinner daily.

"Are you out of the Jackson *Clarion Ledger*?" he asked.

"We don't carry that paper, sir," said the huge woman who had somehow squeezed herself into the small cashier's kiosk. "Only the Coast paper, the *Herald*."

"Really?"

"Very few people ask for it."

"Do you know where I can get one?"

She shook her head. "All the shops in the airport stock the same papers. The only place I know that might have it is that newsstand off Canal downtown."

"All the way in town?"

"'Fraid so."

Brent stepped back to the rack and picked up the Biloxi paper as well as a *Wall Street Journal*. "Well, this'll do, I suppose," he said, uncertainly.

"Are you sure?"

He nodded, handing her some change and folding the papers under his arm. He resumed his now-habitual scrutiny of the people around him as he crossed the terminal to the ticket counters. Once in the line for an agent, he lowered his face to read the front pages.

"Photo identification, please?" he heard the ticket agent ask the man ahead of him in line.

Brent stopped breathing. Photo I.D. Shit, he'd forgotten. His passport photo might not work without the hairpiece.

He stepped out of the line and raced back to the restroom where he'd changed.

Two yellow caution signs blocked the doorway. The janitors were working. Brent brushed around the signs and entered.

A woman in a gray blue uniform stepped out of one of the stalls. "This is closed until I get through, sir."

"I don't need to use the facilities, ma'am. I threw something away by mistake. Have you emptied the trash?"

She pointed to her cart. His racket case and gym bag were balanced on top of her supplies. "I just dumped it in there."

He reached into the plastic bag, then stopped. "May I?"

"Sure."

He pawed through the collection of damp paper towels feverishly.

"What'd you lose?" the woman asked, watching him curiously.

"Medicine," Brent said without looking up.

"It happens," she said, turning back to her work.

Then he felt something more substantial and drew out the discarded hairpiece. He stuffed it in his pocket and said, "Got it. Thanks."

When the woman looked up, all she saw was his back.

In another restroom, Brent positioned his hairpiece as best he could since he didn't have any tape to hold it in place. Then he put his contacts back in. He checked his look against the passport photo. Damn. Maybe good enough to pass—and maybe good enough to be recognized, too.

With his head down, he hurried back to the end of the line and pulled out his newspaper. He stood as calmly as possible while he progressed toward the counter, intent on the front page.

"Sir?"

Brent looked up, startled to see that he was next. He quickly stepped up to the efficient smiling agent, and handed over his ticket folder.

The agent looked at the ticket and punched something into his computer terminal. "The 8 P.M. flight had a weather delay and we're waiting for another aircraft to arrive, Mr..." the agent hesitated, looking for the name on the ticket.

"Wex..." Brent began, then corrected himself, blushing with his error, "Wheeler."

The agent looked up at him and then back at the ticket. "The aircraft should be here shortly, Mr. Wheeler. Do you have photo identification?"

Brent reached in his jacket pocket and pulled out his passport. The gate agent looked from the photo to Brent and back again. "This isn't very recent."

"It's almost expired. I need to get a new photo."

He looked at Brent again and handed him back the passport. "Bags?"

"No," said Brent, exhaling with relief. "Just carry-on."

"Will it fit under the seat?"

"In the overhead bin."

"Have your bags been in your constant control since you packed them?"

"Yes," Brent said, impatient to be out of the public eye, "and no one has given me anything to carry for them."

"You travel often, I see."

Brent nodded.

"Window or aisle?"

"Window, near the back of the plane, at an exit. Alone, if possible."

"You're in luck for the moment. Not too many booked on the flight."

As the agent handed him the ticket, he smiled. "Gate 38, anticipated boarding time 9:45. Have a nice trip, Mr. Wheeler."

At the first restroom he came to, Brent pulled off the hairpiece and took out his contacts.

■ ■ ■ ■

After Trey had hung up from talking with Brent, he'd turned the police scanner back on. The transmissions had been coming in loud and clear since he'd moved the antennas to the top of a slash pine in the yard. Nearly the entire State Patrol had been out the previous night on a saturation operation catching drunk drivers, but tonight they were back to their normal five units for the entire nine-county district even though the roads were still icing up.

He reached for the wool sports coat Brent had selected—a black herringbone tweed—and began easing it over the corpse's right arm. As he lifted the body to slide the coat underneath, he caught the unmistakable scent of Brent's aftershave. It stopped him cold.

Goddamnit, why was Brent doing this to him?

That pig Morgan, that's why. Christ, why didn't I kill him when this first got started?

In his fury, Trey tugged at the left sleeve, ripping it along the seam before he jammed the limp arm into place. Then he slung the body over his shoulder and moved toward the car, dropping the corpse into a sitting position on the ground at the driver's door, then hoisting it from under the armpits to get it behind the wheel. The corpse's height made this a tricky maneuver, and Trey finally had to tilt the seat back to put it in place. Once in and upright, Trey securely fastened the seat belt about the cadaver.

With the strongest 100 percent cotton cord he'd been able to find, Trey tied down the steering wheel and wound the line around the seat so that not only would the front wheels be held in place but the body would remain in position. He secured a second cord around the gear shift lever and fed that line behind the seat. Then he opened several bags of Zapp's potato chips and stuffed them under the driver's seat to provide some extra fuel, a trick he'd picked up in an arson school the State Patrol had paid him to attend. After reinserting the keys in the ignition, he checked the controls, turning the heater and fan on.

Carefully inspecting everything, Trey closed the door as he threaded the gear shift cord through the small opening at the top of the window. Under the hood, he double-checked the lead he'd attached to the cruise control. A tiny alligator clip dangled at its end. When that clip was attached to anything metal on the engine block, it would provide a ground to the accelerate mode of the cruise control and the car would pick up speed continuously.

Trey dropped the hood gently into place but didn't secure it. He jacked the rear end up and rolled under the car on the dolly with his flashlight in hand. He'd rigged two blasting fuses, the second as a back up, to run down behind the shelf behind the bucket seats, into the trunk, and through a loosened shock absorber inspection plate and over the top of the tank past the fuel transmitter and the filler, staying away from any moving parts of the suspension that could brush them off. Two fuses burning near spilled raw gasoline would ignite the fuel vapors.

He checked the loosened gas tank and the tissue he'd stuffed around the shock absorber plate to stop any fumes from entering the passenger area and igniting prematurely. Satisfied that everything was in place, he rolled out from underneath, lowered the jack, and filled the gas tank to the brim.

Trey locked the barn and walked to his house to get some coffee, searching the quiet, darkening fields for unexpected visitors. Hunters often strayed onto the property and he couldn't risk a visitor this night. Filling a blue and gray State Patrol commemorative mug with hot coffee, Trey warmed his hands around the cup for a moment, then picked up his night vision glasses and surveyed the surrounding fields and woods from his kitchen door. No one was in sight.

Coffee in hand, he headed back to the barn, passing the plain gray twenty-five-foot van he'd borrowed from the Patrol for the weekend. With the doors slipped away to the sides, the van was lined up perfectly behind the Mercedes. With not a movement wasted, Trey unlocked and rolled up the van's back door, pulled out the car ramp. He reeled out the cable of the winch that was secured to the front wall of the van, and secured the cable to the rear bumper of the Mercedes. Trey turned on the power and slowly pulled the car and its ghostly driver into the van.

■ ■ ■ ■

With over two hours to wait, Brent decided to have dinner and walked to the concourse again, his head down to avoid anyone's glance. For a city known for its food, there was hardly anything worth eating at the airport.

Maybe that was the point, Brent thought.

He stopped at a fairly large, generic restaurant off the central concourse with a view of nothing in particular. He chose a circular table in the back corner and when the waitress, a thin, sallow-looking creature, finally appeared, he ordered a bourbon and water. She returned promptly, bringing his drink with the menu, but quickly disappeared, probably chapped that her table was being taken up by a single drinker who looked like a lousy tipper.

The menu was designed for the nervous flying stomach rather than the gourmand. His bourbon had introduced an uncomfortable state of confusion rather than the calming effect he'd been seeking, but Brent settled on an innocuous shrimp pasta and Caesar salad, beckoning the waitress with a wave of the menu and ordering another bourbon along with his main course.

The order placed, Brent looked at his watch. 7:20 P.M.

What was happening in Saragossa?

He picked up the *Biloxi Herald* and opened to the second section where they printed news stories from around the state. Other than the antics of the legislators as they slogged through the legislative session, there was nothing from Jackson except a story about a man who had spearheaded an aluminum can collection effort and raised enough money for a little girl dying of cancer to go to Disney World. There were no Jackson obituaries—just a list of names and addresses of people who had died in other parts of the state—and the only reports of car wrecks were in the coast area. There was no local news from Jackson.

He checked his watch again. 7:35 P.M.

By the time his main course arrived, he wasn't particularly hungry; his stomach was too tight to eat very much. He picked at the pasta, searching the paper for crime stories and glancing through the business sections.

Trey could be trusted, Brent thought. He'd never failed him.

Besides, Trey stood to lose a lot if he screwed it up. More than he, in fact.

Trey was talented, loyal.

That greedy bastard Reed Morgan. It was all his damn fault. Maybe Trey had been right—maybe they should just kill Morgan. Then Gibbs goes to Washington and I go with him.

A group of businessmen in dark suits came toward him, and Brent quickly raised his paper to shield his face.

The homeless guy could be buried, no one would know.

He looked at his watch. 7:45 P.M.—plenty of time to call it off.

"Final boarding for Delta Flight 267 to Chicago," quietly permeated the restaurant.

He cautiously lowered the paper. The men were seated and conversing among themselves. Pushing the pasta dish to the side, Brent raised his glass and caught the waitress's eye, signaling for another bourbon and water.

No. This was his last chance to walk away from everything. He'd better take it.

Brent stayed out of sight in the back of the restaurant until it was time to get to his flight. He hugged the sides of the wide concourse, keeping his face obscured, slowing only when he passed an automatic teller machine tied into his bank system. A last chance to get more money out of his bank account. He reached for his wallet.

Then he stopped. Someone might see the transaction on the statement.

He started to put his wallet back when he thought again. The time never showed on his statements, just the date. It was perfectly normal for him to get cash.

He withdrew four hundred dollars, the cash limit for a day, and hurried to his plane. Boarding time—10:15 P.M.—flashed behind a frazzled agent trying to calm the passengers who fidgeted in front of the counter.

Another damned half-hour.

In the waiting area, Brent chose a spot at the end of a row in front of the windows, his back turned to all approaching people. He picked up a *Newsweek* abandoned on the side table and flipped through it. Keeping his head down, he glanced at the reflections in the huge window, but didn't recognize himself until he raised his hand to touch his head.

He was stunned. The change in his physical appearance hadn't altered his mental image of himself. It took a moment before it sank in: He was barely recognizable. For the first time in the last several hours, his stomach muscles relaxed ever so slightly. He moved his head from side to side, checking his look from each angle. Captivated by his new image, Brent sat back in his chair, contemplating the limited availability of the Jackson newspaper.

A plane pulled up to the gate and the jetway moved out to connect to it, spawning a round of applause behind him. The gate agent picked up his microphone. "Boarding for flight 1187, nonstop service for New York, LaGuardia Airport, will begin in ten minutes."

New York. He was clutched with a panicky thought that if he went on to New York that night, he wouldn't know what had happened, or more important, whether the police were looking for him. There wouldn't be a chance of finding a Jackson paper up there.

How would he find out whether it had worked?

Better stay here.

Brent quickly gathered his things and stepped up to the counter.

"I just called my home and an emergency has come up. I can't leave tonight. Will this ticket be good on another flight?" He pulled the folder out from his inside coat pocket and handed it to the man.

"It's good on any flight. I can cancel you for tonight and make a reservation for another day, if you'd like."

"I don't know when I'll be leaving."

"Well, let me cancel this, Mr...." the agent checked the name and then handed the folder back, "Wheeler. Whenever you plan to fly, make your reservation, and be certain to allow enough time to change the ticket beforehand."

"Thanks." Brent slid the ticket back in his pocket, picked up his bags and strode off down the concourse, preoccupied with the change in his plans, and lapsing for a moment into his usual self-confident way. Passing the teller machine again, he remembered his two credit cards and stopped. Inserting one, he withdrew the cash limit, then stood there, listening to the machine chug through its machinations. Shoving his hands into his coat pockets, he felt the crumpled transaction slip from his earlier withdrawal from his bank account. He pulled it out and looked at it.

NOLA Airport
03/05. 9:38 P.M.
$400.00
500 4862419

His credit card popped out, followed by the transaction slip for this second withdrawal.

NOLA Airport
03/05. 10:16 P.M.
$400.00
4630 0200 7886 5148

He was about to insert his other credit card when he stopped. 9:38 P.M. 10:16 P.M.

10:16 P.M. placed him in New Orleans less than two hours before the accident, assuming Trey was on schedule. It took more than two hours, even at breakneck speed, to get to Saragossa and that would put him there around one in the morning, if he left right now.

Maybe he should wait and withdraw the rest a little closer to midnight, just in case he ever had to prove where he was when the murder occurred.

He slipped into a men's room, hung his bag on a door and sat down in a stall. The only other patron left a few moments later and Brent read his newspaper to pass the time. At 11:20, a janitor came in and began cleaning, starting at the end of the room and working his way toward Brent. When he was two stalls away, Brent flushed the toilet and left hurriedly, picking a moment when he was certain the man was busy with a commode.

There were hardly any passengers on the concourse—mostly gate agents finishing up their night's work. If he waited too much longer he wouldn't be able to get a cab, so he stepped up to the teller machine and inserted the last credit card.

### 03/05  11:42 P.M.

Better.

Brent hailed the only cab at the arrival platform and threw his suit-bag and briefcase in. "Canal Street—can't remember whether it's the Marriott or the Holiday Inn, but there's a big newsstand across the street from it."

"That's on Royal. It's the Holiday Inn."

"Fine."

■ ■ ■ ■

By midnight, everyone was off duty and there had been no reports of disturbances near any of his possible accident scenes. Trey changed into black tactical unit clothing and left the farm, carrying a portable high-band radio to supplement the low-band in the van. He drove directly to the most isolated of the locations, one where at least three wrecks had occurred in the past ten years—drivers coming down the hill had missed the sharp curve and shot off the road. He didn't pass anyone on the way. Backing up into a curve, he lined up the van with the roadway, and parked.

Leaving the van idling, in several seconds less than his best practice time, he opened the back door of the van and pulled the ramp down. Trey scanned up and down the road one last time before he vaulted into the back. With the front chock blocks removed, given the slope, the car would have rolled out, nose first, on its own. He played out the cable until all four wheels were on the road and then jumped down and blocked the rear wheel again. He threw the disconnected cable into the van.

From the passenger side, he started the car, turned the lights on high beam, then reached into the back seat and lit the fuses. He closed the door and hustled forward to raise the hood. He attached the alligator clip to the manifold, let the hood slam, removed the rear wheel chock and tugged the gear shift cord to move the shifter from neutral to drive. The Mercedes was off on her last ride.

The car moved straight across the field, accelerating all the while until it disappeared over the edge of a shallow creek bed and crashed. A minute later, the gasoline that had sloshed out of the fuel quantity transmitter ignited and flames erupted just as Trey was pushing the ramp back in the truck. Less than fifteen seconds later, Trey was gone.

Back at the barn, Trey pulled the moving van in to clean it, listening for a burst of traffic over the now silent scanner. But there was none. Half an hour later, with four gallons of extra gasoline, he climbed into the pickup and drove past the scene. With his night vision goggles he could see smoke billowing out of the bayou. The fire was still burning.

Perfect. Goddamn perfect. Wanna make a guy disappear? Trey thought. I'm your man.

Then the truth hit him.

Brent was gone without a trace. He was safe.

How long would it be before he heard from him? Trey wondered. He returned to the barn to scrub down the cooler and try one more time to get the smell of the guy out of the cab of the pickup truck. Around four A.M., after several hours of silence on the radio, he left for Jackson in the Patrol van, and parked it in its spot at headquarters, then headed back home in his own car. He drove carefully on the slippery roads, listening to his scanner for police traffic while WSM, 650 AM out of Nashville, clear as a bell in the dead of night, filled in the background with Hank Williams.

# FIVE

Lt. Col. Jimmie Anderson, assistant chief of the State Patrol in charge of the uniformed branch, lived in Jackson. But his home place, where his mother still lived, was sixty miles southeast of the city. That's where the entire family had gathered, from as far away as California and Arizona, for their mother's 80th birthday. He'd stayed overnight, but at 5:30 A.M. he started back to headquarters, hoping to attack the mound of paperwork he knew was waiting for him while it was still quiet around the office.

Fairly far off the beaten path—there wasn't a direct route from his mother's to Jackson—he was meandering around familiar back county roads when he rounded a sharp curve and noticed the blackened fronts of trees across the field. He drove on, trying to remember if he'd seen them on his way down but couldn't, and a mile down the road, turned back, interested in what had caused the damage. They'd had wrecks at that curve numerous times but the county refused to spend the money for a guard rail.

He parked on the edge of the road, pulled on his jacket, and picked up his portable radio. Fields sloped away to his right as he ambled toward the trees and the creek.

"Oh, Christ," Jimmie muttered, when he saw the charred heap sitting on the far side of the creek, smashed into a fallen tree, with no more than an inch of water around its wheels. He radioed headquarters to send the unit on duty and clambered down the four foot embankment, stepping carefully onto the sand.

The driver had been reduced to a crispy cadaver. Here and there, no skin at all remained and the blackened bones showed through. The corpse sat on a rack of metal seat springs, all that remained of the driver's seat. Since no doors were ajar, he presumed that there hadn't been any other passengers who escaped, but he circled the area quickly just in case.

The front end had been smashed beyond recognition, but from the emblem on the trunk and its roof design, Jimmie was certain it was an old Mercedes, late 60s or so. All the paint was burned off, even from the car tags, so he had to get the license number by feeling the raised shapes on the cold plate. Of the wrecks they'd had on that curve, he couldn't remember one this bad.

Jimmie keyed his portable radio. "A-2, Jackson."

"Jackson."

"Run the tag on Edward-Boy-David-2-1-7. An old Mercedes. Don't know the color. And let the backup know he needs to wear waterproof boots if possible."

The backup who arrived was C-84, Trooper Lester Billings, a tall, skinny, but powerful kid, one of the brand-new troopers they'd just commissioned. He hadn't been on the Patrol long enough to know much about working wrecks other than what was in the procedure manual.

"Go back and get some evidence bags," Anderson shouted when Billings appeared. "And gloves. Bring me some, too."

Jimmie Anderson had been wearing a State Patrol uniform for twenty-five years, and though he'd seen a few burnt cars and bodies in his day, this one might well be the worst. He was standing by the driver's door blocking the view when Billings climbed down. "Worked a wreck yet, Billings?"

The trooper shook his head.

"Well, this is a helluva one to start on." Anderson stepped away to give Billings a full view, interested in how the rookie would react. No matter how many grizzly slides of car wrecks they showed to desensitize the cadets, nothing prepared a trooper for something like this. But Billings did the Patrol proud—no retching or gagging when he saw the corpse. He stood there transfixed at the sight until his whole body shivered involuntarily from the cold and gore.

"This one is extra-crispy, needless to say." Jimmie looked Billings in the eye. "So what do you do first?"

Billings still hadn't said a word.

"Billings?" Jimmie stepped toward him, and the movement caught the young man's attention.

"Sir."

"I repeat, what would you do first?"

He looked blank. "Umm." He shivered again and then looked Anderson in the eye. "I'd call for the coroner, sir."

"Right."

The portable radios crackled, "Jackson, A-2."

"Go ahead," said Jimmie.

"The tag comes back to Brent Wexler, 303 South Union Street, Jackson."

The name struck a familiar chord with Jimmie, but he couldn't place it. He whistled when he heard the address. The driver was connected with money. That area was one of the nicest in Jackson.

"Run the driver's license on him and tell me how tall he is." He let his hand drop a bit, then keyed the radio again, looking at Billings who had moved toward the door and was inspecting the corpse more closely.

"And get in touch with the coroner—you'll probably have to roust him. Tell him we don't need an ambulance, just a bag and a hearse. And call a tow truck. Tell them we'll need to pull a car out of a creek bed in a few hours. They'll need a long cable and a slide-back wrecker."

"Ten-four," the operator said.

"And send a reconstructionist over here as soon as possible," Jimmie added.

Fascination with the grim spectacle was overcoming Billings' revulsion, a promising sign to Jimmie.

"What happened to his head?" the rookie asked.

"Some of it might have exploded with the heat. We shouldn't touch this guy until the coroner gets here." Jimmie looked back across the hill. "How do you think it happened?"

Billings' eyes followed a direct line from the wreck to the curve in the road. "Missed the curve, maybe asleep at the wheel or drunk, shot right off and landed over here. Kaboom."

"Probably right."

The radio operator called back. "The subject should be 6' 1", 190 lbs. DOB 8-22-42. Three speeding tickets—80 in 55, 60 in a 40—both dismissed—and one 75 in 50, guilty."

Jimmie was looking into the car at the bones as he answered, "Thank you, ma'am." He clicked off the radio and sized up Billings. "How tall are you?"

"Six feet even."

"Got any rope in your trunk?"

"Should have." Almost instantly, Billings climbed out of the ditch and was moving across the hill, away from the scene and Anderson's scrutiny.

Jimmie keyed the radio again. "A-2, Jackson."

"Go ahead A-2."

"Check and see if there are any other Wexlers at that same address."

"Standby," said the radio operator, then came right back on. "A-2, the coroner is on his way, but he has to come from Stokes. Says he'll be there in 35-40 minutes."

Anderson picked up a pair of the gloves and was at the passenger side front door when Billings returned. He pulled back slowly on the metal rim of the handle. The hinges were brittle, creaking as though they might break. The slight barbecue smell was stronger inside the car, and it drifted out with the push of air, disgusting to the young trooper who wasn't ready for something so familiar. There wasn't much left of the interior, though if it had been a new car, there wouldn't have been anything at all. The completely combustible nature of automobiles was a testament to something, though Jimmie wasn't certain what.

Billings offered him the rope and Jimmie dangled it next to the trooper, marking off a length the same as his height. He leaned in and, stretching the rope from the top of the skull to the hip area, then across the exposed femur and from the knee area to the gas pedal, he estimated the height. "Six feet plus a bit."

In the charred debris beneath the right hand lay an Ole Miss class ring, a single cufflink, and a watch, the band for which had disintegrated. The back of the watch was engraved "For Brent 6-20-67, all my love, Grace."

He pulled back out from the car with the jewelry. "Make some notes, Billings. The wreck was cold when I arrived. Get my actual time from the radio log. The ring, cufflink, and watch were near the right side of the body. You'll find the other cufflink near the left side, I bet. Maybe a wedding ring."

Jimmie leaned back in and checked the key. "Key was in the on position," he called out to Billings as he wiggled it out of the ignition lock.

Attached to it were several other keys and a six-sided medallion. As he drew back out of the car, he felt the raised ridges of some kind of design, and flipped it over, wiping away the soot from the inscription. "To My Friend Brent—Gibbs Carver, Governor."

"Oh, shit," he muttered, shaking his head then staring off across the brown field speckled with shoots of spring green. Jimmie picked up the radio and was about to key it when the operator's voice boomed out again, "Jackson, A-2."

"A-2, Jackson, go ahead," Jimmie said.

"A-2, I have the info on the residence," the operator chirped. "One other person, Grace Josephine Wexler, DOB 1-20-44, possibly the wife. No violations, no accidents."

"Thanks. Call A-Adam and find out if she's familiar with the first subject. And ask about the second, too."

He put the portable radio down on the roof of the car and

walked around to the trunk. The lock had burned out, and after wiggling the lid a bit, Jimmie was able to lift it, carefully avoiding breaking the hinges. "Check the window mechanism on the passenger side and figure out what position it was in, Billings."

While Billings inspected the door frame, Jimmie sorted through the residue of the trunk's contents, ascertaining that there had been at least two suitcases and a small tool kit.

"The window was down a couple of inches at most, Colonel."

"What about the heater?" Jimmie asked.

"The heater knob is burned off but the lever is in the middle. I'd have to check with the dealer to be certain which way the controls work."

"Good idea, Billings."

Billings held out the hinges of a small case as well as a flat gold bar engraved BW. "What's are these? I found them behind the seat."

Anderson glanced at it. "Probably a tag on the handle of a suitcase. It's gold most likely. Pretty nice case, I'd say. Fits."

"Jackson, A-2," the radio operator called out.

"Go ahead."

"I have the Commissioner on the line. She confirms the first subject is a friend of Unit 1. She wants you to call her ASAP."

Anderson noticed that Billings had been getting a closer look at the corpse while he'd been talking. "Tell A-Adam, I'll leave for a hard line phone in two to three minutes. The nearest one is about ten miles away, I think." He put the radio back in his pocket. "Billings, you'll have to take over."

The young trooper quickly pulled his head back out of the car. "Sir?"

"You can do it. I've got to talk to the Commissioner—looks like this guy might be a friend of the Governor's."

"Uh, sir, I'd hate to make a mistake."

Jimmie shook his head as he gathered up the evidence. "You'll do fine. Standby for the coroner. Should be here shortly. Not a bad guy—kinda skinny and morbid—but it goes with the territory. Tell him I have the watch, ring, one cufflink, and keys with me, and I'm heading to Grace Wexler's house for identification. He'll be glad to hear I'm handling that part because dealing with the living isn't his specialty. You might have to help him get the bones into a body bag."

Billings, who had been taking notes, stopped and looked at Jimmie, incredulous.

"It'll be kinda messy with this water but wear gloves—think of it as a deer carcass. You do hunt, don't you, Billings?"

"Yes, sir."

"Good. I've got confidence in you—you can handle it. The reconstructionist should be here soon too. Pay attention to what he does—you could learn something. Search around the inside for more evidence while you wait."

Billings nodded nervously, "Yes, sir."

Jimmie moved across the hill as fast as the bumpy terrain would allow. The nearest pay phone was at Bertha's Best, and he wanted a land line for the conversation he had to have with Laura Owen.

■ ■ ■ ■

The two hours from 5:00 to 7:00 A.M. before Will got up were sacred for Laura. The still darkness, slowly emerging toward daybreak seemed safe, orderly. Ranger, their Golden Retriever puppy, usually got up when she did, ate her breakfast, and promptly went back to sleep with Will. While coffee dripped into the carafe, she began her stretching exercises on the big oriental rug in the main room. Laura was petite by most descriptions, medium weight for her frame, and in good health but not in particularly good shape. Exercise had never been one of her strong suits. She ended the twenty-minute session with a maneuver that twisted the spine—the best stretch of all and her alternative to a whirlpool bath. Then she lay down for a few moments of rest, the last she knew she'd get until late that night.

But there was no rest period that morning. The phone rang and she leaped to get it before the second ring, not wanting Will to wake any sooner than absolutely necessary. Jimmie's voice was softer than normal.

"Commissioner, I've got to speak sort of quietly. Bertha and the boys at the truck stop are trying to figure out why I raced in here and picked up the phone."

"No problem, I can hear you fine."

"Sorry if we woke you earlier, but I needed to know about Brent Wexler's connection to the Governor."

"I'm an early riser," Laura said. "I was already up when the radio room called." She moved about around the kitchen in her sweatpants and sweatshirt, fixing her first cup of coffee. "What's the deal on Wexler?"

"Found his car totally destroyed by fire off the road to Saragossa, northbound. The driver was burned beyond recognition. There isn't enough left of his face to identify him by looking at him."

A vision of the mangled Acura in the middle of the road with red and blue lights flashing eerily in the darkness flooded into Laura's mind—and then her husband lying on a hospital table surrounded by doctors and nurses.

"Commissioner?" Jimmie asked.

Laura snapped back. "When did it happen?"

"Had to be last night, probably late and no one passed by to see the fire. There were several identifiers besides the car—a watch, ring, key chain, cufflink. What tipped me off was some kind of medallion inscribed by the Governor. Mrs. Wexler can probably do the identification just on the jewelry."

"Won't you need more?" Out her kitchen window, Laura could see a small light colored creature creeping along the edge of the dense woods, but it was still too dark to know if it was an armadillo or an opossum.

"Not if it's clear cut. No need to put the family through an autopsy if it isn't necessary."

"I assume you'll be the one to talk to her?"

"The coroner usually does that, but I..."

Laura cut him off. "I'd like you to handle it, Jimmie. This man was the Governor's closest friend and his chief fund-raiser. I don't need some over-zealous body snatcher upsetting her."

"Yes, ma'am. I'm headed her way right now."

"I met Grace Wexler at the Governor's birthday party. She seemed like a very strong woman."

"As soon as I've talked with her, I'll call you back."

"I won't call the Governor's office till I've heard from you."

"Are you sure the Governor wouldn't want to break the news to Mrs. Wexler himself?"

"Probably would if he were here, but he left yesterday afternoon on the state jet for Washington. Something about the air base closures. Won't be back until tonight."

"Then I'll be on my way."

"Thanks, Jimmie."

"Part of the job, much as I hate it."

■ ■ ■ ■

Grace Wexler had been up for quite a while when Jimmie pulled his cruiser into the driveway of the Wexlers' Northwoods mansion and she'd just come in the back door from her morning walk when he rang the front door bell. She stepped briskly to the wide oak door, not hesitating to open it at that early hour. She was taken aback, however, at the sight of a uniformed State Patrol officer on her doorstep.

"Mrs. Wexler?" Jimmie took off his slightly faded blue Smoky-the-Bear hat.

"Yes, I'm Grace Wexler. Is something wrong, officer?"

"I'm Colonel Jimmie Anderson of the State Patrol, ma'am, and this morning I discovered a car that had been involved in an accident. The car was registered to Brent Wexler."

"Brent's my husband. Was he hurt?" She gripped the sides of the door to steady herself.

"I'm afraid the driver was killed, ma'am, if the driver was Mr. Wexler."

"What do you mean 'if?'"

"Could I come in, Mrs. Wexler, so that we could sit down?"

"Certainly, I'm sorry I didn't..." Grace's voice trailed off.

Jimmie stepped through the door, the heels of his boots clicking on the black-and-white checkered marble entry floor. In her confusion, she let him lead the way to a large living room, made significantly cozier by two colorful rugs covering the hardwood floors.

Grace took several deep breaths as she sat down. "Now tell me why you're uncertain who was driving."

"The body was burned beyond recognition, ma'am."

Grace stared blankly at Jimmie Anderson's face until a faint, "Oh, my God," passed her lips.

"The car was found off the road, Highway 133 to Saragossa. Is there a reason Mr. Wexler would have been on that road?"

"Yes. He, I mean, we, have a farm in Saragossa. He called me yesterday from New Orleans. He'd been on a trip—skin-diving in Honduras—and had just gotten in. He said he was going to drive up to the farm after he had dinner with a client. I remember telling him not to leave if it was very late. The roads have been so slippery when the temperature drops."

"Yes, ma'am, they have. It looks as if Mr. Wexler fell asleep at the wheel and missed a curve, a deep curve, in the road."

"Where?"

"About a mile past the Little Foot River. The road curves to the left and there's a creek through there, down to the right. That's where we found the car. In the creek."

"I know the place," Grace said, shaking her head. "It's on Brent's so-called shortcut, though I never believed it saved any time. He seemed to hate main roads when he was headed to the farm."

Jimmie pulled the baggie from his parka pocket and opened it. "I found these with the body."

As the ring and watch tumbled out, Grace let out a quiet gasp and extended her hand for them. "These are Brent's—I gave him the watch as a wedding present—since he didn't want to wear a wedding ring." She gently wiped some soot from the clock face and then focused on the other pieces. "And this is his class ring—he always wore it, proud of his education and his football career." She closed her eyes for a moment as the information sank in. The husband she hadn't loved was dead, and she was free of him. She'd thought about this eventuality so often she was surprised at the uncertainty of her feelings.

Grace opened her eyes to see Brent's key chain in Jimmie's outstretched hand. "That's Brent's too. Gibbs—Governor Carver—gave him that key ring after the first election. They're best friends, you know. Gibbs will be crushed, absolutely crushed."

A silence filled the room as Grace stared blankly over the mantle at a painting of a cowboy on the edge of vast prairie. At some level it registered with her that the officer was rolling the brim of his hat in his hand as he sat silently. The movement brought her back to reality.

"I guess I have to attend to some details," Grace finally said. "But for the life of me..." she paused and looked at Jimmie. "'For the life of me', isn't that a strange expression at a time like this?"

Jimmie nodded, and she appreciated his quick smile. "Anyway, I have no idea what those details are."

"Let us help you with that, ma'am. The only thing that must be done immediately is to decide which mortuary you want to handle the funeral arrangements."

"Reynold's, I suppose. They've handled everyone in my family."

"If I could use the phone, please, I'll get that word passed along to the trooper at the scene."

"Certainly, there's a phone in the hallway, and another in the kitchen—down the hall to the right, if you want more privacy."

She watched him take off his parka and lay it and his hat neatly on a chair. "Can I bring you anything?" Jimmie asked.

"Oh, thank you, no. I'll be fine."


Jimmie dialed headquarters from the kitchen and told them to pass the information on to the coroner. Then he called Laura once more. "I'm at Mrs. Wexler's now."

"Was she upset?" Laura asked.

"Commissioner, I've been doing this for a long time. I've

seen 'em scream, seen 'em faint, and seen 'em rejoice. Calmly dazed might best describe Mrs. Wexler."

"Did she identify what you needed?"

"Yes. Mr. Wexler told her he'd be heading up that way. They'd spoken earlier in the day."

"You know, all things considered, that's probably good news, Jimmie. Thank you for doing that."

"Don't mention it. Part of the job."

"I'll see you at the office."

"Ten-four."

When he walked back into the living room, he saw Grace staring at the cowboy painting over the mantle again. He squatted down by her chair, holding the armrest for balance. "Is there someone I can call to be here with you?"

"No, thank you, I'll be all right." Then Grace paused, clearly about to say more, so he waited right where he was. "This isn't the first person I've buried—I mean besides my parents. Our only daughter died several years ago from cancer and it broke my heart. She spent her last days out at the farm. I cried every tear that was in me over her grave."

"I'm so sorry. No one should ever have to bury a child."

"Do I need to do anything?"

"No. The funeral home will call you after a while, and the car will be towed to whatever salvage yard the wrecker company uses unless there's somewhere in particular you want it taken."

Grace shook her head. "No, I don't really care about that—whichever they use is fine."

Another pause. Jimmie waited. "Thank you for being so kind," Grace added. "It's quite a change."

"Ma'am?"

"I said you're quite a change. I know a patrolman who wouldn't have an ounce of sympathy at a time like this."

"Who's that, ma'am?" asked Jimmie, steeling himself for a blast about a ticket incident.

"Trey Turner. He works for my husband—in fact, he lives

at the farm where Brent was headed and handles all the repairs and odd jobs. I doubt he'd be very comforting when he delivers news like this."

The name Wexler finally clicked. It wasn't Wexler's connection with the Governor that had nagged Jimmie, but his link to Turner, a trooper who'd come on the Patrol after he had. He was an investigator now, a fearless, solitary type. Through Turner, Wexler had made a sizable contribution to the foundation for families of troopers killed in the line of duty.

"Regardless of my feelings, he and Brent were close. I guess I should let Trey know," Grace said, clearly uncomfortable with the prospect.

"I can handle that if you'd like, ma'am. It's the least I can do for you." Jimmie stood up, stretching his aging knees and shaking his left leg so that his pants fell straight over his boot.

"Thank you, I'd appreciate that."

Jimmie put on his parka. At the door, he drew a business card from his shirt pocket and handed it to her.

"Please call me, Mrs. Wexler, if you need anything. Commissioner Owen specifically asked me to make sure you know we're ready to help. She was very sorry to hear of Mr. Wexler's death."

"Please thank her, but I'm sure you all have more important things to think about than me."

"Not really. We're here to serve."

"Well, thank you again," Grace said.

Jimmie opened the door and the cool air hit their faces.

"And thanks for calling Trey."

"Don't mention it. I'll have someone drop off copies of the reports as soon as they're finished." Jimmie nodded and walked to his patrol car, fitting his hat in place as he went. As he grabbed his door handle, he looked at Grace, framed by the front door, her arms tight across her chest holding back the cold, not a tear in her eye.

"It's 7:28, Momma," Will said, looking at his watch, a Christmas present from his grandmother that he'd completely ignored for two months. Luckily it was waterproof because now he refused to take it off, even for a bath.

Laura was acutely aware of how late it was. She had the phone to her ear and was pacing around her kitchen, hoping Vic would answer soon.

"Have you made your bed?" Laura asked.

"No."

"No, ma'am," Laura corrected. "Why don't you time yourself? See how long it takes you."

"Ah, Momma."

"Go on," Laura said.

When he finally picked up, Vic sounded as if he'd been running. "Regis."

"Vic, this is Laura."

"Sorry, it took so long. I was getting more coffee."

"I've got some terrible news. Brent Wexler was killed early this morning. The Patrol just got identification from Mrs. Wexler."

Vic was silent.

"Vic?"

"My God, Laura, what happened?" he stammered.

"Looks like he fell asleep at the wheel and went off the road near his farm. The car burned completely. The location was remote enough that no one saw the fire. Nothing left, so I understand it, just charred bones."

"How did Grace identify the body?"

"Watch, ring, a key chain inscribed from the Governor. Wexler had called last night and told her he might be headed that way."

"Jesus, dear Lord."

"Sorry, Vic."

"You can't imagine what this means."

"Maybe not entirely, but I've got an idea. This either kills the Senate race or puts it all on your back."

"That sums up half of it...." Vic paused a moment. "Carver

didn't go to the bathroom without calling Wexler first. I don't know if he'll recover. They talked over every decision Carver made. They spoke two, sometimes three times a day."

"I knew they were friends but..."

"It's a lot more than that. Wexler's the money. He has been from the start."

"Anything I can do?"

"Not that I can think of right now," Vic murmured. "God knows how this will affect things."

"Well, let me know. And promise me you'll tell me what I can do for you."

"Promise."

■ ■ ■ ■

At State Patrol headquarters, Blake Coleman looked over at Robert Stone. "Now tell me again how that loser got away?"

"We screwed up," Robert admitted. "I can't put it off on any of the other agencies involved."

"Any chance we can recover and still get him?"

"We're working on it. I don't like losing him any more than you do."

Blake looked away from Robert at Jimmie Anderson who was peering in his door, holding a cup of coffee. "Come in and make yourself at home. Busy morning, I hear."

Jimmie took a careful sip from his steaming cup. "My lucky day, I guess."

Robert looked back and forth between them. "Is there something I don't know about?"

"The Colonel, here, worked a wreck this morning on his way in. It just so happens that he picked the worst one-car accident in recent memory," Blake paused and gave Jimmie a thumbs-up, "as well as the most influential fatality."

Jimmie rose from his seat slightly and bowed. "Thank you, thank you. Word travels fast."

"All the way to Washington and back before you get from the grieving widow's to here." Blake turned to Robert. "Brent

Wexler, the Governor's best friend and chief fund-raiser, was killed this morning. Tell us about the wreck," he said to Jimmie.

"More like a barbecue. The car was headed north into Saragossa, went off the curve of a county road, crossed a field, and crashed into a fallen tree in a shallow creek. Must have burned like a son-of-a-bitch. We've had several wrecks there, but the county's always refused to pay for a guard rail. The wreck was cold when I got there about quarter of six this morning. Probably started burning hours before."

"You got a call?" Robert asked.

"No, I happened to be traveling by, coming from my mother's, and I saw the singed trees."

Blake stopped playing with his Styrofoam coffee cup when all the edges had been broken off in little pieces. "How'd you know it was Wexler?"

"Car, ring, and watch were engraved. The body, such as it is, was the right height. I couldn't believe it when I saw a keychain inscribed from the Governor."

"What was he doing in Saragossa in the middle of the night?" Robert said, puzzled.

"He's got a farm there. He was coming up from New Orleans. Apparently, he called his wife last night to say he'd be leaving the city after dinner. Mrs. Wexler said that road was his 'shortcut.' Did you know Trey Turner lives at his place and works for him?"

"Yeah, but I've never known what he did for him," Robert said.

"From what Mrs. Wexler says, he's a jack-of-all-trades and takes care of the farm. I asked Deborah to track him down for me."

Robert started to ask a question but was interrupted by the intercom buzzing.

Blake picked up the handset, listened a moment then handed it across the desk to Jimmie. "Speak of the devil. It's Turner, calling from the road near Forest." Blake glanced Robert's way. "What's he doing over there?"

"He's probably working a chop shop case," Robert answered. "You know, I feel sorry for the guy. Wexler might have been his only close friend. He kinda stays above it all out here."

"But I bet he doesn't have much of a reaction to the news," Blake said. He looked at Jimmie. "Do you mind if we listen?"

Jimmie shook his head.

Blake positioned his fingers over two buttons on his phone. "Ready?"

As Jimmie nodded, Blake punched down the two simultaneously and brought his finger up to his lips, signaling quiet. Robert moved silently to the door to prevent anyone from opening it and interrupting.

"Turner, Jimmie Anderson here. How's it goin'?"

"Fine, Colonel. What can I do for you?"

"'Fraid I have some bad news. Your boss, Brent Wexler, was killed in a car wreck early this morning."

There was silence.

"Turner?"

"I'm here," he said. "Where'd it happen?"

"Highway 133 to Saragossa just north of the Little Foot River."

"I know it well. That's right near my place at Wexler's farm. Was it bad?"

"The car went off the road at that curve and landed in the creek. Completely destroyed by the fire."

"Jesus." After another long pause, Trey said, "He called last night from New Orleans to say he was coming up, but I didn't check to see if he'd made it in. I was in a hurry to get off this morning."

"I visited Mrs. Wexler earlier and she asked me to pass the word on to you."

"Damn," said Trey, then nothing more.

"If we can help anyway, let us know," Jimmie added.

"Thanks, I appreciate that."

As Jimmie handed the phone back, Blake shook his head. "Now there's a warm and fuzzy kind of guy."

"Absolutely cold-blooded," Robert said. "Which reminds me—why was Turner's car here this weekend?"

"He borrowed the department moving van," Jimmie answered. "I was in the radio room when he checked it out on Friday."

A knock on Blake's door was immediately followed by Laura Owen. "Ahh, everyone I need to see. Good morning, Gentlemen." She settled into the corner of the couch. "How was the family reunion?" Laura asked Jimmie.

"Great. It was my mother's 80th birthday—she was queen for the day."

"Count your blessings that she's well and living independently," said Blake, wryly.

"I do. Every day," Jimmie said. "I don't know how you do it with your mother-in-law at home."

"Sorry you ended up with the wreck this morning," Laura said. "But given who the driver was, I'm glad someone who knew what to do was on the scene."

"Actually, the one I feel sorry for is C-84-Billings—from the last class. He had the early shift and the poor kid got to work it."

A dark little chuckle came from Blake. "Imagine a toasted torso to start your career—he'll be warped forever. I never had one of them the whole time I was on the road."

"So Blake switched to investigations to get his," Robert said, smiling at Jimmie and Laura.

"I've never seen you putting in for a transfer, Stone," Blake responded.

"Does Billings need any help?" Laura asked. Blake knew the tone: Let's get this conversation back on track.

"The reconstructionist and the coroner were both on the way when I left to talk to Mrs. Wexler. There isn't a whole lot to do in a case like this. Just bag it up and..." Jimmie stopped.

"Bury it?" Laura finished his thought.

"Yes, ma'am." Jimmie said.

Laura's pager went off and she checked the number, then rose from the couch. "The Governor's office calls." She looked at Blake. "I'll need all the details as soon as the reports are in."

"Don't worry, we'll handle it," Blake said with total confidence.

"And when the dust settles," Laura said from the doorway, "we need to talk about how it's going with the troopers on the pay raise business and which legislators they've contacted."

He thought she'd left when she reappeared. "But with this wreck thing, let's make it go as smoothly as possible—particularly for the Governor. He's got too many other things on his plate right now. We don't need to load on any more and upset him, do we?"

"No, ma'am," Blake said.

■ ■ ■ ■

As usual, death brought out the best and the worst in people. When Grace returned from the bank where she'd inventoried the contents of the safe-deposit box and removed all the legal papers, she found that the florist had delivered three bouquets, and a visitor was already waiting in the driveway. Grace had known the woman for years—a widow who'd made attending funerals a full-time occupation—but she was hardly a close friend. Grace didn't recall inviting her to stay, but somehow the woman slid in with the flowers and Grace directed her to the living room while she went to the kitchen and called Sarah Carver.

"I was just coming over to see you," said the Governor's wife.

"Come quickly," Grace said, speaking as quietly as she could. "People are already arriving."

"Oh, my God. I'll be there in ten minutes."

"I'm calling Fannie to see if she can manage the kitchen," Grace said, "and then I'm taking the phone off the hook."

The food, fruit, and flowers—the three F's of funerals—arrived all afternoon, borne by a steady stream of well-intentioned but uninvited mourners. The professional mourner maintained her key position in the living room, dispensing what little information she'd gleaned from Grace or Sarah.

Sarah juggled the phone and doorbell, politely turning away as many people as she could, freeing Grace to make arrangements with the funeral home. But night's approach and the end of the workday brought a fresh crop who, having expressed their condolences, grazed their way around the overflowing dining room table, some eating a full meal. It was nine before the last person left, and Grace quickly turned out every light to discourage any others and went to the kitchen.

Fannie was putting away a final load of dishes.

"Anything left that's worth eating?" Grace asked.

"I saved you some of Miss Sarah's special crab and some sort of rice dish I thought you'd like," Fannie said.

"Sounds wonderful."

Fannie opened the refrigerator and pulled out a plate covered with plastic wrap. "Everything else is wrapped up for tomorrow."

"I'm hoping there won't be a crowd like today. Shouldn't be," Grace said, sinking onto a stool.

Fannie set the microwave timer to heat Grace's food. "I'm awful sorry about Mr. Brent. I know you two weren't..."

"It's still sad," Grace said quickly. "Thank you, Fannie."

"Now if you need me tomorrow, just call."

"I probably will—why don't you plan on it," Grace said. "But you go on tonight, I'll finish up here."

"You sure you'll be all right by yourself?"

"I'm sure."

"And you'll set the alarm?" Fannie asked.

"I won't forget."

After a quick shower, Grace climbed onto her bed to read over the papers from the safe deposit box, starting with a copy of Brent's will—a mirror image of her own. Everything was left to her except the money set aside for the establishment of a charitable trust in her daughter's name for which she was trustee.

She sorted the papers into piles: insurance policies, deeds on the houses and land, stocks and bonds, partnerships, and appraisals. Then she sat back against the pillows and high oak headboard, holding up her mug in two hands and looking over its rim as she sipped the warm tea, and surveyed her holdings. A broad, exhausted smile spread across her face.

This chapter of her life was finally over. She was free of Brent and he'd left her rich enough to enjoy every minute of it.

■ ■ ■ ■

A black late model Cadillac shot past a trooper who was driving one of the new Fords that didn't have the bar light or bubble gum machine on top to give it away. His radar clocked the car at 79 in a 50 mile per hour zone. He punched the button for the blue light on his dashboard and sped up to catch the guy, adding the siren after another quarter mile. The driver finally looked back and saw him.

By the time the trooper had gotten out of his car, ticket book in hand, the driver's door opened and a man so wide that his feet splayed to the sides as he walked, emerged from the Cadillac, his face red with anger rather than shame. The trooper was now close enough to recognize the legislative decal issued by the Patrol. The sight of the emblem checked the adrenaline surging through him.

Pay raise.

The man barged toward him. "I'm a State Representative and I can't be arrested during the legislative session," the man bellowed. "Don't you know anything?"

Without the insult, the officer might have waved him on and turned back to his car but he kept advancing. "I don't believe issuing a ticket is the same as an arrest, sir," the trooper said evenly, taking a deep slow breath. A vision of the training officer from hell, up in his face every day at patrol school, yelling at him to provoke a rise, brought an extra ounce of calm. He didn't take the bait.

"Could I see your license, please?"

"I'm late, I said," the man replied, growing more impatient.

"And you were speeding, twenty-nine miles over the limit, sir," the trooper said, increasing his grip on his ticket book to redirect some of the tension. "If you let me see your license, I can get you back on your way quicker, sir."

The big man dug in his back pocket and pushed his billfold toward the officer. He turned his ticket book over and noted the name so he could tell the Captain.

"When do you go in session today, sir?" he asked, handing the license back.

"At eleven," the man said, becoming distinctly calmer when he realized the trooper had quit writing.

"It's only 75 miles to Jackson from here. You can do it in an hour and a quarter at 60 miles an hour. I'll radio ahead and tell them you're on the way."

"If I can ever help you," the man sputtered.

The trooper smiled. "Just drive safely."

■ ■ ■ ■

Senator Gabriel Collel glided down the broad hallway in front of the senate chamber, dispensing smiles, winks, and wisdom as he made his way toward two senate staff members who were talking with Laura at the rotunda railing. His full head of silvery hair, topping a tall, militarily erect posture, made him a striking presence. For twenty-six years, he'd walked the same halls, building that presence bit by bit, bill by bill. Most people gave him wide berth.

Laura had tangled with Collel often in his tireless campaign against her, and she had loathed each encounter with the man. Just the thought of running into him made her edgy. And here came her nemesis.

"So she deigns to mix with the hoi polloi," Collel said, sarcasm dripping from every drawled word. "It's Madame Commissioner, coming to save her boys."

"Hello, Senator," Laura said, as coolly as possible while extending her hand to greet him. It was a challenge to keep

Collel from getting under her skin, requiring a certain artifice that she wasn't entirely comfortable with.

"And how goes the war?" Collel said, putting his hands in his suit coat pockets rather than shaking hers. He completely ignored the two staffers and looked only at Laura. The staffers melted away, leaving Laura alone with Collel. "Any converts lately?"

"A few," she said, letting her hand drop to her side. "Can I count on your vote, sir? The State Patrol is certainly deserving."

"Dream on, my dear," Collel chuckled spitefully. "We don't have the money for that sort of across-the-board raise."

"I beg to differ, Senator. You do have the money, sir, and you definitely have enough to give the Patrol a raise. It's only a matter of priorities."

"You haven't even convinced your own governor. How can you expect me to go along with it?"

"The Governor agrees the Patrol needs a raise. His only concern is giving a raise to some employees and not to all. But my point is that the patrol is different. They've been treated differently in the past, both to their advantage and their detriment."

"A tough case to make."

"But a case worth making, I believe," she said, forcing herself to remain cordial.

Across the rotunda, a number of state representatives were scurrying into the House chamber, probably for a roll call. Collel looked to the left and hastily added, "You'll have to do better, as far as I'm concerned. Good-day, Madame."

Laura was surprised he'd given up so quickly. As she watched him depart, she was secretly proud of her parries.

Then she saw Jimmie Anderson and two Troopers Federation representatives coming her way. Collel hadn't departed because of anything she'd said—he'd left because he didn't want to talk to the men.

■ ■ ■ ■

Brent hadn't trusted his change in appearance one iota. For a day and a half, he'd hidden away in his hotel room, keeping the housemaids at bay with the excuse that he'd picked up a virus. He whiled away the hours reading the *Times Picayune* and a variety of other newspapers the concierge sent up, and watching news programs and movies. He picked at his room service meals, dozing off and on, unable to sink into deep sleep. Despite all his years of hard work, plus the accumulation of substantial assets, money, and power, he was trapped in a Holiday Inn, too scared to show his face on the streets of New Orleans.

When the Royal Street newsstand man confirmed that the *Clarion Ledger* was in, Brent rushed out like a bald, aging Huck Finn, fascinated by the chance to experience his own death.

The lead stories were about hog farm legislation and casino-related crime.

Goddamn, he didn't even make it above the fold.

He flipped the paper over quickly. "Fiery death," the headline said in the lower right. There was no full-face photo of him, they used a shot from election night where he was on the dais with Gibbs Carver, the two of them stretching their arms high in victory.

The State Patrol had concluded that Brent, who was returning very late from New Orleans, must have fallen asleep at the wheel and, with the slippery roads, ran off the road and crashed. His car was engulfed by the ensuing fire. In the Reynold's Funeral Home notice on the obituary page, he found Grace's arrangement for one night of visitation and private burial on Wednesday.

The twelve column inches couldn't have been clearer: the front page coverage was due to his close friendship with Governor Gibbs Carver. Indeed, Grace's prominence as a volunteer and philanthropist outweighed Brent's considerable business success. All his money and influence had made Grace and Gibbs who they were, yet his indispensable role in their lives was ignored.

Poof! He was gone.

Brent packed his bag, paid his bill in cash, and hailed a cab to catch the afternoon flight to New York. Fatigue and depression made him even less recognizable, but with his wig on for the last time, he hugged the thin shadows of the concourse, boarded the plane at first call, and slunk into his seat in the back.

# Six

To manage the anticipated crowd at the evening visitation without disturbing other bereaved families, the funeral director had placed Brent's elegant oak casket in the largest room at the back of the second floor. There, the thick carpeting, dark colored upholstered furniture, draperies, and textured wallpaper would soak up as much sound as possible. The room was overflowing with flower arrangements and funeral sprays—each one displayed so the senders could easily locate their offerings. The blossoms created an enticing bouillabaisse for the nose, only to be ruined by the barrage of perfumes that arrived with the mourners.

Most people came to be seen. The women arrived in their more somber cocktail dresses, the men came in well-tailored dark suits. They officially registered their grief in the white ledger book at the door, paid their respects to Grace, and then mingled with the others. It was a motley combination of politicians, contractors, suppliers, and socialites. The funeral directors noted with disdain that the whole affair was far from the quiet, dignified visitations occurring in the other salons.

Grace stood by the closed casket alone. Her dark hair, black when she was younger, now streaked with gray, framed her still-handsome face, intentionally made paler with powder. Her brother and sister-in-law positioned themselves nearer the front, to deflect many of the needless questions about matters that were nobody else's business but somehow became fair game when a person died. Grace was tired to the bone, having been up long into the morning hours, analyzing her financial position and contemplating her next step.

But Grace Wexler was used to standing alone. Possessing utter self-control and poise, she had never needed to circulate at parties or meetings. People came to her, usually seeking her support, financial or otherwise, for their latest cause. Some simply wanted to be seen by her side. Cordial and animated, she rarely shared details of her personal life and her few close friends guarded her privacy as ardently as she did. Even so, Grace had kept plenty to herself, bearing her soul about the most disturbing things to no one.

Early in the evening, Grace saw Trey Turner enter the room and watched him make his way toward the casket. Though she never made eye contact with him, she could feel his presence. She ably avoided the morbid questions of a stout Jackson matriarch about the condition of Brent's body until the woman finally gave up and rustled away. Trey stepped forward.

"I'm very sorry, Mrs. Wexler," he said quietly. Trey had never called her by her first name and she'd never suggested he should.

"Thank you, Trey." Grace forced herself to reach forward, gently placing her hand on his arm and feeling him recoil ever so slightly. Grace sighed through a small smile. "But I'm also sorry for *you*—you've lost a good friend."

Trey pulled his arm away. "He gave me a chance when no one else would, ma'am, and I'm thankful for that."

Grace nodded. "He was generous with his friends."

"If I can help, Mrs. Wexler, please let me know."

"If you'd look after the farm for the next few days—keep it locked up—I'd appreciate it. I have lots of decisions to make, but I'm going to take my time. I'll probably run down there someday soon, but honestly I don't know when."

"I understand. I'll keep my eye on things for you." He paused and looked past her at the casket. Not a trace of emotion crossed his face. "I wouldn't want to tackle what you have ahead of you."

"I'll manage. Not having to worry about the farm will help immensely. I really do thank you."

"Consider it taken care of, ma'am."

Trey had turned to walk away when Grace drew him back with another touch on his arm. "Oh, Trey, I looked over the hunt club deed last night. Brent included a provision that allows you first option to buy the house and some or all of the land whenever it's sold."

She couldn't tell if Trey had been aware of the option, but he faltered before answering. "As much as I love the place, I doubt I can afford it."

"Maybe we can work something out," Grace suggested. "The one thing I do know is that I don't want to keep the hunt club. I may hold onto the farm, but not the hunt club."

"I'm honored Brent let me have the option."

"Let's see what happens."

"Thank you again, ma'am."

Trey was upset with himself as he turned away. He hadn't expected the option business to come up and wasn't certain if he'd handled it right. He headed straight out, and was almost to the door when he felt a tap on the shoulder and turned to see Reed Morgan in line to pay his respects.

"Commissioner," said Trey, with a brisk nod.

"This is terrible, Trey. What really happened?"

Trey considered ignoring the man's question but drew closer and spat it into his ear, "Probably had a few too many to drink, worrying about you going south on him."

Morgan paled. "I would never have done that."

"He knew you too well to believe that. Brent made you who you are and your greed jeopardized everything."

"I was working it out. I told him I would."

"Too late now," Trey hissed, and turned away, not stopping to speak to any of the hunt club members he'd so often assisted, or to little Miss Junior Executive, over in the corner, who was already hitting on a new prospect.

Grace reached out for Gibbs Carver when he approached. He looked past Grace to the casket and burst out sobbing, draping himself over her shoulder.

"You were his best friend, Gibbs," Grace said hugging Carver tightly. "I know how he treasured your trust in him."

Grace pulled back from his embrace to receive a comforting hug from Sarah. The two women were a lot alike. For years both had been expected to perform in their husbands' parades and they'd always acquiesced. Sarah alone recognized—somewhat enviously—how the tragedy of Grace's daughter's death had opened the door for Grace's metamorphosis. The strain and distance between Grace and Brent had pushed Grace off onto her own separate course, and she'd blossomed as her involvement in the Cancer Clinic deepened.

"I'm sorry Gibbs is acting so selfish," Sarah said, drawing close and looking directly at Grace. Like Grace, Sarah was trying to ignore her husband's display. "How did it go this afternoon after I left?"

"Just fine. But I couldn't have made it this far without you. Our professional mourner was actually helpful in the end, entertaining people I didn't want to talk to anyway."

"That woman..." Sarah said, glancing around at the crowd. "She's by the door."

Sarah shook her head, "Eleven tomorrow?"

Grace nodded. "Right here in this room."

"We'll be here a little early," Sarah said. "Call me if I can do anything in the morning."

Grace looked at Gibbs' pitiful face and with a nod toward him, silently suggested Sarah worry about him. Sarah stepped up to him with a handkerchief. Getting a grip on himself, Carver gave Grace one final hug then turned to walk out through his supporters, all respectful of his deep distress.

Promptly at 10:30, the funeral home director persuasively dispersed the crowd, and fifteen minutes later, having cleared up several last minute details, Grace was on her way home. She'd lived virtually alone for so long, it was a familiar feeling to enter an empty house. The only difference this evening was the abundance of fresh flowers and the welcome relief that Brent was gone forever. Grace slept better than she had in years.

■ ■ ■ ■

Sally Coleman turned on the light in the hallway and slipped back into their bedroom. Blake was dead to the world, sprawled across more than half their double bed.

"Honey," she said, shaking Blake's shoulder as gently as she could.

He lurched awake, looking around in momentary terror for what was wrong.

"I'm sorry. I didn't want to wake you, but I need you to help me with Mother," his wife said quietly.

"Something wrong?" Blake said, throwing back the covers, still disoriented.

"She tried to get to the bathroom by herself and fell."

"Is she hurt?"

"Maybe bruises, but I don't think anything's broken. She's too heavy for me to get her up by myself."

Blake pulled on some sweatpants and followed his wife through the house and outside to the tiny apartment they'd added for Mamie Tower, designed to accommodate her inevitable shift to a wheelchair. Mamie had resisted leaving her own house, but Blake and Sally's brother had recreated her old bedroom, arranging her pictures and furniture in exactly the same way so that when she walked in, her book and reading glasses were in the same place they'd been in the bedroom she'd slept in most of her married life. The move was a complete success with never a word of regret.

Mamie was sitting against the wall of the bathroom with a sweet but confused smile on her face. "Sorry to get you up, Blake. I just don't have enough strength in my arms, I don't guess."

"Don't worry about that, Mamie," Blake said, stepping into the bathroom. "I'm not good for much around the house but getting you back to bed is one thing I can do. Scoot forward for me, and I'll help you up from behind."

With his arms under each of hers, Blake lifted her to the level of the wheelchair and swung her into the seat.

"My knight in shining armor," Mamie said. "Thank you."

"Don't know about the armor but I'll always help you, you know that. Anything else?"

"No," Sally said. "Go on back to bed. I'll be there in a minute."

Sally returned to the smell of coffee perking and bacon sizzling.

"I was wide awake," Blake said when he saw her surprise. "Decided to get a jump on the day."

"That's a big jump—it's only 4:15."

"Scrambled or fried?" Blake asked.

"Scrambled," Sally said, moving toward the refrigerator. "I'll do the muffins."

Blake started cracking eggs into a bowl. "Have you thought any more about the nursing home for her?"

"Not really," Sally answered, distinctly uninterested. "Aside from this little problem, it's working out fine."

"Wouldn't it be better if she were around more people during the day?" Blake gently prodded. He pulled a plate from the microwave and transferred four crisp bacon strips to a paper towel.

"She doesn't seem to want company," Sally said, splitting open the muffins and spreading a thin layer of margarine on each side. "She didn't get around much when she was able, if you remember. And she doesn't want to go, so I'd rather put the extra money in savings for the time being. You never know how long you'll be chief."

"At least three more years. And if I'm playing my cards correctly, we'll get a raise."

"I hope so, but you never know," Sally repeated.

Blake nodded in agreement. "You're right about that. Finished?" He reached for the tub of margarine to add some to the frying pan. Sally smiled, then laid down her knife and stepped behind him, circling his waist with her arms. "What are your plans after we eat?"

Blake switched off the burner and turned around, bringing his hands up to her face. "Will the eggs spoil if we don't cook them now?"

"Not if you put them in the refrigerator."

He kissed her first on the forehead, then the bridge of her nose, reaching for the bowl and maneuvering her toward the refrigerator, continuing his kisses down her nose to her lips, chin, and neck as they moved. He broke away only long enough to put the eggs away, then settled back into his mission. He took Sally by the shoulders and, turning her toward the bedroom, gently directed her forward as if he were leading her around the dance floor.

All the way down the hallway, Blake's lips never left the back of Sally's smooth neck, his arms engulfing her while he unfastened the six buttons of her nightgown. At the edge of their bed, Sally's gown slipped off her shoulders and dropped to the floor. She purred with contentment.

■ ■ ■ ■

The morning service at Reynold's was brief. Since Brent had no family, there was only Grace, her brother and his wife, Gibbs and Sarah Carver accompanied by Sandy Quinn, and the minister. He was the new pastor of the Methodist church they'd attended for years, but he really hadn't known Brent that well. The service was conducted in the visitation room since with so few, there was no need to use the chapel.

It was over in thirteen minutes.

Grace rode with her brother and sister-in-law out to their

family farm where he and his family now lived. The cemetery was half a mile from the house across the fields at the corner of four pastures. Her brother's children were all in school, so the only additional faces at the grave side were the two older black men who had worked for Grace's parents and now worked for her brother, and the funeral home people. They stayed in the background until the ceremony was finished.

It was cold for March—even the sun's full light didn't offer much warmth. They stood about the grave shivering, and Grace hoped the minister would be brief. Jody was buried there and visiting her grave was always upsetting. Gibbs Carver had remained composed until he placed his boutonniere on the casket, and then a final sob burst forth. He quickly stifled it, seeing the somber but passive faces of everyone else. Grace's sister-in-law took the minister and Sarah back to the house to start lunch. Gibbs started for his car, but stopped when Grace didn't follow.

"I'm waiting until it's filled in," Grace said. "Daddy never left the dead alone, unburied."

Sandy Quinn looked to the Governor for a signal. Carver nodded, and silently, the men remained by her side.

■ ■ ■ ■

"Okay, Will, think where you were when you had the beret on last," Laura said as she loaded the dishwasher with Will's breakfast dishes. "You put everything on after dinner. You went to see how you looked in the mirror. Then what?"

"I don't know."

"Where did you find the blue shirt?"

"In my room, on the shoe bin. Momma," he pleaded, "I'm going to be late."

Laura glanced from her son's anxious eyes to her watch. She couldn't help smiling at the pencil thin moustache she'd painted above his lip. "No, you're not. Just calm down. Let's try your room again. Empty out the shoe bin, all the way. I'll be right there."

He raced away.

She wiped the pancake skillet clean, and then appeared at the door to Will's room. Surrounded by a collection of shoes, rubber snakes, Nerf pistols, and baseballs, was her son wearing her black wool beret at a particularly jaunty angle, balancing an old palette of Semmes' on his arm, and brandishing a paintbrush in his hand. "Found it!" he smiled.

Primos Restaurant was noisy, filled with its regular breakfast crowd, plus a large contingent of irregulars, with the many voices bouncing off the beige plaster walls and Fifties bric-a-brac. Everett had gotten there early enough to grab one of the circular booths on the raised level. He endured the glares from several other customers squeezing their larger groups around smaller tables, annoyed at a single man taking up an entire corner with just a silver coffee pot and cup in front of him. He kept an eye on the front door for Laura while he scanned the *Clarion Ledger*.

She slid across on the red Naugahyde cushion before he even realized she'd arrived.

"Sorry I'm late, but Will had to go to school in costume."

"What kind of costume?"

"It's French Day. He went as an artist—but by this morning, he'd managed to misplace my black beret."

"I came early to stake out a table and I'm glad I did, or we might have had to go to elsewhere." Everett handed her the front section of the paper.

The waitress appeared with a menu under her arm and a new pot of coffee. She turned over Laura's cup and filled it with inky black liquid. "Ready to order now or do you need a moment?"

"Two eggs scrambled, bacon, hash browns, wheat toast, and orange juice," Everett quickly responded.

Laura scanned the menu for something tasty with slightly less cholesterol, but the aroma of bacon and sausage from the kitchen was overpowering. "Ahhh...one egg scrambled—dry, sausage, wheat toast, and orange juice."

"Hash browns?"

A real test of willpower. "No thank you, ma'am." Everett looked at her. He knew, and she knew, that the hash browns were unbelievably good.

"Okay, hash browns," said Laura, relenting. "Small order." The waitress smiled and disappeared.

"How's your last week at the Auditor's Office going?"

"As they say, 'When it's over, it's really over.'"

Laura nodded. "Been there myself."

"It's weird. People ask me questions about cases—they want information, in fact, they want all they can get out of me, as though once I'm out of the door, they can't call again."

"And they won't. You're the only person I've heard from since I left. The Auditor treats me like a traitor. It's so stupid to act like that, if you ask me."

"Only five more days of the cold shoulder and that's it."

"Aren't you going to take some of your accrued leave before you go?"

"I could have, but I've got too many loose ends to tie up."

"Sounds like you ought to leave them untied, if that's the way they're acting."

"There'll be plenty left undone—but I've got some papers and files to copy, bits and pieces I want to take with me."

"Such as?"

"Transportation Department files."

"Good planning," Laura said, her eyes lighting up at the thought. "I've been thinking, if the IRS comes to you to find out about Transportation audits, I figure they've found income they can't pin down, don't you?"

"That's the only reason I can think of."

"And those guys only go back a few years, right?"

"Their limit is five unless they find something that gives them a reason to go back farther and then they go back two more. The guy who was in my office was asking about recent stuff, I do know that."

"So how could Reed Morgan fleece the state? I mean, I thought they'd beefed up internal controls over at

Transportation."

"It's not easy to do, but not impossible," Everett answered. "He's king in his district. Morgan could have greased the skids on certain projects, maybe gotten advance information to contractors, sent business to certain people. There are plenty of possibilities. But I doubt it's too intricate—Morgan isn't exactly a rocket scientist."

"Then the next question. Assuming we don't want anyone to know we're looking into this, what records can we get our hands on that will be helpful?"

"That's the problem. The annual reports don't have much, particularly the recent ones. And the public records room at Finance and Administration isn't browser friendly. You've got to know exactly what you're looking for—the date and the voucher number—to get copies of anything."

"How do you find anything?"

"Write a search program for the state financial database and work from that."

"So what kind of queries could you design for this hide and seek in the dark?"

"I'm downloading as much data as I can, then I'll sort it a bunch of ways and see what I can see."

"How far back?"

"Ten years, which'll cover the years the IRS is interested in."

"Go as far back as you can, just to be safe. Can you still get into the data?"

Everett nodded. "My password's good until next Monday."

"So you can work on this at home?"

"Already am."

Laura smiled. Just like old times; nothing had changed. Finding the needle in the haystack was something she was really good at. Even though she loved running the Patrol, she wasn't a cop and never would be. "Will you still have access to the Finance records room?"

"The woman who runs it loves my stock tips. And she repays me with dinner every so often. I doubt she'll know I've left the Auditor's Office, particularly if I keep showing up from time to time."

"Do you have the annual reports?"

"I've been scrounging around for a complete set. I'm only missing a couple and then I'll have every year since Morgan was elected."

"Why don't you let me look at those? I think I still have my notes from that Inspector Generals' seminar three or four years ago at the Federal Highway Administration. It was all about bid rigging and other ways to steal. Let me see if the annual reports give me a feel for how Transportation operated. Something might hit me."

"I'll bring them next week when I start working at the Patrol."

■ ■ ■ ■

Brent's lawyers were an old Jackson firm, which had handled both the corporate work for Wexler, Inc. as well as his personal business and estate planning. Grace never had much to do with them except on the occasions when her signature was required, and then she'd signed wherever the sticky red arrow pointed. She'd called Franklin Gilliam, the senior partner who had handled Brent's affairs, to review the will and discuss her options and probate obligations. Eager to please, Gilliam arranged a morning meeting.

As Grace stepped off the elevator, she could see several people congregated in the conference room—its interior wall was glass. She introduced herself to the receptionist, who directed her to the glass room.

"I thought I was meeting with Mr. Gilliam."

"You are, ma'am. He'll be joining you in just a moment."

Somewhat tentatively, she crossed the reception area and entered the room. Everyone stood as she walked in and introduced themselves. Gilliam appeared a minute later in an expensive dark business suit. The gray at his temples was particularly apparent. Considering the thinning but jet black hair on the top of his head, Grace figured Gilliam was finally going natural.

"On behalf of the entire firm," Gilliam said to start things off, "we want you to know how very sorry we all are about Brent's death. Everyone in this room worked with him, some of us on a daily basis. It was a privilege, always."

One of the attorneys launched into an anecdote about Brent and another followed as soon as the first had finished.

Grace cleared her throat. "Thank you all for your condolences," she said, smiling as politely as possible. She hoped her limited response would end the expensive chit-chat.

Gilliam nodded, looking down at the pile of documents in front of him. He folded his hands, and, with a patronizing tone that a less discerning listener might have mistaken for inordinate deference, cleared his throat and began. "The will, though not simple because of the way he set it up to shelter assets from estate taxes, boils down to this: Everything was left to you except for a bequest of up to five hundred thousand dollars to form the Josephine Ethel Wexler Trust, with you as trustee, the proceeds of which are to go to the charitable causes of your choice in memory of your daughter."

At the sound of her daughter's name, Grace's eyes moistened. She pulled out a handkerchief and carefully dabbed them, avoiding ruining her mascara. When she realized that everyone had become silent, waiting for her, she looked at Gilliam and spoke so softly it was nearly a whisper, "Excuse me, go on, please."

"Wexler, Inc., the house, the farm, and the hunting camp, as well as the insurance proceeds of two million dollars, are yours. We've already prepared the papers...." the lawyer patted a red file folder in front of him, "for your signature to get the ball rolling on the life insurance claim, as well as a claim against the automobile policy for the value of the car that burned in the wreck."

"The bad news is that there's over a million dollars owed in mortgage liability, secured by the house in Jackson and the farm."

Grace took a deep breath and exhaled slowly. The actual mortgage balances were the information she hadn't had. Gilliam nodded to the tax attorney who picked up his worksheets, glanced at the bottom of the right-hand column and then addressed her. "Mrs. Wexler, given the way Mr. Wexler structured his estate, all the assets are covered by the marital deduction, so there won't be any estate taxes."

"Thank goodness. That's the first good news I've heard in days."

"But that won't be the case at your death except for the charitable contribution, of course. As your own reads now that Mr. Wexler has predeceased you, everything over the unified credit amount will be taxed."

"What do you suggest?"

"As soon as possible, and I know it's hard to think about this now, I need to sit down with you and discuss what your options are so that we can draft a new will."

"I'd appreciate that. We could meet next week, if you have the time."

"At your convenience," said the tax attorney, respectfully. "When you have your calendar in front of you, please give me a call and we'll set up a time." He handed her his business card.

"Thank you," Grace said, looking expectantly for the next speaker. Gilliam nodded imperiously to man in his early forties who hurriedly began. "Mrs. Wexler, I've handled Wexler, Inc., matters for several years now. The company is very sound and in a strong position, due in great part to Mr. Wexler's hands-on approach. I can't say how the company will do without him, but I'm certain—in fact, I know—there will be several groups interested in acquiring the company. Mrs. Wexler, the best time to pursue offers is now, when the buyers believe you're dealing from a position of weakness."

"I don't know what I'm going to do yet. I might keep it."

Gilliam looked at Grace over his reading glasses. "Grace, I must tell you that keeping the company is not advisable. Who will run it for you?"

"For the time being, Leb Bailey will. He's been running it

up to now, Franklin."

Gilliam stifled the scoff that had partially erupted from his mouth and looked at her long and hard. It was clear she meant what she'd said. With an unctuous smile, he quickly backpedaled, trying to protect their substantial retainer. "And we'll be right here to help in any way we can."

"I'm certain of that." Grace sat forward, straight in her chair, garnering everyone's attention. "I do want to sell the hunting camp," she said, looking directly at Gilliam, who'd been a member since its inception. "Brent gave an option—a right of first refusal, as I read it, to Trey Turner. So must I offer it to him before I do anything else? How does that work?"

Gilliam's eyes widened. "I don't have that in my files. Brent must have had someone else draft it. Can I see what you're referring to?"

"Certainly." Grace drew a document out of her case. Franklin Gilliam looked it over, obviously surprised and anxious. A younger attorney moved instantly to his side and read over Gilliam's shoulder. After a few mumbled words and nods, they looked back at Grace who had been waiting patiently, watching.

"This seems to be valid," Gilliam said, disappointed. "But you're only obliged to offer it to him, and Trey will have ten days in which to decide. Don't forget Turner can only exercise his option if he pays your asking price, so set your price. I know for a fact that the club members are interested in making an offer."

In fact, the hunt club members had been caucusing nearly constantly since Brent's death, discussing their situation. No one wanted anything to change, particularly not until the current hunting season was over. In the lives of a substantial number of Mississippians, few obligations took precedence over hunting.

"What about the club? I couldn't find a lease or any type of agreement in Brent's papers."

"I have a copy of the lease right here." He opened his notebook, handed the paper to the only female attorney in the room, and asked her to make a copy.

Grace's eyes widened noticeably.

Annoyed at the affront, the woman left the room, not daring to take the matter up in the presence of a client. Gilliam continued, oblivious to both his faux pas and Grace's recognition of it.

"There's a provision that disbands the club at such time as the land is sold and rebates a *pro rata* share of any membership dues already paid. I can speak for the club, though—they authorized me to—they may well seek to purchase the property themselves. Of course no one knew about the option clause, but I don't think that changes anything. We'll talk with Trey and then make you an offer."

The female attorney had returned with the copy and as she handed it to her, Grace couldn't resist the temptation to mouth the word "typical," polishing it with a weary grin. The woman smiled awkwardly as she took her seat. At least two of the other attorneys were shaking their heads in apology.

"How much per acre can I get, do you think?"

Gilliam shifted his weight and cleared his throat. "I've got an interest in that, Grace, so you'll have to have an outside appraiser. But I know that neighboring land has sold recently for six hundred an acre. The camp should be in that range."

"Good. Selling it will wash out the mortgages."

"With a considerable amount left over."

Grace looked through her papers, tapping her long fingers on her note pad. "I've got to deal with Wexler, Inc., and I know I'll have lots of questions."

Gilliam spoke up immediately. "Just call me—I'll make sure your questions get routed to the right person."

"Thank you. I'm going to try to go by there tomorrow. Well, gentlemen," she looked at the female attorney, "and lady, I've got lots to do and I don't need you all billing me for any more time...." Grace looked down at her watch, "than necessary. If I could sign the insurance papers, I'll be out of your way."

A murmur of appreciation rolled about the room as she stood

up. Gilliam appeared with the red folder in hand, offering his thick black Mont Blanc fountain pen to her, pointing to the blue arrow that identified the place for her signature.

"What am I signing?" Grace asked.

"You're swearing to Brent's death, that's all."

Grace signed her name quickly and straightened up to go.

"And here," Gilliam said, flipping to another page.

"What's this one for?"

"The claim for the wreck," Gilliam answered quickly.

Grace scrawled her signature again. "I assume you'll send copies of these to the house?"

"Certainly. We'll have the runner take them out there this afternoon."

"Regular mail will do fine," Grace said a bit sharply. "Franklin, did I just pay for all these people to sit in this room? I only called for you."

"Uhhh..." Gilliam stumbled, not quite certain what to say, nor able to return Grace's chilly stare. "No, Grace. This won't be billed time."

She gathered up her brown case. "Thank goodness."

She turned and strode out to the elevator with him at her heels, speechless. When the doors had opened and there was only a second left, Gilliam blurted out, "Have you really thought this Wexler, Inc., thing through?"

She hadn't, but Gilliam's attitude annoyed her so much she said, "Often. Contrary to what Brent may have told you, not only can I smile but I can think, sometimes even at the same time." The doors closed between them.

■ ■ ■ ■

Corporal Billy Cook, the Troopers Federation representative who had piped up in the Captains and Majors meeting when Laura had forbidden slow-downs, had been the first volunteer to take on a field trainee for a month. He'd been assigned a very enthusiastic graduate from the last class. The rookie had a massive upper body and could bench press three hundred pounds easily.

The two men drove slowly through struggling downtown Claytonia, on the western edge of Polk County, with its huge sign announcing its only claim to fame as the birthplace of Governor Gibbs Carver. It was close to 10 P.M.

"I wonder if the Governor's ever had a bill collector after him," said Cook, bitterly.

"Never has and never will," the young trooper replied.

The town square was deserted, as it was every day by two minutes after five o'clock, no longer the center of life for the sixty-five inhabitants. Claytonia almost straddled the county line, halfway between the Polk County and Taft County court-houses, and all but forgotten.

"He certainly moved on as soon as he could," Cook said.

"I'd move out of this area if a chance came along," said the rookie, who lived on the other side of the district. "None of the schools are worth crap, and it's only two years till my oldest is in kindergarten."

"Madeline's home-schooling the girls," Cook told him, "so I think I'm here to stay."

Green's Grocery and Washeteria appeared—a cinder-block building with a tattered awning that shaded a parade of folding chairs, rockers, and an illuminated Coke machine—a beacon in the night. Across the dirt parking lot was the only pay phone in town, and a car was pulled up close enough for the driver to talk from his front seat. Another was waiting behind him.

"This is where I'll be," Cook said, pointing to the corner of the lot where he had a clear view of the road. "Need a Coke or something?"

"Yeah, let me get one," the trooper answered.

Cook pulled up by the drink machine, leaving the car running with the headlights illuminating the front of the building. Above the door to the Washeteria, someone had painted in scrawling letters, "Gibbs Carver washed his clothes here." The word 'clothes' was crossed out and the words 'dirty laundry' were scrawled beneath it.

"I'm surprised his brother hasn't had that removed," Cook

said.

"His brother?"

"He's a Polk County supervisor, big fish in a small pond."

"He hasn't done much for the place from what I've seen," said the rookie, pulling a cold can out of the machine.

Cook gave a gruff laugh. "Not a single new business that I can think of has moved here in ten years."

"Traffic tickets must be the biggest part of their monthly revenue. They must live off of us."

"You got it," said Cook. "A slowdown would bring a county like this to its knees. That's exactly why it would be such a great pressure tactic. Carver's brother would be all over the Governor within a month."

"Too bad the Commissioner's so adamantly against it," his trainee replied.

Like that's really going to stop me, Cook thought. And you, my brand spanking new trooper, are going to cover my ass, though you don't know it.

"What do you think about her anyway?" the rookie asked.

Cook wondered whether he ought to answer the question at all—innocent off-hand comments seemed to have a way of being repeated. "I'll give the devil her due. No commissioner in my time has worked as hard. And I don't always agree with her but at least you know where you stand. After all the double talk we've heard, it's a relief."

Drinks in hand, they drove on toward the County Line Lounge, a joint that featured bands every weekend, drawing customers from all around. Its once-risqué neon sign—a curvy female holding a small serving tray above her shoulder—flashed its icy blue and pink lights up and down the highway. The parking lot was filled and more cars lined the shoulder of the road.

"This should be a productive little outing for your first solo venture," Cook told the rookie. "Must be quite a party tonight."

"Looks like it," said the trooper. "We ought to be able to write up at least three or four drunks each and fill up both the Polk and Taft jails."

"You work the Taft County side, I'll cover Polk," Cook said, speeding up now that they were past the lounge. He dropped his trainee at his car which was parked around a bend in the road where the shoulder was wide enough to pull cars over. "Keep in touch over the radio," Cook told him. "And rule number one: Never hesitate to call for backup. I can be here pretty damn quick if you need me."

Back at Green's, on the Polk County side, Cook parked at the edge of the lot, heading into the street, ready to go, putting his blue light on a slow steady pulse. It wasn't five minutes before a car came his way. He stepped out into the road and motioned the car to pull off into the parking lot.

"May I see your license, sir?" Cook asked when he approached the driver.

The smell of alcohol on the man's breath was unmistakable as he shifted in his seat to pull his wallet from his back pocket. He offered it to Cook.

"Just the license, sir," Cook said. He watched the man fumble around, trying to get the card free from its plastic cover.

"Did you like the band tonight?" Cook asked as he read the man's name and address.

"It was gr..." the driver started to say but the woman in the passenger seat punched his arm to stop him from talking. The man looked at her, confused, and then turned back to Cook. "Is something the matter?"

"Sobriety checkpoint, sir. Could you step out of the car, please?"

"Sure," the man said, with inappropriate bravado.

"Hold your hands out to your sides, point your fingers," Cook said, once the man was standing in front of him. "Now bring your right finger in and touch your nose, sir."

The driver missed by several inches, managing to jab his left cheek.

"Not so good," Cook said.

"Let me try again." The driver brought his hand toward his nose more slowly but undershot this time, landing on his right cheek.

Cook leaned lower so he could see the passenger better. The woman was cowering in her corner, defiantly looking out her window, trying to avoid any involvement in the matter. She pulled a light sweater tighter across her ample chest for protection from the cool night air.

"Ma'am," Cook said, his voice deep and commanding. The woman looked at Cook, her eyes alert. "Are you in better shape to drive?"

"I probably am," the woman said, disgusted.

"Then why don't you step out of the car and show me," Cook suggested, handing the license back to the man. "You do know how to drive, don't you?"

"Yes, sir, Officer," the woman said promptly, surprised.

She opened her door and trotted through the glare of the headlights as quickly as her clear plastic spike heels would allow. She passed the finger-to-the-nose test with flying colors.

"Thank you, Officer," the woman said, opening the driver's door. "I tried to get the keys from my husband to begin with," she added.

"Drive carefully," was all Cook said.

"Move over, Phil," she commanded.

Cook watched down the road and waved his flashlight for the woman to pull out.

His portable radio crackled, and Cook turned up the volume to hear the rookie calling in a driver's license to the substation.

Cook keyed his mike. "Looks like the drunks are going your direction. I haven't seen a soul," he lied.

"Must be. I'm taking this one to the Taft County jail to run him on the intoxilyzer."

"Want any help?"

"No, I can handle it," the rookie said.

"I may move down to your spot since you're having such good fishing," Cook said.

"Be my guest. I'll be back in a while."

Crossing into Taft County, Cook pulled into the spot they'd scouted earlier. A car was parked on the shoulder, probably belonging to the drunk the rookie was locking up. Traffic seemed to pick up for a while—the band had probably taken a break—and Cook stopped several cars. But no one appeared impaired until a sporty foreign car approached, moving considerably faster than appropriate for the narrow road and dark night, the engine whining as the driver pushed it through its gears.

Cook flagged the car over. The driver was a defensive lineman-no-neck type. A pencil thin woman with heavy eye make-up sat in the passenger seat. Cook thought he'd encountered the man before but he couldn't remember the context.

"I'm Jim Guy, the Quick Deal man," the driver said breezily, as he handed Cook his license. "You might have seen me on TV."

"Now I remember," said Cook. "Would you step out of the car, Mr. Guy?"

The woman got out of the car, too, and watched from her side, impassive, as Cook went through the same nose touching drill with Guy that he had with his earlier customer. The Quick Deal man did no better. Cook looked over the car roof at the woman. "Are you able to drive a standard shift?"

The woman nodded.

"And are you sober enough to drive?"

She nodded again.

"Let me see," Cook said.

The woman promptly extended her arms and brought her right forefinger to the point of her nose, and then her left, without hesitation.

"Fine, then you follow me in his car while I take Mr. Guy in."

"Officer..." Jim Guy began.

"We'll see what sort of a quick deal we can get for you at the Taft County jail," Cook said, escorting Jim Guy to his patrol car.

When they pulled into the sheriff's office, his trainee was coming out. "Gotcha one?"

"Yup," Cook said. "The Taft county side is hot. You ought to set right back up where you were."

■ ■ ■ ■

Nat Tomaselli was leaning back in his chair, musing about which kind of fresh pasta he was going to fix that night while he waited for the Missing Persons Bureau of the New Orleans Police Department to come back on the line. His battered stainless steel desk at the I. J. Riley Memorial Center, a food kitchen on Ramparts that served hundreds of homeless people every day, was covered with drafts of a grant application he'd put off writing until the last minute. He'd hit a writer's block, fresh out of ways to rephrase the same desperate needs. Taking a break, he'd called the police about Myron DeLaureal, one of the regulars who hadn't shown up to eat for several weeks. Nat felt badly that he'd waited so long to call them, but one thing after another had interrupted him. Besides, the cops never paid any attention to his calls anyway as far as he could tell.

The silence on the line was shattered by the particularly grating Cajun accent of the clerk who'd put him on hold minutes earlier. "Now, Mr. Thompkins, you say you don't have a permanent address for this man?"

Nat decided to ignore the woman's mistake with his name, infuriating as it was. "Not what you'd consider permanent. He's been a regular at the center for at least two years. He would have told us—he would have told me—if he were leaving the area. I know this man."

Indeed, Nat credited Myron with saving his life one very cold Christmas four years earlier when Nat, down on his luck and love, had become sufficiently drunk to warrant being thrown in jail for disorderly conduct and public drunkenness, a state of behavior not unknown in the Crescent City. Myron had been meandering past the jail when Nat was released, and taking pity on the dazed and hungry young man, panhandled enough money for the two of them to eat, and listened to Nat's sad story of unrequited love and lost opportunities. Whether it was the vision of becoming like Myron, or the catharsis that came with finally unloading his sorrows, Nat never knew, but he walked away with renewed determination.

After a couple of years, when Nat had gotten a grip on his life again, he shelved his management job at a fish meal plant in Empire, Louisiana. Then, working through a community organization, he took over managing the I. J. Riley Center on the edge of the Quarter, his effort to repay the debt he felt he owed to that nameless man. It was months before Myron wandered in, but Nat recognized him immediately and tried to strike up a conversation. Myron didn't respond to Nat's overtures at first, but Myron kept coming back, and over time something akin to a relationship developed. Friendship would be too strong a word because Myron was stingy with the details of his life. Eventually Myron had told Nat enough about his descent to his current ignoble state so that Nat, wanting to rescue this man who'd been his own savior, began searching for Myron's relatives. After much research and effort, Nat had located some of Myron's family in a city cemetery. But since then, he hadn't figured out what tack to take in his crusade to save Myron.

"Okay, Mr. Thomas, let me get the info."

"Tomaselli. Nat Tomaselli."

"Have it your way. Let's go."

"Myron DeLaureal. Born July 19, 1945, I think. I don't know his social security number."

"Description?"

"About 6 feet 1 or 2 inches. 150-160 pounds. Caucasian. Blue eyes."

"Family?"

"Dead as far as I know."

"Last seen?"

"About three weeks ago."

"Where?"

"At the I. J. Riley Memorial Center."

"Have you checked the hospitals?"

"Yes."

"And the morgue?"

"Yes."

The clerk grunted as if intrigued for the first time. Then she continued, "Your name?"

"Nathaniel Tomaselli."

"Slow down."

"N-A-T-H-A-N-I-E-L  T-O-M-A-S-E-L-L-I."

"Relationship?"

"Friend and director of the I. J. Riley Memorial Center."

Nat could hear the clicking of terminal keys. "Okay. He's in the computer."

"What next?"

"If he turns up, make sure you let us know. If we find him first, we'll let you know."

"Can I check from time to time?"

There was silence followed by an overworked sigh. "Sure."

"Your name, please, ma'am?"

The clerk hesitated. "Just talk to whoever answers."

"But your name, please?"

The clerk hesitated again.

"Just so I can say who entered the record and when."

She gave up. "Officer Breyard."

"Spell?" He could tell he'd annoyed her.

"B-R-E-Y-A-R-D."

"Thank you, officer. I really appreciate your time."

# SEVEN

Blake was watching the movements in and around the parking lot when Sandy called. The Patrol was not unlike a very busy anthill with the chief and commissioner sitting at the top, usually clueless about the activity below. In fact, most chiefs and commissioners preferred not to know, and some actively avoided learning what was happening inside the swarming mound. But not Blake. He tried to keep his finger on the pulse of everything, and his fifth floor window gave him one of the vantage points he needed.

"Chief, Quinn here. What was the exact location of Wexler's wreck?"

Blake frowned. "The Governor doesn't want to visit the scene, does he?"

"No. He's busy with the Legislature today. I'm taking Mrs. Carver and Mrs. Wexler out to her farm to look around in a few minutes. I thought I ought to know where the wreck had occurred in case Mrs. Wexler wanted to see it. Or avoid it, as the case may be."

Sandy was as likable a guy as anyone you could meet, yet his easy-going nature masked a cautious, thorough mind. He was constantly checking and rechecking to be certain nothing went wrong on his travels with Governor Carver or the First Lady.

Blake watched a wrecker pull one of the new cars into the shop. He hadn't heard about a wreck so there must have been a mechanical breakdown. Why wasn't the car going directly to the dealer for warranty work?

Sandy coughed on the other end of the line bringing Blake back to his conversation. "Why are you going along?" Blake asked.

"All I know is, right after Mrs. Wexler called yesterday evening, the First Lady asked if an officer could drive with them. I looked over the roster and decided to do it myself."

Blake snapped into gear, his attention switching from the parking lot to the First Lady. "Hang on, I think Jimmie Anderson's around and he can tell you." Blake was about to punch the hold button when he added, "Stay on the line when you're done with Anderson. I want to check something and then I'll need to talk to you again."

He hooked Sandy up with Anderson and dialed Investigations.

"Stone," Robert answered immediately.

"Busy?" Blake asked, not bothering to identify himself.

"Got all the Captains in. We're working through our list of legislators."

"Are we making any progress?"

"It's slow, but we're touching them," Robert said. "There are several we don't have an angle on—Gabriel Collel and his buddies, for instance."

"He's so down on the Commissioner, we ought to just write him off. Not antagonizing him may be the best we can hope for."

"Well, let us know if you have any brilliant ideas."

"Do you know where Trey Turner is today?" Blake asked.

"He's coming in from the Greenville," Robert said. "Should be here by now."

Blake scanned the lot for Turner's maroon Bonneville and

didn't see it. "Undercover?"

"Nope."

"I don't see his car. Make some excuse to get up with him—I need to know where he is."

"Why, may I ask?" Robert inquired.

"Because Mrs. Wexler asked the First Lady to have a trooper go with them out to the farm. Based on what Mrs. Wexler said about not wanting to run into Turner alone, and given what the Commissioner said about things going smoothly, I'd like to be sure that doesn't happen."

"Gotcha covered."

"If they're going to cross paths," Blake added, "let Quinn know—he's taking them."

"You bet."

"Call me when you guys go to lunch," Blake said. "I'll join you."

Blake searched the parking area again then punched the blinking light on line one.

"Quinn," Blake said.

"Yo."

"Be on the lookout for Turner. I don't think Mrs. Wexler likes him much. We think he's on his way back from the Delta but you never know. Hate to have them meet up if we can avoid it."

"I can understand that. He's quiet but not real friendly."

"Been around him much?"

"Some. When the Governor was hunting, or visiting Wexler at the farm. Turner's great with a gun, but piss poor with people."

"Hasn't he been working for Wexler for years?"

"Fifteen at least. Wexler probably liked big silent bodyguards."

"Did he need one?"

"Nah. But if the Governor had one, Wexler wanted one. He considered himself a wheel. You know he's the reason Carver was elected, don't you? That man raised an incredible amount of money."

"I did know that much," Blake said.

"Wexler didn't have the right personality to be the candidate," Sandy said. "He was a little over the top on arrogance, but he wanted to be Governor so bad he could taste it."

"They all do, though damned if I know why."

"Ain't that the truth. Anything more?"

"No. Drive carefully."

"Thanks, Chief."

Blake's gaze swept over the parking lot one more time for Turner's car, but it still hadn't appeared. His intercom buzzed.

"I forgot to tell you," Robert said. "I rescued Mrs. Nora Sandifer and her charming daughter, Leigh, in that driving thunderstorm late yesterday afternoon."

"Should I know Nora Sandifer?"

"She's Senator Terrell Sandifer's wife."

"You're kidding."

"Nope. I was about fifty miles north of Jackson, headed to my parent's house. The road narrows on top of that levee."

"I know the place."

"Well, I make the turn and there, blocking half of the northbound lane was a dark red Toyota Corolla without any lights on. I nearly landed in the ditch trying to avoid it. The two women were inside, both waving frantically."

"Idiots."

"That wasn't the word I used at the time but it'll do. Of course, they wouldn't let me in the car until I'd shown them my badge. I got soaked to the bone."

"What was the trouble?"

"Out of gas. I moved their car and took them home. They seemed very appreciative."

"No offense, but somehow I don't think that's going to translate to a vote in our favor. He's too close to Collel."

"Maybe, but you never know."

Grace breathed an audible sigh of relief when there weren't any cars at Trey's house. She, Sarah, and Sandy wound through a field and past the pond to the main house, a much more welcome sight than Grace had expected. Long beds of perennials had been planted in front and the entry had been redesigned with broad flagstone steps and large clay flower pots at the edge of each one. There were several comfortable wicker chairs and tables grouped on the porch.

Brent and Grace had named the farm Sunset Hill because of its open western view over gently rolling countryside. Twenty years before, they'd bought six hundred acres from a hay farmer and cattle man who had continued to graze his cattle and keep up the fence lines. There were four rundown structures originally—a horse barn, a main house, a one-bedroom gatehouse, and at the opposite end of the property, a cattle shed for branding and treatment.

Their daughter, Jody, short for Josephine, was ten years old when they bought the place. Brent immediately set about expanding the main house into a rustic but handsome one-floor hacienda with long, screened porches on both the eastern and western sides, perfect for watching the sun rise and set. Each summer, they moved out to the farm. Jody stayed outdoors, busy every moment, riding horses, or exploring whatever animal, insect, or flower came into view. Grace read to her heart's content—on the porch, in the hammock, or wherever she pleased—enjoying the respite from the myriad social obligations Brent normally required her to attend.

All was well—their happiest days as a family—until Brent let Trey Turner move into the gatehouse and renovate it. By then, Jody was fifteen, lovely and virginal, an unfettered spirit still captivated by the outdoors and wildlife, unscarred by the normal ravages of teenage hormones.

But Trey unnerved Grace. Right from the start, he and Brent exhibited an unsettling familiarity with one another to the point of completely anticipating each other's moves, something even she hadn't achieved in all their years of marriage. Daily battles erupted and the issue wasn't resolved satisfactorily until the inevitable change in Jody's interests, when she traded in horses and the great outdoors for boys and social events. That's when she and Grace stopped their annual pilgrimage for the summer and stayed in Jackson year round.

Grace retrieved four empty moving boxes from the back of her Volvo station wagon, and headed toward the house, pulling out an old set of keys she hoped would work. As she unlocked the door and stepped into the large airy main room, she saw that all the furniture had been changed, there was hardly a piece she recognized. She was speechless, completely unprepared for the inviting room she saw before her.

"Grace, what a wonderful retreat," said Sarah from behind her. "Gibbs always raves about it and now I know why."

"I'm impressed, too. It's totally different than the last time I saw it."

"You know they had all their top-top-secret meetings out here," Sarah added.

Grace turned to Sandy. "Then you must know your way around."

"Yes, ma'am," he said, a little uneasy at being more familiar with her property than she was.

"Why don't you check the kitchen and that end of the house," Grace suggested. "I want to see about any papers and financial stuff."

Sarah and Sandy headed toward the kitchen and Grace went to the master bedroom. Part of the west sleeping porch—Jody's porch as it was called—connected to the bedroom, and Brent had converted it to an office. A huge armoire containing a television and sound system dominated one end and at the other was his desk. It was orderly—papers were in expandable folders and labeled, and the two-drawer file cabinet, though chock full, was also neatly organized. On top of the broad oak table, next to a laptop computer, was an in-box with bills, receipts, and letters. Grace leafed through the pile, then decided to take it all with her.

She'd finished boxing up the papers and was disconnecting the computer when Sandy appeared at the door. "Can I help you with anything, Mrs. Wexler?" he asked.

"I hate to bother you, but if you wouldn't mind, I need to get all this out to the car."

"Certainly."

After Sandy left with a load, Grace stepped into the dressing area and looked through the long rack of Brent's clothes, depressed by the thought of all there was to clear out. The tall-boy dresser was filled with socks, underwear, and shirts—enough for four full wardrobes, easily. She presumed Goodwill would be overjoyed to see her coming. Maybe they'd even send their truck all the way out to the farm once she told them how much stuff she was donating.

"What size is Gibbs?" she called out to Sarah.

"Pardon?" said Sarah, coming to the door.

"What size is Gibbs? Maybe he could use some of these."

"44 Long."

"That's too bad. These are 42s."

"They'd be a little tight, I'm afraid. He's expanding these days, not contracting."

"I'm just going to give it all to Goodwill. Lock, stock, and barrel."

"That'll be a nice little haul."

Grace's eye caught the cufflinks box. She noticed that Brent's favorite set was missing—a pair of diamond-studded gold ones engraved "BW." They had been a present from Jody when he'd escorted her to the debutante ball. He'd added the diamond studs after she'd died, taking the stones from a sixteenth birthday ring he'd given her. It was a pity, she thought, that they'd been lost in the fire. Grace scooped up the odds and ends of jewelry and a set of keys hanging next to the dresser and dropped it all into her purse.

Sarah was looking through the sport jackets. "Strange how fast things change," she said to Grace as they left the dressing area.

"This certainly wasn't something I expected," Grace said, a hint of relief in her voice. "No one really knows how it was between Brent and me except you. I'm really sick of pretending to be sorry. I wonder what else this year will bring."

Grace looked all around her. "Don't you think this room could use something other than maroon as a base color?"

"Definitely. A light blue or pale yellow."

They wandered out to the west porch, and sat in the tall maple rockers. The afternoon sky was filled with billowy clouds. "Sandy was awfully nice to cart all that stuff out to the car for me."

"He's a most obliging person." Sarah looked off in the distance as a large bird circled over a pond. "This is paradise, Grace. I wouldn't be too quick to give it up."

"I was just thinking the same thing myself. I'm not filled with the difficult memories I thought I'd have—so much has changed. It's very pleasant, comforting actually, to be back in Jody's favorite place." Grace paused and watched the same bird Sarah was tracking, still circling in the distance. "I bet something's died and that's a vulture." She looked at Sarah, a twinkle in her eye. "Kinda like me."

Sarah laughed. The sun had moved behind a bank of clouds, outlining its edges in a bright golden glow. Everything was quiet, peaceful, making Grace regret her long absence.

"My only hesitation about this house is that I don't like Trey Turner being around."

"Who's Trey Turner?"

"A trooper. Lives in that little house out by the road and the barn. He worked for Brent, helped out around here, and also down at the hunting camp. But I never liked him—not from the start." Grace looked back at the horizon. "Frankly, that's why I asked you to bring someone along. I don't want to be out here alone with him."

Sandy arrived on the porch just as Grace finished her sentence. He stood by the screen door, his hands jammed down in his pockets, looking out over the back lawn.

"Do you think he'll want to stay in the house?" Sarah asked.

"I assume so. He owns it. One of our pitched battles was about selling it to him."

"I take it you didn't want him to live out here?" Sandy asked.

Grace shook her head and said no more, distinctly uncomfortable talking about another trooper in front of Sandy.

"Ma'am, there are five hundred troopers on the Patrol, and they aren't all friends of mine. Don't know half of them, wouldn't want to know some others."

Grace relaxed a little. "Well, Trey and I never got along. My only hope is with the hunting camp. Brent gave him first refusal rights on the house and land in Second Creek."

Sandy whistled. "They must have been very good friends."

"You could say that." Grace shrugged with disgust. "I want to buy him out—even if I have to swap his house here for the hunting camp house and twice as much acreage."

"How much land is in the camp?"

"About three thousand acres."

Grace watched Sandy's mouth open slightly in awe.

"I don't want to see him again. Ever. He's the source of half the bad feelings I have about the last fifteen years, and I'm willing to pay dearly for a solution."

"Don't let him know that or he'll hold out for an even better deal," Sandy suggested.

"I'll keep that in mind. But one thing will change, he's not going to be the one doing odd jobs around here any more."

"Is that barn by his house yours or his?" Sandy asked.

"Mine."

"All it'll take, I wager, is a stranger whistling in and out of there a few times and he'll decide to leave," Sandy said. "The one thing I do know about him is he's always protected his privacy. Always."

"You wouldn't live out here by yourself would you?" Sarah asked.

"Not until I can find someone decent to live in the front house. Maybe I'll add on to it so it could accommodate a family. Someone with children, someone normal."

Sandy spoke up. "You wouldn't have any trouble with that. There are lots of young troopers, decent sorts who would love a place like this...." he paused, "if you're not too gun-shy of troopers."

"I'll vouch for anyone Sandy recommends," Sarah chimed

in.

Grace smiled. "Maybe it'll all work out." She watched the clouds change their shapes in the western sky, understanding exactly why Jody had wanted to spend her last days in this very spot.

With one final look around, Grace rose from her rocker. "Let's head back—I still need to stop at the barn on our way out..." she looked at Sandy, "if Trey's not there."

It took three tries but one of the keys finally fit the side door to the barn. Sandy went in first, searching and finding the light switch before Grace and Sarah stepped in. The farm truck was right in the middle of the open area with the bulldozer and small front-end loader off to the side, out of the way.

"Did you butcher your own meat?" Sandy asked, inspecting the stainless steel table and the meat lockers first. There were locks on each refrigerated unit.

"I think Trey did. I haven't been in this place in ten years, and Brent and I never talked about it."

Grace opened the truck door and pulled down the visor. A collection of gas tickets and papers rained down.

"These have Brent's name on them. Do you think I can take them?" she asked Sandy.

"Do you own the truck?" he asked.

"I guess I do now."

"If it's got your husband's name on it, I think you have a right to it."

Grace was stuffing all of it in the pockets of her jacket while Sandy nosed around the freezer and cooler some more. "I bet some meat's moved through here."

"Brent was a big hunter, don't forget. Every day, in every way."

■ ■ ■ ■

The padlock chain wasn't twisted the way he always left it.

Trey drove through and locked it behind him then rolled

another fifty yards, and stopped at a massive grouping of azaleas, bursting with hot pink blooms. He pulled back a branch and knelt, looking at the counter for the pressure trip line he'd installed across the driveway. It had been Brent's idea—a bell in both houses signaled when cars came in and out. The counter was Trey's personal addition.

Four. Trey looked down the drive, across the open field toward his house. Four axles—two cars in, and still there. Or, one car in and one car out.

Finding no one at his place, he drove on to Brent's. No cars. So, one car had come and gone.

As Trey unlocked the door, he could feel his whole body tensing. He felt violated, not knowing for certain who had been there. It was as if a thief had gone through his own house.

But the discomfort bloomed into insult and anger when he caught the hint of perfume disturbing the familiar odor he'd been expecting. That bitch, Grace.

Trey flicked on the light switch that controlled two lamps next to large easy chairs in front of the fireplace. He cast quickly about the main room but found nothing out of place.

"Hello?" Trey called out.

Getting no answer, he moved directly to Brent's rooms off the far corner. Brent's smell would be there. His smell and the soft wool of his suits.

The clothes were undisturbed, neatly hanging on double racks one above the other in the closet of the dressing area. He stepped in close to inspect each article, intentionally letting the fabrics brush across his face and hands.

He breathed slowly, sucking the fragrances deeply into his body.

In the bathroom, Trey looked through every drawer and cabinet but only took the extra bottles of Brent's brand of aftershave. He was almost smiling when he flicked on the wall switch that controlled the desk lamp and saw the office.

The desk had been cleared off. Brent's computer was gone. The stacks of correspondence had been removed. Empty drawer after empty drawer confirmed that every bit of paper had been taken away.

"Goddamn whore," he bellowed, the sound bouncing from every wall.

Trey sank into the tall leather swivel chair. In the fading evening light, the illumination from the desk lamp transformed the window into a mirror. He turned swiftly away from the sight of his reflection.

He was alone. After all these years devoted to one person, he was alone.

All because of that stupid-ass Morgan and his expensive little sluts. Jesus Christ.

And now Grace was taking the rest of Brent away from him.

"What about me," Trey screamed, angry and disoriented. "Goddamnit, Brent, what about me?"

Hunting, building, clearing. Years of work constructing Brent's life, and now it's being taken away.

Trey leaned forward and turned out the light. As his eyes adjusted, he could see the deep red tones just above the western horizon and he settled back into the chair, pulling his legs up and resting the heels of his black boots on the desk.

That bitch gets all this. And all the insurance money. And the hunting camp. And the business.

And what do I get? $250,000 to wait until he calls for me.

How long he sat there, Trey didn't know, but when he finally rose from the chair, night was all around him. He locked up and climbed back in his car, and drove slowly toward his house, looking at the star-studded sky.

Where was Brent right now?

What the hell else would he lose?

Morgan and his little sluts.

And Grace. Goddamn her.

Goddamn them to hell.

■ ■ ■ ■

No legislative session was ever easy—particularly not an extended 120-day session—everyone's nerves frayed early and stayed frayed. The Governor was no exception. Brent's death had severely aggravated Carver's short temper. He was even more despondent than Vic had anticipated, and when things didn't go exactly as he wanted, he was likely to explode in rage, unable to keep any emotion in check.

But the pay raise business had mushroomed, throwing everything out of kilter. Every legislator had been inundated with calls about troopers and police officers on welfare, and the push for a substantial pay increase for them was fueling the call for a pay raise for the rest of the state employees. Every major plank of Carver's budget—education reform, criminal justice reform, expanded health and home nursing care reforms, and the big capital improvement bill—they were all on the chopping block and being chopped.

"This wouldn't be happening if she weren't Commissioner," said Carver, angrily reaching for a pen to sign correspondence.

"That's not true and you know it. This has been boiling under the surface for years."

"And it would have stayed that way, most likely."

Vic was shaking his head. "I tell you this has nothing to do with her. And she's right about one thing—we can use some of the revenue created for the crime bill to fund the pay raise."

"Sorry, I won't budge. If my programs are fully funded, we'll bargain about other things."

"That's an impossible position to take," Vic countered. "We never get everything we ask for, never."

"Well this time we'd better, particularly the capital improvements bill. Harry Curlett and those guys have their pens and checkbooks poised, waiting to see which construction projects survive. I'm working my butt off with the Senate to reinstate what the House has already cut. And it's not a pleasant experience  making deals with senators like Gabriel Collel, I assure you."

"But there's more than just raising campaign money at stake. You need to come out as a strong supporter of law enforcement before the *Wall Street Journal* arrives to do their profile."

"They called?" asked Carver, his face brightening.

Vic nodded. "Earlier this morning."

"When are they coming?"

"Within the month, maybe as early as next week."

"My position on crime is strong and the criminal reform bill says it all. You get this message back to Ms. Commissioner: When my complete agenda is passed and funded, I'll consider a pay raise. But not until then."

Vic winced. That was an impossibly difficult hoop to jump through. But he decided to let it drop for the moment.

"Now, on another subject," Carver continued. "Who are we going to get to handle the fund-raising?"

"Well, there isn't a crowd lining up," said Vic, with a sigh. "No one can afford to devote as much time as Brent did."

"Can you handle it for a while?" Carver was adrift without Brent Wexler to confer with and even as much as he trusted his chief of staff, Vic was no substitute for his old buddy, nor did he show any interest in trying to fill the bill.

"I'll have to do it until we see if someone else emerges."

"Maybe we can fire up a few people at the luncheon on the 28th."

"Perhaps, but we may have to hire someone, though I hate bringing in a stranger for that job. By the way, what should we do about getting Brent's campaign papers?"

"I'm sure Grace will gladly hand anything over that even remotely smells like campaign. She never liked all this...." he waved his hand about his office. "She just did it because Brent controlled the purse strings."

"How estranged were they?"

"Totally. Remember what they used to say about Richard Nixon and Pat? As soon as the doors closed and they were out of public view, the smiles faded, the hands pulled apart, and they separated to their own rooms? That's Brent and Grace in a nutshell—except they went to separate houses. Take my word for it, she'll want to get rid of whatever he kept."

"I just hope there aren't any surprises."

"What do you mean?"

"I've never really known how Brent kept up with everything, and my biggest worry is that he collected more money than we disclosed. An awful lot showed up on the streets at the last minute."

Carver quickly resumed signing papers, avoiding Vic's glance. "Brent knew the campaign laws inside and out. I trust he followed them to the letter. In fact, he gave me a lecture about it at my birthday party...."

The Governor stopped writing, a wistful look crossing his face. "Remember that night? Brent and I came down here to take a break. He talked about the federal election laws and the changes we'd have to make. It was as if he was teaching me how to do his job because he wouldn't be around to do it. And then he dies. So strange."

"What'd he say?" Vic asked.

"He talked about how much more careful we had to be in a federal race."

"But he was confident," Carver went on. "Even talked about getting a townhouse in Georgetown and being up there with me."

■ ■ ■ ■

Grace parked outside the stately two story brick building with its B and W carved in stones set between the first and second floors. As she mounted the steps, she screwed up her courage. All her bravado at the lawyer's office about running Brent's business herself was just that, bravado. She didn't know beans about building roads, bridges, or foundations, and she wasn't certain she wanted to.

The young receptionist hopped up the moment Grace opened the door.

"Good morning, Rita. I appreciate your help with all the calls that have come in."

"We miss Mr. Wexler so much, ma'am," the receptionist said. "I'm just glad I could help some way."

Grace smiled. "So many will miss Brent. It's amazing the number of people he knew."

The phone rang and Rita quickly shunted the call to an engineer.

"I'm going back to Brent's office. Could you let everyone know that I'd like to talk to the entire staff as a group later on."

"Certainly, Mrs. Wexler. When would be a good time?" The phone rang again and Rita excused herself, handled the call, then looked back up.

"How about lunch? Order in sandwiches for everyone. We can lock the door, take the phone off the hook and talk. Right here, if you think it's okay." Grace's hand swung around the two story foyer which, with some people sitting on the open stairway to the second floor, was large enough to accommodate all of them. They managed to cram onto the stairs for an annual photograph at the Christmas party each year.

"This'll be fine. The conference room is really too small for all of us."

"I leave it to you," Grace said. "Let everyone know and call me to tell me the schedule."

Another call came in. Rita raised her hand in apology. "What can I order for you?" Rita asked when she put the phone down again.

Grace didn't really want even a sandwich, having grossly overeaten funeral food for the past several days, but she needed to set the pace. "How about tuna on whole wheat, lettuce, tomato, no mayo. And a bottle of water."

Rita nodded. "I'll tell everyone noon, right here."

"Thanks." Grace moved toward the hall where Brent's office was. "Let Leb Bailey know I'm here and see if he can come down in a few minutes."

"Certainly, Mrs. Wexler."

Brent's office was large but not extravagant. For all his interest in money and power, he was rarely ostentatious about it, except for his penchant for displaying his connections. The wall behind the large dark cherry table and matching credenza, was decorated with photographs: Brent and the governor; Brent and various politicians; Brent and his hunt club friends; Brent and the Roatan snorkeling group around a table. There were few family photos, and those were mostly of Jody, with the exception of Grace's formal portrait taken the year she was president of the Opera Guild.

Sinking into Brent's huge leather chair, Grace was instantly filled with the ridiculous feeling of being a little tiny girl at Daddy's big desk. One by one, she opened the drawers and took stock of how Brent had arranged his life. In the single wide desk drawer were personal bills to be paid: a staggering bill from a fashionable men's clothier; a VISA bill with three pages of charges, some as small as $3.21, a Chevron credit card bill; and the cleaners. All Wexler contracts were in one file drawer in the credenza, fund-raising materials were in another, and personal papers were in a third, including bank statements and paid bills. She flicked on the computer and while it powered up, flipped through the bulging Rolodex, finding scores of names she'd never heard Brent mention.

When the intercom buzzed, she jumped with surprise, then pushed down the red light, hoping that was right. "Yes?" she said, tentatively.

Rita's cheery voice answered. "Mrs. Wexler, Franklin Gilliam is on line two."

"Tell him I'm busy," Grace answered automatically, then changed her mind. "No, I'll take it. By the way, is lunch arranged?"

"Yes, ma'am," Rita answered, "and almost everyone will be attending. Two of the project managers are at job sites and can't get back, but all the rest of us will be here."

"Terrific. Ah, Rita, buzz me when it's noon, will you?"
"Certainly."

She waited a few more seconds, then punched the flashing line. "Hello, Grace Wexler speaking."

"Grace, Franklin Gilliam," his voice flowing ever so smoothly through the phone to her. "Glad to find you there. How's it going?"

"Fine, Franklin. What can I do for you?"

"I just spoke with the insurance company. They've got the life insurance claim and expect to process it within sixty days, maybe less. I thought you ought to know in case that would affect any financial decisions you might be making."

"I appreciate that information, Franklin." She waited for him to continue.

After an awkward moment, Gilliam added, "Well, I guess that's all for now."

"Great. I'll be talking to you soon, I'm certain."

Grace hung up and looked at the computer screen. What she saw was totally foreign from the set-up on her home computer where she kept all her correspondence and financial data for the Cancer Clinic fund-raising. Rather than mess anything up, she shut off the monitor, deciding someone else could show her around. There was a polite knock on the door and Caleb Bailey, the chief financial officer of the company appeared.

"Grace, nice to see you today."

Grace stood and came around the end of the desk, her hand extended. "Hello, Leb."

Leb Bailey had worked for Brent from the beginning. He was the one behind the scenes, the detail man, moving haltingly from pocket protectors to Mont Blanc pens without any apparent mid-life crisis. He'd lived entirely in Brent's shadow, physically thinner and shorter, and always dressed in unremarkable but neat suits, absolutely avoiding the public salesmanship that marked Brent's success. He sat in the upholstered chair that Grace offered and placed his note-pad and a small stack of papers on the edge of the desk.

"Thank you for coming to the visitation. I know you must have been devastated by Brent's death. I'm so very sorry for all of you."

Leb seemed near tears, speechless, and Grace hoped a short silence would help him gather his wits. It did. "How can I help you?" asked Leb.

"I've got to decide what the best thing is for this company and for all of you who've worked so hard. I suspect you know better than anyone exactly what makes this place tick and I want your advice." Grace had moved back to her chair behind the desk. Realizing Leb wasn't bubbling with suggestions, she took a different approach. "Everyone has presumed I should sell immediately. What do you think?"

Leb hesitated before responding. "I'll be as honest as I know how. I've got some other options, but I love this job and this company. I've been paid well but I've earned every dollar. If you'd asked me ten years ago, I'd have said sell to the highest bidder or merge with another company, because we can't make it without Brent. But today, I'm not so certain, regardless of what appearances might indicate. It won't be easy to go on, but you don't have to fold your cards either if you want to be in the road-building business. It'll be your choice."

"What role did Brent play in daily operations?"

"He handled the big picture. By the time we got into bridge building, the engineering required had surpassed his technical abilities. No, I take that back, not his abilities, his interest. He relied entirely on the design and engineering staff for things that he used to do himself. For the last five or six years, Brent has been totally involved in politics and fund-raising, staying visible, making it rain."

"That's how the company got contracts? Brent's schmoozing?"

"Yes and no. The private stuff, yes. He's stayed right in the middle of development companies that are building office complexes and upscale subdivisions. But the bread and butter, the road building projects, are public bids. Brent's been all over the South, meeting and greeting and touting our successes and the Wexler, Inc. reputation has grown. But that's just it, it has grown and blossomed. Maybe we can survive by continuing to do good work."

"What about the rest of the staff? What do they think?"

"We've got a great group and no one wants to leave, but they aren't sure what will happen if they stay. They've got kids and houses. You can understand."

"Well, I'm not going to make any hard and fast decisions immediately. I need to learn my way around, I need to understand what it is I'm selling and why, if that's what I ultimately do. How long can we operate if no new business walks in the door?"

Leb handed Grace a balance sheet, running the fingers of his other hand across a small calculator as he did. "With cash reserves and receivables—assuming they come in as scheduled..." he flipped to another list to check something and back again, "and there's no reason to think they shouldn't with these clients—we can go six months, no changes in operations. But after that we'd be in trouble. We've got several bids out now and we have to either withdraw or commit to completion."

"Translate this balance sheet for me, Leb. If you were going to sell Wexler today, what would it be worth?"

"You'd be selling the name, the building, the equipment—say one and a half to two million."

"And how much was Brent making each year?"

She saw his look of total amazement and realized how ignorant her comment made her seem. "I signed on whichever line on the tax return the accountant pointed out, I got my household check, my charitable contribution money, but I wasn't told much more."

"Brent was taking $350,000 plus expenses. That doesn't include any equity shares in real estate developments."

"I certainly can't make nearly as much selling the business and collecting the interest," Grace said, rather cavalierly.

"Not with the taxes you'll pay when you sell."

Grace looked at the pained, almost hurt expression that filled every corner of Leb's face. "And I'm forgetting about all the rest of you," she said.

Leb shrugged his shoulders as if reconciling himself to the inevitable. "You don't owe us anything, Brent gave us all more than many of us could have hoped for. It will just be hard to make a big change. Every last one of us will land on our feet, I'm sure, because we're the best in the business, and the competition knows it. It's just hard to face change."

She looked down at the printouts he'd handed her. "Well, let's get started. Just how do you run this place?"

"How much do you want to know?"

"As much as I need to know. But for starters, I've got a

drawer full of bills. Are these company expenses or personal?" She pulled out the VISA bill and handed it to him.

Leb looked at the statement. "This one is personal but sometimes, a charge gets on the wrong bill and I reimburse it." Leb handed her a list of payables and pointed to the Wexler entry. "There's $128.52 for reimbursed expenses. Brent gave me receipts to back that stuff up."

"So I ought to go through the bills I get, don't you think?"

"It may not be worth the trouble," Leb said. "He was pretty good about keeping things separate."

The intercom buzzed and Grace picked it up. "Yes?"

"It's 11:45, Mrs. Wexler," Rita said.

"Thank you, Rita—I wasn't keeping track of the time. I'll be right there."

Grace put down the phone. "It's almost time for the lunch meeting. I'm going to tell them that I'll make my decision within two months and that everyone is guaranteed salaries for the next six months no matter what. Safe to say that?"

"Yes'm."

"Thanks, Leb. You've been very helpful—as I was sure you would be."

■ ■ ■ ■

Everett had spent his first morning at the Department of Public Safety in the comptroller's office, then after lunch, he took the stairs up to the fifth floor two at a time for exercise.

"How'd the morning go?" Laura asked, sitting back from her desk full of paperwork, pen still in hand.

"Great, but I'm ready for investigations."

"Is this gonna work? Half here, half there?"

"I'll make it work."

"Okay," Laura said. "Robert's rearranged the file room and made you a carrel down on three."

"I really appreciate this."

"We're the ones who are getting the deal, Everett. Robert's got a doper he's trying to get a forfeiture on—that'll be your first assignment."

"I'm gonna like this place, I know it."

"Now, tell me where you stand on Reed Morgan."

"I've got all the Transportation Department data in my computer but haven't had any time to analyze it. And I have a complete set of the annual reports, all the way back to the beginning of Morgan's term."

"Where are you going to start?"

"I don't know yet. If Morgan was on the take, the money could have come from anywhere."

"Can you recall exactly what the IRS guy asked you?"

"You know those guys. They never ask a direct question, and they never volunteer anything," Everett said. "He wanted to know how the department worked—what kind of authority an individual commissioner had in making contracts, about heavy equipment purchases, and what kind of audit work had been done over the past ten years. After I answered his questions with what little I knew, I sent him to the state agency division since we'd never opened a case on the department."

"Not that we hadn't thought about it."

"I didn't say anything about our suspicions. He wasn't giving me much, so I didn't load him up."

"This is way out of the Patrol's territory, you know."

"I know."

"I found my notes from that bid-rigging seminar," Laura said, "so give me the annual reports and I'll look at the big picture. You can play around with the vendors who sold to Morgan's district."

Everett nodded.

"But we've got to be pretty damn discreet, okay?"

"Promise. Extracurricular only."

■ ■ ■ ■

Will's eyes never left the dessert chef's hands as a brownie was transformed into edible art at the food bar at Bravo! restaurant. Laura and Will were regular customers, usually eating at the bar where Will could see everything being prepared, especially the brownies. With masterful strokes, the man zigzagged the plate with lines of strawberry icing, then vanilla, and finally, chocolate, and presented the finished product to Will with a special flourish.

"So what shall we do at your birthday party?" Laura asked after he'd demolished half the creation. If only he'd eaten his pasta with such gusto.

"Can we have a treasure hunt?" mumbled Will.

"Don't talk with your mouth full. What kind of treasure hunt do you mean?"

He carefully swallowed his bite of dessert and took another huge gulp of milk. "You know, you write clues and we go from place to place to find them."

Laura thought for a moment. Ten little boys. That would mean at least two, maybe three separate hunts. And not all of them could read. "Okay. I'll figure out something. Is that all?"

"Then we can play."

"Anything in particular?"

"You wouldn't let us."

"What?"

"Never mind."

"Will, don't do that," said Laura, exasperated. "Either say the whole thought or don't say anything at all."

"A water balloon fight."

She smiled. "Of course you can have a water balloon fight. But I'll have to get someone to help fill and tie them."

Will scraped the last of the icing off the plate and licked his fork. "Frank could help. He already said he'd come."

"And I'll think of one more helper. You ready to go?"

Will nodded, yawning.

Will dozed off in the car on the way home and Laura led him, half asleep, through the paces of changing his clothes and brushing his teeth. Ten seconds after he landed in bed, he was breathing deeply in sync with Ranger, who had curled up at his feet. Will ran full-out all day long, every day, and fought a brave battle against sleep every night, and then crumpled with exhaustion and was out for nine solid hours. Just like his father. If only Semmes had lived to see these days.

In the kitchen, Laura hit the speed dial button for her mother, a hundred miles away in Natchez. It rang at least eight times before kicking over to voice mail.

"Hi, Mom. Just wanted to check in. I'll be up for at least an hour if you get this. We're fine, and Will's very excited about the trip to Disney World. He's got a calendar in his room and one in the kitchen, and he's slashing out each day that passes. Talk to you soon—love you."

She filled the coffee maker for the morning, switched the load of clothes to the dryer, and started the dishwasher. With the satisfying hum of the machines and a glass of white wine, she turned out the kitchen lights and went down the hall.

The office was still decorated with Semmes' architectural drawings—she wasn't ready to take them down—but she had put away most of his books to make space for her own work. A six-foot-long table top resting on three steel file cabinets served as the desk—plenty of room for the computer, fax machine, telephones, and a work area. Will had commandeered the nearby drafting table for his markers and colored pencils.

Laura pulled the stack of annual reports from the Department of Transportation toward her and turned on the computer. Everett had managed to locate a copy for every year since Reed Morgan had been elected. Each was a dense listing of expenditures, organized by district—Eastern, Western, and Central. For all practical purposes, the districts were individual fiefdoms, and what the district commissioner wanted was what happened, either expressly or by intimidation.

Her private telephone line jangled unexpectedly, breaking the silence. She swiveled around, reaching for the phone.

"Did I wake you?" Charlotte Hemeter asked.

"Heavens, no, Mom," said Laura, yawning. "I'm sitting here trying to make sense of some annual reports."

"I was just thinking about that terrible wreck."

"Which wreck?" asked Laura, her mind flashing on their

wreck and Semmes lifeless body.

"The Governor's friend, a couple of weeks ago. Did you have to do anything about it?"

"Unfortunately, yes. And the Governor is devastated. The man was his best friend—absolutely his closest confidant."

"I'm so sorry. But who I keep thinking about is the poor man's wife—she must be in shock."

"Probably is."

"Hope it wasn't too hard on you, dear."

"Mom, there are so many horrible wrecks all the time, I've gotten past seeing Semmes in each one," she lied.

"So you say."

Laura changed the subject as fast as she could. "Will is almost unable to contain himself about this trip. He asks about it constantly. Wants to know every detail. He's making a list— well, I'm keeping the list of all the things he thinks he needs— Legos, army men, cars, and trucks."

"What about clothes?"

"He doesn't think he'll need any of those, but I told him I'd throw some in, just in case. Especially clean underwear."

"I probably shouldn't have told him so far in advance."

"Oh, no. It gives me tremendous leverage when he acts up."

When she finally hung up, she picked up the annual report and started in where she'd left off. Midway through she found a list of highway construction projects, their bids, and the final award. She skipped to the Western District contracts and started down the list. There were projects of every size—from big, multi-million dollar projects to smaller ones costing as little as fifty thousand.

Laura leaned back in the chair and closed her eyes. Wine had not been a good choice.

It would probably take her the rest of the month, working in the evenings when she could, to sort through the reports and get all the data she needed into a spreadsheet program. At least there wasn't any particular hurry.

She clicked the Internet icon and listened to the little electronic squeals while the connection was made. Her e-mail showed three unsolicited offers, the news digest, and a message from Naomi.

LAURA:

HOW'S THINGS IN THE SUNNY SOUTH? IT'S BEEN COLD AND RAINY HERE FOR WEEKS IT SEEMS.

I'M STALLING JOHN ABOUT A DATE FOR THIS WEDDING. HE'S AIMING FOR LABOR DAY, OUT ON THE EASTERN SHORE OF THE CHESAPEAKE. HE WANTS A BIG BLOWOUT WEEKEND PARTY WITH A WEDDING IN THE MIDDLE SOME- WHERE. I'M THINKING CHRISTMAS TIME, JUSTICE OF THE PEACE, AND A PLANE TO THE BAHAMAS. WHAT DO YOU THINK?

BONSOIR, NAOMI


NAOMI:

WHY ARE YOU STALLING? YOU'VE GOT TO RESOLVE THAT BEFORE YOU EVEN THINK ABOUT HONEYMOONS. DOUBT JUST EATS AWAY AT YOU. TRULY INSID- IOUS.

THINGS HERE ARE IN AN UPROAR. THIS PAY RAISE MAY BE THE DEATH OF ME WITH THE GOVERNOR. HE'S SO PISSED HE CAN HARDLY SEE STRAIGHT. MEANWHILE, I'VE GOT TO ADMIT THAT I'M FALLING IN LOVE WITH VIC. AT LEAST I THINK THAT'S WHAT'S HAPPENING, IF I REMEMBER CORRECTLY. THERE I WAS, AT THE CAPITOL, LOBBYING FOR MY BILLS, TALKING BUSINESS WITH REPRESENTATIVES, AND HE SHOOTS ACROSS MY FIELD OF VISION, HEADED TO THE SPEAKER'S OFFICE. I LOSE MY TRAIN OF THOUGHT AND MY STOMACH TURNS TO BUTTERFLIES. WHAT IS THIS? I FEEL LIKE I'M EIGHTEEN.

LAURA

# EIGHT

Trey was expecting Franklin Gilliam, Brent's lawyer, to be the first one at breakfast at the Red Crown Hunt Club, he usually was. "It's going to be different without Brent," Gilliam said to Trey.

"Certainly is," Trey said, pouring off the fat from the broiler pan covered with bacon strips and sticking the pan back in for extra crispness.

Sticking closely to the routines he and Brent had created, Trey had headed straight to the camp Friday afternoon with ample breakfast provisions for the twelve who had reserved beds that weekend. But the atmosphere was entirely different, distinctly uncomfortable. Gilliam told Trey that he had informed the members of Grace's intentions and Trey's option to buy the house and as much of the land as he desired. He'd left Trey with little doubt that the members had found it a dispiriting revelation, given the critical role the camp played in their lives. But Trey discovered that the news cast him in a different light among the membership. Until now, Trey had been a man who, to all but Brent, was no more than a very capable manservant and a useful conduit for getting tickets fixed.

The members had arrived Friday night more reserved than usual but as the liquor loosened their tongues, they began trading years of "Brent stories" and related escapades. Not knowing how future ownership would play out, they'd included Trey in their reminiscing. He'd listened, not caring to tell any of his own, but absorbing as many of the details about the other parts of Brent's life as he could.

Saturday morning, Gilliam wasted no time. "I think Grace wants to sell this place. What are your plans?"

"Mrs. Wexler and I talked about it briefly at the visitation. I'm not entirely certain about the process." Trey pulled a large iron skillet to the front burner, spooned in some butter to melt, and began breaking eggs into a bowl.

"The way it works is this. If the land is ever put up for sale, Brent gave you the right to buy it at that time. I know the club wants to stay together if we can, so depending on what you do, we may make an offer on the place."

"Hmm." Trey pulled the bacon out of the broiler, setting the pan on the stainless steel counter.

Trey preferred to keep his distance from Gilliam who was a charter member of the club. For fifteen years, part of his annual dues had paid Trey's salary, but Trey knew the lawyer had no clue about him except that he worked for the State Patrol, was an excellent hunter, could fix anything, and was always willing to clean and dress the game and fish. Gilliam couldn't possible understand what motivated Trey, and none of the other members had ever bothered to draw him into conversations. But Trey knew this about Gilliam: the man was persistent. "So, what do you think you'll do?" Gilliam asked.

"I don't know yet. Haven't had time to think about it really."

"I had the distinct impression that selling this place was first on Grace's list."

Trey, moving efficiently through his breakfast preparations, concentrated on his cooking and didn't respond immediately. Then he asked, "Have any idea what she's gonna do with the farm?"

"She's planning on keeping it, I think—maybe developing it."

Trey pursed his lips, while he pushed the eggs around the pan. "Too bad. Mrs. Wexler and me—we don't gee-haw, if you know what I mean."

"Grace Wexler doesn't have many friends, truth be known," said Gilliam. "There's a lot of people who are after her name and her money, but I can't think of many people who would call her a friend. She never got over Jody's death, near as I can tell. She pulled back inside herself from that day on."

Trey flipped the bacon strips onto paper towels to drain and laid out another pan full. The damned bitch, he thought. "Maybe I can sell her the house up there and use the money to buy this place." He shoved the pan in the oven and left the door open slightly to monitor the popping bacon grease. "I don't need anything this big, though," he said, waving his spatula around the spacious room.

"We're still going to need a base camp, and we'd sure like you to keep running things. Maybe we could work something out."

"Maybe. 'Preciate the offer." Trey began shoveling eggs onto a platter. He did need this place, this routine, even more than the club members needed the house. But he wasn't about to let Gilliam or anyone else know that. "Maybe we can work something out."

He thought Gilliam seemed to relax with the conciliatory tone in his voice. A moment later, two more members straggled in, and Trey began dishing out breakfast.

■ ■ ■ ■

"Commissioner," the switchboard operator said when Laura punched the speaker phone button, "Senator Sandifer is here and he doesn't have an appointment. He wants to know if it's possible to see you for a moment."

Laura looked up at the comptroller who had just gotten settled. All his papers were spread across the end of her desk so they could work out a series of alternatives on the pay raise for Holden Bowser, chairman of House Appropriations. "Yes, send him up. I can break away from what I'm doing."

The comptroller's eyes widened. He needed final decisions as quickly as possible.

"Could be important," Laura said apologetically.

"I'll run back to my office. Call me when you're done."

Sandifer was a stalwart friend of Gabriel Collel's and just like Collel, he'd opposed every move she'd made. Laura punched in Blake's extension, hoping he might know why Sandifer was stopping by, but Blake didn't answer. Neither did Jimmie. She trying to reach Robert when her intercom rang again.

"Commissioner, Senator Sandifer is headed down the hall to your door. I couldn't get him to wait out here."

"Is he angry?"

"Didn't seem to be."

There was a knock on the door.

"He's here," Laura said quickly. "Bye."

She moved across the large office to the door, tucking in her linen shirt as she went, calling out, "Come in."

The door opened. Senator Sandifer was a Santa without the smile. His belly entered first, followed by a round face dominated by a bushy moustache, and the entire structure was balanced precariously on tiny feet—an oversized incarnation of the Monopoly man. But there was no humor in him. Laura presumed the moustache hid a snarling upper lip.

"Good morning, Commissioner. I hope I'm not disturbing you."

"No, Senator."

"I've always heard about this office but never visited," the senator said, glancing about the huge room, taking in the photographs of Will, and the discreet display of her certificate of appointment and three plaques, commemorating her community service. His eyes came to rest on the oil painting behind the couch, a brightly colored landscape. "Very nice."

"A friend's painting from his Van Gogh period. He visited one day and thought the brown walls needed a little lift."

"It certainly lifts, as you say."

"Can I get you some coffee?" Laura asked, motioning toward two leather chairs at the edge of the sitting area.

"No, thank you. I just have one matter of business."

Laura tensed. "Is there something I can do for you?"

"No. I want to commend one of your officers. A man named Robert Stone. He helped my wife and daughter when they were stranded with a flat tire on a rainy night."

"Colonel Stone never mentioned it to me. Let me call and see if he can join us."

"I'd appreciate that. I realize this is short notice, but as I was driving in today, I just decided to take the chance."

After Laura spoke with Deborah, she returned her attention to Sandifer. He was looking at the photograph of Will on the side table near him.

"He looks like a charming little boy," Sandifer said quickly.

"He is. Not sure what I did with my time before he arrived."

"And you won't know what to do when he's gone. Mark my words."

"So I hear. It's already slipping by a little too fast for my taste," Laura said. "Senator..." she began, ready to mention the pay raise.

Sandifer cut her off. "My mother used to say she couldn't live with me and she couldn't live without me. Apparently I was a little headstrong."

Laura smiled. "I know exactly what she was talking about." She took a quick breath and began again, "Have you..."

"Mothers are far wiser than we ever give them credit for. And I didn't realize it until long after she was gone. One of my great regrets."

There was a quiet knock on the door before it opened. As Robert strode in, Sandifer stood to greet him, his hand outstretched. "I cannot thank you enough, Colonel Stone, for helping, well, rescuing would probably be a better word, my wife and daughter. Nora and Leigh have been insisting that I find you to thank you personally. I'm so very glad you were here today."

"It wasn't much," Robert said, taking a seat on the end of the couch closest to the Senator. "A dark, rainy evening can be unnerving. I'm glad I happened along and could be of assistance."

"Your parents live north of us?"

"Yes, sir. They're in Como."

"I know it well," Sandifer said. "They're in good health I hope."

"Yes, sir. Still at home, still farming and canning."

"Senator..." Laura began yet again.

"Never neglect them, Colonel," Sandifer said. "We never have our parents long enough, as far as I'm concerned." He pulled a pocket watch out and opened it. "My grandfather's. Looks like I must be going. We have several matters on the agenda this afternoon."

Sandifer stood and bowed slightly to Laura as she and Robert rose from their seats. "I've enjoyed getting to know you, Ms. Owen. Keep up the fine work." He turned quickly to Robert, extending his hand again. "My heartfelt thanks, sir."

With a nod, he stepped to the door, gave them both a quick smile, and was out of the room.

"What a performance," Laura said.

Robert shook his head. "Couldn't be beholden, could he? At least not publicly."

"And not a substantive word was exchanged. Incredible."

■ ■ ■ ■

Trey had left the hunt club on Monday, going directly to a tactical team stake out and eighteen cold, damp hours in and out of a bayou watching some dopers in a ramshackle tenant house. He returned to Saragossa to find Grace's letter under his door. She was very generous, offering to trade the title to the farmhouse and his ten acres for the hunting clubhouse and one hundred acres. He still had the option to buy as much additional land as he wished.

Grace wanted the place pretty badly or, more likely, she wanted him gone. He considered holding out for more but that might entail hiring a lawyer and he might not net any more than she was offering. The only glitch was that she wanted the whole matter finished and closed within twenty days.

After taking a much-needed shower, he wandered over to Brent's house to go through clothes and personal items one more time. Even before he reached the front door, he caught the unmistakable odor of fresh paint. A new alarm keypad dangled from a freshly cut opening next to the door. Drop cloths created a path to the bedroom where the furniture had been piled in the center, covered in more drop cloths, and the walls had a coat of white primer on them. The dressing room was empty, no suits on the racks or clothes in the drawers. All the knickknacks, photos, and keepsakes were gone too.

"Goddamn bitch," he muttered repeatedly, storming through the rest of the house. Every room and every closet had been cleared of Brent's personal effects, the last taste of him was gone. Half the books in the library were gone and all the photographs, except those of Jody, were missing.

Nothing of value was left, except the view from the west porch over the fields and the lower pond. It was a sight he'd seen time and again, drinking beer, and listening to Brent. He could never grow tired of it.

He left the house and walked away, turning back at the far side of the circle, seeing a fortress he couldn't invade.

"Goddamn bitch!" he yelled. "You can have your goddamn house and your goddamn land!"

■ ■ ■ ■

Paperwork was what Master Sergeant Levi Davis hated most about his job but the promotion had brought more money and he couldn't complain. It meant the difference every day between the cheapest and something better, whether it be a dishwasher or a vacation. The huge stack of weekly reports, now nearly done, was his own fault—he'd let himself get behind, so he couldn't expect much sympathy and wasn't the type to ask for it anyway.

Coffee would help though. He could hear three or four voices in the kitchen and picked up his mug, heading that way, ready for some news. Three veteran troopers were leaning against the counters trying their best to fluster the one female assigned to the road in their troop, but she wasn't biting. Levi hadn't poured half a cup when the radio operator called through the open door.

"The Chief's on line three for you, Levi."

A trooper whistled. "The bossman. Better hustle, Sergeant."

Levi finished pouring his coffee, added creamer and sugar, and stirred it, deliberately taking his time.

"The shit has hit the fan somewhere," one of them added.

"You can handle it, we've got confidence in you."

"The price of fame and glory," Levi quipped as he left the room rather than take the call there.

No one else was in the master sergeants' office, so Levi closed the door.

"Hey, Chief," Levi said. "Whatcha know good?"

"Just keepin' my head down," Blake answered. "What's the word on a possible slowdown? Is Cook still stirring it up?"

"No, and he's sure not slowing down. I've got his weekly reports right here. Thirty-five tickets last week, thirty of them hazardous, five drunks. And he worked three wrecks. I can't complain."

"Hardly," Blake said. "Anyone else still talking about it?"

"Nope. Seems like the Commissioner's remarks and that photo in the food stamps line might have done the trick. What are you hearing?"

"Generally good. Several legislators have just fallen into our laps. It's amazing what happens once you start keeping track of these guys—paths seem to cross real regularly."

"Working those watering holes, are you?"

"Every little bit helps."

■ ■ ■ ■

"Happy Birthday to you," Laura sang as Will raced toward the kitchen with a big Lego box under his arm and Ranger right behind him.

"You're the best Momma in the world!" Will said, hugging her tightly. Ranger squeezed into the middle and started pawing at Laura's sweatpants, barking for attention.

"And you're the best seven-year-old I know," Laura said, giving him a kiss and hug. "That's not all your presents." She looked toward the counter.

Will whipped around to see two more on the middle stool where he always sat.

"Can I open them?"

"Of course you can, but not until you let your dog out and give her some water. I've got to finish these pancakes."

Laura had lifted the last batch off the iron skillet when the back door slammed and Will raced by.

"Potato guns!" he shrieked a moment later, after tearing open the box, and instantly brandishing the plastic pistol. "How many are in here?"

"Plenty."

Will ripped open another present. "A Nerf football!"

When Laura turned toward him again, she had a plate covered with pancakes and candles flickering on top. "Happy Birthday to you," she sang again. "This'll have to do until Saturday when we have your real cake."

He dropped the football on the floor and leaned forward to blow out the flames.

"Make a wish, first."

He thought for a moment and blew them all out in one puff.

"I really wish Daddy was here," Will said, as he climbed up on his stool.

"So do I, Sweetheart." Laura pulled the candles out of the pancakes and scraped off the flecks of dried wax. "Everyday I miss him. But he'll always be right here with us, helping us build our lives. You know that, don't you?"

"I guess so, Momma." Will dropped his head so he wasn't looking at her directly. "But sometimes, it's hard to imagine. Am I bad if I can't remember him?"

Laura cradled him in her arms. "No, Sweetheart, don't ever think you're bad. It's hard to remember when you haven't seen someone in a long time."

Will hugged her tightly.

"Just never forget that he loved you more than anything in the world."

"More than he loved you?"

"Yup, more than me. You were the light of his life."

Laura held on a moment longer, savoring her son's sweet hug, until Ranger began barking outside. Then she reluctantly let the moment end.

"All right, my suddenly bigger boy, dig in to those pancakes and milk. We've got school and work waiting, and I haven't even gotten dressed."

■ ■ ■ ■

For the moment, Grace was splitting her days: mornings at home trudging through the endless correspondence, thanking people for their many kindnesses, and afternoons attending to her substantial obligations to charity organizations or at Wexler, Inc., where she felt distinctly like a fifth wheel, turning with the movement but not contributing to forward progress in the least.

After a working lunch with the hospital foundation board, she stopped by the office for the mail and to return phone calls. The mail had already been separated, but she looked at it before passing it along. Personal matters and bills she kept, business items went to Leb for his perusal, unsolicited bulk mail went in the trash, and letters of condolence went to the ever-replenished stack that she answered from home after Rita logged each one onto an alphabetical ready-reference list.

Two credit card bills, covering part of February through early March, were on top, chronicling Brent's last days. He'd shopped all over New Orleans, but mostly at Canal Place.

There was a huge charge at Brooks Brothers—$2,750—which was over and above another bill of nearly $2,000 from The Rogue, a Jackson clothier; $11,026 at Adler's Jewelry Store; plane tickets for the Roatan trip, hotel room and meals at the resort, scuba gear rentals, over $400 worth of something at a clothing store or gift shop during his vacation, gasoline, a car rental, and two nights in Tegucigalpa which she didn't recall him mentioning when they had talked; and on the last day, he'd spent $25 at the airport gift shop, $50 at some place called the Catfish Corner, and had gotten a $400 cash advance. Then nothing.

As long as the details of Brent's life were entangling her in probate matters and tax issues, she might as well find out what he'd been spending his money on. Grace called Brooks Brothers and Adler's and asked the accounting departments to send copies of the actual sales slips. She also closed Brent's account with The Rogue, and requested an itemization of the last bill.

■ ■ ■ ■

"Laura, Vic here. How's it going?"

"Okay. How 'bout with you?"

"The session's a nightmare, Carver's still depressed about Wexler, at least four people are talking about running for the party nomination, and your pay raise is killing me. Other than that, fine."

"You know we have the votes in the House."

"I know. Carver's in a permanently foul humor since he can't derail your train."

"But the Senate vote isn't a certainty," she added. "Far from it. Collel is working full time to kill the measure."

"I know that, too. One of the rare occasions when he and the Governor are on the same side of an argument."

"Strange bedfellows."

"But that's not why I called. Isn't today Will's birthday?"

"It is," Laura said, surprised but pleased that he'd remembered. "Candles on his pancakes this morning."

"No party?"

"Saturday afternoon at the house. I'd love to have some adult company, if you're free."

Vic looked over his calendar. He had a 2:00 P.M. meeting with several of the lobbyists to work on the education bills. "What time?"

"Two to five."

He hesitated again. Surely he could rearrange it. "I'll be there."

"Wear shorts or jeans and pray for sunshine. If it rains, I have no idea what we'll do."

"What's he want for his birthday?"

"Squirt guns, laser guns, Super Soaker long-range water guns..."

"Do I detect a theme?"

"You do. It's a Y-chromosome thing."

"How about rocket launchers? Those pump action things that shoot foam missiles. My nephews have some."

"You'd be a hero, I can assure you."

"Consider it done. I'll bring an extra for you."

■ ■ ■ ■

It was almost lunch time when Trey got back to headquarters, needing to knock out some paper work to get the secretaries off his back. He walked into the criminal records room to make copies just as Everett was leaving his little carrel.

Everett smiled and nodded over the file cabinets as Trey approached the machine. They hadn't been introduced, but Trey knew Everett was the Commissioner's pet. Probably a plant, if he had to guess. While Everett packed up in his usual orderly fashion, Trey sent sheet after sheet through the copier without jamming it, trying inconspicuously to catch a glimpse of Everett's work before it disappeared into the file cabinet.

The door opened at the far end of the room and Nima Gales, the chief criminal analyst for the section, appeared. Her clear voice—the one that sent shivers down every investigator's spine when they asked her to do one too many things—rang out, "Move it, Everett, we're holding the elevators for you."

"Coming." Everett looked around and seeing only public documents out in his carrel, left everything as it was and hustled away. As soon as the door shut, Trey stepped up to Everett's desk, his stomach tightening when he saw the Transportation Department annual reports. When he was certain everyone had left, he pulled on the top drawer of the cabinet Everett was using. He'd forgotten to lock it.

Everett's papers were neatly organized in folders and only a glance was necessary to recognize that Everett was looking into expenditures for the Western District of the Transportation Department—Reed Morgan's district. As Trey flipped through the printouts, the knot in his stomach grew sickeningly tighter. The most recent printout, dated the day before, was a list of suppliers ranked according to the size of the payment. The audit had never stopped.

"Sonovabitch," he muttered, slamming his hand into the corner of the filing cabinet.

The door buzzed open and Nima returned, a streak of fuchsia and sea blue, as she raced to her desk. Although she was on the other side of the room and couldn't tell what drawer he had open, Trey nearly dropped the sheaf of papers he was holding. A set of keys jingled as she found what she was looking for, scooted back out the door, never acknowledging Trey's presence.

Collecting his wits, Trey examined the dates of the purchases in question, leafed through the rest of Everett's papers, then carefully put everything back the way it was. Distractedly, he finished copying the file he'd brought in, then made his way to his desk in the investigator's bull-pen, hardly noticing the game of dominoes in full play right next to him.

Reed Morgan must never talk, he thought. If he's dead, they'll stop auditing. It should have been handled this way from the start.

That sleazy bastard has cost me half my life, he's not about to get the other half, too.

Trey checked out a video camera from the property room, and disappeared from headquarters, heading downtown to the Transportation Department where Morgan had his official office. His car was in his reserved spot not more that ten yards from the back door. Trey cruised the parking lot, found a place where he could watch, and settled in.

Shortly after four o'clock, Reed Morgan appeared, hustling his big body to his Mercury, then roaring out of the lot, tail-gating every car ahead of him all the way to the airport. Trey stayed as close behind him as he could. Deftly swooping in between passengers unloading their cars, Morgan parked in the curb lane on the upper level and was hurrying in when the police officer patrolling the area shouted to him to move it.

"Look, I'm Reed Morgan."

The name rang no bells with the officer, but before he could say anything, Morgan added, "Western District Transportation Commissioner," with a tone sufficiently confident to impress the officer. "I'll only be a minute. I'm picking someone up and they're expecting me. Already late."

The patrolman nodded and turned away, crossing the traffic lanes to stand near the outside edge and watch.

Trey didn't move. He was far enough back so he wasn't blocking anything or drawing any attention, not even with a video camera trained on the entrance. Moments later, Morgan and a trim young woman in the dark blue straight skirt and jacket of an airline stewardess, emerged, his thick arm bearishly pulling her to him, ignoring her struggle to keep her rolling luggage upright as he embraced her. He waved at the cop as they sped off, Trey pulling out behind them.

Trey tailed them to a Vicksburg Casino and watched them disappear inside. It was too risky to follow Morgan in—he'd pick him up another time.

■ ■ ■ ■

To refill water balloons without breaking them, Vic had to dredge up long forgotten talents. Two had burst in his hands, drenching his shirt and shorts, before he'd remembered the exact parameters of the science. He worked as fast as possible, knowing that his team would be back any moment for another round of ammunition.

His five little boys included Will. They were sneaking south toward the enemy, keeping low to the ground, each with two balloons. A deck and pergola obstructed their view so they stayed as close to the house as possible, creeping behind the bushes, trampling the vinca. The only noise was Ranger, penned up and barking. Suddenly, the two groups were face to face, and with screams and war whoops, twenty balloons were lobbed from side to side with several direct hits.

"More, we need more," the boys screamed, racing back to their outposts for another round.

Vic dispensed the last of his balloons and joined Laura who'd been watching the event from an Adirondack chair on the lawn, guarding the presents and the cake from stray missiles. He shook out his wet shirt as he approached. "Did you consider the usual bowling alley party or a pony ride?"

"It was Will's choice," Laura said. Screams of delight erupted from the other side of the house. "I think they're having fun—and you seemed to be enjoying it yourself."

Vic smiled. "But I can't imagine that war games as a birthday party theme will do much for your reputation."

"Whatever social acceptability I ever had disappeared when you made me Commissioner."

Half the boys with Will in the lead came running across to Laura. "We need more balloons, Momma."

"Sorry, guys," Laura said. "You'll have to switch to potato guns. I put everything you need on the deck."

"Potato guns!" With everyone trailing behind him, Will ran for the deck.

"Make sure everyone knows how to use them," Laura called after him.

"What I was trying to say," Vic began again, "was that

maybe you need to be more..."

"Conventional?"

"I guess, but I don't like the sound of that word, now that I hear it." He looked around: The boys were laughing hysterically as they pelted each other with tiny pieces of potatoes, Ranger's tail was wagging furiously, straining to be let loose, the sun was shining, the grass was that luxurious spring green, and Laura looked totally relaxed. It was heaven, or as near as he'd been in a long time.

"Scratch everything I said." He settled into the chair beside her. "This is one party Will won't ever forget."

Laura smiled. "This is the good life."

"So I see," Vic said. "I'm beginning to figure out just how sweet it is."

■ ■ ■ ■

Lt. Carl Rankin, a criminal investigator with the State Patrol, and his wife, Linda, ambled away from the Heywood National Guard Armory where their twentieth high school reunion was in full swing.

"Want to go to the Truck Stop and get something to eat?" Carl asked. He was a large man who, when he bothered to eat, insisted that the food be worth eating. In his opinion, the Truck Stop had the best barbecue south of Memphis, or east of Kansas City.

"Didn't you get anything at the party?"

"That stuff was horrible. Who was in charge of the food?"

"It wasn't that bad," said Linda, laughing. "You just ruined your appetite wasting your time on that idiot Grady Kellogg."

"He's a state senator who votes on my salary, even if he is a jerk. We're contacting every one of them, waste of time or not.

"He was so drunk he won't remember a thing about it tomorrow, and he probably doesn't care anyway. I never did like him."

"Wonder where Helene was?"

"I saw her leave when Grady arrived. She finally came to

her senses and threw him out. He's been sleeping around when he's in Jackson."

They stopped talking to listen to the whine of car tires spinning uselessly on the other side of the building.

"Let me go see who's stuck," Carl said, heading that way.

As he rounded the corner, Carl could see smoke coming from the rear tires of a shiny red pickup. He quickened his pace, and when he reached the window, he had to rap loudly to get the driver's attention. Senator Grady Kellogg turned his blood-shot eyes and silly smile toward him. The spinning stopped.

Carl pulled open the door and before the senator could object, jerked the keys out of the ignition. "You're not getting anywhere, Grady. Shove over and I'll get you out."

"You don't need to do that," Grady mumbled, reaching toward the steering column.

"On second thought, I'll drive you home," Carl said. He turned to Linda. "Do you know where he's living?"

"Angler Apartments, I think," Linda said.

"Apartment Six," Grady mumbled.

Carl stepped toward Linda so Grady couldn't hear him. "That place is a dump," Carl said.

"It's cheap, and it needs to be," Linda whispered back. "Helene is taking him to the cleaners, which is better than he deserves."

"Follow me over there, will you, Darlin'?"

"You ought to keep the keys and leave him here."

"Just follow me, okay?" Carl asked, easing into the cab while pushing Grady over to the passenger side. "I'll get him in the apartment and that's it."

# NINE

"But what if I can't *go* to sleep?" Will whispered as Charlotte Hemeter disappeared to the newsstand. He sat on the edge of his chair at the airport, unable to lean back because of his backpack and unwilling to take his backpack off for fear of leaving it behind. It was filled with Legos, tapes and a tape player, and a small battalion of green and brown plastic soldiers, with a contingent of army trucks and tanks.

"Grandmom will read to you just like I do," Laura said as calmly as she could manage. It was his first big trip away from her, other than periodic weekends with his grandparents at their homes. As the day had grown nearer, he'd become more and more jittery about the prospect. A few days before, he'd even suggested canceling the entire thing, but the lure of Mickey and Goofy won out in the end.

"But she doesn't know how to tuck me in."

"What does she do when you're at her house?"

"Well," Will hesitated, "she doesn't do it right."

Laura leaned closer and drew him to her across the armrest. "If you can believe this, Grandmom has a lot more experience tucking in little boys than I do. I think she'll take very good care of you."

"But..."

"Do you want to stay home?" Laura asked, carefully mixing sufficient concern with a slightly stern look.

Will didn't answer immediately. Then as his grandmother appeared around the corner about twenty yards away, he reached over and gave Laura a hug. "I just wish you were taking me."

"And I wish I were taking you, too, but I can't go this time." She looked straight in his eyes and added, "Tell you what. You learn your way around and then we can go back and you can lead the way. Okay?"

Will nodded, then over her shoulder, noticed a plane coming to dock at the next bay. "Can I go watch?"

"I'll be right here. Just stay where I can see you."

"I'm going to watch the plane, Grandmom," Will said to Charlotte. "Don't get on without me." In the blink of an eye, he was at the window, his nose pressed to the glass. "I wouldn't dream of it," said Charlotte, as she settled in the chair next to Laura. "What are your plans while we're gone?"

"Work."

"No social engagements?"

"Nothing definite. Maybe dinner with Vic Regis."

"Is this something new?"

"Yes and no. We're friends."

"And maybe more than friends?"

"I can't imagine my luck is going to change. It's been a year since Semmes died, and I can count on two hands the number of invitations I've had from anyone."

"It'll come, dear. But I hate to tell you this, it's not easy. You're dangerous competition for all the other women grasping to hold onto their husbands. It happens to me, even at my age."

"You're kidding."

Charlotte shook her head. "I can name five women who won't let me have a conversation with their husband without standing over us. And I'm not famous like you."

"Infamous is a better description."

"No, famous, young, attractive, and available."

Laura grinned at her mother, brushing aside the praise. "I think my capital's sunk pretty low lately. I've heard through the grapevine that another mother from Will's school said, 'You don't mean you're a personal friend of hers,' referring to me like I had some sort of disease."

"Well, I certainly wouldn't waste a second on someone like that."

"I don't. And I shouldn't exaggerate, she's really the only one. Plus, I can't stand her snotty little kid anyway."

"Your job is pretty intimidating."

"That's what I think. People figure a woman taking this job must be a Nazi or something abnormal. And no man in his right mind would mess around with the head of the state patrol."

"Except Vic?"

"Well, he can't hold it against me. He recommended me for the job."

Laura watched Will, his face still plastered against the window to get the best view of unloading and loading. She had a whole, wonderful life, with or without a husband. "I'm sure not going to quit just to get a date," she added.

Charlotte looked like she was about to offer some more advice when Laura continued, "This is the best ride I've ever had. Better than anything at Disney World," she said as Will headed back toward them. "And you never know when you're on your last great ride," she added a bit wistfully.

"What last ride, Momma?"

"I was telling Grandmom not to miss the 20,000 Leagues ride," said Laura without missing a beat. "I read somewhere that they might close it."

"Delta Flight 1611, now ready for boarding," the gate agent said. "We'd like to pre-board any families with small children or passengers needing assistance."

"Do you think I qualify?" her mother asked.

Laura was shaking her head when Will said, "Come on, Grandmom," and took Charlotte's hand.

"Might as well give it a go," said Charlotte, as they all stood up.

"Bye, Mom," Laura said, giving her mother a hug.

"Enjoy yourself a little, if you can. Relax."

"I'll try." She knelt down in front of her son. "Now you be a big help to Grandmom and don't wander off. It scares the living daylights out of me when you do that, and Grandmom will be the same way."

Will nodded, straining to get into line.

"Promise?"

"I promise."

"I love you," Laura said as she hugged him.

"I love you, too, Momma."

■ ■ ■ ■

Leb Bailey heard that Wexler, Inc., wasn't getting the nod on the roadwork for a development outside Atlanta and immediately headed off to find Grace, papers in hand.

"This is a real disappointment. It was going to be an easy job—in and out—no problems. I talked to the people last week and they seemed fine. They assured me Brent's death wouldn't be a factor."

"Should you and I fly over there and meet with them?"

"No, it's probably too late. You could try calling. The only other thing I've thought of is to contact the public relations firm Brent used and ask them to make some calls."

"Good idea."

Leb's brow furrowed. "Problem is, I can't reach 'em. They must have moved. Brent always handled them himself, in fact, I've never seen or spoken to either of the partners. I thought maybe he had a file on them in here."

Grace rolled back from the desk and pulled out the credenza drawer. "What name?"

"Crimmins and Westerly. I think the two guy's names were Bob Crimmins and Broderick Westerly. Brent said Crimmins had been sick for the last few months, and we really haven't used them as much."

"Those names don't ring any bells," she said as she flipped through the files. "Wait..." At the very back, out of alphabetical order was a file with their name. She pulled it out and handed it to Leb as she turned to the Rolodex, finding a practically untouched card with their number. "Here's a number for them, want me to call?"

Leb nodded while he looked at the file, disappointed in what he found. "This is the same stuff we have in accounting—just the invoices."

By now, Grace had gotten through to a telephone company recording that the number she had reached was not in service. She punched in information for Atlanta and was quizzing the operator while Leb came around the end of the desk. With dizzying speed, he entered a whole series of numbers on the desk calculator, and stood back as he hit the subtotal button, then noted it on the cover of his file.

"Thank you, ma'am," Grace said, shaking her head as she looked at Leb. "Nothing." She punched Rita's number on the intercom.

"Has a Bob Crimmins or Broderick Westerly called or written?"

"I don't believe so, ma'am, but I'll check. Just a moment."

Leb looked befuddled. "We've paid these people over a million dollars in the last six years for consulting work. Got great results. How could they not be in the phone directory?"

"Maybe they moved."

Rita peered in the door. "No calls or letters from either person, Mrs. Wexler."

"Thanks, Rita." Grace turned back to Leb. "Let me talk to the developers. I'm certain it's a matter of their being nervous about the future of Wexler, Inc."

Leb handed her the job file and launched into an explanation of the work and their proposal.

"Forget the details, tell me what you know about the developer. Have we worked for them before?"

"Several times. Buzz Hadley is his name."

She remembered immediately. "He sent lovely flowers to the house."

"That would be him. A real gentlemen."

"God, I hope I thanked him." She called for Rita again. "Check whether I wrote Buzz Hadley in Atlanta a thank you."

"I remember that one going out."

"Good."

She looked back at Leb. "I think I've even met him."

"Probably. Brent hit him up pretty good during the last campaign. Maybe he flew in for some reception at the Mansion." Leb grimaced a bit. "For that matter, Brent hit everyone up pretty hard."

Grace knew how heavy-handed Brent had been—she'd witnessed some of the arm twisting herself. But no one could argue with what he'd accomplished. "I'll call him now. Stay here while I talk to him in case I get some question I can't answer."

Leb nodded as he shifted to the couch and picked up the other extension to make his own calls. "This Crimmins and Westerly thing bothers me. The phone company should have had a forwarding number at least," he said.

Grace got through to the developer immediately and after the requisite reminiscing about Brent, was able to reassure him about the future of Wexler, Inc., sufficiently to hold off a negative decision while the engineers re-crunched the numbers. She hung up to Leb's admiring smile.

"You're as good as Brent was with that sort of stuff. We should have hired you instead."

"I must have picked up more from Brent than I knew. What did you find out?"

"You're not going to believe this, but the phone company says there's never been a Crimmins and Westerly at that number. Up until two years ago, Peach State Record Company had that listing, but they moved."

Grace's success with Buzz Hadley faded. "How much did you say we've paid them?" she said, flipping through the Crimmins and Westerly invoices.

"About a million over six years." Leb got up and approached the desk, tapping his pencil on the edge as he spoke. "I think I'll do some more checking."

"Hmmm," she murmured, preoccupied with Leb's discovery. His movement toward the door snagged her attention. "Get the project manager to call the Atlanta people back. See if we can shave any costs down."

"Will do." Leb disappeared out the door.

Grace slipped the public relations firm file into her leather carryall to take home and answered the buzzing intercom.

"Mrs. Wexler," Rita said with crisp efficiency, "there's a man here from Mutual of New Hampshire, a Mr. Hubert Kingsbury, to see you."

"Mr. who?" Grace had stalled on the phrase Mutual of New Hampshire and never heard the man's name.

"Kingsbury."

It clicked. Mutual of New Hampshire was Brent's insurance carrier and it was time for the settlement. "I'll be right out," Grace chirped.

With a broad smile, she strode toward the unfamiliar man in the foyer who was standing near the staircase on the far side of the room. He was slight, mid-forties or maybe more, dressed in a dark, well-worn suit. He watched her approach, not taking a step to shorten her trek or lessen the time he had to take stock of her.

"Mr. Kingsbury?" Grace said, extending her hand.

"Yes." His grip was unbearably strong, a surprise given his stature. It wiped the smile from Grace's face.

"I'm Grace Wexler. Won't you come in?"

"Thank you." He handed Grace a business card from his pocket, which simply said "Hubert P. Kingsbury, Mutual of New Hampshire," but there was nothing to identify his position.

"I assume this has to do with my husband's death?"

"Yes, ma'am. I want to extend my condolences. I never met your husband, but I've experienced what you're going through and I'm very sorry."

"Thank you." Grace showed him a chair in front of her desk

and sat next to him. After a moment of painful silence, she asked, "Would you like something to drink? Coffee?"

"No, I had more than my share on the plane."

"You just arrived?"

"An hour or so ago."

"What can I do for you?"

"We're processing payment on your claim now. I've held off visiting you, Mrs. Wexler, to give you a chance to attend to other things, but we need to get your statement of the events the night Mr. Wexler died. All we have is the State Patrol's report of Colonel Anderson's meeting with you."

"Well..." Grace began.

"May I record this?" Kingsbury interrupted. "We'll transcribe it and send you a copy to attest to in a day or so."

"Certainly," said Grace, suddenly uncomfortable and shifting her position in her chair.

Kingsbury pulled a small hand-held recorder from his breast pocket and placed it on the desk, clicking it on. He mumbled some identifying information and then addressed Grace. "Please start with the events of March 5th."

Grace spoke slowly and deliberately, relating everything she could remember about Brent's call, but leaving out her remark that he didn't have to check in with her. It didn't take long, there wasn't much to say.

"And he was driving to the farm not to your house here in Jackson?"

"Yes."

"Is there a reason for that?"

Grace fidgeted some more. "Brent spent most of his time at the farm."

After a long pause, Kingsbury asked, "Were you estranged from your husband?"

Grace cringed at the question, and she knew Kingsbury had noticed. But she recovered quickly, her anger with his inference supplanting her fear of him. "I don't know whether the word is estranged or not, Mr. Kingsbury. My husband and I did better when we led our own separate lives."

"How so, if I might ask?"

"We never recovered from the death of our only child ten years ago."

"I'm sorry," the man stammered. This was clearly new information to him.

"Is there something more I can tell you?" Grace asked, taking back control of the conversation.

"No, I think I have all I need." He picked up the recorder, then put it back down. "One more thing. How were you able to identify the body?"

"The State Patrol had found several things that survived the fire—a watch, ring, key chain."

"Were these things Mr. Wexler usually wore or had with him?"

"Ye...," Grace faltered, suddenly remembering the new Rolex watch. "Yes, I believe so."

"Well, that's all I need. Thank you for your time, Mrs. Wexler," Kingsbury said, clicking off the recorder and standing as he put it in his coat pocket. "I'm sorry to have put you through this."

"That's perfectly all right," Grace said. "You're just doing your job. Brent had a substantial policy and I can understand your concern."

"Yes, ma'am. Thank you again."

When he was gone, she slumped in her chair and stared out the window, exhausted.

■ ■ ■ ■

In his office on the first floor, Carver straightened his tie twice and then suddenly took off his suit coat and rolled up his sleeves. Vic knocked and walked in, looking at him askance.

"Andrew Hilboldt has just arrived," Vic said. "Are you ready?"

"Yes, indeed."

"Don't you want to put your coat on?"

"I think I want the hard at work look."

"But he's the first appointment of the day," Vic protested. "And I'm already hard at work."

"Okay, I'll bring him down."

A second after the door closed, Carver rolled his sleeves back down, cursing the rumpled appearance. He had just gotten his suit coat back on and was looking over his messages, when Vic knocked again and the door opened.

Carver stepped around the end of his desk to greet the reporter, both hands out for a warm handshake.

"I'm honored, Mr. Hilboldt," Carver said. "Won't you sit down?"

■ ■ ■ ■

Laura had planned to spend most of the nights Will was gone, working on the Transportation Department reports. As it turned out, her son's absence was far more disorienting than she'd expected. The first two nights were frittered away entirely on busywork with her finances and re-papering the kitchen drawers and shelves.

She lingered over a huge salad while she finished the last fifty pages of a mystery, and then took Ranger, who was equally confused without her playmate, on a long walk. It was after nine when she sat down at her computer. She stalled a little longer by checking her e-mail. Naomi had written.

LAURA:

JUST A QUICK REPLY— I GUESS I'M STALLING ABOUT SETTING A DATE BECAUSE MY STOMACH'S NOT TURNING TO BUTTERFLIES LIKE YOURS IS. THAT'S HOW I THOUGHT IT WAS SUPPOSED TO BE. I DEARLY LOVE JOHN, BUT HE DIDN'T SWEEP ME OFF MY FEET. WE SORT OF GREW INTO LOVE AND NOW HE'S THE BEST FRIEND I'VE GOT.

AM I WRONG ABOUT THIS? IT SEEMS FOOLISH TO FANTASIZE ABOUT A HANDSOME STRANGER SUDDENLY SWOOPING INTO MY LIFE, BUT I DO.

HASTA LUEGO, NAOMI

NAOMI:

WAITING FOR TRUE LOVE OR SETTLING FOR SOMETHING GOOD BUT NOT TINGLY—THAT'S A TOUGH ONE. THE ONLY THING I CAN THINK TO SAY IS THAT THE TINGLY STUFF DIES DOWN, BUT A GOOD FRIENDSHIP LASTS FOREVER.

IF YOU DO DECIDE TO GO AHEAD WITH IT, PERSONALLY, HAVING BEEN THROUGH A BIG DEAL WEDDING, I'D SAVE MY MONEY AND GO TO THE BAHAMAS. THERE'S A PLACE WHERE SEMMES AND I WENT TWO CHRIST-MASES BEFORE WILL WAS BORN. OUT ON ELBOW CAY. HAD TO TAKE A BOAT FROM MARSH HARBOR TO GET THERE. IT'S THE EDGE OF THE WORLD AND IT'S HEAVEN ON EARTH. AND GREAT FOOD. I WILL NEVER FORGET IT, NEVER.

WILL'S AT DISNEY WORLD WITH MOM AND I AM TOTALLY AT A LOSS WITHOUT HIM. IT NEVER OCCURRED TO ME HOW MUCH HE STRUCTURES MY LIFE.

VIC IS TAKING ME TO THE MOVIES TOMORROW NIGHT. I'M NERVOUS AS A CAT AND I FEEL SO FOOLISH. I, WHO NEVER THINK ABOUT CLOTHES, HAVE BEEN TRYING ON OUTFITS. CAN YOU BELIEVE THAT?

LAURA

Unable to avoid working on Everett's Transportation Department inquiry any longer, Laura began flipping through the annual reports and picked out the most recent one. Five or six companies seemed to be the main bidders in highway projects. She noticed Wexler, Inc., bid often.

What will happen now that he's dead?

The last section was actual expenditures on construction, listed by project number. Laura chose the first one in the Western District and grabbed the next report on the stack, the year before the one she'd been reviewing, and flipped through until she found the bids for that project. Boshers, Inc., had been awarded the contract for $3,628,482.70.

She checked the actual expenditure, and then pulled her feet off the desk and sat up straight, reaching for the calculator. The job actually cost about $145,000 more than bid, a 4 percent job overrun. Not too bad. She compared the bids, award, and final cost on another project, but this time found a 15 percent cost overrun.

Laura counted the number of bid projects in the western district for a year. Thirty projects with four or five bids for each one. And payments covering several different years on the big projects. Times twenty years. It would be a massive amount of data.

She turned to her computer and clicked on the spreadsheet program, then sat back to think about what data would be relevant. If she included all the bids, awards, and expenditures, she could see if there were any patterns—who got the bids, how large the cost overruns were. It was long shot, but there might be something.

Laura decided to create a spreadsheet for every project. It was slow going at first, and she made a lot of mistakes. But as the muscle memory of her fingers on the keypad came back, she made better progress. When she turned out the light just before midnight, she'd entered the data for an entire year. Only nineteen to go.

■ ■ ■ ■

"I love previews," Laura said, automatically sinking into the second seat on the row so that Vic could have the aisle seat to stretch out. Vic was as tall as Semmes, so she assumed he'd prefer the extra legroom. "I hope there are at least four."

This was their first real date but she knew so much about Vic, she could anticipate most of his moves. What she didn't know was whether they'd be able to turn their competitiveness on and off. It gave her an odd off-balance feeling.

She took a handful of the popcorn he offered, and ate one kernel at a time, the only way she could avoid devouring an entire bucket before the movie even started. When she went back for a second helping, her hand brushed Vic's, sending a thrill through her.

"I make no guarantees about this movie," Vic said, sinking lower into the seat and bringing himself closer to her. "I haven't had time to read the reviews."

"Can't imagine why," Laura said, selecting another from her handful to eat. "But I'm not very discriminating. Movies are my ticket away."

"I know exactly how you feel. I can't wait for this session to end."

"Remember," Laura reminded him. "No shop talk tonight."

"My apologies. Have you heard from Will?" he asked, quickly changing the subject.

"He's having the time of his life. Apparently, he loves MGM Studios. That's been his favorite place so far."

"Must get that from you. What about your mother?"

"She says she's keeping up," Laura whispered as the house lights went down.

There were five previews. And the movie, a remake of a forties thriller, was so well paced, it was over before she realized it.

"How about getting a bite to eat?" asked Vic.

Laura looked at her watch instinctively, then caught herself. "Sure. Your choice."

"I chose the movie, you choose the restaurant."

"Do you eat sushi?"

"Never had the courage to try it, though I like Little Tokyo."

"Then allow me to introduce you to the tastiest morsels ever created."

"Do I have to eat raw fish?"

"Only if you want to. The asparagus rolls are to die for."

"Okay, I'm in."

"What's your all-time, all-time favorite movie?" asked Laura. She was peeling and eating the last of her steamed soy beans, the only food remaining on the table. They'd polished off the salad, soup, and all the different sushis Laura had ordered..

"Impossible. There are too many."

"Okay, all-time favorite, last five years."

"*Pulp Fiction.* Did you see it?"

"Missed it," said Laura, shaking her head in regret. "I've had a pretty steady diet of G and PG movies lately."

"So what's yours?"

"That's tough."

Vic chuckled. "It was your question."

"I know, give me a moment. How about *Last of the Mohicans* with Daniel Day Lewis."

"Magua, the best damn villain in movie history. Who played him?"

"Wes Studi," Laura answered immediately.

"But that's more than five years old."

"Details, details."

"Your details. Try again."

"Okay. *The English Patient.*"

Vic nodded. "Nice to know we agree about the really important stuff."

"Remember in *Mohicans* when they were running through
the woods?"

The waitress came and removed all the dishes. "Dessert?"
she asked.

Vic patted his stomach as though it couldn't hold another
bite.

"One green tea ice cream and two spoons," Laura said.
"You've got to try it."

"Whatever you say, it's all been delicious." He put his arms
on the table and leaned a bit closer. "I'd like to be in those
woods. They filmed it in North Carolina, I think."

"Around Asheville."

"In fact, I'd like to be anywhere except here."

Laura knew what he meant, but feigned hurt.

"I didn't mean it that way," Vic stammered, reaching for her
hand. "I just wish this legislative session was over, the Senate
race was over, everything."

"I don't know how you stand it."

"I'm not doing very well actually. With the campaign starting, the session's twice as bad. And I particularly don't like
being at cross-purposes with you."

"But we're not," Laura said, tingling with the warmth in his
touch and his remark. She looked around to see who was nearby only to discover they were the last ones in the restaurant.
She hadn't noticed anyone coming or going

"You and I aren't, but you and the governor are, and I'm his
mouthpiece. What I say in that capacity, you don't always want
to hear. That's what I regret."

"I know where he's coming from," Laura admitted. "He's
got a bigger agenda these days and I don't always keep that in
mind."

"You shouldn't have to, that's not your job."

"In a way it is. I'm a member of his cabinet."

"But you've got a responsibility to those troopers, too. And Carver never remembers that."

"If he wins this senate race, will you be off to Washington?"

"I don't know," Vic said slowly. He was looking square in her eyes and squeezing her hand gently. "It will depend on a lot of things."

Laura smiled.

"Don't forget though, a Senator needs someone to keep the home fires burning."

The ice cream arrived, and their spoons were a blur.

Vic slid in behind the wheel, pushed the key into the ignition, then turned to Laura and kissed her gently before she had an opportunity to object.

Laura didn't retreat. When she raised her hand and gently stroked his cheek, a wave of relief spread over Vic, mingled with the excitement. After they broke away, he looked at her for another long moment, offering a sweet warm smile, then cranked the engine, and headed toward her house.

Her late husband Semmes had been Vic's good friend before either of them had met Laura. They'd grown up down the street from each other and until their interests—Semmes' in architecture and Vic's in law and politics—had sent them into different spheres, they'd been close. Semmes had met Laura first, and though Vic had always been intrigued with her, he'd never intruded on his friend's relationship. Wooing her now after Semmes had died, wasn't easy because he knew how much they'd loved each other and he wasn't certain he could ever measure up to Semmes.

"Will you come in for a drink?" Laura asked as they pulled into her driveway.

"Are you sure?"

"I'm sure about the drink."

"Love to."

Ranger met them at the door, jumping all over both of them.

"Know anything about wine?" she asked, pointing to a rack above the refrigerator that held a dozen bottles. "Semmes bought all those at Martin's Wine Cellar, one of his regular stops on the way home from a New Orleans business trip. The best I can do is tell red from white, and identify the sweet ones."

"You have a preference?"

"Red, but I'll drink whatever you want."

Vic looked at the bottles one by one, and then handed her a zinfandel. As she was uncorking it, Ranger appeared with a rope toy in her mouth and Vic took up the challenge, tussling with the puppy as she backed into the living room.

Laura brought the wine and glasses into the living room. She pulled two large chairs closer to the fireplace and lit the fire while Vic and Ranger continued their battle. But when he settled in the seat next to Laura and dropped Ranger's toy, the retriever immediately moved to the side of his chair, sitting straight up with her tail swishing behind her. She raised her paw and placed it on his arm, her soft brown eyes pleading for more attention.

"That's enough, Ranger," Laura said, starting to get up.

"Sit back down, she'd not bothering me." Vic scratched behind the puppy's ears, looking at the shelves to either side of the hearth. His old friend Semmes was everywhere. Not only had he picked out their wine, but there were several photographs, two models of buildings he'd designed, and architectural books in the shelves and on the coffee table.

Vic looked at Laura. She'd followed his gaze and was now focused on a photo of Semmes holding a much younger Will on his shoulders, a faint wistfulness in her expression.

Maybe she isn't ready for this.

He reached for his glass. "To a lovely evening," he toasted, hoping to break her reverie.

"And to the next," Laura said, with a smile so inviting Vic couldn't help but think that she wanted this as badly as he did.

But then she added, "He died a year ago tomorrow."

"I know. I hadn't forgotten. He was one helluva friend."

"So it's kind of hard for me right now."

"I hope I didn't make it harder."

"No, not at all."

He raised his glass and said, "To Semmes. I'm certain he's building something wonderful for all of us."

"To Semmes," Laura repeated, her eyes glistening slightly.

Vic finished his wine and reached for the bottle. "One more glass before I go?"

"Absolutely," Laura said.

■ ■ ■ ■

Laura looked into the waiting area of the Governor's Office in the Capitol before she opened the door. A mother was standing at the visitor's log book patiently watching her young child—a little girl in a red and white polkadot rain slicker, who couldn't have been more than four—sign her name. A representative from the Coast was seated next to a gentleman in a business suit on the blue couch, deep in conversation—a constituent, Laura presumed. A lone man, about Laura's age, in a comfortable wool sport coat and tie, sat in the armchair next to them, writing in a small notebook.

She stepped in the room, smiling at the little girl. "Good morning, Representative," Laura said, nodding toward the legislator.

"Commissioner," he said with a nod but didn't get up from his place. The constituent didn't even glance her way, never slowing up his sentence.

The man looked up from his notebook. She knew he was watching her as she crossed the room.

"Vic just paged me," Laura whispered to the receptionist who had a handset perched between her shoulder and her ear. The woman nodded and gestured for her to go in.

Laura felt her stomach flutter slightly in anticipation. She hadn't seen or talked to Vic since their date two nights before. He was hanging up the phone when she entered. She dropped her satchel and raincoat in a chair.

"Hi," Vic said, his voice only slightly softer than usual. She knew instantly it would be business as usual and she wasn't certain whether she was relieved or disappointed.

"Who's that guy in the reception area?"

"Glasses? Dark hair?"

Laura nodded.

"*Wall Street Journal* reporter."

"How'd the interview go?"

"Great, so far. At least I think so."

"What's the focus?"

"Carver's leadership on this base-closing issue," Vic said quickly. "I'm glad you were in the building."

"What's going on?" she asked.

Vic rolled his eyes and pointed toward the door to the Governor's office. "Polk County is in there—four of the supervisors, the representative, and Senator Grady Kellogg, railing about the State Patrol. Not only is Claytonia the Governor's hometown, but Kellogg's on Appropriations with a rather tight grip on two of our bills, so Carver decided to let you explain."

"Explain what?"

"Why your men have quit writing tickets in Polk county."

"They haven't, at least not that I'm aware of. We've been trying to stay on top of any slowdowns. Why didn't they call me?"

"Some people like to start at the top."

"This is the first I've heard of it," Laura said, reaching for the phone on Vic's desk. "You've got to believe me about this."

"No time for a phone call," Vic said, pointing the way toward his private door to the Governor's office.

"They don't pay me enough," Laura muttered.

The conference table in the Governor's Capitol office seated eight, and every chair but one was filled when Laura entered the room. The conversation stopped abruptly.

"Commissioner Owen," Governor Carver said, straining to keep from sounding angry. "Let me introduce you to the supervisors from Polk County—Mr. Buchanan, Mr. Alvis, Mr. Wagner, and my brother, Mr. Leo Carver. You know Representative Tims and Senator Kellogg, I presume."

All the men had stood up and Laura shook hands with each one. Tims and Kellogg just nodded.

"I've just been told that tickets in Polk County have dropped by over fifty percent," Governor Carver said. "What's the cause of this?"

"I didn't know anything about this, sir," Laura said, trying to sound as earnest as possible. "In fact, we've been monitoring tickets carefully to make certain there wasn't any sort of slow-down. I'll have to check into it. Whatever the reason is, it's not acceptable."

"You're right about that," Mr. Leo Carver grumbled. "Our revenue's down by several thousand dollars. And that may not sound like much to a lady with a big budget, but it's about..."

"About 25 percent of your monthly expenditures," Laura interjected. "I understand completely. I only wish you'd called me directly—I might have saved you a trip up here."

"They're borrowing to make payroll," Representative Tims added.

Senator Kellogg, Laura noticed, was strangely silent. "All I can do is find out what has happened and correct it," Laura offered.

"Could there be a mistake?" Vic asked, trying to give her some room to maneuver.

"I'm as baffled as everyone, but as soon as I can get to a phone, I'll get some answers."

"Vic, I don't know what to say—I really didn't know any-thing about this," Laura said, pulling at his sleeve as they left the room. "I didn't want to say it in there, but we've been watching the tickets like hawks—I can't imagine what's going on."

"Just get some answers as fast as you can." He stood behind his desk, hand on his hips, looking over the array of pink mes-sage slips that had appeared in the few minutes he'd been gone.

"I'll call you within the hour," said Laura, turning the brass door knob. She was about to walk out, but she couldn't resist adding, "Sure is hard to come up short at the end of the month."

Vic took a deep breath. "That point will not be lost on the Governor, I assure you."

Laura drew back the door a sliver and peeked out. She waited until the Polk County people were all the way out of the reception area and the Coast contingent had been shown into the Governor's office. Then she slipped across the reception area, smiling at the *Wall Street Journal* reporter as she went.

■ ■ ■ ■

Grace happened to be at home that same rainy morning when the postman dropped a damp pile of mail through the slot onto the foyer floor. There were a few notes, innumerable solicitations from charities, catalogs, credit card and long distance companies trolling for business, and replies from all of the stores she'd contacted. She sorted it all, disgusted at having so much paper arrive, day after day, only to land directly in the trash.

At Adler's, Brent had bought the Rolex watch she'd noticed at Gibb's birthday party, two sets of cufflinks, and a tie clasp. The Brooks Brothers charges were for two 42-long sport coats, five shirts, two pairs of slacks, two pairs of shoes, and a new trench coat. The Rogue bill was more of the same, a small but complete new 46-long wardrobe. She didn't recall seeing any of this when she packed up his clothes to give away a month earlier. But then again, she'd been more concerned about whether she had enough garbage bags, not with what was going in them. Still, it was a pity that so much had burned up in the wreck.

She stopped and looked at the Rogue bill again. Brent didn't wear 46 long.

She dialed the store and asked for the salesman who'd signed the sales slip with the note, 'Always a pleasure to help you, Mr. Wexler.'

"This is Grace Wexler, Brent Wexler's wife."

"Mrs. Wexler, I'm so sorry about Mr. Wexler. He was a great guy."

And a terrific customer, Grace thought. "Thank you."

"How can I help you?"

"I was going through some bills and found yours. The last

purchase my husband made was for several suits."

"That's right."

"But they were 46-long and he wore a 42."

"Those were a present for someone. He's been picking out three or four suits every year for the same gentleman."

Grace's surprise left her silent.

"Is there anything more I can help you with?" the salesman inquired.

She groped for something appropriate to say to end the conversation quickly. "I'm sorry, I was just trying to think who was a 46-long and now I feel so stupid. It was for his uncle. I've seen Brent present them to him. I'm sorry to have bothered you."

"No problem, Mrs. Wexler."

"Thank you."

Who could Brent have bought clothes for? Grace put the sales slip under a paperweight on her desk and walked toward the kitchen.

It could have been worse, she thought, he could have been buying clothes for a woman.

■ ■ ■ ■

"You're on the speaker phone, Levi," Blake said. "I've got Jimmie Anderson and Robert Stone in here."

"What's up?"

"The Commissioner just got raked over the coals in the Governor's office," Blake said. "Seems that tickets are way down in Polk County—so low they had to borrow for payroll. The Governor's brother brought the whole board of supervisors up to the Capitol to complain."

"First I've heard of it," Levi said. "You'd think they'd start by calling here."

"What's the deal?" Blake asked.

"The only guy over there is Cook—we've been short two men this month. But Cook has been working his tail off."

"Not in Polk County, he hasn't," Blake said.

"I've got his last weekly report, right here. Three DUIs, twelve speeding tickets, two wrecks. I've been watching him, you know."

"But where did he write the tickets?"

Levi flipped to the yellow copies attached to Cook's report. "Taft, Taft, Heywood, Taft, Taft, Taft, Taft, Taft, Heywood, Polk, Polk, Taft, Taft, Taft, Heywood."

Jimmie Anderson shrugged his shoulders, his hands up in puzzlement.

"What are the dates on those Polk tickets?" Robert asked.

"April 1 and April 1," Levi answered. "I'm gonna put you on hold and get the earlier reports.

No one spoke for a moment. "If I had to bet, Cook hasn't written but three or four little tickets in Polk all month," Blake said. "And it wasn't accidental."

"He's not that dumb," Jimmie said. "He was in the meeting, he heard what the Commissioner said."

"He didn't disobey anything she said," Robert interjected. "He didn't slow down...."

"You still there?" Levi said.

"Find them?" Blake asked.

"I did," Levi said. "But the yellow ticket copies already went on to key-punch, so I can't tell where his tickets were without running a report, if key punch has got them entered. And if not, I'd have to search through the piles of tickets over there to find them."

"Don't bother," Blake said. "I'm going to assume it was coincidence."

"Hell of a coincidence," Levi said.

"Don't go any further till we call you back."

"Should I talk to Cook?"

"Not yet," Blake said. "Let me think about how to handle it."

Laura appeared at the door just as Blake was hanging up. "Find out anything?"

"Not really," Blake said, noticing that Laura was strangely calmer than he'd expected, given the urgency in her voice when she'd called him from the Capitol. "The trooper who works Polk County has been pumping this month—lots of tickets—but we don't know where, exactly."

"Was this part of your war plan?" Laura asked.

"Absolutely not," Blake said quickly.

"Well, it sure did get the Governor's attention."

"But will it help or hurt," Robert asked. "That's the question."

"And not just any old question, it's a seven million dollar question," she corrected. "What do you plan to do?"

"Unless we could prove it was intentional," Blake said, "I think it's pretty risky to jump all over a trooper who's really busting his ass about the geographical distribution of his tickets. That's not to say that he shouldn't know we're aware of it and watching."

"So what can I tell Polk County?" Laura asked.

"I'll go over there with Cook," Jimmie said, "and assure them it wasn't intentional, and that he'll be working overtime in Polk County for a while."

"That should solve their problem," Laura said. "Now I've got to think about what to say to the Governor."

"Be honest—tell him what Jimmie's going to do, and let him wonder," Blake said.

"Do you think it's happening anywhere else?"

"I hope not," Robert said. "It would ruin the effect, I think."

"Make sure, will you?" Laura said as she left.

# TEN

An overnight letter from Mutual of New Hampshire was delivered to Grace at home before she left for the office. It contained a transcript of her conversation with Hubert Kingsbury and a statement for her to sign, attesting to the accuracy of her remarks. The cover letter explained that it would take only seven days from the time they received the notarized statement until they transferred the settlement to her account. They requested information on the bank account to which the money should be wired.

She read over the transcript, recoiling at her hesitant response to Kingsbury's question "Were these things Mr. Wexler usually wore or had with him?" Brent did wear those pieces but as little as she saw him, maybe he wore other things, too. But it was accurate, Grace thought, absolutely accurate, as far as she knew.

Grace typed out a reply with her account information and, since the attestation required a notary, called Franklin Gilliam's office to see if someone there could witness her signature. She wanted to get the whole thing off her hands and out of her house as quickly as possible.

"Of course we have a notary for you, Grace," Gilliam said. "We're always glad to help."

When she arrived thirty minutes later, she was directed to a conference room and the designated firm notary, a secretary Grace didn't recall meeting but who seemed to know her, appeared moments later. Just as they were finishing up, Gilliam stepped in.

"I didn't know I'd be interrogated about Brent's death," Grace said, skipping the pleasantries when she saw him. "You should have warned me, Franklin."

"What do you mean?" Gilliam replied, startled by the sharpness of her tone.

"The insurance company sent a man to ask me questions a while ago. I have to swear to the answers to get the settlement."

The secretary waited patiently for a moment to slip away but Gilliam was blocking the door. She coughed and got their attention.

"Is there anything more you need, Mrs. Wexler?"

"Could you make copies of all for this for me?" Grace replied, her voice kind and smooth.

"Make two copies, please," Gilliam told the secretary, then he looked at Grace. "May I have one for our files?"

"Certainly," Grace nodded.

The secretary slipped out.

"I'm sure it was just routine," Gilliam said, sliding into a chair.

"Routine or not, it was very unpleasant."

"I'm sorry you had to go through this," Gilliam apologized. "I wish I'd known at the time."

Grace wanted to be gone, but trapped there, she changed the subject to something less odious. "How's the hunting going?"

"Fine," said Gilliam, always glad to talk about Second Creek. "Trey's letting us use the house until turkey season's over, but we've broken ground for the new camp. It'll be finished by the fall, I hope."

The door opened and the secretary returned giving the original and a copy to Grace and one to Gilliam.

"Anything else?" the young woman said tentatively.

"Could you get this original out by overnight mail for me?" asked Grace. "They're waiting for it to process the claim."

Gilliam answered for her. "We'd be happy to."

The young lady left again, closing the door behind her. Gilliam looked over the transcript, raising his eyebrows as he read. "This is rather crude of them, I must say, but perhaps it was necessary. I think they could have handled it differently. There are ways and there are..."

"Well, it's over," Grace said, interrupting Gilliam's embarrassed drivel, and rose to leave. "That's the only good thing about it."

■ ■ ■ ■

Trey made several trips down to the Transportation Department, ostensibly working on car titles for his cases. He got lucky again and caught Morgan driving away from his office. His first stop was one of the near-nightly receptions for legislators and public officials thrown by lobbying groups at the Trade Mart. Morgan didn't stay long. He made another mad dash to the airport to pick up his honey, and the two made a bee-line again for Vicksburg.

Perfect time to check the lay of the land.

Morgan's driveway turned into a poorly paved area between the house and a high chain-link fence in back, which separated the property from the Interstate. Thick overgrown ligustrums and weed trees masked the boundary fence and deflected some of the nearly constant traffic noise. The house to the south was on a double lot and the extra lawn, rimmed with equally thick azaleas and philodendrons, separated the larger, pumpkin-orange house from Morgan's neglected one. To the north, across the road, was a small dark house that seemed unoccupied—Trey hadn't seen any lights or cars on the many occasions when he'd been watching Morgan's house.

He pulled on a pair of gloves and with a set of lock picks, let himself in the back door in less than thirty seconds.

Doubt that getting into Grace's house will be this easy, he thought.

If Morgan had a cleaning service, they clearly hadn't been there recently. In the dining area was an eight-sided table covered with the remnants of what looked like a poker game—overflowing ashtrays, beer bottles, highball glasses, and greasy bowls with the broken pieces of potato chips and pretzels.

Trey never figured the guy for such a slob—he was always nattily attired even for his roly-poly shape.

To the left, a hallway led to three rooms—the west and front bedroom, which was relatively tidy from lack of use, a small crumbling bathroom that needed renovation, and a second larger bedroom, obviously where Morgan slept.

Bingo.

Only Morgan's closet, which filled one entire wall, was in order, his suits neatly hanging from the rack and polished shoes lined up below. The rest was chaos. Overwhelming the room was a king-size bed, its designer brown and navy sheets unmade and badly in need of changing, with a matching night table and lamp next to the near side, its top drawer yawning open.

A .22 automatic Colt Woodsman lay in the back of the drawer. He pulled it out and checked the magazine. A full clip. Brand spanking new and loaded. How convenient.

Either this was the one he had with him hunting, or there'd been a special on at the gun shop—one for the house and one for the car.

Opposite the bed was a matching dresser covered with personal articles and the contents of pockets emptied night after night. Magazines and newspapers were strewn about near the side of the bed, and a television cabinet housing a 25-inch TV and VCR was in the corner. Videos were stuffed above and around the equipment.

Jesus Christ, how can he live like this? Well, it won't be for much longer, Trey thought, with a dark chuckle.

He inserted one of the unmarked tapes and turned on the set.

It was obviously a home-recorded scene. A woman, clad only in a lacy garter belt and black stockings, was tantalizing a grossly overweight man who was squirming in ravenous ecstasy. When the man turned his face toward the camera, Trey recognized Morgan.

What a dickhead.

Trey pulled the tape out, totally repulsed by what he'd seen, and slipped in another. A different woman was hovering over Morgan—this one wearing some sort of tiger skin body suit—and Morgan's arms and legs were tied to the bedposts. Trey shook his head in disgust.

He started to grab another, but he checked his watch. There wasn't time to watch every one. He popped the second tape out and stuffed it in his jacket.

He moved to the bathroom, picking his way through the double-mirrored medicine chest and the drawers of the vanity. Well, well, well. A miracle of modern medicine and cosmetology. Dentures, contact lenses, a hairpiece, hemorrhoid medicines, heart medications. It must take him an hour in the bathroom every morning.

Trey went back to the bedroom and from the side of the bed, counted his steps down the hall, through the kitchen and up to the back door, checking the hazards and obstructions along the way.

Quick and efficient.

Then, just in case, he went back to the bedroom and counted his steps to the front door, noting that unlike the back door which had only one lock activated by pushing the button in, the front door had an additional dead-bolt above the knob. It was set, but the key was dangling from the lock.

What an idiot. The stupid slob deserves to die.

Trey let himself out and checked his watch on the way to the car. Five minutes total. Not a soul in sight.

He drove past the park, looking across the interstate at Patrol headquarters.

The sonovabitch has ruined enough of my life. It should have been handled this way from the start and then Brent would never have left. At least this will stop the audit and keep Brent safe. Wherever he is.

How soon before I hear from him? Trey wondered. He'll take his time. He's got to make certain everything is over. Then he'll be in touch.

■ ■ ■ ■

Everett knocked quietly on Laura's door, which was standing ajar. She was leaning back in her chair with her feet up on the desk, engrossed in something, pen in hand. She looked up when she saw him and motioned for him to come in.

"Give me one more minute. I can't make this sentence work."

Everett took a seat on the couch and unpacked his laptop, then pulled out a pile of papers while it powered up.

"You want some coffee?" Laura asked as she headed toward the door, papers in hand. "I've got to get this out to Deborah to retype."

"Sure," Everett said. "Black."

When she returned and put down the two cups of coffee, Laura closed the door and took a seat next to Everett.

"I hope you're finding more than I am."

"I don't know yet. Let me show you what I've got." He handed her a batch of printouts. "I'm making some assumptions: the first is that the IRS has zeroed in on Morgan, not the other two."

"Can you assume that?"

"If I were doing their work, I'd have checked the other two commissioners before I went out asking questions in public and looking for documentation. Wouldn't you?"

"Probably."

"So, let's assume Morgan's the only one with unidentified income, which is why they came to see me in the first place."

"Okay."

"So assuming he's different from the other two, I decided to look at things all three districts purchase and see if there are differences."

"Like heavy equipment?"

"Exactly. And other things. Here's a list of items where all three basically purchased the same thing."

"But Morgan purchased a different brand."

"And paid a little more. The guy's no dummy. He knows it wouldn't fly if he bought the same item at a higher price, so he goes with a different vendor."

"But are these prices inflated?"

Everett handed her another sheet. "I've compared the prices of the items Morgan bought to prices paid by other agencies or counties for the same things. The differences become even clearer."

Laura ran her finger down the list. "But this is nickel and dime stuff."

"Yeah, but a thousand here, a thousand there, and sooner or later you're talking real money."

"I know, but it would be too dangerous having so many people know," Laura countered. "Is he that stupid?"

"Possibly. What do we do with this?"

"I don't know," said Laura, sitting back. "Let me think about it."

"And what about the annual reports?"

"I'm half way through, working from the present backward, and there's nothing out of line."

"I wouldn't bother doing any more, then. All the activity has been in the last five years. Before that, nothing unusual."

"No," Laura said. "I think I'll keep going. You've convinced me he's a crook and he didn't get rich from what you've picked up. That's just spending money."

"You really think so?"

Laura nodded. "Besides, I've got a rhythm going. Once Will's in bed, I turn on some music, and punch in a few numbers. I like the feeling of chasing someone—a real case, for a change."

■ ■ ■ ■

Grace finished a late breakfast of leftover Chinese steamed dumplings with garlic beef and rice while she browsed through the newspaper at the kitchen counter. Eating what she liked, when she liked, was one of the greatest pleasures of living alone. As she pushed the front section aside to pick up the local news, her hand brushed against a baggie of remnants from the wreck which a trooper had delivered several days before. Now curious about them, she pulled a white plate down and emptied out the contents to get a better look.

A clasp had separated from one of a pair of oval Ole Miss cufflinks, another unmatched plain cufflink was undamaged, three tie tacks came through unscathed except for soot, and the rest seemed to be name plates from Brent's luggage. He'd always liked gold and what it instantly said about a person's disposable income. But since men weren't supposed to wear bracelets and necklaces, he'd given plenty to Grace over the years and insisted she wear it. His own jewelry was the usual older male fare—watches, cufflinks, and tie clips.

She slipped off the stool and went to the foyer where she'd put the first bag of articles Jimmie Anderson had found and then searched her closet for what she'd collected from the farm. Adding them to the pieces on the counter, she sorted them into pairs and types. It added up to a decent amount of gold, maybe a quarter pound, worth the time and trouble to sell.

Two hours later while she was searching for the right necklace to wear with the dress she had on, Grace remembered the cufflinks Jody had given her father, the ones he wore the most often.

They hadn't been in the pile of jewelry or the fragments.

Where could they be?

Even if he'd been wearing them, something would have survived the fire, the other items had.

And that Rolex he'd bought, where was it?

The insurance company's question—Were these things Mr. Wexler usually wore or had with him?—came roaring back at her. Had she been mistaken to answer as she had?

■ ■ ▨ ▨

Blake watched the parking lot with his proprietary air while he talked on the phone. He saw Jimmie Anderson's reflection in the glass and signaled him to come in without even turning around or missing a beat in his conversation. Blake pointed at the Patrol moving van that was backing up and slowly crawling toward the entrance, asking with his hand movements whether Jimmie knew who had checked the van out.

"Trey Turner," Jimmie mouthed silently.

Blake nodded. "Well, gotta go," Blake said into the phone. "Duty calls." After a few more remarks and growing impatient, Blake finally hung up and swiveled back to scan the parking lot. The van was gone. "Know why Turner wanted the van?"

"He's moving. He's trading Mrs. Wexler his house at the farm for a hunting camp house and a hundred acres. Somewhere near Second Creek."

"Sounds like he got a deal."

"I'd say so. He's buying two hundred more acres."

"How do you know that?"

"I'm on the loan committee at the Credit Union this year. He's financing the extra acreage. I bet Mrs. Wexler's happy. She didn't like him at all."

Blake shrugged. "He's not the most likable guy, but I could always count on him to volunteer for the really tough stuff. Never been to his home or anything. What's the camp that he bought like?"

"Apparently it's got a pretty nice place that has served as the clubhouse. He's moving in this weekend." They both fell silent as they watched the activity in the lot.

"We've got to a decision to make," Jimmie said, picking up Blake's Casey Stengel baseball. He tossed it up and down a few times, making it spin in the air. "Billy Cook is the finalist from his troop for the reconstruction school and classes start on Monday. Do we let him attend?"

"What he did almost cost us the pay raise," Blake said.

"Or, tipped the balance for the pay raise."

"And he lied to Levi," Blake scowled.

"Maybe, maybe not," Jimmie said quietly. "But he's real smart, and except for this one incident, he's been a real good trooper."

Blake was staring at the empty space where the van had been. Trey's car was parked next to it. "Okay," he said rather absently, "tell him he can be in the class."

"Will do."

"Are you teaching it?"

"Mostly." Jimmie carefully replaced the ball on its stand. "But we're taking some field trips to the junk yard and a body shop. Want 'em to analyze actual damage. And I have an insurance fellow coming in to talk about policies, fraud, etcetera. I think they'll learn something."

"Sounds like a good program."

"Hope so," Jimmie said. "Well, gotta go."

"Later," Blake said with a wave and turned back to stare at Trey's car. An awful lot of moving was going on in a quiet man's life, he mused.

■ ■ ■ ■

Will Owen dashed between two passengers pulling carry-ons, his arms stretched wide, smiling from ear to ear. "Momma!"

Laura knelt down as he ran through the crowd toward her, hungry for one of his hugs. "I'm so glad to see you, Sweetheart." She looked over his shoulder at her mother coming out the jetway, weighed down with an extra bag filled to overflowing.

"I'm glad to see you, too," Will said, planting a big kiss on her cheek.

She pulled back to get a better look at him. "How was your trip? Were you sweet to Grandmom?"

"Uh-huh. Disney World was really cool."

"I think you've grown. In fact, I know you have."

Will snuggled back into his mother's arms, holding tighter than before.

"He probably has," Charlotte said with an equally large smile. "I've never seen a child consume as many pancakes as this young man can. Even the waitresses couldn't believe it. And three glasses of milk."

Laura stood up to give her mother a hug. "Let me take that, Mom."

"I'll let you—gladly. It's filled with all our mementos."

Will's hand slipped into Laura's as they headed down the concourse.

"What was your absolutely most favorite thing?" Laura asked her son.

"Muppets 3-D," he said instantly.

Laura looked at Charlotte.

"I agree," her mother said. "And how did you make out?"

"It was awfully quiet around the house with just Ranger for company."

"Did you remember to feed Ranger?" Will asked with sudden urgency.

"Of course. And she's just fine. Slept on your bed the whole time."

Will beamed, then hopped on the escalator to the baggage claim. Laura and Charlotte followed him.

"Any social occasions?" Charlotte asked.

"Vic Regis and I went to the movies and out to dinner," Laura said, over her shoulder.

"Where did you say we were going for dinner?" Will asked from the bottom step.

"I didn't."

"But you just said something about dinner."

"I was talking to Grandmom about going out to dinner while you two were living it up in Disney World."

"Oh. Well, what's for dinner tonight?"

"Your favorites: stuffed potatoes, scrambled eggs, and brownies for dessert. Now let me finish my conversation with Grandmom. Please?"

"A pleasant evening?" Charlotte asked tentatively.

"Very."

"I'm glad."

They'd reached the luggage carousels, and Will slithered into a spot right at the opening.

"Did you go to the cemetery?"

"No," Laura said. "I just couldn't."

Charlotte slipped her arm into Laura's and stood beside her. "I didn't go for a long time either."

▪ ▪ ▪ ▪

When Grace stepped out onto the second floor of the bank building parking garage late Tuesday morning, her feet did an uncontrollable little jig, until she caught hold of herself and walked sedately the few remaining yards to her car. The two million dollars in insurance proceeds had been transferred by wire the day before and against her accountant's advice, she'd paid off all the mortgages immediately. She'd always hated debt of any sort, and now that she was out from under Brent, she was getting out from under everything else.

The only decision left was what to do about Wexler, Inc. Grace enjoyed the respect she suddenly commanded, distinctly different from the careful deference paid her as Brent's wife. Now luncheons were with the husbands rather than the wives, talking about politics and business rather than charities and social occasions, and for the present it seemed more stimulating. And she liked getting a paycheck, though in her mind, she didn't really deserve it. All she said was "I agree" to anything Leb Bailey suggested.

There was still a skip in her step when she got to the office and picked up her messages and mail.

"Leb wants to talk to you when you get a chance," Rita said in between calls.

"Tell him to come down whenever he wants."

She dropped her leather satchel by the desk and was looking through the mail when she heard a quick double knock. "Come in, Leb," Grace sang out.

Leb appeared with a file folder and papers under his arm and a frown on his face.

"Why so glum?"

He handed her the folder and documents, then dropped dejectedly into the chair in front of her desk. "We just lost another bid and I can't understand this one any better than the others."

"Which project?"

"A portion of Highway 293 in the Western District. The other contractor has to come from halfway across the state, our money was practically the same, we can start sooner. I just don't understand it." The puzzled look seemed to have become embedded in his face lately. "Maybe it's the uncertainty of what you're going to do that's bothering them even though we guaranteed completion. These were quick emergency deals, over and done within three months."

Her jaw tightened. "It's my fault. I should have decided about the company immediately. What kind of a merger offer did we finally get from Alabama?"

"A draft stock purchase deal came in this morning. I took the liberty of sending a copy to the law firm. To my untutored eye, it's excellent. They'd been talking about just acquiring the assets and didn't want the liabilities, but I was apparently cool enough to make them change their tune. Wexler would become their road division, absorbing all thirty-two employees. They'll buy all your stock. No one loses. All we'd have to do is change the name on the front door."

"How soon do I have to decide?"

"Theoretically, fourteen days, but if you're going to accept, I'd do it sooner rather than later. They'll want to come in and do their evaluation but I think that once the word is out about the sale, the tide will change on these bids. I don't need to tell you that with every lost job, the value of your stock drops. And, beyond that I don't want them to get cold feet if we rack up a pile of losses during the negotiations. They've got a clause in their offer protecting them if the business environment changes substantially."

"You're certain everyone would be okay?"

Leb nodded.

"You too?"

"I think so," Leb answered.

"I'm going to take it, I think. The insurance money came in today. I'd rather not spend my days building roads—hospitals, maybe, if I'm going to build anything."

Leb smiled. "Well, when you open up a new business let me know."

"You'd be the first, I can assure you." Grace flipped open the file folder. "What's the next step?"

"We—I mean—you must respond in writing."

"Do you think the law firm's had time to look it over?"

"Probably," Leb said, heading toward the door. "I'm going to make a few more calls about that bid and see if I can find out where the problem lay."

"Wait..." Grace added. "Here's your mail. By the way, what have you found out about Crimmins and Westerly?"

Leb stopped and turned toward her. "Nothing. Never been a company with that name, as far as I can tell. I don't have any final answers because I keep hitting roadblocks. The post office won't give me information about the P.O. box that was used without some type of search warrant."

"Where did the money go?" she asked.

"To an account at Georgia Guaranty National Bank. They're worse than the post office. At least the post office acknowledged there was such a box number, the bank wouldn't admit they had an account even though I was reading the account number from their own stamps on the canceled check." Leb's fretful grimace returned. "Do you want to know what I think happened?"

Grace put her hands up to halt him, a scowl contorting her face. "Sounds like my husband paid himself an extra million that was never reported to the IRS. Unless I'm missing something."

"That about sums it up."

"Are you and I now party to tax fraud?"

Leb shook his head. "We don't know anything for certain

and we certainly didn't know about it when it happened."

"But now we do know. Aren't we obliged to find out the truth? Or disclose this to someone?"

Leb, clearly uncomfortable and uncertain, muttered, "I don't know what our obligations are—either to the IRS or our purchasers."

"I'm meeting with the accountants soon about our personal tax returns...."

"I don't know that I'd mention it," Leb interjected. "You're talking about a lot of tax liability for something that might never have come to light."

"Have you said anything about this around here?" Grace asked.

"Not a word."

"Then let's keep this between us for the time being," Grace suggested. She knew Leb didn't need the problem exposed any more than she did. "Give me a few days to think this through."

"We've taken improper deductions for business expenses on the corporate returns, too, you know. I just submitted our tax return last week and there were payments to Crimmins during that year," Leb added quietly.

"And if they trace this money to Brent, what will my tax liability be?"

"Nearly a quarter million."

"You already computed it?"

He nodded.

"I wonder what else I don't know," she muttered. She reached for her satchel and pulled out an envelope from the bank. "This was forwarded from the Saragossa address. It's not an account I'm familiar with. One of those bank audit forms."

"I'll handle it." Leb added the letter to his pile and scurried out of the office.

She was looking over the stock purchase offer when she heard Leb's distinctive knock again. "Yes?"

He stepped back in, the bank letter in his outstretched hand. "This must be personal, it's not one of ours."

"Hmmm." She looked at the document, one of those standard forms auditors send out to verify balances in randomly selected accounts. "Sorry. Thanks."

As Leb slipped out the door again, she picked up the phone and called her newly acquired friend in the bank's investment department who had been embarrassingly eager to help her when they'd met earlier that morning.

"Can you tell me about one of my husband's accounts? I just got one of those audit confirmation notices and I've never seen anything about this particular account."

"Certainly, Mrs. Wexler, give me the number."

She read the ten digits off and waited while his computer brought the record up.

"That's closed."

"When?"

"Last December."

Grace drew out a clean piece of notepaper and a pen, fumbling nervously to take the top off. "Can you tell me anything about it?"

"It was a checking account, styled Brent Wexler Committee. Mr. Wexler was the only signatory, statements went to Saragossa, Mississippi. That's about all I can tell you from what's in the computer since there's no current activity."

"It was probably a campaign account, but I need to find out. Can I get copies of statements?"

"Yes, but there's a charge for them."

"Doesn't matter. I'd like to get every statement available."

"Checks, too?"

"You have those?" Grace asked, impressed with the possibilities.

"We keep microfilm copies of every day's business. It takes a lot of time to back track. If I might suggest, let us get the statements first and once you see them, if you want backup, we'll get it then."

"Sounds like a good idea. Why don't you do that for me."

"How soon do you need them?"

"Whenever, the sooner the better," a phrase she'd become all too familiar with lately.

"I'll see what I can do, Mrs. Wexler," the bank officer said. "Thanks so much."

She sat transfixed, every nerve in her body on alert, holding the phone.

"If you'd like to make a call, please hang up...." the telephone company's recorded message droned in her ear. She put the handset down.

Whatever this account was, it couldn't be good news. Not with the way things had been going.

■ ■ ■ ■

The three rows of seats squeezed into the galleries on both sides of the House chamber were packed with lobbyists in suits and ties, feigning rapt attention as they waited for the morning session to adjourn so they could escort their quarry to lunch. Laura stood at the edge nearest the hallway, a spot that allowed her to see the entire chamber and also gave her quick access to the back stairwell if she got a signal from one of the members on the floor.

The debate over the Patrol's appropriation which included the pay raise had gone on far longer than either she or Holden Bowser anticipated. Laura needed a decisive vote from the House to counter the anti-Patrol sentiments stirring in the Senate. Senator Collel was doing a remarkable job of consolidating his forces against her: All nose counts from that end of the Capitol indicated the pay raise was in deep trouble, at best.

"The question has been called," the Speaker of the House of Representatives intoned. "Is there any further debate on this bill?"

A loud chorus of "No's" was shouted from the floor.

"I'll recognize the Gentleman from Ferriday."

"Mr. Speaker," Holden Bowser said. "I believe the appropriation for the State Patrol is ready for a vote and I urge the members of the House to vote in favor. As you vote, don't forget what the State Patrol does for us and for all the citizens of

Mississippi. If we are to have and maintain the quality of law enforcement we have come to expect, we must support these men and women in a most important way: We must give them a living wage. I urge passage." It wasn't until he'd returned to his seat that he dared look up at the gallery and saw Laura. She mouthed the word, "Thanks."

"Will the clerk open the machine?" asked the Speaker.

Laura watched the board light up and then closed her eyes to listen, holding her breath.

"Has everyone voted, has everyone voted?" the Speaker called out, his eyes shifting from the board to the Chamber.

"Voting is closed. With 101 Ayes to 21 Nays, the bill passes."

Her eyes flashed open on the board, looking to see who had been against them. Then she looked back to Bowser. He nodded his head, satisfied.

■ ■ ■ ■

One of Trey's chop-shop cases had led him to a run-down repair station in the Delta. In the late afternoon, he dropped by the Greenwood Patrol substation, talked to the investigators there, and made a few calls, including one to headquarters announcing his plans to stay overnight. He checked into the Ramada Inn, ate dinner with a couple of guys from the Greenwood troop, then went back to his room.

By 8:30 P.M., he'd changed into black cargo pants with a dark turtleneck and a dark jacket, and was headed south to Jackson. At Canton, he detoured southeast to the Natchez Trace and pulled into the turn-off for the old West Florida Boundary. It was empty that late at night and Trey made his final preparations relatively calmly.

He switched his license plate to a Tennessee tag he'd found in a salvage yard that morning, unscrewed two of the extra antennas from his car, and checked his .45 Smith & Wesson. He stuffed thin black leather gloves into one leg pocket, a dark cap into the other, and put the video tape he'd pilfered from

Morgan's in a special pocket he'd added to the lining of his jacket. By 11:00 P.M., he was at his post outside of Morgan's house. The Wednesday night poker game was still going strong. All he could do was wait.

Like a movie theater disgorging its patrons moments after the show was over, all the players left at 11:35 P.M., the entire group ambling down the front walk talking, their voices loud but indistinct in the quiet neighborhood. At the edge of the street, they gathered around one man, his arms waving as he talked until laughter erupted. Then they separated. The chilly spring air made them hurry to their cars with a final round of noisy good-nights, oblivious to the darkened windows of the houses all around them.

Morgan was moving back and forth between the kitchen and the card table.

Surprising. The slob must be sick or something.

A few moments later the lights on the north side of the house were doused. Nope, it wasn't a cleaning binge, just a twinge of conscience.

Now to the bathroom to get out of the costume—first hair, then eyes, then teeth.

Trey slid down in his seat to wait until Morgan turned off the television. The security patrol had never paid any attention to his car but he didn't want to take any chances.

Morgan watched television longer than usual—it was nearly 12:30 when all was dark. Trey waited fifteen minutes more.

12:45. Finally.

Trey pulled his gloves from his leg pocket, checked his weapon one more time and replaced it in his special fanny pack, designed to conceal a gun. The special Velcro opening allowed fast access—rip it back with one hand, grab the gun with the other. Then he slipped out, checking first around the side of the house to be certain the television was off. Using his ever-handy picks, he unlocked the back door, pulled out his gun, and stepped in quietly, closing the door behind him.

The house reeked of cigarette smoke and liquor. His foot

brushed a black garbage bag full of trash, but he settled the load before it clattered onto the kitchen floor. He eased the safety off his gun, ready, listening intently to the unbroken rhythms of snoring from the bedroom. In two steps he was at the hall, instinctively flattening himself along the wall. Three sliding steps and he was at the door to the bedroom. He peered around to see Morgan sprawled across the bed, his toothless mouth wide open, gulping in the stale air.

Watching the profile of the large belly rise and descend with each breath, Trey stopped.

The night table drawer with the gun was closed. Should he try for suicide? The investigations were usually always neater.

Whatever he did, he had to do it quickly.

Two long steps later, he was standing at the side of the bed, his .45 in his left hand pointed at Morgan, as he eased open the night table drawer an inch. It stuck after two inches.

All that goddamn trash he has in there.

Morgan noisily gulped in some more air and shifted in the bed, throwing his right hand out to the side. Trey held his breath as he repositioned his gun, jiggling the drawer from side to side. It moved another inch and stopped again.

Enough of this.

Trey yanked the drawer and pulled it out as Morgan woke up. Morgan's eyes popped open wide at the sight of Trey and then the gun.

"What..." was all he could croak before Trey jammed the .45 into his mouth.

"Shut up, you ignorant carcass."

Trey's right hand felt for the Colt. He brought it up, placed it against Morgan's quivering cheek as he eased the .45 out of the man's mouth.

Morgan choked and moved his right hand.

"Don't move another inch, you goddamn piece of shit," he growled. "You've ruined my goddamn life and now I'm going to goddamn ruin yours."

Trey pushed the Colt into Morgan's mouth. It didn't seem possible for Morgan's eyes to open any wider, but they were almost bulging out of his head, as the man lay frozen in terror.

Trey took one deep breath and pulled the trigger, the noise hardly more than a loud cough.

Morgan's huge frame jerked reflexively, then lay still.

Trey stepped back, a gun in each hand, grunting, his body suddenly quivering with satisfaction and excitement. His breath came in quick pants.

"Gotta set this up right, gotta focus," Trey said to himself as he shook his head to clear it. He stashed his own gun in his pack, and then put the .22 into Morgan's right hand, wrapping the thick fingers across the stock. Then he let the arm go so the gun, held loosely in the limp hand, would clatter to the floor alongside the bed.

He looked around the room, probing for any missing ingredient. He left the drawer of the night table hanging open, stepped to the video player, pulled out whatever was in there, and inserted the homemade porno-tape.

Twenty-three steps later he was at the back door, turning the knob and re-locking the door in one smooth movement. He slid quickly but carefully from shadow to shadow to his car. Then he dove in behind the steering wheel and cranked his engine, looking about for house lights but seeing none.

"That takes care of that bastard," Trey said, talking to himself again. "Less than three minutes, and not a scintilla of evidence left behind."

In another minute, he was out of Morgan's neighborhood. No cars followed him. He floored it as he moved onto the interstate. "Ooo-eee! Should have tied him up like his girlie friends do and slit his gut open. Let him watch himself bleed to death. That's what that dead sonovabitch has been doing to me. I'm goddamn bleeding to death."

Back on the Natchez Trace, Trey passed the first three parking areas, all frequented by Jackson lovers, and pulled in a more isolated spot to change the car tag and put the aerials back up. By 2:30, he was asleep in his motel in Greenwood.

# ELEVEN

Kilgore, Brown, and Dudding, the accounting firm Brent had retained for years, handled both the Wexler, Inc. accounts as well as personal tax return preparation for Brent and Grace. Like the lawyers, Grace had rarely dealt with the accountant directly, except to respond to a tax work-sheet they sent every January asking for documentation on contributions, medical, and her business expenses. Then in April, a messenger arrived with the returns and she dutifully signed on the dotted lines.

Dedereaux Kilgore was an average-sized, cerebral type in his late fifties who always dressed in well-tailored suits, no matter what the occasion. He greeted Grace warmly as she emerged from the elevator into the opulent foyer of their offices.

"Thanks for seeing me, Dede," said Grace, extending her hand to him, "I hated to sound so ignorant over the phone, but as you well know, Brent handled all our affairs."

"That's what we're here for," he said, smiling, ushering her down the hall.

Grace was nervous about her mission, uncertain whether she could get the answers she needed about Brent's puzzling finances without attracting unwanted attention. The arrival of the tax returns for signatures had been the perfect opportunity. As they walked, she pulled the tax return package from her carryall and waved it his way. "I just don't want to sign the tax returns until I know what I'm signing."

"I understand completely. I shouldn't have presumed you would."

He opened a door and showed her into an airy conference room where several brown accordion files were stacked on the far side of the long oval table. Moments after she was seated, a young woman appeared and asked if they wanted anything to drink.

"Just water for me, thank you," Dede said. "Grace? Coffee? Coke?"

"Hot tea, if you have it, please." She smiled at the young woman and then turned to Dede.

"If only I knew what all this meant and what information Brent had provided you, I'd feel better about signing."

"Well, how about if we work through the tax preparation packet that he submitted." He looked through his bifocals at the labels on each folder. "Shall we go page by page?"

"That would be great," Grace said, relieved.

Dede flipped to the first page, a series of questions about financial transactions during the year. Grace stopped him immediately.

"I don't know what he bought or sold this year. No idea."

"But his broker knows," Dede quickly added. "He provided confirmation slips on every transaction."

He flipped to the second page which listed social security numbers and biographical data, muttering, "Standard stuff."

Grace looked perplexed. "You forget that nothing's standard for me. Could I take some of these with me?"

"They're yours. I've been holding them as a courtesy for Brent, but I don't need the backup. We've got the information we require. Just hold on to them in case of an audit."

"This..." she said, patting the file, "will solve several problems."

Dede marched on. "This page covers sources of incomes—the usual salary, investments..."

"Can I assume that he submitted forms from every company that paid dividends and interest?"

"By law, Form 1099 must be sent out by the end of January, and Brent supplied those. You've already given me all the K-1's we were expecting, so I think we're okay. We always check them against previous returns," Dede said. "But all you can do is all you can do."

Grace smiled. "Do you have a list of bank accounts?"

"That's page...," Dede flipped through the packet, "ahh, page seven." He turned it around and slipped it toward her so Grace could read it.

She scanned it, tensing when she didn't find the Brent Wexler Committee account. "Is this a complete list?"

"I believe so. At the very least, it's everything that pays interest."

Grace looked at the accounts while she spoke. "What if I've missed something? You never know what I might find as I dig through the records. Can I amend a return later?"

"Of course. There might be a penalty, if any taxes were due and not paid, but yes, you can amend."

Grace looked down at the papers, not making eye-contact with Dede. "And what if, as I'm going through all these records, I find something in years past that Brent missed, should we amend those years, too?"

"My advice would be to amend only if it's material. It's a lot of trouble and not worth it for pennies."

"What's your definition of material?"

"In your tax bracket, anything that results in a thousand dollars of liability."

She winced. She'd known the answer, but hearing it confirmed brought her predicament home.

"Is something wrong?"

Grace shook her head. "No. There's just so much to handle all at once."

"I know it must be difficult. If it makes you feel any better, it's unlikely you'd be audited," Dede continued. "In a case like this, they'd only assess penalties if there was evidence of willful violations."

The word willful sent adrenaline surging through Grace's system. She started to ask another question and then stopped, smiling as broadly as her nervousness would allow.

■ ■ ■ ■

April had been consistently balmy, an assurance that a long hot summer was ahead. Since the accident reconstructionists had been working in a classroom for a solid week, Jimmie decided it was a perfect occasion for a field trip. He wanted to keep these men interested and learning as much as possible. The reorganization and upgrading of the reconstructionists promised to be a real plus for the Patrol since, in a normal year, there were as many as 80,000 accidents across the state and the Patrol handled a substantial percentage of them.

After lunch, the class met at a salvage yard to look at wrecks. Jimmie had pulled the files on several of the mangled car bodies, ready to quiz the troopers on what they could figure out from the battered heaps. Wexler's car was one of his examples. The troopers walked all around it, feeling for indentations since it was hard to discern that sort of thing without a paint job, sizing up the situation carefully. Jimmie called on Billy Cook, who had consistently been one of the most eager. He supposed that Cook was trying hard to dispel any second thoughts the administration might have about him.

"What do you think?" Jimmie asked.

"One-car wreck. From the shape of the front end it must have hit a tree or something very solid," Cook said. "I suspect he had a full tank of gas at the time of impact to cause a fire to burn long enough to do this much damage. Must have happened in a secluded spot because no one found it to put it out."

"Pretty good," Jimmie answered.

"Frankly," Cook added, "it looks like a torch job to me."

"Why do you say that?" Jimmie asked, curious because the

possibility had never crossed his own mind.

"Not many wrecks get this bad without some help...." Cook said, looking cautiously at Jimmie, "or am I wrong, Colonel?"

"You're absolutely right and normally I'd agree, but there wasn't a shred of evidence indicating foul play and none's emerged since then."

"I didn't mean it *had* to be a torch job, just might be," Cook said, backing off.

"I understand. Tell me, what would you look for?"

"Where the fire started, for one, to see whether extra fuel had been added and ignited."

"Right you are." Jimmie turned to the rest of the troopers. "A guy did that once, right here in Jackson, and it was obvious as hell that the fire started in the passenger area. In fact the fuel line hadn't even been broken." He turned back to Cook. "But in this case, the fire spread from the gas tank forward. Anything else?"

"Ignition. Was the car turned on when the crash occurred?"

"It was."

"And the crash scene itself. Were there any indicators that it was anything but a wreck?"

"None. Went off the road, in the creek, smashed into a fallen tree, and ignited."

"Next I'd check with the family and business."

"Wealthy, upstanding, successful."

"Well then, I'd agree with you." The other troopers chuckled as Cook came full circle back to Jimmie's position.

"But you're absolutely right," Jimmie said, "you should trust your instincts and check into a case fully if something doesn't seem right to you—even if it's just the percentages. Any more questions?"

A tall, slow-talking trooper spoke up. "How would you fake a wreck, Colonel?"

"Depends on what I wanted to accomplish."

"Say you wanted to total the car and collect the insurance."

The trooper next to the questioner elbowed him in the ribs. "Need some quick cash?"

More laughter spread through the group.

Jimmie smiled. "In a case like that, it depends on where you are and what you have to work with. Flat land, hills, water, what time of year. A good hot fire can be a good cover. Got to be air in the passenger area to keep it burning and a little extra accelerant never hurt. But it can't be obvious. That torch job I mentioned a moment ago? The scene, taken as a whole, didn't make sense. The car was on the side of the road, no wreck, no reason for a fire. Everyone was suspicious."

"How'd he get caught?"

"The letters he wrote home did him in," Jimmie explained.

"Not bright."

"No," Jimmie said. "But they usually aren't."

■ ■ ■ ■

The week was ending with a bang. Grace and Leb had spent the day with the Alabama company executives and the combined retinue of lawyers, hashing out details about the stock sale and ending the session with handshakes all around. It had been a nail-biter to the end. Wexler, Inc., had lost two more state bids, but they'd picked up several large private contracts, so they'd guessed the gains had balanced the losses. In sixty days, at most, everything would be final.

She came home to find a large manila envelope from the bank, so thick it almost hadn't made it through the mail slot. The packet contained three years of bank statements on the account called the "Brent Wexler Committee," with a note attached that the rest were off-site at a storage facility and would be sent the following week. It was a non-interest-bearing account with no service charges if the balance was over $1500.

The first statement from January, three years earlier, showed an opening balance of $31,562, which had been drawn down to $1,712 by a series of $9,950 cash withdrawals between February and June. Then the deposits began again, so that the balance had built up to over $400,000 by early July. More withdrawals, mostly cash, came in a frenzy all during late July and August, then stopped. The balance built back up to $100,000 by late October. In the first week of November, the withdrawals began again, always in cash. The activity dropped off to almost nothing for the rest of the year, and remained low for the next two years, until a single cash withdrawal for $6,237.00 in December of the previous year zeroed out the account. The final statement in January of the past year, showed the account closed.

Even though she felt certain it was just campaign stuff, the cash withdrawals astonished her. She racked her brain about the materials Gibbs so insistently requested, but couldn't remember anything relating to a bank account. Finally, she called it quits and went up to her room to take a hot shower.

The water pounded down on her neck as Grace scrubbed away at her scalp. How could she have been Brent's wife and known so little about his affairs?

How long ago had it been that she'd stopped asking what he was doing and where he was going?

If this was anything like the Crimmins and Westerly business, maybe he'd hidden even more money from the IRS. What if they found it?

The business issues, the negotiations, the money, the property—it had all been so exciting, even discovering the cheating had been rather titillating. But now, with this, she was torn between the allure of discovering and the safety of hiding her eyes. It was all getting too close to her, and she wanted the questions to end.

Grace leaned against the tile in the corner of the shower, replaying her last conversation with Brent.

He was going to have dinner and then drive home. Dinner with a client.

Why are you telling me your schedule? she'd asked. Not sure, Brent had said. The ramblings of an aging man.

Dinner. She didn't remember it being on a credit card, he must have paid cash.

But he never paid cash for business expenses. He always

turned in credit card receipts. Grabbing her robe, Grace hurried down to her office and flipped on the desk light, pulling out the file of bills that covered Brent's last expenses.

No dinner on March 5th.

Who was the client?

Where did they eat?

Her finger raced down the credit card statements. $50.00 at the Catfish Corner. That had to be dinner. He'd called her when he landed and it was late in the afternoon. If he was entertaining a client there, two people couldn't eat and drink for $50.00 unless it was an awfully chintzy meal.

Maybe this was the drink bill and the other guy picked up the tab.

Couldn't be, Brent never let anyone else pay.

She sank back in her chair, staring blankly into the windows of the patio doors.

Where were the diamond cufflinks Jody had given him? Where was the Rolex? And who had he bought 46-long clothes for?

In the kitchen, she made herself a cup of chamomile tea, locking the house up while she waited for the kettle to boil. Then she went back up to her room, picked up a book, and read for another hour before she turned out the light and tried to sleep. But nothing worked. She lay wide awake, paralyzed by what she couldn't figure out.

Who could she talk to about all of this? Did she even dare ask anyone?

The exhilaration that should have come with the success of selling Wexler, Inc., her freedom from Brent's control, the incredible amount of money that had insured such a sweet future, everything had been obliterated by the looming suspicions that Brent had left unfinished business all around her.

Grace felt tricked, cheated. She'd been married to a man she didn't know. She'd shown herself to him, exposed every foible and imperfection, but he'd never let her see who he was. Not really.

And he'd left her with a mess.

At least he'd left money to cover it.

Her eyes opened wide. But was that true? Was there enough money to cover the things she still didn't know about?

■ ■ ■ ■

Blake was in the headquarters radio room when Catherine Britton, Director of the Crime Lab, called him. He was engrossed in a test run of the new laptop computers for direct access to the FBI's National Crime Information Center.

"Jackson Police are bringing Reed Morgan's body in," Catherine reported.

"The Transportation Commissioner?"

"Yes. They need an autopsy."

"How'd he die?"

"Bullet through the mouth and brain."

"Who found him?"

"When he didn't show up for a one o'clock meeting, they sent someone over to the house."

"Jesus, was it suicide?"

"I can't say. We don't know enough. The Jackson police are doing the crime scene."

"Where?"

"His house. Some place on Enterprise in Belhaven."

"When's Doc going to do the autopsy?"

"Soon as he gets here. He's teaching a class at the Med School right now. Shouldn't be too long."

"When he comes in, tell him I'll be there, but not to wait."

"Okay. By the way, I called Commissioner Owen first."

"Where was she?"

"At the Capitol."

"What'd she say?"

"I think her exact words were, 'Leave no stone unturned. Morgan was born a scumbag.'"

"That about sums it up," Blake said. "Thanks, Catherine."

Blake hung up the phone then jerked it back and punched in Robert's office number. When he didn't answer, the line

flipped over and rang on Nima's desk in the records room.
"Investigations, Colonel Stone's office."

"Nima, this is Blake. Where's Robert?"

"Raced out of here a minute ago. Said something about the dentist."

"Hmmm." Blake watched a criminal record pop up on the screen, his eyes sparkling with satisfaction. "Look, is Everett there?"

"Yes, sir. He's working away on something."

"Tell him to meet me on the fifth floor. I'm in the radio room, but I'm heading up there now."

"Sure thing."

Blake was nearly at his office when he heard the stairwell door clang shut and Everett emerged, having run, two steps at a time, from the third floor. "Come on in, Everett, and shut the door, please." He dropped his substantial stack of pink message slips on his desk without even glancing through them, and sank into his chair. "Reed Morgan is dead."

Stunned, Everett said, "The Transportation Commissioner?"

Blake nodded.

"When?"

"Jackson police are bringing the body in for an autopsy." Blake half stood up to peer through the west windows at the Medical Examiner's loading dock where a gray suburban with Hinds County Coroner in bold letters on the side, was backing up to the loading dock. "In fact, he's arriving now. What can you tell me about him?"

"Not too much, yet. Laur—the Commissioner—and I are analyzing some of his data now."

"The Commissioner's working on this, too?"

"Yeah. She's doing the highway projects. I'm searching the records on purchases. So far, it looks as though Morgan always paid more than everyone else for his stuff."

"How much more are we talking about?"

"Nothing big that I've seen so far, but I pumped in a bunch of data the other night that may tell a different story, just haven't printed it out yet."

"What about the Commissioner? Has she found anything?"

"She's going backward from the present. It's slow going and she hasn't found anything at all yet. But she's still working."

"Can you be prepared to talk about it in the morning?"

"Sure, and if I can spend the afternoon pulling more records, I can have an even better picture."

"Do that. Make this your first priority."

■ ■ ■ ■

Laura caught up with Vic as he headed toward the Senate and pulled gently on his jacket sleeve. "There's something you need to know," she said quietly so the others in the hall wouldn't hear her.

Vic turned around at the sound of Laura's voice with a shy smile. "Good or bad?"

"Bad, though there may be a thin silver lining. Reed Morgan was found dead in his house."

"Jeez," said Vic, grimacing. "How'd he die?"

"Gunshot through the mouth. That's all I know."

"Damn," Vic said, then looked up and smiled, nodding to someone down the hall, behind Laura. Vic looked back at her. "And the silver lining?"

"Carver gets to appoint his replacement."

"You're starting to think like a politician," Vic said, putting his arm around her in a fraternal sort of way, a terrific cover for his gentle squeeze of her shoulder. "I'm impressed."

"Better get to Carver before someone else tells him," she said, leaning into him to feel the warmth of his body.

"On my way. Keep me posted."

■ ■ ■ ■

Blake got to the autopsy suite after the medical examiner had already started. There were two other observers, both detectives from Jackson Police Department's homicide division, as well as the crime scene specialist from the lab who doubled as the examiner's assistant. A video camera mounted on the wall was filming the proceedings and a microphone hung down over the center of the table to pick up the pathologist's remarks as he proceeded.

Dr. Lawrence Hershel looked over his shoulder as Blake slipped in, his bushy black and gray eyebrows rising over the rims of his glasses to welcome his latest spectator. He'd already finished his external examination and the inspection of Reed Morgan's torso and vital organs. "Just in time for the good stuff, huh, Blake?"

Blake stepped right up to the table, peering all around the eviscerated corpse. "Sorry I'm late, Doc. Find anything so far?"

The pathologist was in his early sixties. A spare man, a bit stooped, his posture shaped by the raised autopsy tables where he'd spent so many hours. He'd been drafted into the medical examiner's position almost against his will, there being no surfeit of board-certified forensic pathologists to handle the autopsies for the state. It would have been much more lucrative to have remained in private practice, but when the previous examiner had retired, Blake had cajoled him into taking the job—at first temporarily—preying on the doctor's sense of civic responsibility.

"The usual excesses of a stressed-out politician—enlarged heart, nearly blocked arteries, ulcer or two, terrible diet, reduced lung capacity," Hershel said. "Nothing that was killing him though."

The pathologist turned back to his work, closely inspecting Reed Morgan's head, turning the skull from side to side to see everything in clear light. The bullet hadn't exited the skull, unlike what happened with bigger weapons. "No bruises, cuts, abrasions, or exit wounds."

He looked in the open mouth. "The bullet entered at the back of the mouth, angled up slightly into the cranial cavity. It was nearly a contact shot so the barrel had to be fully in the mouth when it was fired."

He pulled an examination light down lower to see more clearly. "There's soot on the roof of the mouth. Hand me a swab, will you?" he said to the assistant.

After taking a sample, Hershel stepped back to assess the entry angle and moved his hands, simulating a right-handed person putting a gun into his own mouth. "Was this guy left or right handed?" Hershel asked, inspecting Morgan's hands. "I can't tell for certain."

The detectives shook their heads, not knowing the answer.

"I need to know," Hershel said.

One of the men quickly moved toward the door, leaping at the chance to get away from the surgery.

Hershel pulled the skin back from the skull and opened it, cutting through the bone with vibrating electric saw specially designed for that procedure. He removed the brain, examining it carefully.

"The path of the bullet is consistent with a small-caliber pistol—like the .22 found at the scene." He was picking carefully around the spongy matter, looking for the bullet's final resting place. Look..." he motioned to Blake and the remaining detective who held back. "It ricocheted off the skull and moved all around like a little knife, tearing everywhere, trying to find a way out."

He followed the sinuous path, teasing apart the brain tissue as he went. "Here it is." With his gloved fingers, he picked out the bullet, a flattened disc not more than a quarter inch in diameter, holding it up for everyone to see. He scratched his mark on the base, the one area not needed for ballistics testing, and dropped it into the evidence envelope that the assistant held out for him.

The door opened from the hall and the detective stepped back in. "Morgan was right-handed."

"Who says so?" Blake asked, never taking his eyes off what Hershel was doing.

"His secretary. Another detective's down there questioning everyone."

"Well, that fits...." Hershel said. "The angle's consistent

with a right-handed person pulling the trigger." He looked up at his assistant. "As a precaution though, we need to test the hands, even though with a rim fire gun, there won't be much gunshot residue."

Hershel put his instruments down and stepped back from the table, taking a break. "Gentlemen, unless something else turns up, I'd say this was suicide."

"Has to be?" Blake asked.

"Not has to be, but there's nothing to indicate homicide. A contact wound, in the mouth, no signs of struggle or forced entry to the house. I don't have any reason to think otherwise."

"But could it have been homicide?" Blake pressed.

"Of course it could—you know that as well as I do." Hershel looked suspiciously at Blake. "You know something about this that I don't?"

"Nah. Just my suspicious nature."

"My report won't get typed up until in the morning. If you find out something I ought to know before then, let me hear it."

"I will."

■ ■ ■ ■

Robert was pulling into the parking lot when Blake got to the top of the steps that climbed the hill from the Medical Examiner's office and Crime Lab to headquarters, a little out of breath.

Blake jerked his thumb over his shoulder toward the morgue. "Reed Morgan died, in his bed, at home, last night after midnight, .22 in the mouth. Doc says it's suicide, but I think not."

"God, a guy leaves to go to the dentist and all hell breaks loose."

"Anything wrong?" Blake asked.

"Lost a filling," said Robert, waving his hand to dismiss that topic. "Where did Morgan live?"

"Right over there on Enterprise, in Belhaven," Blake said, pointing southwest of headquarters. "I told the Commissioner

I'd check on it myself. Wanna come?"

"Sure."

"She wants to know as much as possible, as soon as possible. With Morgan, it was never simple."

An unmarked Jackson police car sat outside Morgan's residence, blocking the driveway. Yellow crime scene tape blocked access to the house and yard. Blake and Robert stepped across the line and walked up to the back door, careful not to touch anything.

"Anyone home?" Blake called through the open door.

"Who's there?" came a voice from somewhere in the house.

"Blake Coleman, Robert Stone—State Patrol."

Lt. Garvey McMillan, Jackson Police Department, came to the door, smiling, his nearly bald head gleaming. "Slumming it?"

"Hey, McMillan. What's happening?" said Robert. They'd both worked with McMillan over the years. He was as good a homicide detective as either knew.

"Same ol', same ol. Little murder, little suicide."

"I just came from the Medical Examiner's and that's what he allowed," Blake said.

"Which?" McMillan asked.

"Suicide," Blake said, drinking in the scene with practiced eyes.

"Hmmm," McMillan muttered.

"That is unless you find something else to tell him about."

"I won't. There's no forced entry, no sign of struggle. But there's no note, either. I'm working it like a homicide, though God knows I don't have time to. We've got plenty of damn-sure homicides piling up downtown."

McMillan swept his hand past the dining table. "Had a poker game last night."

"Who was playing?" Blake asked.

"Don't know for sure yet, but his secretary said he'd called Senator Collel to make certain the game was on," McMillan said. "As soon as I get some help, I'll run him down."

Blake and Robert exchanged quick glances. Gabriel Collel

in their sights. How fortuitous.

"We could handle that for you, if you want," Blake offered. "I practically live down there, lobbying on this pay bill thing."

"If you've got the time," McMillan said.

"You're covered."

"Have you talked to his wife?" Robert asked.

"Not yet, but I heard she wasn't exactly broken up about it when she heard the news. They hadn't lived together in years."

"Can we look around?"

"Be my guest. You want the case?"

They shook their hands. "No, no, no. Just wanted to see the scene."

Robert walked ahead tentatively, looking over the kitchen counters as he went. "Kinda sloppy housekeeper, wasn't he?"

"That's a nice way of putting it."

"Body found in the bedroom?" Blake asked.

"Yup. To the left off the hall."

Robert was careful to stay on the paper that had been spread over the carpeting.

"Check out the lava lamp," called McMillan.

When they got to the bedroom, they couldn't miss the red globs oozing up and down the lamp by the bed. Robert looked past the bed and dresser to the closet. He walked over, keeping his hands in his pockets. "This guy might've been short on dusting but he knew his clothes."

"How can you tell that without checking the labels?" Blake said, stepping into the room.

"Any decently dressed guy can spot quality," said Robert, ragging a bit on Blake.

"Give it a rest, Stone," said Blake, coming over to the closet. He looked at the labels and sizes. "Too bad he was so much bigger than you. You might've been able to make a deal for the whole shooting match. But you can't alter 46-longs to fit you, no way."

"I ain't into dead men's clothes," Robert said. "Even good ones."

Blake looked at the stacks of videos all around the television and stepped back to the door. "McMillan," he called out.

"Yo," came from the kitchen.

"Anyone looked at the videos yet?" he called.

"I did that first. Check it out."

Blake pushed in the tape and turned on the VCR and the TV. The tigress jumped into action across the splayed figure of Morgan, who was straining at his bonds.

"A little more active than when I saw him earlier today," Blake said. "Who's the woman?" he called out to McMillan.

McMillan appeared at the door. "How the hell should I know? Never get a look at her face. Not on any of them."

"There are more?" asked Robert.

"Bunch of 'em. But this was the only one where he's tied up. And that's all fake. Look at the ropes. He could slip out of those so easily. Musta gotten off on watching himself because you never see the woman's face."

"Where could this have been taped?" asked Blake.

"Not here, that's for certain," said McMillan. "Looks like a No-Tell Motel. Could be anywhere."

"Not all those places have cameras in the ceiling," Blake said.

"A little overweight, wasn't he?" said Robert.

Blake started to switch it off. "Is there any reason to watch more?"

"Not that I saw. I'm gonna take all of them and see if there are any identifiers at all. I don't think it has anything to do with this, though. It's pretty tame stuff."

They wandered around the house a little while longer but found nothing more of interest. McMillan was in the kitchen rummaging through the trash. "We're headed down town, Mac. I'll be back in touch as soon as I know something about the poker game."

"Thanks for the help."

"Sure thing," Robert said.

As soon as they were out of earshot, Robert asked, "What's your problem with it being a suicide?"

"Remember that Transportation stuff Everett was working

on?"

"Yeah."

"Well, his theory seems to be checking out. Looks like Morgan might have been on the take."

"That does complicate things. Why didn't you tell Mac?"

"The Commissioner's working on it, too, and she's the one who sees all the angles on that stuff. Besides, Mac said he was working it like a homicide. We can tell him later if we've got something to say."

"Now where do we find Senator Collel?"

"We can start at his office."

Blake picked up the microphone. "A-1, Jackson."

"A-1, go ahead," the dispatcher answered.

"Page A-Adam and tell her to meet me and Colonel Stone at the Capitol."

"Will do."

■ ■ ■ ■

Laura was standing under the portico when Blake and Robert drove in, cornered by a Capitol police officer who wanted to be on the State Patrol but had failed the physical twice. She walked over to the car to escape him.

"Anything new?" she asked.

"Yes and no," said Blake. "He liked kinky sex."

"How kinky?"

"Not too. He liked to watch. The interesting thing was he was playing poker last night."

"With who?"

"Your friend, Senator Collel."

Laura smiled. "Light at the end of the tunnel."

"My thoughts exactly," Blake said. "We've decided not to overwhelm him, so only one person is going to talk with him. Robert got the short straw."

"I happen to know he likes my kind just about as much as he likes you, Commissioner," Robert said, grinning.

"Enjoy," said Laura, her eyes twinkling, "I always do." Then she looked at Blake. "I'll tell the Governor."

■ ■ ■ ■

"Senator Collel?" Robert called out tentatively, after knocking on the partially opened door to his office at the capitol.

"Come in," ordered a voice from the other side of the glass. Robert poked his head in.

"Yes?" the silvery-headed man asked brusquely. His extremely erect posture was evident even while seated in a chair.

"I'm Robert Stone with the State Patrol." He handed the senator his card.

"I know who you are," Collel said, not even glancing down. "If you've come about the pay package, you can save your breath."

"That's not why I'm here, though I hope we'll have your support...."

"You won't, not while that woman's out there," Collel barked back.

"I'm sorry you feel that way."

"Get on with your business then."

"I've come to talk to you about Reed Morgan."

"What about Commissioner Morgan?" Collel said, emphasizing Morgan's title as though he was someone who deserved the honor. "Does this concern his death?"

"Yes, sir," Robert said, taking a seat even though Collel hadn't offered one. "We understand from his secretary that he'd called you concerning a card game."

"He did," Collel said with the beginnings of a more cooperative tone.

"Did you play?"

"Yes."

"Where?"

"At Morgan's."

"Who else was there?"

"The State Auditor," Collel said, "the Lieutenant Governor,

and the Chief Justice."

"How late did you stay?"

"I was at home, in bed, by midnight."

"Everyone left at the same time or did anyone stay later?"

"We all left at once."

"And was it a friendly game?"

"It always is," Collel said.

"Did Mr. Morgan win?"

Collel shook his head. "He never does."

"How high were the stakes?"

Collel shifted in his chair as he spoke. "There's never more than a couple hundred dollars in the game. We have a three hundred dollar limit on how much a person can lose."

"I see," Robert said. "Did you notice anything about him? Was he cheerful? Despondent?"

"He seemed quite fine to me," Collel said. "And I've known him a long time."

"Do you know any reason why he might have taken his own life?"

"None whatsoever. Last person on earth I'd suspect of suicide."

Robert looked up from the notes he was taking. Collel's scowl had disappeared. "I guess that's all, Senator," he said, standing up. "I appreciate your help."

Collel stood also, extending his hand. "If you need anything more, you know where to find me." His voice was definitely more pleasant.

"Thank you, sir."

Blake was at the rotunda rail when Robert emerged. "The Lieutenant Governor, the State Auditor, the Chief Justice, and Collel were playing poker with Morgan that night. Regular game, they all left at the same time, Morgan wasn't depressed in the least even though he lost. Apparently, he always loses."

"I guess we'd better verify that. How about I talk to the Lieutenant Governor and you find the Auditor?"

"Should I mention anything about the audit?"

"Not now," Blake said. "In fact, all I'm going to do with the

Lieutenant Governor is ask him about the game. I want to leave us room to go back later."

■ ■ ■ ■

Trey watched Grace drive out shortly before 7:00 P.M., dressed for the evening. Remembering how Brent always had to beg her to go out, he doubted she'd be gone long. He quickened his steps, wanting to try the alarm as soon after she departed as possible, just in case she'd changed the code since the last time he'd been there with Brent. If he set it off, the alarm company might think she'd set it incorrectly and not be suspicious.

The red light switched to the nice green glow of go as soon as he tapped in the last digit. He moved quickly from room to room, discovering that Brent's room off the patio was now Grace's office. He closed the blinds as he entered so he couldn't be seen by anyone wandering onto the property. From Grace's deep blue upholstered swivel chair, he perused what was at her fingertips. Four stacks of papers were held down by millefiori glass paperweights: a batch concerning the Cancer Clinic, a pile of current bills, what looked like tax information, and lastly, correspondence. He flipped through the letters, finding a mix of condolences and thank yous, but nothing else. Grace's calendar, open on the middle of the desk, listed appointments scattered over the entire month of April and then two weeks blocked out for Florida.

Her file cabinets weren't locked, and the one to the far right was filled with folders marked "BW" and a subtopic. The probate file bulged with copies of the legal documents and court orders. The insurance file was deceptively thin, containing the policy, a claim for both Brent's life insurance as well as the auto insurance on the wrecked car, and a transcript of her statement to the company. Slipped in the back, however, was a notice of electronic transfer of the proceeds from the life insurance policy one week earlier.

Two million from the insurance for his handiwork. Jesus. And the farm, the hunt club, the business, this house. The damned bitch got everything. All because he'd orchestrated Brent's departure.

In a folder marked "Brent," were copies of store invoices, invoices to Wexler, Inc. from a company named Crimmins and Westerly, and photocopies of bank statements for something called the Brent Wexler Committee. Estate stuff, surely.

Trey flipped on the computer but realized he didn't know enough to browse her files without leaving a trail. He turned it off and left the room, opening the blinds to leave everything as it had been.

He walked back to the garage door. Counting his steps and timing the whole thing, he moved from the alarm key pad, through the kitchen, into the hall, up the stairs, into her bedroom, over to her bed. Forty-five seconds, being very cautious.

Her dresser, clothes, and accessories were in a huge walk-through closet between the bedroom and the adjoining bath. Right in the middle of the dresser, in plain view, were the jewelry boxes, filled with necklaces, bracelets, and earrings. He reset his stopwatch and acted out every move he would make, from entering the house, to killing Grace, to filling his fanny pack with as much jewelry as possible. Then down the stairs, through the kitchen, out the back door, and disappearing.

Two minutes. Very do-able.

He'd made her rich, but he wasn't about to let her enjoy it.

■ ■ ■ ■

"I wish this evening wasn't ending," Vic said, as they turned into Laura's driveway. The concert had been great, the dinner was delicious, and they'd managed to talk about their work while easily sidestepping the troublesome issues where they were at odds. He reached toward her and softly stroked her cheek. He was struggling to not rush her.

"Me, neither," Laura answered quietly, kissing his hand. "I'd invite you in but I've got to get the babysitter home. I promised he'd be back before midnight."

Vic looked at his watch. "Ten minutes to spare. He can go

with me."

She took her time getting out, and Vic came around to hold the door.

"So chivalrous."

"Hardly," he said, losing some of his resolve and wrapping his arms around her for a long deep kiss. "It was a subterfuge," he whispered when he finally pulled away.

"You can hold my door any time."

Frank, Will's favorite sitter, was watching a videotape of *Close Encounters of the Third Kind*, and Will was asleep, sprawled across the couch.

"I tried everything I could think of to get him to sleep in his bed," Frank whispered.

"It's just fine," Laura whispered back, smiling at her son in his blissful sleep. Ranger rushed to her side, then to Vic's, her tail wagging furiously. Laura pulled out her wallet and counted out several fives. "Vic's going to give you a ride home."

"I can walk," Frank said, reaching for his jacket.

"No, it's too chilly and late. I'd feel better knowing you got home safely."

"I insist," Vic added, kneeling down to pet the Retriever.

Frank stuffed the dollars in his pocket with an acquiescent shrug. "Anytime, Mrs. Owen."

Laura looked quickly at Vic, then back to Frank. "I'll call you."

Vic held the door open for Frank, and as the young man stepped outside, Vic reached for Laura's hand. "I enjoyed it. Sometime soon again?"

Laura nodded, stepping toward him on tiptoes with a gentle kiss. Vic brought his arm around her and began another long kiss.

Then Will sneezed behind them.

Laura pulled away quickly, practically pushing Vic out the door.

"I'll talk to you tomorrow maybe," Vic whispered meekly. "Monday for certain."

When Laura turned around, Will was staring, albeit sleepily, at her. Her heart skipped at least one beat, maybe three.

"Let's get you to bed, my little man," she said as evenly as possible, not knowing what he'd seen.

She moved toward the couch but Will darted toward the hall, with Ranger at his heels.

"Will!" Laura called after him, alarmed.

When she reached his room, he was already in his bed, turned away from her, with the covers pulled over his head. Ranger was desperately trying to get her hind leg up onto the bed.

Laura lifted the puppy up, then sat down beside her son. "Will, Sweetheart," she said, stroking his back.

"Why were you kissing Mr. Vic?" came a small voice from under the covers. Ranger was settling herself right next to Will, pawing at the lump that was his head.

Laura took a very deep breath. "Because Mr. Vic is a very special person."

Will didn't say anything, nor did he move the covers.

"Sweetheart, I like Mr. Vic a lot. And when people like each other a lot, sometimes they kiss."

"Are you and Mr. Vic going out again?"

"I don't know," Laura answered very solemnly, her skin prickly with fear. She started to ask, "Would that be okay?" but swallowed the question, not wanting to give Will the impression that he had a veto over her plans. She eased back the covers and he let them go, uncovering a very troubled face.

"Do you still love Daddy?"

"I'll always love Daddy. Always."

Will didn't say anything in response.

"But he isn't here with us anymore," Laura added.

"Do you still love me?"

"More than anything." She leaned over and wrapped her arms around him for a hug. "You can only go out with Mr. Vic if Frank can stay with me," Will said emphatically.

"Okay," Laura said, quietly breathing a huge sigh of relief. "I'll try to arrange that."

When Will was finally asleep again, Laura flipped on her computer, too keyed up to go to bed.

**NAOMI:**

**I'M PARALYZED. VIC BROUGHT ME HOME TONIGHT AND KISSED ME GOOD NIGHT AND WILL SAW US. HE RAN AWAY FROM ME. I GOT WILL TO TALK ABOUT IT, BUT I DON'T KNOW WHAT HE REALLY THINKS. I'M SCARED AND I'M EXCITED. I DON'T KNOW IF WILL IS READY FOR THIS. I DON'T KNOW IF I'M READY FOR THIS.**

**LAURA**

# TWELVE

When Everett, Blake, and Robert arrived for their meeting in the morning, Laura's door was opening. A stocky man no more than forty wearing brown tweeds was leaving, his face serious, his manner nervous. The man seemed to recognized Everett and scurried away with only a perfunctory, "Good morning."

"Well, it's never dull around here," Laura remarked, taking a place around the coffee table where the morning paper lay open with its splashy coverage of Reed Morgan's death. "That fellow who just left was the IRS agent who was auditing Reed Morgan."

Everett snapped his fingers. "That's why he looked familiar. He's the guy who came to ask for old audits."

"Ahhh," said Laura. "He read the paper this morning and thought he should donate some off-the-record information in confidence, and stay out of the Jackson Police Department investigations."

"Damn," said Blake, exasperated. "Wish I'd known. There are some things I'd liked to have asked him."

Robert shifted, uncrossed and recrossed his legs, clearly

impatient to get on with it. "What did he tell you?"

"What are those three 'B's' y'all talk about? Booze, bimbos, and bucks? Or is it three 'G's'? Gambling, girls, and gin. Seems as how Morgan had a steady stream of lady friends in addition to Mrs. Morgan. She lives at the home place outside Vicksburg, and he stayed here. Always had lots of extra money. I can't remember whether the IRS guy mentioned booze or not."

"Did you tell him the autopsy results?"

"He already knew."

"Word travels fast. What'd he think?"

"He doubts it was suicide. He'd recently told Morgan that there were taxes due, but they weren't proceeding criminally. Morgan was overjoyed, he had plenty of money to cover the tax bill, his problems were over. The IRS guy thinks Morgan got caught with his pants down."

"By whom?"

"That, he didn't know exactly, though he has some suspects. For years Morgan has been paying the rent on apartments for his lady friends. In fact, he's paying part of the rent for two different women right now. The agent thought Mrs. Morgan knew all about it, but that she wasn't going to stop him. Morgan was her meal ticket."

"Did he tell you who the girlfriends were?"

Laura handed Blake a plain piece of paper with two names typed on it.

"Chickenshit." Blake read the names and handed the paper to Robert.

"At least he spoke up," Robert chided. He called Nima and instructed her to get every record she could on the two women, including driver's license photographs.

There was a knock on the door, and they all turned to see Jimmie Anderson poke his head in.

"Sorry..." Jimmie said instantly and started to close the door.

"Come on in," Laura called out. "We're talking about Reed Morgan."

"Know him well," Jimmie said.

"You do?"

"If you ride his roads enough, you get to know the guy." Jimmie pulled another chair into the circle.

"I just had a visitor, an IRS auditor who doesn't think Morgan's suicide was necessarily suicide."

Everett sat forward to get Laura's attention. "Where did he think the extra money came from?"

"The golden touch," Laura answered. "Apparently, he never made a bad investment. Consistently turned one thousand dollar stakes into huge profits. Over and over again. The agent didn't know who Morgan was getting advice from, but he wants to find the guy and hire him himself."

"What about the Transportation Department?" asked Everett. "Did he suspect any kickbacks?"

"From the work he did, he didn't see any evidence of that."

"Did you contradict him?" Everett inquired.

"I didn't say a thing. I thought we ought to all talk first."

"Well, as we both know, he's wrong," Everett said with an edge of contempt for the man's work. "Or lazy."

"Do you have something more since we last talked?" Laura said.

"I've been working nonstop since yesterday."

"That explains the dark circles under your eyes."

Everett nodded. "Two hours sleep." He pulled papers out of an expandable file folder and handed two lists to each of them. Jimmie looked over Robert's shoulder at his.

"The top one is a list of suppliers who seem to sell items to the Western District at a higher price than they sell the same item to counties. I emphasize the word "seem" because I don't have enough documentation to be absolutely certain."

"And this second sheet?" Robert asked, flipping the page over.

"Those are approximate per-mile costs for each of the districts—Western, Central, and Eastern, taking everything spent and dividing it by highway miles. Western is way out of line, but, like I said, these figures are rough."

There was long silence as they all flipped back and forth

between the pages. "Do you know anything about these vendors?" Blake asked.

"Not much."

"We'll start digging a little bit."

"Have you got anything more?" Everett asked Laura.

"Nothing yet," Laura said. "I've gone back through thirteen years, with seven more to go and there are no obvious patterns with the highway projects. At least nothing I can see from the gross figures in the annual reports."

"Which seven are left?" Blake asked.

"The first seven. Ancient history almost."

"How long will it take you?"

"A couple of nights."

"Need some help?" Everett offered.

"You stick with what you're doing and let me slog through what I've got left."

■ ■ ■ ■

A number of faces turned as Blake and Robert took seats in the left Senate gallery. Laura had sent them to monitor the debate, fearing her own appearance would only enrage Collel and provoke him to even greater heights of advocacy in his campaign against her.

But with or without her, Collel was in rare form as he moved to amend the State Patrol's appropriation and remove the pay raise provision. After handling every conceivable question from the floor, he closed his remarks quite simply: "I was opposed to teachers getting a raise when other employees didn't, and I warned you then about just what is happening today. And the disparity between our teachers and those of the surrounding states was even more dramatic than the situation that confronts us with the police. We are setting an horrendous precedent, gentlemen and ladies. You must vote to amend this appropriation and strike the pay raise."

Robert leaned toward Blake. "So much for softening him up."

The Secretary of the Senate began the roll call. Since the Senate had steadfastly refused to switch to voting machines, all fifty-two senators had to be polled separately. It didn't seem hopeful, hardly anyone would look at them.

Moments after the final vote was cast, the Secretary handed the tally sheet to the Lieutenant Governor.

"On the motion to amend and strike the pay raise, the Ayes have 28, and the Nays have 24," the Lieutenant Governor announced. "The motion passes and the pay raise is stricken from the appropriation."

Collel smiled proudly, his eyes sweeping the galleries and coming to rest on Robert and Blake.

"That son of a bitch," Blake muttered.

Immediately, Senator Grady Kellogg jumped to his feet, his hand up. "Mr. President."

"The Gentleman from Heywood is recognized," said the Lieutenant Governor.

"I move the matter for reconsideration," Senator Kellogg said.

Blake leaned toward Robert and whispered, "That's the guy Rankin drove home. Found him knee-walking drunk, trying to drive."

"So noted," the Lieutenant Governor said.

"We've got the weekend to find three people to switch," said Blake.

"Two would give us a tie."

"But I don't trust the Lieutenant Governor to break it in our favor," Blake said. "Maybe now's a good time to reopen the Morgan matter—gives me one hell of an entrée."

"And I'll get Rankin up here to work with Kellogg on finding the votes."

■ ■ ■ ■

When Trey saw Grace on television handing over a check for half a million dollars to the Medical Center, he knew the perfect moment had arrived even if he hadn't done enough background work on her habits and schedule. After dark the next night, Grace's car was parked in the drive instead of in the garage. Trey figured there was a chance she was going out, so he set up in the bushes and waited.

And he was right. Wearing gray slacks and a black wool sweater, suitable for an evening out, Grace left the house shortly after Trey had eased into the shadowy recesses of the garden. Not taking any chances that it might be just a quick run to the grocery store or for carry-out, Trey pulled on his gloves and left his perch immediately. He entered the house and reset the alarm behind him, then went directly to the door that led from the breakfast nook to the terrace to unlock it.

But it was already unlocked. What a trusting fool she was.

He surveyed the place quickly. Grace's office was cluttered with papers, but the rest of the first floor was neat as a pin. Upstairs, the only room that looked used at all was her bedroom. The closet door, not five steps from the main door to the room, stood open, and a few clothes were strewn about, the hurried preparations for leaving, he supposed. The jewelry box was open. He started jamming pieces in, but there wasn't enough room in the extra pocket of his special fanny pack.

Crap. I don't know shit about jewelry.

He spread everything out and picked what he thought were the best pieces and left the rest in disarray across the top of the dresser. It would look like a burglar interrupted in the act.

Trey crept toward the window and sat in the darkness, out of sight, waiting.

Game's almost up, thought Trey. This bitch is not going to get to enjoy her goddamn money—the money *I* got for her.

If I can't have what I want, she can't either.

Two and half hours later, Trey watched Grace pull into the garage and heard the garage doors rattle shut. Home for the night.

He moved from the window to the bedroom door, pulling on a ski mask that he'd altered so that his ears were partially exposed and he could hear better. He listened for movement downstairs.

Grace was opening the back door. Then silence. She must be tapping in the code to disarm the alarm. He watched the red light on the bedroom alarm keypad switch to green.

But it stayed green. She wasn't resetting it immediately.

Trey's breathing quickened as he considered the possibilities. The garage door was down, so most likely she wasn't going out again. But why didn't she rearm?

Maybe she's going for a walk, or out on the patio.

He exhaled slowly. Maybe she's just not going to bed right away.

Trey heard her quick steps across the entry floor, and then it was quiet. Where was she? In the living room or on the stairs? He reached down and pulled a short hunting knife from the sheath strapped above his ankle. His pulse quickened when he caught the rustle of Grace's clothing—the slither of the silk lining in her slacks—as she mounted the stairs. He counted backward, estimating her steps. Fifteen, fourteen, thirteen, landing, twelve, eleven, ten. He gripped the knife ever tighter. Nine, eight, seven. He raised his knife. Six, five.

Then the lights of another car played against the far wall of the bedroom. Grace stopped on a stair, nearly at the top.

Someone's coming.

Trey looked around the room. There were only two windows on the second floor where he could drop to the roof of the garage and then down to the ground. Both were in guest bedrooms across the landing.

Grace was moving again, but descending

The car was swinging around the circle. It would stop at the front door.

There was still time to kill Grace and get out the back door.

This bitch is not going to get away from me, Trey thought.

He took a deep breath, and lunged around the corner to the stairs.

Grace was three steps from the bottom on a small landing. He saw her head turn as he started down. She screamed, but not loud enough to be heard outside. In the next instant she was racing for the front door.

Shut up, shut up, Trey thought as he clambered down the stairs.

The car had stopped. People were getting out. Grace was pawing at the intricate antique lock, now whimpering rather than screaming. Trey vaulted the railing of the final three steps.

You're gonna die, right now, you rich little twat.

The first car door slammed as Trey's feet hit the floor.

The bolt slid back and Grace jammed down the lever to open the door.

He was raising his knife when he heard the second car door close and footsteps approaching the front of the house.

Too late, damnit.

Trey turned and raced through the kitchen to the door he'd left unlocked and sprinted into the darkness.

Grace flung open the door and ran from the house toward Sarah Carver and her security guard, Master Sergeant Julia St. Clair. "He has a knife! He's in there!"

"Where?" Julia asked, pulling her gun from the shoulder holster under her jacket, and bolting up the steps.

"He ran toward the back," Grace gasped. "He has a knife."

"Call 911," Julia commanded, "and stay out here."

Sarah fumbled in her purse for her cell phone and jabbed in the number.

Within minutes the house was surrounded by police officers. While two searched every inch of the house, the others fanned out into the neighborhood on foot and in their patrol cars. The crime scene unit arrived, dusting for fingerprints at the back door and in Grace's closet where she'd discovered most of her jewelry was missing. Julia had alerted the Mansion, and Robert arrived shortly thereafter. He'd just come in from running and was still in his sweats. At his suggestion, they contacted the security company for instructions on reprogramming the alarm code.

In the kitchen, Grace picked through the remaining pieces of jewelry with Sarah's help, trying to make a list of what was missing.

"And you're certain the alarm was on when you returned?" Robert asked.

"Absolutely. I turned it off but didn't reset it because Sarah and Julia were on their way."

"How does the system work?"

"It's an old system with contacts on every door and window. You can't get in the house without setting it off, and I can't set it to leave without every door and window being shut, which drives me crazy. There's a closet for silver and other valuables that's always armed. You have to shut that off separately."

"Who knows the code?"

"Only me. And Fannie."

"The maid?"

Grace nodded. "She's worked for me for twenty years."

"What's the code?"

"My daughter's birthday."

"Your daughter?"

Sarah interrupted. "Jody died ten years ago."

"I'm sorry," Robert said. "Does the alarm company have the code?"

"They might. I don't really know. Brent was the one who had the system put in, but except for the rare false alarm, I don't have much to do with them."

"Tell me about the man again."

"Dark clothing, ski mask with the ears partially cut out."

"Anything unusual about the ears?"

"Couldn't see much. I didn't focus on them."

"Did he have anything in his hands?"

"No, except the knife."

"A long knife?"

"Not really. Kind of thin, about eight inches maybe." Grace stood up and went to the knife rack and pulled out a filet knife. "About like this."

"And no gun."

"I didn't see one. He had a pack on his waist."

"I'll talk to the alarm people. My guess is that someone stole the code from their files or just guessed—children's birthdays are really high on the list of most often used codes. Must've heard about your gift to the hospital and figured you'd have lots of valuable things around here. He couldn't have been here long because that sort goes for the jewelry first and you interrupted him."

"But why was the alarm still on when I got home?"

"I can't figure that one out yet," Robert said.

"Grace, why don't you spend the night at the Mansion," Sarah offered. "Gibbs is out of town, so it's no imposition. And it's safe."

"That's awfully nice of you. But if I leave now, I'll lose my nerve forever."

Robert looked at the Jackson Police lieutenant. "Do you have any spare cars you could park here for the night?"

"Probably so. Several of these guys are going off duty. One of them could leave his car here and get it in the morning."

"And I'll see if I can get a Patrol car, too," Robert added. Then he looked down at the jewelry. "What did he take?"

"Mostly junk. He took several good pieces, but left some of the best ones." She held out a palm full of earrings, studded with diamonds, rubies, and emeralds. "Must have been in a hurry."

Robert nodded.

■ ■ ■ ■

By 10:30 P.M., Laura had finished her data entry for the night. She lacked only the first two years that Morgan was in office and she hadn't noticed anything startling along the way. But then again, she hadn't been paying much attention either. Laura had discovered that listening to rhythm and blues with headphones while she punched in numbers dramatically increased her productivity. She hit the print button to generate a report in descending order by percentage of cost overrun, and headed to her bathroom to wash her face and brush her teeth.

Ranger padded out of Will's room when she passed back by,

interested, as always, in a biscuit. She snatched the pages off the printer tray and proceeded to the kitchen and the tin of dog treats, dropping the report on the counter to free her hands to pry off the lid. Ranger sat down next to her, with full attention focused on the treat can, her tail swishing a little arc on the floor behind her.

Laura's eyes caught the top of the page just as the lid came free. Wexler dominated the entries.

She brought the biscuit tin down with a sharp click.

There was a 45 percent overrun, and a 42 percent, then a 71 percent. Only one other contractor showed up among the first twenty entries.

Ranger, still waiting anxiously for her biscuit, repositioned herself closer to Laura, eyes roving constantly between the tin and Laura's hands.

Something was wrong. Maybe too much Otis Redding during data entry.

Laura started toward her office when Ranger let out a little bark, breaking the silence of the quiet house. The Retriever's eyes were still trained on the biscuit tin, periodically stealing a glance at Laura.

"Did I forget you, Ranger?" Laura asked, turning to the can. Ranger snatched the biscuit, slobbering on Laura's fingers in the process, and trotted off to a private corner in the living room to devour it.

Laura was printing out a second report in entry order when the phone rang.

"Commissioner?" said Robert.

"Hi, Robert."

"Sorry to disturb you."

"That's okay. I'm working on the highway contract stuff. Something up?"

"I thought you ought to know that the First Lady went out with Grace Wexler this evening and when they returned to Mrs. Wexler's home, there was a burglar inside who threatened Mrs. Wexler with a knife. He escaped but with all the radio traffic, the media picked up on it and it will probably be in the paper tomorrow."

"Did he take much?"

"Jewelry. And not all of it. Mrs. Wexler must have interrupted him."

"But everyone's okay?"

"Yes. Julia St. Clair was with the First Lady. Julia went after the guy but he'd disappeared."

"I guess it's not safe to announce you have an extra half million bucks to give away."

"My thoughts exactly. But in this case, the burglar knew the alarm code. Might have been someone from the security company."

"I'm sure that's happened a time or two."

"Anyway, just thought you should know. The First Lady called the Governor, because we didn't want him to hear it from someone else. We've decided to park a car at the house for the night."

"Good idea. Anything else going on?"

"That's about it for now."

Laura went back to her papers, and pulled the reports closer to compare the numbers. Except for a couple of minor transposition errors—nothing that would significantly affect the results—the report was correct.

She picked up the ascending order report while a corrected copy printed out. All the Wexler projects showing huge overruns occurred during the third and fourth years Morgan was in office. After that, Wexler's projects were sprinkled among all the other projects.

Wexler dies in a car wreck. Morgan dies—maybe suicide, maybe murder.

Two more years of data—about two hours of work. She looked at the clock. It was nearly eleven.

Laura logged on to check her e-mail hoping that would give her a second wind.

LAURA:

NOW I CERTAINLY DON'T HAVE ANY BASIS FOR GIVING YOU ADVICE—I'VE NEVER EVEN MET WILL—BUT YOUR LIFE HAS TO GO ON, MY FRIEND. SOUNDS

LIKE YOU TOOK A STEP OUT THE DOOR AND I'M VERY GLAD TO HEAR THAT. THE SOONER WILL KNOWS THINGS WILL CHANGE, THE BETTER, I THINK. IS WILL GETTING TO KNOW VIC? DO THEY LIKE EACH OTHER? MAYBE VIC SHOULD BE AROUND A LITTLE MORE, NOT JUST SHOWING UP TO TAKE YOU AWAY FOR THE NIGHT.

I THINK JOHN IS WARMING UP TO THE BAHAMAS IDEA. PARTICULARLY AFTER I FOUND THEIR WEBSITE AND HE COULD SEE THE VIEW FROM THE TERRACE.

ADIOS, NAOMI

NAOMI:

THANKS FOR YOUR ADVICE. I HAVEN'T SEEN VIC, BUT WE'VE TALKED EVERY-DAY, SOMETIMES SEVERAL TIMES A DAY. ONCE OR TWICE, THE REASON FOR CALLING ME HAS BEEN SO TRIVIAL THAT I'M CERTAIN IT WAS JUST AN EXCUSE. WHICH, OF COURSE, IS DELIGHTFUL. AND I FINALLY TOLD HIM ABOUT WILL'S REACTION TO SEEING HIM KISS ME. I'M STILL SHY ABOUT SUCH PERSONAL STUFF IT'S SO MUCH EASIER TO TALK BUSINESS, BUT HE NEEDED TO KNOW. I HOPE HE'S NOT RECONSIDERING. IT GETS PRETTY COMPLICATED WHEN CHIL-DREN ARE INVOLVED.

LAURA

Laura inserted an old Credence Clearwater Revival tape in the tape deck and put on her earphones. That ought to do the trick.

The data entry was finished in an hour and a half. She printed out new reports. Wexler's overruns had begun with the first job he'd been awarded.

What balls this guy had.

Just to be certain, she chose a few Wexler projects during the same years in the other two districts and plugged those numbers in.

The overruns were standard. Nothing out of line.

Laura used the average cost overrun for all the other construction projects and applied that percentage to the Wexler projects. Then she subtracted the calculated lesser amount from the actual amounts to get an estimate of the extra money paid.

$496,000 over four years. He was a greedy bastard and a clever one.

Just not clever enough.

# Thirteen

Brent Wexler, a.k.a. Bob Wheeler, had settled temporarily in Villars Sur Ollon, Switzerland, close to his money at the Banc de Chessiere. For six weeks, he'd stuck to a routine that kept him out of sight. His rented chalet, plain by picturesque Swiss postcard standards, was at the end of the last paved village road. The only people he saw with any regularity were the couple who operated the Villars post office, the clerks in the grocery, his favorite ski instructor, and the local woman who cleaned three times a week. The latter stayed an hour at most since the chalet was very compact—only a main room, bedroom, bath, and the kitchenette. She took the washing and ironing home after each visit.

Once the newspaper started arriving, the daily trek to the post office each morning to collect his mail became a scheduled event, with a stop at the grocer afterward. He'd return straight away to the chalet and read the *Wall Street Journal* front to back, scouring it for business opportunities. Brent's plan was to ease back into the world of commerce through the door of small investments in limited partnerships and start-up companies. He had to be a player—in something, somewhere.

The bank president had taken him to lunch a couple of times and called fairly regularly, always under the guise of giving him financial information about European business ventures that might be of interest. Brent had the distinct impression the man was on a mission to keep Brent's sizable account, though his friendliness seemed genuine.

In the afternoons, weather permitting, Brent donned his wraparound sun glasses and skied to the train or the gondola for the ride to the top of the mountain. He'd pushed himself hard at skiing and it was paying off. He'd improved enough so that by the time the good snow was disappearing from the lower slopes, he'd be ready for the more challenging higher descents on the Diablerets.

Skiing wasn't hunting and never would be, but it had its share of thrills, like the woman in the hot pink ski suit. She'd appeared on the train to Bretaye the previous afternoon, alone, and he'd followed her when they'd reached the station, looking for an opportunity to talk. But she'd gotten her skis off the rack and was pushing off for the lift before he'd even found his equipment. The next time he caught sight of her was two hours later when she whipped past him, headed for the village. He took up the chase, but only got close enough to watch her approach the back entrance to the Villars-Palace Hotel and disappear within.

Clearly, the woman was an athlete, not just an exercise princess. Hot on skis, and maybe, hot in bed. He'd find out if he ever got her there.

■ ■ ■ ■

Lt. Colonel Jimmie Anderson awakened with a jolt, his dreams both vivid and vague, rapidly disappearing with each new moment of consciousness.

The wreck in Saragossa was on his mind, maybe because of all the talk about Wexler and Morgan. He got out of bed as gently as possible and moved around in the dimness of the bedroom, the blinds drawn tight against the glow of the security light on the pole in the yard. He quietly collected his clothes.

"Where are you going at this hour?" Elisabeth Anderson mumbled from her side of the bed, feeling for the alarm clock.

"I'm sorry I woke you, Honey."

"What's wrong? It's only quarter to five."

"I can't sleep. Gonna ride a while. I'll call you."

"Will you be home for dinner?"

"Unless something comes up."

"Be careful," she said, drifting back to sleep.

With his boots, uniform, and Sam Brown belt, Jimmie closed the bedroom door behind him and headed down the narrow hall to the bathroom and shower. He was more comfortable in his uniform and driving his car than he was at home in jeans, sitting in his recliner—a function of how he'd spent the better part of his adult life. Around five, when reddish light was breaking on the deep blue horizon, he tossed his thermos on the front seat of the patrol car and climbed in. He figured he'd find some of the men at one of the diners and catch breakfast with them. He cranked the engine, and when the radio jumped into life, Jimmie picked up the mike out of habit, then put it down, deciding not to report in immediately.

Forty minutes later, he rounded the bend where Wexler's wreck had occurred and pulled over. With a stainless steel cup full of coffee, he got out to survey the scene, leaning against the front of the hood, his boot on the bumper while he carefully sipped the steaming liquid. The midnight blue sky was giving way to the day. It would warm before long. Spring had been entirely too short this year.

It didn't look like the people who owned the fields were planning to raise anything but hay this season. Jimmie put his cup on the hood and started across. The farther from the road he got, the more the slope increased, dropping off to his right enough to make him walk off kilter.

Too bad the car hadn't drifted off course, or it might have landed down further without a crash. Like the other wrecks on this curve.

Really bad luck. But, when your time's up, it's up. That's all that could explain it, Jimmie thought. The order—or disorder—of things.

■ ■ ■ ■

At 7:45, after finishing eggs and grits at a truck stop south of Jackson with two young troopers, it hit him. On that sloping terrain, Wexler's car had driven straighter than one might expect given the loose grip of a sleepy or drunken man. None of the cars leaving the road had gone as far as the creek and none had stayed near the ridge. Cars had rolled, some had stopped farther down the hill but none had landed in the creek.

A surge of adrenaline pulsed through him.

How had he missed it? He'd analyzed hundreds of wrecks, worked out the angles and slopes plenty of times. This was basic stuff.

Jimmie excused himself hurriedly and raced to headquarters, not slowing down until he was talking with the major in charge of Driver's Services, one of the few people in the patrol who actually understood what the accident computer data base contained. It took much more wrestling with the antiquated records system than expected, but an hour later, Jimmie had the case numbers of the other wrecks at that location. He searched through the mountains of paper files until he had all the reports in hand. None of them had stayed on course straight across the field to the creek. He drove back to Saragossa just to be certain. Peering over the expanse, it was now painfully clear that there had to be more to Wexler's wreck than an accident.

At the junkyard, the burnt-up Mercedes was still on the lot, sandwiched in between the skeletons of other disasters, but now straddling a yawning mud hole, a product of the recent rains. Jimmie looked over the exterior, finding nothing surprising but knowing the underside might tell the tale if any evidence was to be found. The manager assured him the Mercedes wasn't going anywhere and let him use the phone to call headquarters.

Eddie Williams, the director of Patrol Communications, picked up his desk phone on the first ring, one of the rare times he wasn't in the shop under a hood or testing equipment. He and Robert Stone had been reviewing bids on electronic equipment.

"Eddie, this is Jimmie. Is the undercover bay being used?"

"Yes, sir. Do you need it?"

"Yes, but not until later in the day."

"I got one of the narc's new cars in there now, but we should be finished with it by 1:30."

"I'm out here at ABC Salvage, and there's a wreck I want to look under. It's sitting in the mud here and I really need some time with it so I thought about hauling it in. But I don't want the word gettin' around."

"Why don't you bring it in tonight? I'll stick around."

"You ever get a lift in that bay?"

"No, but we got a couple of jacks."

"Book it. And I'll need the slide-back wrecker."

"Gotcha covered."

"Thanks, 'preciate the help." Before he heard the click, he said, "Eddie?"

"Yes, sir?"

"Put me on hold and see if Robert's in his office."

"He's right here."

"Should have known. Put him on, will you?"

"Sure thing," Eddie replied.

"Stone, here," Robert said.

"Robert, this is Jimmie. I'm over at the Salvage looking at Wexler's wreck. I don't think it was an accident."

"Say what?"

"I said, I don't think it was an accident. I've been out there twice this morning. The angles are all wrong. Don't know why I didn't notice at the time."

"What do you mean, Jimmie?"

"I'm saying that car couldn't have landed where it landed without some help. More I won't know till I look at it."

"So what do you want to do?"

"I wanna bring it in and look underneath."

"Jesus Christ, Jimmie, I don't believe this."

"I think I know how sensitive this is gonna be, so I thought I'd do it after hours and put it in the undercover bay."

"Good idea," Robert said.

"Will you tell the Commissioner?"

Robert laughed. "Man, I ought to make you go through the chain of command. I believe Coleman would get the honors that way."

"I'll tell the Commissioner myself if you want, but it'll be a while before I'm back there and she'd rather be informed early in the game. You know that." When Robert didn't respond, he added, "And no one's better at easing bad news in on her than you."

"Flattery will get you everywhere. You're just lucky I'm such a nice guy today."

"Thanks, Robert. I owe you."

"Consider it on your tab."

Robert hung up the phone and looked at Eddie. He knew the man was dying to know about his conversation but was too polite to ask. "Shit."

"What's going on?" asked Eddie quickly.

Robert's head was swimming with all the tangled possibilities that flowed from Jimmie's hunch but he hesitated only a second. Eddie was one of the most trustworthy people in the department, and he was going to have to help. "Remember the Governor's friend who died in the wreck in Saragossa?"

"The poor guy who was charbroiled?"

"That's the one." Robert splayed the fingers of both his hands and tapped the tips together. "Jimmie thinks it wasn't an accident."

Eddie's eyes didn't shift from Robert's. "Holy shit."

"Exactly." Robert stood up to leave. "I've got to find the Commissioner PDQ. Later."

"Let me know if I can help," Eddie offered.

"Just keep this under your hat, okay?"

"You got it."

Robert sprinted over to the main building, arriving on the fifth floor just as Blake and Laura were converging on the coffee pot. Laura still had her briefcase in hand—she'd been down at the Legislature since early morning.

"Can I pour you a cup, Robert?" Blake asked.

"Sure," then added, "We all need to talk."

Laura's faced clouded. "Oh, God, what now?"

He discreetly shepherded them away from the secretaries. "Your office or mine?"

Laura said, "Mine" at the same moment that Blake said, "Hers" since Robert's office had become a rat's nest of equipment and files. For more than one person to sit down, piles of gadgets had to be moved. Laura's office was the biggest in all of state government, a ridiculous six hundred twenty-five square feet, and even as disorganized as she was, there was always a place, several, in fact, to sit down.

"Okay, so it's a little messy. I'll work on it," Robert said.

Robert closed Laura's door behind him. "You're not going to believe this, and I don't have the details yet, but since it was Jimmie talking, I trust his conclusions. He doesn't think Brent Wexler's wreck was an accident, and he's bringing the car in to inspect it more carefully."

Laura had taken a seat on the couch, habitually drawing her legs up underneath her. On hearing Robert, she planted her feet on the floor and sat up.

"You're kidding, aren't you?" Blake asked.

"Nope."

Laura didn't move a muscle.

"All he said was that the angles were wrong, that the car couldn't have ended up where it did unless it had some help."

"Why this sudden realization?" asked Blake.

"Don't know that. We didn't talk for long. He only said he was sorry he'd missed it on the first go around."

Laura finally spoke up. "Can we keep this quiet until we have more than Jimmie's hunch? The thought of foul play involving the Governor's close friend is hardly thrilling. As my fellow lawyers say, 'This is not a practice-builder.'"

Blake turned to Robert. "Who knows about this?"

"Us, Jimmie, and Eddie. We're going to pull the wreck into the undercover bay after dark tonight."

Blake looked at Laura. "It can stay a secret."

"Then it goes no further than us five until we know something. Understood?"

"We may need a mechanic."

"Try and get by without one," said Laura. She got up and walked to the south window. The squatty roofs of Jackson's undistinguished downtown were in the distance. And the Capitol. Robert and Blake waited for her to break the silence. "I don't need to tell you that this could be a nightmare."

"Commissioner, I don't envy you. I can hear it now...."

"Young Lady" said Laura, imitating Carver's deep voice as she came back toward them, "is this some sort of ploy to get your pay raise? He's going to go berserk."

"'Spect so."

"I know so," Laura said. "You'll never guess what else I've discovered. I finished the highway numbers about two o'clock this morning. Wexler was overpaid for every contract in Morgan's district for the first four years Morgan was in office."

"And not from the other districts?"

"Doesn't look like it. I only checked a few contracts but they were normal. He was only doing it with Morgan."

"How much are you talking about?"

"$500,000 or so. I assume he split it with Morgan but even then, if that much had been invested, he'd have two and a half, three million by now."

"Nice work if you can get it," Robert said.

"I just hope we can prove it," Laura continued. "If we can, the balance may shift a little in my favor. Everett's already gone to check out the actual files. But we've got to keep this quiet. All of it."

"You've got it," said Blake. They stood up to leave. "Before I forget," he added, "Rankin's working the pay raise and he thinks he has two senators who will switch their votes."

"Good," Laura said. moving toward her desk. "As soon as

you know something, let's talk again and work out a plan for dealing with Carver."

■ ■ ■ ■

The only lucky thing that happened that day was that no one was around when Jimmie and Blake drove the wrecker into the lot at 6:15 P.M. They had Brent's car jacked up in minutes and Jimmie was rolling under the charred chassis to look at the gas tank. Eddie popped the hood and nosed around the engine, while Blake inspected the driver's area. Robert got another dolly and started in from the other side. None of them had spent much time around a Mercedes, and never a model as old as this one, so even if it had been in good shape, it was foreign territory. A crumpled roasted hulk presented a real challenge.

As the minutes went by with no results, Blake started musing about the possibilities. He and Robert had gone out to the scene with Jimmie earlier in the afternoon, taking a transit with them to survey the slope accurately. Though no one even knew if formulas existed to compute time and distance combined with the angle of a graded surface, once they looked it over and talked about it, common sense led them all to the same conclusion. The car must have been steered by someone or something, and it must have maintained adequate speed or even accelerated. A crush test would tell them final speed, but whether they could ever determine how it had happened remained to be seen.

Blake had to face the possibility that there might not be any decisive evidence on the car or in an exhumation and autopsy. In fact, if Wexler had committed suicide, there probably wouldn't be anything at all to find. Blake didn't know Wexler, but relying only on what he'd observed in his cursory background check of the people around the governor, he hadn't pegged Wexler for the suicide type. No self-doubts, too prominent, too successful. Unless he'd made some terrible mistake that he couldn't live with...

"Here's somethin'," Jimmie called out cautiously, breaking

Blake's reverie. "Maybe."

Robert scooted his dolly toward Jimmie's position.

"What d'ya find?" asked Blake eagerly, getting down on his knees to look under the car.

"Gas tank was loosened at the top fitting where it's mounted."

"Couldn't it have loosened in the crash?"

Jimmie rolled around checking other parts. "Could have."

"How loose is it?" Robert asked.

"Real loose," Jimmie answered.

The air was filled with clanks of metal on metal as the two probed around the chassis.

"Well, nothing else back here is like that. I doubt it happened as part of the crash," Robert said.

"I wouldn't jump to any conclusions, Robert," Jimmie said thoughtfully.

"Look who's talking about jumping to conclusions," Robert chuckled from his side.

"The gas could have ignited easily," Blake said, ignoring their banter, "particularly if it were helped along. Any evidence of that?"

"Not yet," Jimmie said.

Robert chimed in. "Don't forget, this is ground zero on the fire. There might not be anything left even if something had been there at the start."

"So, assuming it didn't loosen itself, what do you think? Suicide or homicide?" Blake asked.

Robert rolled out and stood up. "It wasn't suicide."

"Why so sure?"

"There's no way to be certain the gasoline will ignite and even if it did, burning up is pretty brutal. It's a lot easier to shoot yourself."

"I think homicide," Blake said with certainty. "Someone killed him and wanted to cover it up. Might be connected to Morgan's death. Have you thought about that?"

"It crossed my mind," said Robert.

Eddie Williams came around from the front of the car.

"Aren't you rushing this? I've seen plenty of strange stuff when we've tried to salvage equipment from a tangled-up wreck."

"I'd agree if the accident had been normal. But it's hard to figure how the car landed where it did all on its own. You need to see the scene."

Jimmie rolled out from under the car and looked up at Blake. "I don't like raising this but I guess I ought to mention it. Mrs. Wexler never shed a tear. Not one."

■ ■ ■ ■

Will was totally occupied in the bathtub, orchestrating battles between a host of plastic and rubber animals and sea creatures when Blake called. He had a mixture of excitement and regret in his voice. "The gas tank fitting was loosened so gas spilled out and exploded."

"Intentionally or as a result of the impact?" she asked.

"I think intentionally but it's hard to tell."

"You're not sure?"

"Nope, never can be. But given the condition of the rest of the car, everyone doubts the looseness resulted from the wreck."

"Maybe he'd had the car worked on recently."

"Removing a gas tank is unusual."

From down the hall came a plaintive cry, "The water's getting cold, Momma."

"Hold on, Blake."

Laura hurried into the bathroom to a chorus of explosion noises only little boys know how to make. She turned on the hot water while letting some of the cold out, swishing the hot to the upper end of the tub. "Okay?"

Will nodded his head vigorously while his shark attacked a gray elephant. Laura went back to the phone. "I'm sorry, Will's in the tub. Where were we?"

"Talking about how gas tanks don't come down very often."

"And I was gonna say, it all depends on how big a klutz you

are. I put diesel in my car once and had to have the tank dropped to drain it. It wasn't properly refitted, which I discovered after I flooded a gas station in Memphis when I filled up."

"Well..." Blake stammered. "We can call the Mercedes service people. They've probably got a record of everything done recently on the car."

"I think you ought to. We need facts, not speculation."

"Well, let's assume the fitting was loosened intentionally."

"Then who do you think did it?" Laura asked.

"Whoever wanted him gone."

"What about suicide? Maybe Wexler wanted to kill himself and covered it so his wife could collect the insurance."

"He couldn't have been certain a wreck would work—too many variables—and, damn, it's a pretty horrible way to go," Blake protested.

"Suicides don't think straight or they wouldn't be committing suicide."

"Okay, theoretically, it could be suicide," Blake said impatiently, "but it's highly unlikely."

Laura didn't respond immediately. She was thinking about the debacle that was emerging. "Then you need to exhume the body."

"Our thoughts exactly."

"You'll need Mrs. Wexler's permission, won't you?"

"That would make things a lot easier..."

Laura cut him off. "Well, I'm willing to bet we don't get it."

"Why not?"

"Put yourself in her shoes. This could be anything—and if it's suicide, the proof might eliminate insurance money."

"Maybe, maybe not. They don't always write policies that way anymore," Blake insisted.

"You don't know that, but regardless, no one will want Wexler's death to be dragged out and inspected, not on such flimsy evidence."

"What about Morgan's death? You don't think this is all coincidence?"

"Probably not, but Mrs. Wexler won't want us to find out.

Figure it this way: If Mrs. Wexler's involved, she'll block us for sure. But if she isn't, she'll still block us because it might be suicide."

"But..."

Laura ignored him. "And the Governor won't want us to do anything that might tarnish his image or that of his best friend, over whom he publicly wept uncontrollably."

"Then we'll do it ourselves," Blake said, his voice deeper and more commanding. "We need an answer. There could be a killer out there somewhere."

"I still bet we won't get any cooperation. In fact, just the opposite—I'll be ordered to drop it. You watch."

"But you can't. There might have been a crime committed. That's what we're here for."

"I'm just telling you the facts," Laura said as calmly as she could. "Remember, this was the Governor's chief fund-raiser. Carver's gearing up for another campaign as we speak, already working the big-givers. If we drop this bomb based on supposition and a loose gas tank, I promise you, he won't like it."

"I think I've got enough to convince the judge," Blake boasted.

"Maybe, maybe not."

Neither spoke for a minute, then Blake started in again. "You can't be serious about the Governor."

"Serious as a heart attack. Look, let's suppose Mrs. Wexler had nothing to do with it. She's buried her husband and she's surviving, walking on. I know very well how painful it is to look back again."

"She's awful damn rich as a result," Blake said. "And Jimmie told me she didn't shed a tear."

"People freeze up from shock."

"No, Jimmie's seen shock. This wasn't shock."

"But we've got next to no evidence..."

"Not true. We've got the car, the terrain..." Blake parried.

"Is this topographical idea a physical certainty? Couldn't the accelerator have stuck and that's why the car shot across the field?"

Blake didn't answer.

"See what I mean? There are so many 'ifs' here, Blake."

"Add Reed Morgan to the mix."

"You're still talking about speculation, nothing more. And it could still be suicide."

"Fine. Do you want to be party to fraud?"

"Momma," called Will. "I want to get out."

Laura covered the mouthpiece of the phone and called back, "I'll be there in a minute, Sweetheart." Then she turned her attention back to the conversation. "No, but I'm telling you they won't want it investigated. They'll want to let sleeping dogs lie."

"Come on, this dog is wide awake. Don't you think the Governor would want to know about his friend? Avenge his death?"

"No," Laura said without hesitation. "He'll want it to go away."

"I can't ignore this, you know that."

"Mark my words, the Governor will remind me that in the Patrol's checkered history, plenty of Commissioners have looked the other way plenty of times. We get to pick our spots and he'll suggest, rather he'll demand, that we not pick this one. And don't forget that pay raise."

"Whose side are you on?"

"Yours, of course," said Laura, immediately regretting her catty responses. "I'm just playing the devil's advocate. Believe me, this isn't going to be easy."

Blake was silent. "I'm aware of that, much better now than ever before. What are you going to do?"

"Try my best, and when that fails, I'll back up and think about it again."

"You know," Blake stressed, "if Mrs. Wexler doesn't agree, we can get that court order. With what we got out of the car tonight, plus what common sense tells us from the scene, and the connection to Reed Morgan, there's enough evidence to convince a judge that foul play might have been involved."

"Particularly if he's not one of Carver's friends."

Blake didn't respond.

"Momma!" called Will again.

"Let's think about this overnight. And I'll talk with Vic about it in the morning. He can help me. Where's the wreck now?"

"Still in the bay."

"Do you need to keep working on it?"

"Not at the moment."

"Why don't you stash it somewhere on the back lot, out of sight?"

"Sure." Blake hesitated a moment, then added quietly, "I'm sorry I got so hot."

"I'm sorry, too, for the way I jumped back. We'll talk in the morning."

"Okay."

Laura trotted back to the bathroom. Will was out of the tub and already in his pajamas, though the backs of the tops and bottoms were damp. He was standing on the step stool combing his hair. The bath mat was soaked.

"You didn't need me," she said, giving him a hug.

"Yes, I did. I couldn't dry myself as good as you do."

"We'll just have to work on that."

■ ■ ■ ■

Hours later when the house was finally quiet, Laura turned off the lights for the night, and cracked the window in Will's room. She pulled the covers around his chin, and paused a moment, envying his peaceful sleep, his security.

But then the Governor invaded her thoughts again. He would go ballistic when he heard about their plans for Wexler's wreck, she knew it. And Vic would have to be Carver's mouthpiece again, caught in the middle.

So how to approach Carver? Vic would know what to do. Unfortunately, this was going to create more work for him, and she knew he was near exhaustion already. But they had to go forward—Blake was absolutely right—and Vic would help her find the way to present it.

Thinking about Carver was giving her a headache. She went to her office and flipped on her computer. While it powered up, she went back to the kitchen and poured a shot of bourbon, not bothering to make lemon tea and honey to mix it in. She knew it might make the headache worse, but if it loosened some of the tension, it was worth it.

LAURA:

OK! I'VE TAKEN MY FUTURE BY THE THROAT. THE DATE IS SET, CHRISTMAS EVE, RIGHT HERE IN D.C. JUST OUR FAMILIES. DINNER AT DOMINIQUE AFTER-WARD. THEN WE LEAVE FOR THE BAHAMAS.

HOPE ALL IS WELL WITH VIC.

AMORE, NAOMI

NAOMI:
TERRIFIC NEWS! I COULDN'T BE HAPPIER.

I, ON THE OTHER HAND, AM GETTING INTO DEEP WATER AGAIN. REMEMBER THE WRECK INVOLVING THE GOVERNOR'S CLOSE FRIEND. SOMETHING ABOUT IT IS FISHY AND TOMORROW I HAVE TO TELL THE GOVERNOR. IT WILL SCREW UP VIC'S LIFE ROYALLY. I WON'T BE SURPRISED IF HE DOESN'T ACCUSE ME OF GRANDSTANDING TO GET THIS PAY RAISE I'VE BEEN WORKING MY TAIL OFF FOR. IT IS NOT GOING TO BE PLEASANT.

LAURA

# FOURTEEN

Twelve days to *Sine Die*, the close of the 120-day legislative session, and it was a white-knuckler to the end for Vic. Usually most everything was resolved by that point. But the governor's budget was in shreds while the trooper's pay raise was still alive. Laura had taken his advice for once and made herself scarce around the Capitol because running into Carver unexpectedly wouldn't have been advisable.

"I'm not calling about the raise," Laura said when Vic returned her call.

"Good, because I'm worn out and don't want to deal with it right now," Vic said. He was already tired and irritable, and he'd only just gotten to the office. "But you need to know that even if the pay is put back in by the Senate on this motion to reconsider, he may use his line item veto and strike it. His capital improvement bill has been gutted as too expensive. So he's planning on saying the trooper's raise is not only too expensive but fundamentally unfair."

"Then what I have to say will probably hammer the last nail in my coffin."

"What now?"

"It's possible that Brent Wexler's wreck wasn't an accident."

"Are you kidding? Please let this be some kind of a belated April fool's joke."

"I'd give anything for it not happening."

"What, the accident or the discovery?" he said, with just a touch of sarcasm.

"The accident, of course."

He took a deep breath. "Tell me what you've got."

While Laura recited what they'd found on the car and at the scene, Vic walked away from his desk toward the window, stretching his phone cord as far as possible so that he could watch who was coming in and out of the Capitol.

"That's all?" Vic asked when she'd finished. He was suddenly buoyed—this would be easily taken care of. Before she could answer, he added, "That's an awfully flimsy basis for reopening something involving a person so close to the governor."

"That's all the physical evidence."

"Is there something else?" Vic looked over at the phone console to see half the lines blinking. He glanced at the clock—it wasn't even 8:15.

"Well, it looks as if Wexler and Reed Morgan were doing a number back when Morgan was first elected."

"Morgan's in this, too?"

"Wexler was grossly overpaid for highway contracts from Morgan's district."

"Have your boys worked out some grand conspiracy theory?" asked Vic.

Laura seemed to ignore the barb. "We don't know what happened yet—that's why we need more information. A fellow who works for me, Everett Passage, has been looking into it for a while. He got started when he was at the auditor's office. The IRS was investigating Morgan and came to him for information."

"Was he the guy who took your place?" There was a knock on Vic's door and the receptionist slipped in with a whole slew of pink message slips and slipped back out.

"Yeah. And in March, he transferred out here."

Vic was astonished. The Patrol auditing Wexler's highway contracts? That was way outside their jurisdiction. "Are you telling me the State Patrol's been investigating the Transportation Department and Brent Wexler?"

"Not officially, and it didn't start with Wexler, it led to him. Everett quit his job with the Auditor over Morgan's case. He'd gotten the green light to work it and then, suddenly, the Auditor pulled him off. Everett thought Morgan had gotten to the Auditor and that really made him suspicious. You know they played poker together."

"Don't you know what your people are working on?"

"I don't control everyone's free time. And I didn't go looking for this one, believe me."

"What do you mean you didn't go looking for it? Of course you did, it's outside of your jurisdiction."

"No it's not. We've got criminal investigative jurisdiction anywhere in the state."

"But we elect the State Auditor to do the auditing."

"And he wasn't doing it."

"Who's supposed to be tracking down robbers and dopers while you're protecting our tax dollars? The Department of Education?"

"Just hear me out. Everett was working on this in his spare time, but when Morgan died, we redoubled our efforts."

"Who is 'we'?"

"I've helped a little with the data analysis," she said, in a voice much quieter than before.

Vic was stunned. He leaned against the window frame and closed his eyes for a couple of seconds. The darkness was relief.

"It looks like he was overpaid a half million or so."

"When was this?" Vic asked as calmly as possible.

"Morgan's first term in office."

"Twenty years ago?"

"Yes. So compounded over...."

"Isn't there a small statute of limitations problem?"

"We probably can't go after it..."

"Thank God for some things," Vic interjected.

"Because the files are missing."

"What files?"

"I sent Everett to the Archives to pull the official records since we needed to see the actual files."

"You've been to other agencies with this?"

"Yes. And every single Wexler contract file he needed was missing."

This was unbelievable. In the middle of this total nightmare about the Patrol pay raise, Laura had started investigating the Governor's dead best friend. What could she have been thinking about? "And were any other files missing?" Vic asked.

"Everett didn't say."

"Didn't say or didn't check?"

"I don't know whether he checked or not."

Vic breathed a sigh of relief. Another opening. "Laura, I don't have the energy to cope with another crisis and certainly not a manufactured one."

"Would you hear me out at least?"

He knew she was getting angry. Maybe he should let her lay it all out and then he could deal with it piece by piece. "Okay, okay."

"Here's what we've got. Wexler was overpaid...."

"How can you be certain he was overpaid without the files?"

"We can't be absolutely certain but ..."

"You need to be."

"Let me finish, please.."

"I'm sorry."

"Those contracts were years ago. But Morgan was being audited by the IRS at the time of his death and he had a lot of unexplained income."

"You know this for a fact?"

"Yes. The IRS agent came to see me the day after Morgan was found."

"And Morgan had committed suicide rather than go to jail."

"But we're not certain it was suicide."

"What? Your people made that determination."

"There wasn't any evidence to the contrary at the time," Laura said. "We didn't have the audit data or connection to Wexler, and we hadn't discovered the problems with the wreck."

"Why hadn't you investigated the car wreck at the time?"

"There wasn't anything unusual to make us look closer. It was a standard crash and burn."

Vic's head was swimming. "And so you're going back in on Morgan?"

"Probably, depending on how this turns out."

This was nuts. Total insanity at a time like this. "Laura," he said as calmly as possible, "your facts are few and far between. The accident could still be an accident, the suicide could still be a suicide."

"Theoretically," she interrupted. "We...."

"Let me finish," Vic said abruptly. "With something this speculative, what I was going to say was, it needs to wait. We can't have this coming out right now."

"But we might have a killer on the loose. We need to *find* him."

"*Might* have, and that's *if* you buy your scenario with all the speculation thrown in."

"But Vic, Brent Wexler might have been murdered. Don't we need to know that?"

Vic didn't answer because he didn't know how to. He just wanted it to go away.

"I've got three top-level troopers who've spent their lives doing a damn good job of catching criminals, the highest ranking officers of the Patrol. What am I supposed to do? Tell them to turn their faces away and ignore this because the Governor is running for the U.S. Senate? They don't give a damn about that election. In fact, if Carver is elected, more than likely they'll be transferred out or lose their jobs."

And if Carver isn't elected, they may still lose their jobs after a stunt like this, Vic thought.

"Vic?"

"I'm here, just thinking."

"I mean," Laura continued, "if this case hadn't involved someone close to the Governor, we wouldn't be wasting time having this conversation. We'd be turning over every rock in the state trying to find out what happened."

"But by God, it does involve the Governor's friend. You've got to figure out how to handle this for him."

"What do you mean by 'handle'?"

"You know, deal with it," Vic said, totally frustrated. "Let's go back to the facts. Who are your suspects?"

"Beyond the connection with Reed Morgan, the people who benefitted from his death—his wife..."

"Grace Wexler isn't the type," said Vic quickly. "Who else?"

"Trey Turner."

"The guy who worked for him at the hunting camp? Isn't he a trooper?"

"He is. They're the main two, but that's just preliminary. And let's say neither of them are involved, has it occurred to you that Mrs. Wexler might like to know the truth? You act as though the Governor's the only one to consider."

"He's the only one I'm looking out for, but I don't think Grace will want to reopen this either. They weren't very cl..." Vic tried to catch himself.

"Not close, eh? Just how 'not close' are we talking? Contemplating divorce? At each other's throats?"

Vic took a deep breath again. If he hadn't been so tired, he wouldn't have let that slip. And Laura clearly knew he'd blundered. "Look, they never recovered from their daughter's death. They kept up appearances, but that was all."

"I bet there was a boat load of insurance money, not to mention the rest of what she inherited."

"She's a rich woman, but she's not a murderer."

"Then she needs to be making this decision," Laura responded. "Not you."

"Then you should have called her first," he shot back.

"What?!"

"I said," Vic repeated, instantly sorry for his quick remark, "you should have called her first."

"I shudder to think what the governor would have done if I hadn't called you first."

Vic ignored the retort. "As soon as you called me, you put me in a very difficult position. It's my job to think in terms of the governor's best interests and he doesn't need to have an investigation of the death of his chief fund raiser reopened right in the middle of a campaign."

"I thought we were..." her voice trailed off, then she added, "friends."

"We are," Vic said, "and I'm trying to help. Listen to me: This isn't the time to go off on a wild goose chase. Save it for later."

There was a long silence, then Laura spoke very deliberately. "You're wrong about this. But I'll leave it this way, and I dare say I'm being more reasonable than you are. I intend to call Mrs. Wexler within the hour. If Carver calls me before I get in touch with her, he can order me off. Otherwise we'll proceed just like we would with any case, except I can guarantee it will be all over the papers sooner rather than later."

"And if he orders you off?" Vic asked, taken aback by Laura's blunt tone.

"I'll obey. And then I'll tell the four people who know about it to cease and desist and why. And then we'll just have to wait and see."

That would be worse, Vic thought. This was getting out of hand. "Hold up a second. I apologize for being a smart ass. Tell me what the options are."

"I don't like being in this spot any more than you do," she said, her tone a little less hostile. "And no matter what you think, I didn't go looking for it."

"I shouldn't have acted like you had," Vic apologized, trying to smooth some of the ruffles out of her feathers.

"If Mrs. Wexler agrees to the exhumation and autopsy, it can be accomplished very quietly. Wexler was buried in a private cemetery, wasn't he?"

"Yes. Mrs. Wexler's family place. Her brother lives there now."

"Okay, we get the body up and examine it. If there's no evidence of foul play, we're at square one and without any publicity if we're lucky."

"But if something's wrong?"

"Depends on what we find."

"What if Grace doesn't agree?"

"We'll consider going for a court order. I'd let you know before that happened."

"Can you really do it without publicity?" Vic asked.

Laura didn't answer immediately, then said, "Maybe—but only maybe. And only if Mrs. Wexler fully cooperates."

"Let me talk to the Governor and I'll call you back."

When Laura hung up the phone her hand had stopped shaking but her heart was still pounding.

What had happened? How had she gotten so mad?

She stared at the painting across from her. Puffy white clouds filled the sky above the green and, in the distance, blue mountains.

In one conversation, she'd thrown it all away. How could she have done that?

■ ■ ■ ■

"She wants to do what?" Carver bellowed at Vic from the bathroom where he was shaving.

"They want to exhume Brent Wexler's body and do an autopsy," Vic replied. It was not unusual for the two of them to handle business while Carver was dressing, but he hated to upset him quite so much when the man had a straight razor in his hand.

"Christ, Vic, what is this woman trying to do? Drive me crazy? Is this pressure to support that goddamn pay raise? Or does she want me to lose the Senate race so that she'll keep her miserable little job?"

"I doubt it—she was well aware that bringing this up could backfire in the worst way."

"By God, she was right about that. If that bill passes in the Senate, it'll only be a whisper. She'll never have enough votes to override my veto. Why don't you tell her that? And while you're at it, remind her that I can certainly find a new Commissioner, maybe one who wouldn't stir up quite as much trouble."

"Don't even think about that," Vic chided him.

"How did this come up?"

Vic had rehearsed this part. "Laura wasn't looking for this. One of the troopers found evidence that the accident wasn't so accidental. And when those guys get their teeth into something, it's hard to pull them off."

"What do they think happened?" Carver asked.

"They don't know. But it looks like foul play."

"But why? What do they know about Brent that would make them suspicious?"

"He might have been bribing Reed Morgan."

Vic could hear the water splashing. At least Carver hadn't cut himself. He stepped out half a minute later, drying his chin and neck, avoiding Vic's glance. "How'd they turn that up?"

Vic's eyes flashed. "You know something about it?"

"No," Carver replied, but a little too quickly to give Vic the reassurance he desperately wanted. "That was a long time ago. We all thought Brent did very well, but maybe too quickly. He always claimed he made his big money on real estate but we never knew for sure."

Vic shifted uncomfortably on the unmade bed while Carver finished dressing.

"When they start investigating, what do they expect to find?" asked Carver.

"Answers, of course. But I'm hoping there's nothing there. The evidence is pretty flimsy."

"Then stop her from doing it at all, goddamnit," Carver barked back.

Vic didn't answer him immediately, then quietly suggested, "I think we have to cooperate."

"Why?

"Because if you order her to stop, it'll fester and sooner or later, it'll come out. And the press would love to know you stopped it. They'd make more of that than the case itself."

"Why in God's name does the goddamn press have to know every goddamn thing I do or think?"

"It's the American way."

■ ■ ■ ■

Blake was the last one to arrive at Laura's office—Jimmie and Robert were waiting for him.

"The Governor agreed to let me proceed," Laura told them. "But we've got to get this over with as quickly and as quietly as possible."

Blake's eyes widened, surprised at the upshot. "What was the price for that cooperation?"

She wasn't about to tell them about her discussion with Vic. "I told them we could exhume the body, do an autopsy, and get him buried again without anyone finding out."

"You're kidding, aren't you?" Blake said.

"No," said Laura, wondering what she'd done wrong this time. The finer points of Patrol logistics were still a little vague. "Isn't that possible?"

"Well," Blake looked at Robert, shaking his head and trying to be diplomatic. "It's not that easy to get a casket up."

Robert jumped in. "We need a backhoe and some sort of winch to raise the lid of the vault—if there was a vault—and then we've got to get the casket out."

"Jesus, I knew I shouldn't have made that deal with Vic," Laura apologized.

Blake sat forward, putting his hands up. "Don't panic yet. Where's the cemetery?"

"On a farm in Pocahontas, Mrs. Wexler's family place," Laura said. "Her brother owns it now, I understand. Vic wasn't with the Governor that day, but from what Carver told him, he thinks it's a small cemetery in the middle of a field, away from the road. Didn't Sandy go with him?"

"Probably," Blake said. "We'll talk to him. They may have a backhoe out there, but we can get one if they don't." He turned to Robert. "Kramer worked a case for that equipment company on 49-South. They owe us, wouldn't you say?"

"Is there anyone who doesn't owe you guys?" Laura asked.

Robert smiled at Laura's remark, then looked back at Blake. "They'll probably give us the backhoe, but what about the winch?"

"I'm sure Eddie can rig that if we can't weasel one from a funeral home."

"I'll get the winch," Jimmie volunteered. "It was my mistake that got us into this mess, that's the least I can do."

"Oversight maybe," said Blake, "not a mistake."

"No, it was a mistake," Jimmie protested. "But I'll handle the winch. My brother-in-law's brother runs a funeral home."

"The morgue won't be a problem unless Doc's out of town. Do it this weekend. Use his Suburban to bring the body in. It won't look unusual for it to be backed up to the loading dock. Catherine can assist him if he wants someone in there with him. It's supposed to be pretty weather—no one else will be in the lab."

With great relief in her voice, Laura said, "So, it looks like all we have to do is get Mrs. Wexler to go along."

"That's your job," Blake responded, smiling.

■ ■ ■ ■

Grace politely probed Laura's reason for visiting, but Laura would only say that it concerned Mr. Wexler's accident and she needed to see her in person. It left Grace dreading her arrival. So many things about Brent had turned up wrong in the last few weeks, this couldn't be good. And the burglary. That man with the knife in his hand had really rattled her nerves. She couldn't shake the vision of him coming at her. And never seeing his face only made it worse—it could be anyone at all.

Unable to concentrate on the thank you notes she'd been writing, Grace wandered to the front of the house to wait. Laura's office was relatively close by and she had said it wouldn't take her long to get there. Grace was daydreaming, completely without focus, when the phone rang again. Governor Carver's assistant put him through. She listened, hardly breathing, to his news that the Patrol wanted to exhume and reexamine Brent's body. Grace barely heard the rest of his babbling about what a respected and concerned citizen Brent had been.

In those few moments while Gibbs rattled on, all the unspecified anxieties that had been building up for weeks formed into a disorderly series of horrible possibilities: The accident wasn't an accident, someone had been after Brent.

But who? Maybe they'd come after her, maybe that's who was in the house? Maybe that wasn't a burglary.

Her panicky thoughts were broken by Gibbs' voice.

"Grace? Are you still there?"

"Yes, Gibbs, sorry."

"You don't have to agree to this, Grace. I don't know why Owen wants to put us through this, and frankly it made me so mad I cursed the day I appointed her. You can put her off—she needs your permission—otherwise they've got to get a court order. Why, I should have..."

Grace's instinct was to face the music, head on.

"Let me see what she has to say, Gibbs," Grace cut in, wanting his tirade about Laura Owen to end, wanting silence so she could think. Gibbs had been rubbing her the wrong way lately. His performance at the visitation and the burial had been outrageously self-centered. Then he'd insisted on getting the campaign contribution records back immediately when she had far more pressing things to think about. If Gibbs hadn't wanted this to go forward, he could have called this Owen woman off himself, but he was a political animal to the core, never getting his own hands dirty.

"Sarah and I'll support you, Grace, you know that."

"Thanks, Gibbs."

"Let me know what you decide."

"Certainly. Good-bye, Gibbs."

From her chair at a small antique writing desk that had belonged to her grandmother, Grace watched a dark blue Ford coming in the drive and muttered, "Damn." Gibbs' rantings had wasted all the time she'd had left to think.

She watched Laura—a small woman, dressed in unremarkable business clothes and dark glasses, hardly the Amazon one might expect from all the ruckus she'd managed to create—park, step out of the car, walk toward the front door, and then suddenly drop out of sight.

Grace jumped up, half running to the door, jerking it open, expecting to find Laura sprawled on the flagstones. Instead, Laura was inspecting the clumps of delicate dark blue Siberian irises and the trumpet of one last daffodil.

Laura looked up, smiling. "My father used to call me his 'daffy-down-dilly.' These are just gorgeous."

Grace let out her breath and composed herself. "They *were* gorgeous this year, though I was surprised that late cold snap didn't bother anything."

"I've been thinking about planting a few hundred bulbs in those fields between the highway and the office, but the maintenance people like plain grass. They cut it and forget about it, don't need to tend anything."

"Pity," Grace said, anxious to get past the gardening and onto the purpose of Laura's visit.

"They'd prefer concrete if I'd let them pave it." Laura stood and climbed the last two terrace-like steps, her hand stretched out to Grace. "Thank you for seeing me, Mrs. Wexler."

"Won't you come in?"

Once inside, Laura commented on the foyer with its broad black-and-white tiles. "My son would hopscotch across this every time he entered the room."

"How old is he?"

"Seven. And he's a little tornado of energy."

"They all are at that age. Can I get you a cup of coffee?" Grace asked, as she directed Laura to a seat in the front room.

"No, I'm fine, thank you. I drink it all day long. A very bad habit and I need to cut back." Laura took her seat. "I'm so sorry about Mr. Wexler."

"Thank you. His death has left a big hole in so many lives."

Laura noticed how long it was taking Grace to settle in her chair. "My husband died in an automobile crash just a year ago," she volunteered.

"I think I remember hearing about that. Wasn't your son hurt?"

"Yes, but his leg healed quickly, the miracle of young bones."

"Then you know how confusing everything can be."

"I certainly do," Laura said, welcoming the chance to talk about Semmes. She was well past that early stage of automatically blurting out something about his death every time she met someone new—*Hi, I'm Laura Owen, and my husband died in a car wreck.* Since the first of the year, she'd dramatically curbed the tendency to talk about it, only responding if someone else raised the topic. But, in this situation, it was a great ploy.

"Beyond losing the best friend I ever had in life and trying to pick up the pieces to go on, there's all this legal stuff," Laura said. "I haven't even closed his estate."

Grace shuddered. "Don't tell me that. Every day I seem to be sending something else to the accountant or the lawyer. I was hoping the end was in sight."

There was a tone, a distance in Grace's voice that let Laura know Grace hadn't experienced the same great loss she had. Laura pushed on, wanting to confirm her impression. "You'd think we would have figured out how to make death easier on those left behind, but instead we make it worse."

Grace glanced at a photograph of Jody that was on the side table next to Laura. "Sometimes the pain never goes away. My daughter died ten years ago, and not a day passes that I don't miss her."

Laura looked closely at Jody's picture, a smiling, active young woman, alluring in her innocence, leaning over the handlebars of a ten-speed bicycle. "That's a heart-breaker. I can't imagine how much that hurts. I doubt I would have been able to go on had Will been killed that night."

"As only a mother can know," Grace said quietly.

"And I'm sorry you had to deal with a burglar."

"Thank goodness Julia was here."

"I heard the editorial the next night on the evening news, and I totally agree that it's a shabby way to treat someone who's been so generous."

"Thank you."

Laura shifted in her chair, ready to make her request. "Mrs. Wexler..."

"Please call me Grace."

Laura avoided starting over again and just smiled her assent. "I need to talk about Mr. Wexler's accident."

"The Governor's already called me. But all I know is that you want to reexamine Brent's body. I don't know why."

Laura stifled the urge to roll her eyes in disgust at Gibbs Carver's intrusion. "Colonel Anderson—Jimmie Anderson—who visited you that morning?"

Grace nodded.

"He was teaching a class in accident reconstruction—that's where they analyze car wrecks—and he reviewed your husband's accident as part of the course. That's when he realized the accident might not have been so accidental. They've inspected the car and discovered evidence of tampering. The gas tank had been loosened, probably to insure that the car burned up completely. And though they don't know how it was accomplished, it doesn't look possible for the car to have ended up where it landed without assistance."

"What are you saying?"

"The circumstances are suspicious enough that an autopsy should have been performed at the time. We can still do one, and we need to."

"Is this really necessary?"

"Yes, I'm afraid so."

"Why?"

"Because if it wasn't an accident, we need to know what happened and figure out who was responsible."

"Are you saying someone killed him?" Grace asked, her nervousness obviously mounting. "I can't believe that could be true, Ms. Owen."

This was not the totally calm and deliberate woman Jimmie had been talking about, Laura thought. "Neither can I, and no one at the Patrol considered it a possibility until this evidence turned up quite by chance. But they can't ignore what they now know."

"What do you want from me?"

"Your permission to exhume Mr. Wexler's casket, autopsy the body, and then re-inter him. The entire matter can be handled without any publicity, I believe."

"And if I don't cooperate?"

"The criminal investigators will evaluate it. They'll probably take the matter to the District Attorney, present their evidence to a judge, and get a court order for the exhumation. It's not easy to get a trooper to turn away from a case."

"And then it wouldn't be handled as quietly, I presume."

"Correct."

"And if you don't find anything?"

"The case will be closed."

"I need to think about this," Grace replied quickly. "How long can I have?"

"The sooner, the better. If we're going to do it without anyone knowing, we'll have to work this weekend."

"I'll call you before the end of the day."

"That'll be fine."


After Laura drove away, Grace sank back into a chair in her living room, staring at the cowboy painting over the mantle. A lone cowboy who'd come a long way across a desolate landscape. Maybe it was a cowgirl in disguise.

Why had Brent done this to her? What had she ever done to

deserve such rotten luck?

What if someone had killed Brent? Who could it have been?

She wandered back through the hall and kitchen to her office, the click of her heels echoing in the big house. Standing over her desk, Grace pawed through the files of invoices, receipts, bills, and bank accounts, not certain what she was looking for.

The insurance. Suddenly she was seized with a near-paralyzing fear that if Brent had been killed, she had no right to the insurance money.

Grace yanked out the policy and raced through the fine print for the exclusions.

It said nothing about homicide, but there wasn't any coverage in the event of suicide.

That wasn't a problem. No matter what Brent had been involved in, he never would have killed himself. He might have been murdered, but he wouldn't have done himself in. Never.

She picked up the phone and punched in Franklin Gilliam's office but hung up as she heard the liquid feminine voice answer, "Gilliam and Gilliam."

She didn't want to listen to Franklin's blather or pay for it.

If she didn't cooperate, Grace thought, Laura Owen would get a court order for the exhumation. The police always won those arguments. She might as well let them proceed.

She dropped into her blue chair, suddenly aware of how tired she was.

Too bad she hadn't cremated the remains, Grace thought.

■ ■ ■ ■

Blake got a courteous little wave from the Capitol Police guard at the gate of the Mansion and drove past the security cameras and the cars parked bumper to bumper along the drive, to the off-limits garage area. Two trusty inmates in their starched white jackets were carrying bags of trash to the Dumpster. They nodded respectfully.

Sandy strolled out of the side entrance to meet him. "Bad

day for lunch. It's a zoo in there."

"What's going on?"

"Something about an education bill they want to pass," Sandy said.

"Pick up anything about the pay raise?"

"They don't say a word around me."

"Figures," Blake said. "Surely there's something to eat, especially with all those people."

"If you like little sandwiches on triangle bread..."

"Perfect," Blake said, hitching up his pants as they walked in. Part way up the half flight of stairs, the two troopers behind the desk jumped up to greet Blake. "Good afternoon, Chief."

"'Afternoon. Keeping the man safe?"

"Yes, sir. How's it going with you?"

While Blake chatted, Sandy disappeared into the kitchen and returned with two plates piled high with food. "Let's go downstairs," Sandy said, punching the elevator button while he got the troopers' attention. "We'll be in the security office if you need us."

The door to the cluttered office had hardly closed when Blake began. "What can you tell me about Brent Wexler?"

"Something wrong?"

"Well, we don't know yet, but it looks like the car wreck wasn't an accident."

"What happened?"

"Jimmie Anderson was reworking the wreck for the reconstruction class and realized something wasn't right. He pulled the car in to check it out and sure enough, the O-ring on the gas tank had been loosened."

"When'd you find this out?"

"Last night. The Commissioner's been over to talk to Mrs. Wexler about exhuming the body."

"Does the Governor know?"

Blake nodded. "He and Regis were informed this morning. They weren't pleased."

"Maybe that explains why he and Vic were a little chilly— no, let me rephrase that. It's been like Antarctica around me all day."

"That doesn't surprise me. But tell me about Wexler."

"He was the man who got it all done."

"How?"

"Everything. Anything. Like late in the campaign, if they needed more money for something, no problem, Wexler drummed it up."

"Big money?"

"They didn't talk numbers in front of me very often. But from what I could gather, we're talking five, six figures."

"Did this happen often?"

"Yeah, all the time," Sandy said.

"Did you go to the farmhouse in Saragossa?"

"Beautiful place. Hardly a farmhouse. You ought to see it. Went to the hunting camp, too."

"Did you hunt with him?"

"On occasion. He was quiet, cunning. A bow hunter. Not a crossbow either, an old-fashioned Indian bow."

"Really?" Blake said, clearly intrigued.

"Tried to interest the Governor, but Carver doesn't have the time, and even if he did, he wouldn't have the patience."

"Did Trey Turner hunt, too?"

"As often as he could. He had to run the place so when other members were there, he usually stayed behind, did all the dressing and cleaning. But he's one terrific hunter with every kind of weapon. The most deliberate, patient person I've ever seen."

"What about Mrs. Wexler?"

"Real sweet lady. She's Mrs. Carver's best friend. They play tennis together. When the Governor's away, they eat dinner, either here or at her house. Now that's another nice place, over in Northwoods. And they go to the movies every chance they can."

"Did Wexler and the Governor go along?"

"Wexler never, but Carver loves the special treatment, being ushered in the backdoor and all. He goes if it's not a chick flick."

"A what?"

"You know, girl movies."

"Get back to the Wexlers."

"They were polite with each other, and she's always smiling and acting like nothing's wrong. But they didn't live together, haven't as long as I've known anything about them. They always arrived in separate cars. No love there, not at all." Sandy paused for a moment, finishing a sandwich. "Not too bad, huh?"

"Delicious. Five or six more and I'll be full."

Sandy turned to call the kitchen when Blake stopped him. "Don't do that, I'm fine."

"Sure? There are probably three or four hundred extras up there."

"No. I've had enough."

Sandy sat back, glancing at the security camera video screens. The reception seemed to be breaking up. "You know, sometimes I think Mrs. Wexler was embarrassed by him. He could be really overbearing, and I think it made her uncomfortable. In fact, I know it did. Several times she stalked off so mad at him, I thought she'd explode. But she never did—at least not where any of us could see."

"Why didn't she get a divorce?"

"He wouldn't hear of it from what the First Lady told me. One time, we'd dropped Mrs. Wexler off at her house, and Mrs. Carver just started talking about how lonely Mrs. Wexler was, that she needed someone to take care of her. Then she caught herself and changed the subject. As good looking and rich as Mrs. Wexler is, she wouldn't have a problem finding someone, I don't think."

"Not hardly," Blake answered.

"How did she react to the news?"

"The Commissioner said Mrs. Wexler got pretty anxious about the whole thing."

Sandy thought for a moment. "Keep in mind two things: she was totally unnerved by that burglary, but she'd also just received and spent two million in life insurance money."

"Spent it all?" Blake asked, surprised.

"Well, she didn't exactly blow it. She gave that half million to the hospital—that was on TV. And then she paid off all the mortgages. She and the First Lady were talking about it in the car the other day."

Vic was steps away from the desk in the Mansion foyer, talking with a well-dressed businessman when Sandy and Blake emerged from the elevator. Vic looked squarely at Blake, tensing.

He'd never known what to make of Blake Coleman. Unlike Carver, who enjoyed joking around with the troopers assigned to him, Vic wasn't oblivious to their compulsory deference. He knew exactly how they operated because he was in the same boat. Their jobs, as his, were to serve the Governor, and their amiable, compliant ways were part of the deal. But when the Governor left office, assignments could change with a new administration, so the troopers who liked working at the Mansion, were always hedging their bets.

Blake, as chief, was the only will-and-pleasure appointment within the State Patrol aside from the Commissioner, and Blake would probably be forced to retire when a new Governor was elected—unless of course, he could be useful to the next man. And useful usually translated as "knowledgeable." Blake Coleman's forté—getting and remembering information—was a double-edged sword.

Blake represented the uncomfortable intersection of two planes of existence. He wasn't a member of the Governor's inner circle—either political or social. But he was a keen observer and player, in both the Governor's official world as well as his own world of the streets. Unlike the previous Chief of Patrol, who was rarely seen around the Mansion except to partake of a free meal, Blake had been paying attention to the people around the Governor, filing away every bit of gossip, and remembering every meeting on the schedule, all in the name of providing security. He seemed to move between the two worlds effortlessly.

And now Blake knew something was wrong with the death

of the Governor's friend. And he probably knew about his relationship with Laura.

They passed each other with wary silent nods of uncertainty.

■ ■ ■ ■

"Ms. Owen? This is Grace Wexler."

"Yes, Mrs. Wexler," Laura said, swallowing a bite of a grilled chicken sandwich.

"I'm glad I caught you. I thought you might be at lunch."

"I am," Laura replied. "I eat at my desk most of the time."

"Oh, I'm sorry to disturb you."

"No, no. I'm glad you called."

"I've decided you can go ahead with whatever it is you need to do with the body," Grace said without a trace of hesitation.

"Thank you, I appreciate your cooperation," Laura replied, all business. She wondered what had brought the change in attitude. "We'll do everything thing we can to minimize any disturbance."

"That's one thing I want to talk to you about. The cemetery's on our family farm where my brother lives. He's got young children, and I'd rather not have them know about this."

"I understand. Does he know?"

"No, but I'll call him now. Please work with him on the whole thing."

"We will."

# FIFTEEN

When Brent had finally managed to introduce himself, the hot pink snowbunny had played harder to get than any woman he'd met in recent years. It had required an entire week of skiing, dining, and courting. Then, when he failed to show up at the gondola after lunch, she appeared on his doorstep, suddenly available.

So predictable.

He struggled to be on top, in control, but she was as aggressive in bed as she was on the slopes. Brent let her have her way the first time, holding himself back long enough to learn her most erogenous spots. She'd ridden him as though there was no pleasure to be had but her own.

But the second time around, it was his turn. He might have trailed her on the slopes but he was virtually indefatigable in bed. When the sturdy woman from the village who came to clean and deliver the laundry knocked, he ignored the summons, not wanting to interrupt his rhythm. The front door opened and then almost immediately slammed closed—their groans and cries must have driven the woman away.

It was nearly evening when they awoke from an exhausted post-coital slumber. The best they could do for food was breakfast—an omelette, toast, and coffee. Miss Athlete didn't appear particularly handy in the kitchen, so Brent took over while she showered and dressed. When everything was on the table, he sorted through the pile of papers while he waited for her.

Brent pulled out the April 17th *Wall Street Journal* and unwrapped it. The word Mississippi jumped out from the headline of the left-hand column story. Above the fold was a flattering head and shoulders etching of a smiling Gibbs Carver. The focus of the story was Carver's forceful rebuttal to the Department of Defense's recommendations for closing military bases around the country, but in fact, it was a profile on a person the writer saw as a comer in national politics. Though Carver hadn't explicitly confirmed that he was running for Barksdale's Senate seat, it was clearly an attractive possibility that he was seriously considering. Carver was testing the waters, one person observed.

Brent read every word on the front page, and then turned to page A-6 where the story continued with forty more column inches.

> **Carver will certainly avail himself of the opportunity to extend his power and control over the otherwise independent Department of Transportation when he appoints a successor to fill the unexpired term of Reed Morgan who was recently found shot to death.**

Brent dropped his cup on the saucer with a clatter, coffee sloshing over the edges. Trey had killed Reed Morgan—Brent was certain of it.

He stared at the paper not seeing any words.

With both of these deaths, they'd catch Trey sooner or later. And then they'd be after him.

When he collected his wits, Brent finished the article. There was nothing else about Morgan.

He reached for the phone on the counter near him. With six hours time difference, it would be just before midnight at the

*Clarion Ledger.* Someone might be there. He dialed the operator.

"Hello, I would like an English-speaking telephone operator, please."

"Yes, one moment please," came the reply in heavily accented English.

His playmate reappeared, completely dressed. He reached for her as she approached the table and began unbuttoning her sweater. She only resisted for a moment—the shower must have revived her. Amidst the alternating clicks and silence as his call was routed, Brent availed himself of the breasts before him, handling the questions in between his licking and suckling, all the while stroking her, first gently, then more intensely.

In the ten minutes it took to get an operator, the telephone number from information, and a connection to the newspaper, his cute little snowbunny had climaxed again, and she collapsed on the nearby couch, curled up in wet exhaustion. This was exactly what he wanted—now he was certain she'd be back for more. His way.

No one answered at the news desk, and Brent was disconnected.

He asked the operator to reconnect him and this time was routed to the copy desk.

After an agonizing series of clicks, Brent heard, "Copy." Brent repeated his spiel.

"Who'd you say you were?"

"I read about it in the *Wall Street Journal* but there weren't any details," said Brent, evading the question as best he could.

"He was found shot to death."

"Was it murder or suicide?"

"I don't think they ever decided, but I'm kinda fuzzy on the details. You need to call back in the afternoon and ask for Terry on the state desk. She wrote the stories."

"Thank you."

Brent hung up the phone and stared out a small window. The lights of chalets dotting the mountainside were coming on and somewhere along the road, a farmer was bringing in the last of his cows, their bells clanging as they were herded home.

What could have happened to Morgan?

His eyes came back to the desk and his new laptop computer. The Internet. Maybe something will be posted. Then he looked at the woman. She'd been watching him, silently.

"Something wrong?" she asked.

"I just found out a guy I knew back in the States had died."

"I'm sorry. Was he a close friend?" The woman moved to his side, hesitantly eyeing the stone cold omelette.

"I knew him pretty well," said Brent, following her line of vision to the food. "Doesn't look very appealing, does it? Let's go to the hotel and eat."

Hours later, when he finally got back to the chalet, Brent logged on the Internet, and searched for the *Clarion Ledger*.

There was a website but no archives and no index. Typical.

He searched again and found a link to the *Atlanta Journal-Constitution* and immediately found the archives. After establishing an account and password, he limited the inquiry to the last six months, and typed in Reed Morgan. There were four hits, three of which involved his death and one was an announcement of dramatically increased funding for road maintenance, more than the local contractors could handle.

He printed out the three articles.

Gunshot through the mouth. Maybe suicide—there was no forced entry. But there wasn't a note either.

What could Trey be thinking? He must have had a reason.

Or maybe it wasn't Trey, maybe it was one of the other people Morgan was shaking down.

Or maybe it was suicide. Maybe the IRS had him and he killed himself.

Brent frantically looked for other Mississippi sites that might have current news. WTBS had archives and transcripts. Brent chose the day the body was discovered.

It happened late at night, after a poker game. No one knew of any reason for Morgan to be despondent enough to commit suicide. His poker partners said though he'd lost a little money, he'd been upbeat all evening. The Jackson Police homicide unit was keeping the file open for the time being, even though the state medical examiner ruled the cause of death was suicide. Brent skimmed the rest of the stories and then moved to the next day.

This is a gold mine, Brent thought. He could log on every day.

Brent systematically scanned the archives for each day since Morgan's death, reading the headlines. Not much of interest had been happening. Drug-related homicides and other violent events seemed to dominate the nightly news. The only follow-up story on Morgan concerned Gibbs Carver's setting the date for the new election. The police finally closed the case.

Brent scrolled on, rarely slowing down, until the words Cancer Clinic caught his eye. Grace had made the half million dollar gift to the hospital in memory of her daughter Josephine Ethel Wexler who had died of cancer as a teenager. The bequest was part of the estate of the late Brent Wexler, founder of Wexler, Inc., who died in a car accident.

He punched in March 6, the day after *his* wreck. It was the third story, after a shoot-out and some wrangle about cable TV contracts. There wasn't any additional information beyond what had been reported in the *Clarion Ledger.*

The late Brent Wexler who died in a car accident. Jesus Christ, is that all there is?

He clicked on the last day's news, now two days old and skimmed the headlines. The weekly news commentary by the station manager caught his eye.

**It is truly a blessing for a community when a citizen, in this case Mrs. Grace Wexler, gives so unselfishly of her time and money. Two days ago, Mrs. Wexler, a tireless volunteer and fund raiser for the Children's Cancer Clinic, presented her own check for $500,000, no strings attached, a critical step in their efforts to expand their research into this horrible disease.**

**But how did we thank her? Mrs. Wexler returned home that night, disarmed her alarm system, only to find a burglar inside her house. Luckily for Mrs. Wexler, she escaped injury and the**

criminal fled. The police have no suspects.

This is shabby treatment for such a generous citizen. We urge the police to act swiftly to catch the intruder.

A Burglar. Inside the house. With the alarm on. Must have scared Grace to death.

Brent poured himself a couple of shots of bourbon, turned out the lights, and pulled his chair in front of the picture window. The full moon was a giant glowing orb over the jagged white peaks of the Alps.

Couldn't have been an ordinary burglar. The way that system worked, it would be very hard to get in without tripping the alarm unless you had the code.

Unless you had the code, Brent thought. The alarm company? Some sleazy little rent-a-cop lifts the code and hits the house?

He swished the bourbon around in his glass, thinking.

Trey. That sonovabitch. He's killed Morgan, and now he's going after Grace.

Jesus Christ. Then they'll start looking for me. He's got to be stopped.

■ ■ ■ ■

Every bed in the Second Creek house was spoken for every weekend when turkeys were in season. The end of those blasted birds was the end of his agreement with the hunt club. It was agony for Trey. He resented the invasion, hated their fake camaraderie. All he could think of was getting them out of his life. Two more weekends and then peace.

He cleaned up after breakfast, then loaded his four-wheeler with rolls of barbed wire, posts, and weatherproof posted signs. Trey had two and a half miles of property line to fence, but it crossed some of the roughest portions of his land. He was stretching three strands of wire from tree to tree, with posts in between where necessary, and tacking up NO TRESPASSING signs every twenty yards. There would be no doubt where his land began.

This wouldn't be necessary of course, if Brent had taken his advice.

Trey was working on the crest of a small ridge. He squeezed the gun and shot a staple into the top of the sign, then shooting another at the bottom.

Why hadn't he gotten word to him? It had been weeks now.

Trey looked south at several tall trees on the hunt club side of the line. He'd come upon many a fine animal in that grove.

Damn. So goddamn foolish.

He walked to the next tree, unwinding the top strand as he moved.

This was a lousy trade. Should have gotten more from that bitch for the place in Saragossa.

His face flushed with the thought of missing his chance with Grace. That rich cunt. He should have slashed her throat right then.

How the hell was he going to get at her again? The code on the alarm system was probably changed that very night.

Trey walked back and picked up the second strand, pulling it tight as he walked.

He'd have to surprise her. Catch her when she was entering the house.

■ ■ ■ ■

Near noon, Dr. Lawrence Hershel emerged from the autopsy suite where he'd examined the exhumed body. A gas mask hung around his neck. He didn't have masks for observers, and the formaldehyde powder used on bones was so strong it would make anyone gag, so they'd waited impatiently outside.

"His larynx was fractured somehow and he was dead before the car wreck. The cause of death will be manual strangulation. He sure wasn't very healthy, though. I'll know more when the serology and the microscopic sections are done.

"Not healthy? How so?" Blake asked.

"Advanced cirrhosis of the liver, tuberculosis, and arthritis, for starters," the pathologist drawled.

Jimmie stepped forward. "Something's wrong. I remember Mrs. Wexler saying he'd just come back to New Orleans from doing something athletic like skiing. No, snorkeling, that was it. He'd just been snorkeling, diving, somewhere in..." Jimmie paused, "Mexico. No somewhere else down there, Honduras maybe. That's it, skin-diving in Honduras."

Hershel shook his head as he looked over his glasses at Jimmie. "I seriously doubt the man in the bag could have done that. He'd have wheezed too much."

It looked as if Blake and Robert were sinking into one of their telepathic consultations. "Do you have enough to positively identify him?" Robert finally asked.

"Everything's x-rayed. If you think there's a problem, I can keep the corpse until we have something else to use for identification. Any dental records or other x-rays?"

"I don't know, but keep this guy in storage, why don't you. I don't think he goes with the headstone in that cemetery," said Blake.

"What about the casket?"

"We've got to close the grave back up first thing in the morning, and we'll know in a few hours whether the bones will be in it or not."

As the medical examiner headed back into the autopsy room, he stopped and added, "By the way, he didn't have a spleen either."

The door swung shut leaving the three men standing in the hallway. Jimmie Anderson was speechless.

"We've got an unidentified dead guy, a disappeared friend and advisor to the Governor, a not-so-grieving widow who's the First Lady's best friend, and a dead Transportation commissioner who was taking bribes from the guy we thought was dead," Blake took a breath. "This is giving me a headache."

"Could be worse," Robert added.

"How so?"

"Well, the Governor could have been the one who died, and then we'd be out of jobs too."

"Wrong, I'd be on the street and you two would be fighting for my chair," Blake said, trying to smile but too preoccupied for the banter. "We'd better get over to Mrs. Wexler's house. Is the Commissioner here?"

"Working in her office, waiting for our call."

"I'll bring her."

"Can we stop for lunch? This could be a long afternoon," Robert pleaded. "Bad form to have your stomach growl."

Blake nodded. "I guess I'm hungry too. How 'bout we meet you at the Gourmet Gulf? It's on the way."

"You're on."

■ ■ ■ ■

"And when we get there," Laura asked, in between bites of her Italian tuna fish sandwich, "I'm supposed to lead off and then leave the rest to you?"

The three men nodded. Their big frames seemed to fill the entire table area of the combination delicatessen, gas station, and restaurant.

"Do you even need me?" Laura said hesitantly, secretly thrilled by the chance to tag along.

"Definitely," Blake answered, popping the last bit of sandwich into his mouth. "She'll feel more comfortable with a woman in the room even if you don't need to say anything much. Jimmie needs to be there because he was the one who talked to her first and he's going to loosen her up by taking all the blame. Robert and I will do our usual two-step."

"But I get to be the good guy since she already knows me," Robert added.

Laura looked from Blake's empty plate to the half sandwich left on hers. "What are you in such a hurry about?"

"Never have been very good at waiting," Blake replied. "When the hidden is half-exposed, it's hard not to rip the curtain back and see the rest of it. Besides, Mrs. Wexler may be in serious trouble, whether she's involved or not."

Laura looked at Robert and Jimmie who were both polishing

off their last bites, and then at Blake again. "So I should wrap this up and finish it later?"

They all nodded again.

■ ■ ■ ■

Grace's brother had reported about all the activities at their cemetery so she knew Brent's body had been taken away. She'd waited at the house, passing time with the mindless task of updating her computerized address book until Laura's call broke her concentration. She moved to the front room to wait for her again. When two cars pulled in the driveway, her worry suddenly quadrupled.

Three men, dressed in work jeans and boots from their early morning labors, accompanied Laura. Grace hoped that none of them had noticed her watching. She opened the door wide, summoning up the most positive demeanor she could muster.

"Hello, Ms. Owen," Grace said, stretching out her hand to greet her. She turned to Robert and Jimmie, "And Colonel Stone, Colonel Anderson, it's nice to see you again." Then she looked at Blake who was now closest to her. "I'm Grace Wexler."

"Blake Coleman, ma'am. I'm Chief of Patrol," he said.

From his eyes and voice, Blake was all business but Robert's smile was reassuring enough that her grip relaxed slightly.

"Won't y'all come in?"

The men stepped aside to let Laura enter first. Grace showed them into the front room, asking, "Can I get anyone something to drink? Tea?"

They all shook their heads. "No, but thank you," said Laura as they all sat down.

Grace looked from face to face, wondering who would speak first.

"Mrs. Wexler," Laura said, "we've completed the autopsy and we're ready to close the grave back up."

"I'm glad that's over," Grace sighed.

"However, we need to positively identify the body, just for

the record."

"How do you do that?"

"Dental records will probably suffice. Could you get those from Mr. Wexler's dentist?"

"I suppose so, assuming he hasn't thrown them out." Grace squirmed as she realized Blake was watching her carefully. "Is there a problem?"

"Well," Laura faltered.

"Mrs. Wexler," Robert said, very evenly, "was Mr. Wexler healthy?"

"Absolutely. Hardly a sick day in his life. Why?"

"Because the medical examiner found evidence of advanced cirrhosis of the liver, tuberculosis, and arthritis."

Grace shook her head, bewildered. "That's not possible. He was just in Roatan snorkeling and skin-diving. He hunted, spent every spare moment running through those woods, even in the summer. He never drank to excess. No, your doctor must be mistaken."

"Had Mr. Wexler's spleen been removed?" Robert asked.

"Not that I know of," Grace answered. She noticed an unmistakable look of satisfaction on their faces.

Blake cleared his throat. "Mrs. Wexler," he said in a deep, commanding voice, "it appears that it wasn't your husband who died in the car accident."

Grace's bewilderment was changing to fear. "My God, what are you saying?"

"That someone else was in that car, and your husband has disappeared."

"It was my mistake from the beginning," Jimmie apologized. "The accident couldn't have been an accident. Not the way it happened. We should have—I mean, *I* should have—caught it immediately."

Murder and who might have wanted to kill Brent had controlled Grace's thoughts ever since Laura had first visited her, but this scenario had never crossed her mind. She sat still, paralyzed with confused fear.

"I know this is a shock, Mrs. Wexler," Blake said, his tone

accusatory as if she were one of his errant troopers. "Where were you when the accident occurred?"

"At... home," Grace stammered, looking around at each of them, on edge with Blake's brusqueness.

"Alone?"

Grace nodded.

"Didn't you tell Colonel Anderson that Mr. Wexler had called you?"

"Yes. In the late afternoon."

"Do you know approximately what time it was?"

"Umm, not specifically." Grace searched the others for help they couldn't give her, becoming increasingly upset. "I was re-potting plants, it was still light."

"What can you tell us about your husband's recent behavior?"

She took her time, grasping to regain some composure and control, then she slowly shook her head, all the while hoping cooperation would make a difference with this harsh man. "To tell you the truth, I don't think I knew my husband very well."

"How so, ma'am?" Robert asked, far more gently.

Grace turned toward Robert, relieved to get away from Blake, scratching the back of her neck, her lips pursed. "Nearly everyday since he died," she stopped to correct herself, "since the accident, I guess I should say, I've found out something new about Brent. None of it is good."

Every eye was on her.

"Will any of what I say remain confidential?" Grace asked.

"What do you mean by confidential?" Blake inquired abruptly.

"Well, will this come out in the papers?"

"Why are you concerned, if I might ask?" Blake pursued, still unforgiving.

"I'm in the middle of selling Brent's business, and I can't have that deal fall through."

"What we write down will be a matter of police, not public, record," Blake answered. "But if the investigation turns up something and someone's prosecuted, certain facts may come out then. However, no one has their pencil out yet."

"I hate to mention this, but the business may not be yours to sell," interjected Laura.

Grace saw Blake flinch, and for a second, wondered what was going on, but immediately turned her thoughts back to her problems. "Oh, Lord, you're right." Grace exhaled, pushing the air through her puffed cheeks, exasperated. "And I've already collected the insurance money, and spent it, and now you tell me he's not dead." Grace paused, then resumed, her voice quieter. "I think I need to talk to my attorney."

Laura launched in again, "Mrs. Wexler, you do need to talk to an attorney because, based on what we learned today, your husband didn't die, at least not in that crash, so there isn't an estate, there isn't any probate. But, please," Laura pleaded, "hear us out. This is a very complicated matter and we need your help right now."

Grace sat silently, now suspicious of everyone's motives. She wasn't certain she should be answering any questions. But if she suddenly stopped, it might look even worse.

Robert leaned forward to get her attention. "How much insurance did Mr. Wexler have?"

"Two million dollars," she replied.

Robert let out a quiet "hmm."

"That's between you and the insurance company, if and when they find out about this," Blake said. "We're not working for them. All we're interested in is finding out who the man in the car was, who killed him, and where Mr. Wexler is."

Somewhat relieved, but, more than anything, scared of defying the stern Colonel Coleman, Grace decided to tell them everything—the cash, the bank account, the fake public relations firm. All of it flowed out of her like a river that had broken through a dam, not always sequentially, and hardly concisely.

When she finished, Robert asked, "What do you know about the very last day?"

"I distinctly remember him saying he was taking a client to dinner and then he'd drive home. He'd been skin-diving in

Roatan. He said something about being more tired than usual and we talked about him getting a check-up. He was very..." Grace searched for the right word, remembering Brent's tone that day. "Sweet might be appropriate. We hadn't been close for a long time, not since the death of our daughter. Actually even before that."

Almost instinctively, she glanced across the room at the photo of her daughter, Jody. "But I can't find credit card charges for either a business dinner or gas for the trip home."

"You looked?" Robert asked, seemingly impressed.

With a touch of embarrassment, Grace explained that she'd been reviewing everything, bit by bit, trying to figure out what Brent had been doing.

"Couldn't he have used cash?"

Grace shook her head. "Not likely. From what I've seen, he charged everything and certainly anything that could even remotely be considered a business expense—even movie tickets on occasion."

"Did you know Reed Morgan?" said Blake suddenly.

"The Transportation Commissioner?"

Blake nodded.

"Not well. Why do you ask?"

"After Morgan's death, we began investigating some of his activities," Laura offered. "There may be some connection."

Grace looked puzzled. "When Brent's business was new and Morgan was first elected, we saw a lot of them. They're from over near Vicksburg. Brent got him started. My husband had a knack for being the power behind the throne."

"Had you seen Morgan recently?"

"No. Reed and his wife separated a few years ago, and his playing around offended me, frankly. Brent stayed away from him, too," she said, then quickly added, "I think."

"Mrs. Wexler," Robert said, "you don't have to answer this if it's too personal, but I must ask what pulled you and Mr. Wexler apart, aside from the death of your daughter. Please don't think I'm prying, but it might help."

She shook her head to indicate it was okay to inquire. "I

can't really say, except we—Jody and I—weren't very important to him. Business, campaigns, hunting, they all came first." She looked to Laura for some female reassurance. "He was driven to be the biggest, the most successful, the most influential, the best."

"Where did he come from?"

"Brent didn't have any family that I ever knew about. I met him at Ole Miss. He was a football hero, a bright student. He told me his father had died of tuberculosis and his mother and sister were killed in an automobile accident. He was in the Adriatic in the Navy at the time. They'd been poor, didn't own any land, came from some place in Arkansas. No home place to go to. Jody used to ask him about it all the time. She wanted four grandparents like everyone else had, but Brent just put her off, never telling her more than their names, and immediately switching to a story about himself."

"What were their names?"

"Eli and Georgia Wexler."

"What had he done in the weeks before his disappearance?" asked Robert, bringing them back to the present.

"Business trips. He was behind that huge birthday party at the Mansion for the Governor. And, as always, he hunted. And went on his annual trip to Roatan."

"Did he go with someone?"

"No. He meets up with a group of old friends every year at the same time, same place."

"Where did he stay?"

"The Islander." She paused, thinking. "He'd been in New Orleans shopping. I've got the bills. Practically a whole new wardrobe for himself."

"Where are his clothes and personal effects now?"

"Everything's gone. I cleaned it all out and gave everything to Goodwill."

"What about his papers?"

"Some are at the office, but most of them are here. As I said, I've been going through them, piece by piece."

"And what was at the hunting camp?"

Grace hesitated a moment—the hunting camp was always an unpleasant topic.

"We know you swapped land and houses with Trey Turner," Jimmie said, no longer apologetic but still soft-spoken, "and that Turner bought additional acreage."

Hearing Trey's name cast a chilly pall over Grace. "There wasn't much at the camp. From what I saw, it looked like the members kept hunting gear there but not much else. I couldn't tell one person's stuff from another's."

"Why is it that you and Turner don't get along, if I might ask?" Jimmie prodded.

"Maybe it was foolish of me, but when Trey appeared in our lives, what little we did as a family ended. He and Brent hunted like wild men, in all kinds of weather, at all times of the year. If there were four days for a little holiday, Brent didn't spend it with us, he went hunting with Trey. I guess I always resented it. Even when Jody was terribly sick, he'd leave and go off to the woods."

"Was Turner on the payroll?" Blake asked, his question so quick and direct that it startled her.

"Yes."

"Do you know how much he was making?"

"From both the hunt club and the farm, about twenty-five thousand a year."

Robert shook his head. "Jeez, on that much he could quit his day job."

"Tell me one more time about the night of the wreck," said Blake. He spoke directly but without the brusqueness.

Grace carefully repeated her activities, this time recalling the National Geographic special on the Outer Hebrides that she'd been watching when the call came in. When she finished, Blake leaned over and talked with Jimmie who then stood up and asked, "Could I use the phone, ma'am?"

Somewhat hesitantly, not knowing what was coming next, she said, "Certainly. There's one in the hall and another in the kitchen down...."

"I know."

"Oh, yes, I'd forgotten."

Blake leaned toward her, his eyes compassionate for the first time. "We're arranging to get you some protection."

"Protection from what?"

"We don't know, ma'am. Your husband isn't dead, though he or someone else went to great lengths to make us believe he was. But Reed Morgan *is* dead."

"What does that matter? I thought that was suicide."

"It was ruled suicide, but it was too neat. And we believe something was going on between your husband and Morgan, so we can't ignore the possibility of a link between the two events."

"But why do I need protection?"

Robert spoke up. "The burglary might not have been a burglary, but an attempted attack on you."

"What makes you think that?"

"For one, if the guy was good enough to evade your security system, why didn't he recognize the valuable jewelry from the costume pieces? And if he used the code to get in, why did he rearm the system? But, if he was here to attack you, he would leave the system armed, so that you would come into the house, not suspecting anything."

"But I still don't understand why you think I'm in danger."

"We don't know where your husband is, but he's missing. There's been no ransom note, so it's unlikely that it was a kidnaping. Let's assume the worst...."

"That Brent killed the man in the car? Is that what you're saying?"

"It's possible."

Grace didn't argue with them, just nodded with fearful resignation. "Go on."

"Your husband disappears. Then a couple of months later, Reed Morgan dies, a man who knew about their dealings."

"You think Brent killed Morgan?"

Blake shook his head. "We don't know that, only that Morgan's dead. If your husband did kill him and he decides you know too much, you might be in danger."

Jimmie walked back in and talked to Blake who nodded and quietly said, "Thanks." He leaned toward Grace. "If you will permit it, Master Sergeant Julia St. Clair will spend the night here and stay with you for the next few days."

"Do you think that's really necessary?"

"We do. Until we know more about Mr. Wexler, we can't be too cautious."

Grace looked at Laura. "What about talking to my attorney?"

"You need to do that right away," Laura said. "But I think you ought to consider talking with someone other than the lawyer handling the probate."

"Why?"

"Because this isn't a probate matter anymore. Do you know any criminal lawyers?"

Grace gasped. "But I haven't..."

"But you're in the middle of it. A criminal lawyer will have a better sense of the problems you're facing."

"I know Collier Weeks."

Laura nodded. "He's the best in town. Talk with him first if you can. I know Collier and I'd be glad to share with him what our concerns are, if you'd like."

"I'd appreciate that."

Blake raised his finger to interrupt. "Mrs. Wexler, is there anything missing that you can think of?"

"From the burglary?"

"No, of Mr. Wexler's."

Grace thought a moment. "I always assumed that everything burned up the car, so it's hard to be certain."

"Maybe something that wouldn't have been in the car."

"The only things I haven't found are a pair of cufflinks engraved BW and set with diamonds, and a Rolex watch he'd recently bought. The cufflinks were very special and they weren't with his clothes and weren't in the ashes that were left. Neither was the watch, though I only saw that once and I doubt I could recognize it again."

"Interesting."

Robert spoke up. "We'd like to look through your husband's papers, maybe analyze the spending patterns. Would that be possible?"

"Yes, you can start right now, if you want."

Laura piped up. "There's a young man who works for us, Everett Passage, who'd be the best at the task. Could we send him out later on today?"

"Certainly."

■ ■ ■ ■

Vic and Carver were at the Capitol working with legislative conferees on appropriations bills. Vic was leaning on the rotunda railing, verbally sparring with a cantankerous legislator, when he saw Laura emerge from the elevator with a preoccupied expression on her face. He extricated himself and intercepted her before she reached the Governor's Office. It was the first time he'd seen her since their argument.

"Laura, let's go in here," Vic said, guiding her with a single touch toward the back door of his office. "What do you have?"

"Not what we expected. The body in the wreck wasn't Brent Wexler's."

"What?" The possibility had never occurred to him.

"Well, we won't have a positive identification until Mrs. Wexler gets his dental records on Monday, but the person killed was too sick to have been Wexler. Cirrhosis of the liver, tuberculosis, arthritis."

"I can't believe this."

"The man died from strangulation. His Adam's apple was fractured. It's going to be difficult, maybe impossible, to find out who he was. Probably some poor homeless person, someone who didn't take much care of himself."

With Vic's stunned silence, Laura continued. "We've just come from Mrs. Wexler's. She was very helpful—she's learned a lot about her husband lately and what she's learned isn't good."

"Like what?"

"Oh, payments to non-existent public relations firms, bank accounts, strange purchases."

"Help me, Laura, what does this mean?"

"We're just guessing but these are some possibilities. Wexler could have killed Mr. X, by accident or intentionally, then tried to cover the deed with the wreck, and disappeared. Or, someone has Wexler somewhere and killed Mr. X to cover it up. Or, Wexler wanted to sail away with a honey and created the wreck to cover his tracks. Or instead of a woman, he made off with a lot of money. And then there's Reed Morgan's death, and Mrs. Wexler's burglar."

"And you think they're connected?"

"They could be."

"What do you do next?"

"We'll work out the game plan tomorrow, but everyone agrees that we..."

The door behind her opened and Governor Carver strode in, looking exhilarated. Vic had left him with the Lieutenant Governor fifteen minutes earlier, so he assumed Carver had prevailed.

Both Vic and Laura stood up. "Hello, Laura," said Carver, his broad smile suddenly vanishing. "This must be bad news."

Vic cut in quickly. "The autopsy showed that the man in the car wreck wasn't Brent."

Carver dropped directly into the chair in front of the window, speechless. Laura began giving him the details, as she had with Vic.

"Have you talked with Grace?"

"Yes. We just left her house."

The Governor seemed to recover faster than Vic from the shock. "Who is we?"

"Myself, Blake Coleman, Robert Stone, and Jimmie Anderson."

"You must have scared her to death. Were all those people necessary?"

"Yes, sir, they were."

Vic squirmed with discomfort. Laura's unfortunate tendency toward bluntness when she was certain of her position could backfire so easily at a time like this.

"She was the number two suspect," added Laura.

"Suspect for what?" Carver asked.

"The murder of Mr. Unknown."

"Don't joke with me," the Governor said with a gruff laugh.

"I'm not, Governor. From a police perspective, this whole thing has already netted her two million in insurance money, the value of Wexler, Inc., the farm..."

"And who's number one suspect?" interrupted Carver.

"Mr. Wexler is now."

Carver's eyes narrowed on Laura. "Now listen here, young lady, Brent Wexler was my closest friend and Grace is as gracious a lady as my wife, Sarah. Just what are you suggesting?"

"At this point, Governor, I'm not suggesting anything. All I know is that someone very cleverly and carefully faked Mr. Wexler's death and Wexler may be alive and well, living somewhere on the money that's missing."

"What money?" Vic asked.

"For starters, we've determined that Wexler, Inc. paid over a million dollars to a nonexistent public relations firm. It looks like a tax dodge, but where the money went, we don't know."

Impatiently Vic prodded, "Something else?"

"The bank account Mrs. Wexler discovered had lots of money going in and, by and large, only cash coming out. The bank's getting her copies of all the transactions."

"Grace knows about this?" Governor Carver had become quiet, looking at Vic, not Laura, as he talked.

"As she told us, and we believe her, she's known something was wrong but it never occurred to her that Wexler wasn't dead. Her looking into the bank accounts and all his purchases is what has convinced us she wasn't involved."

In a quiet, resigned voice, Vic spoke. "I assume this will be all over the papers tomorrow?"

"No, not if I can help it. As long as possible, we want to investigate without anyone knowing that Wexler wasn't killed. Of course, Mrs. Wexler is going to consult an attorney to see whether she has to disclose anything immediately. I've suggested someone other than the firm handling the estate."

Carver jumped back in, an edge returning to his voice. "What would she have to disclose? She didn't start this, she hasn't done anything wrong."

"Not intentionally. But think about it, sir. She's received and, so she tells us, spent almost all of the two million in insurance proceeds for the death of a man who isn't dead. She's sold land she didn't have title to, and she's negotiating for the sale of Wex..."

"I see, I see," Carver waved his hand for her to stop.

Vic ventured another question. "How long will this take?"

"No idea. Particularly considering the Reed Morgan connection."

"What Reed Morgan connection?" Carver asked.

"It appears that Wexler might have been paying off Morgan," Laura said, puzzled that Vic hadn't alerted Carver to the issue.

Carver looked back at her sternly. "Wexler was an upstanding businessman, generous to a fault. You'd better be certain before you make any off-the-wall accusations."

"Nothing I've said has been off-the-wall, sir, I assure you," Laura said equally sternly.

Vic scrambled to break up their volley. "Well, then, how long can you keep this under wraps?"

"If it only involved the people within the State Patrol, forever, if necessary. But several others know."

Vic noticed that Laura was avoiding looking at Carver.

"We'll have to ask questions that might make people suspicious," Laura continued. "It'll all depend."

Silence descended over all three and Laura rose to leave. She gave Vic a quick look—all business, not an ounce of warmth in it. Then she turned to Carver and said, "Believe me, sir, I didn't go looking for this one, and I'll do everything I can to keep it as far away from you as possible."

Carver gave her a weak smile. She pulled the door closed behind her with a stately thunk. The two men sat for a moment in stunned silence.

"I've relied on you," moaned Carver. "Don't fail me now. Everything, every single thing, is riding on it."

"Do you know what this other bank account could be? Could it be a fund raising account?"

Still staring off in the distance, Carver shook his head.

"Don't bullshit me, Gibbs," Vic said, anger beginning to mount. "I don't want Laura getting a bunch of cops involved in a chase if it's going to be embarrassing."

Carver still didn't answer.

"I deserve better than silence, goddamnit."

Carver looked straight at Vic. "I don't know what she could be talking about, and that's the truth."

Vic stared straight back at him, saying nothing.

# Sixteen

The early morning was chillier than normal for April—downright cold, in fact. Robert and Jimmie called it invigorating, but with each passing year, Blake was less and less enthusiastic about wintery temperatures.

They bumped onto the wet spring-green field in the medical examiner's Suburban with the empty casket jouncing about in the back. Huge showy pink azaleas, almost past their peak, encircled the cemetery, heightening the lush green of the field grasses.

Blake passed close to an enormous cow, pregnant with a calf ready to drop any minute. If he'd been alone he would have answered her nervous lowing with his own deep moo, but he held it back. "We've got to be done and out of here by eleven," said Blake. "I promised Mrs. Wexler's brother there would be no trace of us when he brought the children home after church."

"Good, 'cuz I'm supposed to be cleaned up and sleeping through the sermon by then," Robert replied.

"This won't take long," Jimmie said. "Particularly since we don't have an audience or a body."

"Good point."

And it didn't. After lowering the casket into the vault and replacing the vault cover, Jimmie scooped up nearly every clod of dirt with the backhoe and dumped it in the grave, so there wasn't much shoveling for either Robert or Blake to do. They had loaded the equipment onto the trailer and closed the cemetery gate by eight-thirty.

Blake, in the Suburban, pulled up alongside Jimmie who was driving the truck with the trailer and backhoe. "Why don't you leave all that in the lot at headquarters, and we'll get it back tomorrow," he said, talking past Robert in the passenger seat.

"Fine. I'm going back there anyway. I want to start working on the wreck tomorrow, but I've got to get it moved while no one's around."

"Need any help?"

"Sure. Always easier with two people. There are about ten cars to move to get to it."

"Plan on it. I'll see you in a few."

Jimmie waved his finger in agreement and headed across the field.

"Find out anything about Trey?" Blake asked Robert.

"He spent the night at his house. At least two club members were there, too. What'd you find in his file?"

"Not much. How old do you think he is?"

"Forty."

"More," Blake said. "He turns forty-seven this coming week."

"In pretty good shape, wouldn't you say? Anything else?"

"He's had very few disciplinary actions. A little overbearing on the road—complaints about rudeness, but not much else. He's done all that SWAT training, bomb removal courses, and he's pulled the trigger in a couple of very tight spots. Did you know he was a Marine?"

"Think I knew that."

"Reconnaissance team and electronics."

"Hmm," Robert said. "He kinda fits the loner profile."

"A real loner. I went through some case files last night too.

He's rarely worked with a partner, something that hadn't occurred to me."

"I wonder why it hasn't cropped up," Robert mused. "If I'm not mistaken, Turner was alone a couple of times when he's gotten some pretty shaky confessions. You would have thought someone would have challenged him."

"Yeah, I remember one of those now that you mention it. We were sweating bullets, but nothing ever happened. Did you find the wife?" asked Blake.

"Still looking. It's gonna be a sonovabitch to watch him. Nearly ten miles of back roads to his place, hardly anyone on them. Can't just inconspicuously fall in behind him."

"Then put a bird-dog on his car. We've got to be able to track him."

"I don't know if I want to take that chance. If he finds it, he'll be spooked. And from what I saw of his house at the farm last night, he's the type who would check each morning. Stickler for detail."

"Have *you* ever bothered to check?"

"No. But I'm not worried about being watched."

"The hell you aren't. But that's my point. No one checks. Go ahead and use a bird-dog," Blake said dismissing Robert's concerns. "Tell me about the house he had at Wexler's farm."

"Neat as a pin. He'd built all sorts of intricate cabinets. There's one pantry shelf unit that I swear is the exact depth for one can of soup. And in the barn where he had his workshop, there's a pegboard with the shape of every tool painted where each one goes. Even his butcher knives and saws were hung up."

"What else did you find?"

Robert shook his head. "It was scrubbed clean. There aren't even fingerprints."

"Well, we've got to keep track of him somehow."

"I could send him on the road."

"Nah. I want to watch him. And at just the right moment, I want him to start noticing things."

■ ■ ■ ■

Grace called Collier Weeks, a former assistant with the U.S. Justice Department in D.C., who had come home and established a thriving white collar crime criminal defense practice. He'd known her for years—their daughters had gone to school together. Given the anguish in Grace's voice when she'd called, Collier skipped church that morning to talk to her. When she stepped out to greet him, her fatigue and anxiety were obvious.

"I'm so sorry I didn't get the message last night. We were out to dinner."

"Don't apologize, I'm grateful you could come this morning."

"What's happened?"

He followed Grace into the house, and she led him toward the kitchen. "Brent's not dead."

"Not dead?"

Grace automatically got a second coffee mug and placed it beside her own. She was filling both without even asking if he wanted any when Julia St. Clair came downstairs.

"Good morning, Mrs. Wexler."

Grace turned and introduced her to Collier.

"I'll be in the back if you need anything, ma'am."

"No, stay here and get your breakfast. We're going into the library."

"Are you sure?"

"Absolutely."

They picked up their coffee mugs and Collier followed Grace. The library was a small room, no more than nine feet by nine with bookshelves lining the walls floor to ceiling. The cushions on the window seats were thick and the pillows plump.

"Who's she?" Collier asked as soon as the door was closed.

"Master Sergeant Julia St. Clair, State Patrol."

"Oh. Why don't you start at the beginning?" Collier suggested, sinking into an easy chair.

"Three days ago, the Patrol realized they'd made a mistake about the wreck. The car had been tampered with they thought..."

"Stop. Who told you this?"

"Laura Owen..."

"I know Laura. She's a straight shooter. I've represented her on a case."

"She spoke highly of you. Well, late last week she came by and explained that the State Patrol had looked at the wreck again and suspected foul play. Ms. Owen asked permission to exhume Brent's body."

"And you gave it?"

"Of course."

"I wish you'd called me then."

"Did I do something wrong?"

"No, but I might have been able to help," said Collier. "But it doesn't matter, go on."

"I needed it to be done quietly. I'm in the middle of selling Brent's business so I figured cooperation would be best. She said they could do an autopsy without anyone knowing and that would be it."

"What you did was absolutely right," Collier said.

Grace sighed with relief.

"What did they find?"

"Someone else's body."

"How did they know that?"

"The man was sick—tuberculosis, liver disease, no spleen. Couldn't be Brent. God, I've already spent the two million dollars of insurance money, and Brent's not..." Grace wiped a tear away from her already red eyes.

Collier was usually good at not exhibiting any trace of alarm when he heard confessions, but this was such shocking news that his widened eyes gave him away. He reached across the side of his chair to put a comforting hand on Grace's arm. "Let's start at the beginning again."

An hour and seven pages of notes later, Collier leaned back and stretched his arms behind his head. "There's one word never to forget, particularly when you can't find me, and that's 'cooperate.' Cooperate all day long. It's the best course of action in this case."

"What about the insurance money?"

"Sit tight for the time being. Just like Laura said, there's been foul play and Brent might in fact be dead. At some point, you have an obligation to tell them, but not yet."

"But I've spent it, figuring I'd live off what I made selling the hunt club. Now I don't even have the right to have sold that."

"I think I can handle that."

"But what about the IRS? Suppose they find out about Crimmins and Westerly?"

"If they haven't already, I doubt they will, but we'll deal with the IRS when it comes up."

"And what about Wexler, Inc., and the sale?"

"Now, that's another matter. How fast a track are the negotiations on?"

"Fast. I've already agreed to sell. They're coming tomorrow to start their due diligence review."

"Can you slow it down?"

Grace shook her head. "I don't know. I'll try."

"You'll need to."

"Maybe I could get sick or something."

"Not a bad idea. Stay here, out of touch." Collier looked at Grace's tearful eyes. "You've done fine. Better than fine. And it will be all right. I promise you. You haven't done anything wrong—certainly not intentionally."

■ ■ ■ ■

"So tell me what new twists and turns you encountered today," said Rachel Stone, putting her glass of red wine down on the edge of their enormous bathtub and slipping far enough under so her shoulders were covered with water,

Robert tipped his own glass up and finished it off, then

reached for the bottle and poured some more. He settled into the water next to his wife, reaching for one of her feet. When she realized a foot massage was in the offing, Rachel repositioned herself with her tiny feet on Robert's chest.

The Stone's master bathroom was the size of a normal bedroom. Besides a steam shower, there was a whirlpool bath nearly as big as a small swimming pool. Both Robert and Rachel loved to stretch out and soak, one of their favorite ways to end the day. The bath was built up on a platform, beneath three large skylights. The steam from the bath often clouded a view of the stars, but tonight, the full moon was hardly dimmed. The only other light was a flickering row of candles.

"Well, the guy we thought was dead, isn't dead," Robert said, gently moving his thumbs into the pad of Rachel's left foot, "and the guy who is dead, we don't know who he is. Then the Senate killed the pay raise, but now we think it's alive again, because the other dead guy was playing poker with a senator just before he kicked the bucket."

"Say that again?"

"I don't think I could." His hand moved up her leg to massage her calf muscle and then continued on toward her inner thigh. "And I don't think I want to."

Robert sat up, bringing both hands up to Rachel's hips and then slipped back into water beside her, his lips finding one of her breasts as she arched her back.

"Mmmm...." cooed Rachel. "You surely know how to make a girl forget about the hospital and all those screaming babies."

■ ■ ■ ■

When Robert arrived at headquarters at 7:30 the next morning, Jimmie's car was already in his spot and the hood was cold. He found him under Wexler's car. Eddie Williams was inspecting the engine inch-by-inch with a flashlight.

"Y'all are at it early," Robert remarked.

"Wish I knew what I was looking for," came Jimmie's voice from under the car.

"Have you figured out how fast it was going?" Robert asked.

"Just talked to the Mercedes service department. They're going to call me back when they find the manufacturer's specs and do the calculations. But it may take a while since this isn't a recent model."

"However fast it was, it wasn't going on gravity," Eddie added. "Something was keeping the throttle open. But damned if I can find it. The cruise control had to be retrofitted because I don't think cars this old had that."

"Where's the control?" Robert asked, picking up another flashlight.

"Right there, what's left of it at least."

"What's that?" Robert pointed his beam toward a portion of the manifold.

Eddie reached in and pulled off a mangled blackened alligator clip and held it up for Robert to see. "Wonder what this was attached to?" Eddie asked.

Robert reached for the clip. "Couldn't you mess with the cruise control circuit boards?"

Eddie's eyes sparkled. "You could make it go faster and faster."

"And crash into the ditch," Jimmie said from under the car.

■ ■ ■ ■

Since eight that morning, Nima Gales, the criminal analyst, had parked herself in front of the teletype machine in the Criminal Records Room, making certain that no one else saw any of the responses to the queries Robert had instructed her to send out Sunday afternoon. Memphis had one missing person that might fit the medical examiner's description, but Birmingham and New Orleans hadn't replied. Baton Rouge had nothing.

She was listening so intently to a Birmingham officer describe a missing person who fit her query that she didn't notice Trey Turner walk in the door behind her. She finished that call and was dialing again when Trey spoke.

"Hey, Nima."

The unexpected voice scared the wits out of her and Nima dropped the phone and knocked another stack of papers off the console. Trey instantly stooped to help her, blatantly looking at her papers as he collected them. Her initial teletype was on top of the pile and the words "New Orleans" and "missing person" leapt off the page.

Nima took the pile from him as quickly as she could.

"Nervous?"

"Tired. It's been a long week."

"It's only Monday, Nima."

"Feels like I never left," she mumbled, her heart still pounding as she took back the papers from Trey. "Thanks."

Trey stared at her eerily, then sauntered over to the copier and switched it on. "Where's that Everett guy? Still busy crunching numbers?"

"Don't know. He hasn't been in today."

■ ■ ■ ■

Late Monday morning, the bank messenger arrived at Grace's house with a large box. Everett, who'd arrived promptly at eight, just before Grace left for Wexler, Inc., signed for the package. He'd been expecting the delivery, but the size of the box made his head swim. There were already mountains of material to review and pump into the computer, and this looked like more than he could handle.

He slit open the packing tape with a pen tip and drew out the first batch of microfilmed copies of the checks. A campaign account. Without another look, Everett dropped it all back in the box, and returned to his task of plugging in dates and transactions, reconstructing Wexler's financial history for the last several years.

Laura called around 11:45.

"How's it going?"

"I don't know if I can do this by myself. There's so much."

"I know the feeling," said Laura. "I'm dug in for a long day myself with the final budget figures. But I'll be able to help as soon as I finish."

"At least I don't have to worry about that other account," Everett said. "The copies arrived this morning and it's campaign stuff."

"Are you sure?"

"Yeah. A lot of the checks are made out to the Wexler Political Action Committee."

"Wexler Political Action Committee," Laura mumbled. "Never heard of it."

"I can check and see if it's registered with the Secretary of State."

"No," she said quickly. "don't you bother about it. Just put it aside."

"Fine with me."

"You know, I was just on my way out to an appointment. I'll swing by and pick it up."

Laura searched under her desk for her shoes and slipped them on, checking her watch. She hurried out of her office to a waiting elevator, calling to Deborah as she held the doors open, "Tell Blake I'm going out for a few moments and see if he can meet me for lunch."

"Where?"

She thought for a split-second. "The Cherokee. At twelve-thirty."

As Laura was leaving with the box of bank records, Grace and Julia pulled up. She patted the box. "The bank copies arrived for that account you found. It's nothing to worry about. Nothing extra at least. Definitely campaign-related, so I told Everett not to bother with it. I'll review it quickly and get it to the Governor."

"Thank God for that," Grace sighed. "I don't think I could handle any more than this Crimmins stuff. I gave all the political and campaign records to Gibbs. He pestered me about it for days. I don't remember any bank statements, just pages and pages of names."

"That's why I figure it won't be important."

Grace motioned to the folders under her arm. "And here's some more from the office. Unfortunately, none of the early construction files were kept."

Laura shook her head with disappointment. "That was our last hope."

"Leb Bailey said Brent had all those old files shredded."

■ ■ ■ ■

Even in the middle of a bright sunny day, it was hard to see in the booths near the back of the Cherokee, Laura's favorite road house. It was never lonely—there was always a sporting event of one kind or another on the two televisions hanging from the ceiling over the bar and in the pool room—and the flavor of their hamburgers was unequaled.

She'd had time to flip through nearly all the pages of checks while she waited for Blake to arrive. Brent had collected contributions from corporations—big checks—and some from names Laura recognized as supporters of Carver's last opponent. And there'd been substantial amounts of cash.

"And what have we here?"

Blake's voice startled her. He slipped into the booth, picking up the laminated menu. "Must be interesting. Didn't your mother warn you about ruining your eyes reading in the dark?"

"That's a myth. Same as having to wait an hour after you've eaten to swim."

A college kid in jeans and a T-shirt appeared with a pad and a pencil behind his ear, and they ordered lunch.

"So who gets to go first?" Blake said, wringing his hands in anticipation.

"Shoot."

Blake surveyed the booths around them, then leaned closer and spoke more softly. "First, our man Wexler was never in any of the armed services."

"That's an interesting twist."

"Second, the Georgia Bureau of Investigation says the handwriting on the bank signature card for the public relations firm looks remarkably like Wexler's. Their documents analyst is going to work on it today."

"Well, now," Laura murmured.

"The Atlanta bank's a little nervous. Their records aren't really up to snuff. The account shouldn't have been opened without more documentation than they had, and their slip-up has put them in a very cooperative mood. They're rounding up copies of all the transactions now. Looks like a lot of it, maybe all of it, was withdrawn as cash. Usually the same amount, $9,950.00. That's fifty bucks under the currency reporting threshold."

"Cash is kinda hard to trace," Laura said.

"You're right about that. What do you have?"

"The unknown bank account Mrs. Wexler found. It had campaign contributions in it."

"That would make sense."

"Yes," Laura said, leaning a little closer to Blake and lowering her voice. "But some of these were big corporate checks exceeding the legal limits on corporate contributions."

Two glasses of ice tea were placed suddenly on the end of the booth. Blake took one, reaching for the sugar, and began doctoring his drink. "I don't like getting this close to the Governor."

"Me neither. But I think Wexler was taking the money and converting it into cash for the campaign. I'd bet big bucks none of it was reported. G-O-T-V money."

"What is 'geo-TV'?"

"Not 'geo', the letters G-O. Get-out-the-vote. That's what all the cash floating around on election day is called."

"Ahhhh. I always wondered about it but felt too stupid to ask," Blake said.

Laura took a long sip of tea, flipping through the pages of checks, looking for something.

A couple of young lawyer types slid in to the booth behind them and Blake motioned for her to draw closer. "But that might account for why Vic Regis got so bent out of shape about the exhumation. He probably didn't want anyone looking around."

Laura looked at him anxiously.

"I'm not saying Vic was involved in the murder," Blake explained. "He just didn't want anyone nosing around, starting some big investigation."

"You know, you're probably right. I wish I could check Carver's campaign filings without raising eyebrows. I hate going behind Vic's back."

They sat back to make room for the food coming their way on the waiter's arm. "That's no problem. I've got it all at the office."

"Why would you have those?"

"How on earth do you think troopers politic for jobs?"

"What do you mean?"

"There must have been ten copies of those reports floating around headquarters. My set came from Bill Kenner when he retired. I went through all the stuff he threw out. Don't you remember all the heat you got from the Governor to promote him?"

"Yeah."

"Kenner got the lists, found the big contributors that he knew, and probably promised to fix a few tickets or something in return for them droppin' a dime on the Governor in his behalf. The Patrol's one of the best customers at the Secretary of State's office buying those lists."

Laura shook her head in disbelief. "I should have known."

They ate in silence, both reaching for extra napkins as juice and grease squeezed out of their burgers.

"So, do you have the final reports that have been filed since the campaign was over?"

"I do."

"I knew I could count on you."

Laura looked back at the sheaf of papers and was about to show Blake some samples when he held his hand up to stop her. "I think you ought to leave everyone out of the loop on this campaign stuff. Then, whenever you have your heart-to-heart with Regis, you can honestly say you're the only one who's worked on it."

"Good point."

"Be careful how you play your cards," Blake said. "All of us are beholden to the Governor, but you more than anyone."

"Don't I know it."

■ ■ ■ ■

"Is there any further discussion before the vote to reconsider the amendment to the State Patrol's appropriation which struck the pay raise for the sworn officers?" the Lieutenant Governor asked, looking around the chamber. The galleries were packed with off-duty troopers, both in uniform and in plain clothes.

"Vote, vote," came calls from the floor.

"Will the Secretary read the roll call?" the Lieutenant Governor said.

Even at a quick pace, reading the fifty-two names seemed to take forever. Robert kept a tally of the ayes, while Blake counted the nays.

When Sandifer was called, the senator hesitated. Robert looked up from his sheet—he wasn't expecting the man to switch his vote, not on an issue so important to his friend and closest colleague, Gabriel Collel. The senator took a deep breath, nodded to Collel who'd turned to watch him, and quietly added his no. Collel smiled, though clearly disappointed that Sandifer had even vacillated.

The Secretary handed the tally to the Lieutenant Governor who stared at the paper a second longer than usual, then spoke. "The Ayes have 26 and the Nays have 26. The Lieutenant Governor votes Nay. The bill as passed is amended to include the pay raise."

Collel slunk back into his chair, staring at the man with all the venom he could summon.

Robert leaned over toward Blake. "Whatever you said, must have worked."

Blake smiled. "No comment.

"Imagine what their next poker game will be like."

■ ■ ■ ■

Brent had kept his face buried in a newspaper for the better part of the flight from Geneva to Atlanta. When he'd felt like resting during the trip, he'd pulled his cap down low so no one could study him. As the crowd waited to pass through immigration, he hung toward the back of the line.

"Welcome home, Mr. Wheeler," an abnormally gregarious agent said as he perused Brent's passport.

"Great to be back," said Brent.

Waiting for his luggage among so many southern travelers was agony even though few people could have recognized him. His continued weight loss had made a significant difference beyond the facial changes. But he was still wary, madly searching every face, praying he'd have enough time to turn away if even a glimmer of recognition registered. Unlike in Europe, he was constantly on alert, looking everywhere, feeling naked and recognizable. It was exhausting.

He waited at the far side of the baggage claim area, back against the wall. The bags were slow to arrive and when his finally appeared, he left it on the conveyor belt for two complete cycles, letting the crowd thin out before he stepped forward to retrieve it. He was the last person from his flight through customs.

■ ■ ■ ■

By 5:30, a brilliant sunset was promising to paint the western sky and Laura left her pencil on her spreadsheets and headed for the conference room to watch it. Turning off the overhead lights, she took a seat at the window in one of the thickly upholstered swivel chairs, putting her feet up on another. With the room darkened, she hoped no one would think to come in. If it hadn't been so windy, she'd have sneaked a beer from her office refrigerator and gone up to the roof where she was certain no one would visit, but that would have to wait for another day. If, Laura thought, she still had her job.

In the distance, she could see a new crane being erected above Children's Hospital. Laura checked her watch. The crew must be working overtime. After a few more minutes of thoughtless reverie, the door opened and Blake walked in. "When I saw the sky, I figured I'd find you here."

"Best view in town. I'm taking a break from those spreadsheets."

"What about Will?"

"He's with his grandparents for the night. All the grandchildren are in town and he wasn't about to miss it."

Blake pulled aside two chairs for himself and stretched his legs out, facing the spectacular colors that stretched out in every direction. "The handwriting analyst in Georgia just reported in. There's no doubt that Wexler signed the bank documents for the public relations firm, Crimmins and Westerly. The Westerly is Broderick Westerly. Same initials."

"That reminds me." She put her feet down and stood up. "Stay here, there's something I need to show you," and before he could respond, she was out the door.

Laura reappeared, closing the door behind her. "This is something from the campaign account. I didn't look at both sides of the checks until I started spreading the numbers."

"I'd rather not..."

"Believe me, I've thought about this. I just want to show you one endorsement—I won't let you see the front side of the check." Laura folded the slick microfilm copy sheet so only one area was visible.

He held his hand up in protest.

"No, you need to see this in case the checks and I ever get separated and you need a parachute." She turned the paper around to reveal "Gibbs Carver—for deposit only" in the strong, slanted rhythms of the Governor's handwriting.

Instead of smiling, Blake's jaw tensed. "That parachute only works if Carver stays as Governor. Once he's out of there, a new governor would bring in his own people, regardless."

"I understand. I'd be the first to go, don't you think?"

Blake didn't hide his discomfort. "We've got to keep control of this thing."

"No question. Could your friend at the Georgia Bureau of Investigations analyze a couple of these handwriting samples, too?"

"I'm sure he could. Do you have comparisons?"

"I have plenty of the Governor's handwriting, but we need to get some of Wexler's."

"Julia can get those for me. GBI's probably shut down for the day, but I'll send the materials out overnight. They'll have it in the morning."

"The more I know, the better off I'll be when I talk to Vic. Did you tell Robert?"

"Yes, but only him. With the rest of them, I'm blowing off this account as a routine campaign matter."

Laura nodded, agreeing. "If it makes you feel any better, under the election laws, false reporting isn't a felony."

Blake smiled for the first time that afternoon. "I never did think the Patrol had enough manpower to spend any time on misdemeanors."

Laura leaned her head back, closed her eyes to the sunset, and exhaled, exhausted. "Has this job always been like this? What happened to all the perks that were supposed to come along with it?"

"You've got 'em—big office, nice car, plane, and more work than you can shake a stick at. Your problem is you bother to look around. Most guys find a way to keep their eyes closed and enjoy the ride."

■ ■ ■ ■

After everyone except the cleaning crews had left headquarters, they all congregated in Laura's office—Blake, Robert, Everett, and Jimmie. The five of them settled around the coffee table, each with notebooks and papers at hand.

"Let's start with the wreck," Robert suggested.

Jimmie spoke up. "The car was moving at approximately 45 mph when it left the bank of the creek and traveled through the air, dropping and crashing into the tree on the far side. The gas tank had to have been full or close to it for the wreck to have burned as completely as it did. But that brings up an interesting point. Catherine's people determined that the octane level of the fuel left in the tank was between 89 and 91 octane."

"Bad gas?" Laura asked. "Or it had been mixed?"

"I'm pretty certain it was mixed," Jimmie said. "The Texaco where Everett says the last tankful was purchased is a good station, quality products. Assuming Wexler always used premium in that car, an octane level of less than 93 would mean regular was mixed in—probably at the last fill-up."

Everett nodded.

"So when do you think the accident happened?" Blake asked Jimmie.

"Working back from when I got there, the car was cold, so it had cooled down after burning at least two hours—that's the minimum we think it took for such a complete burn. It was near freezing that night and the car could have cooled down pretty quickly. Let's figure two hours for the fire, two hours to cool down. I'd say it started at 2 A.M. at the latest. Probably earlier." Jimmie shook his head, disgusted. "This never should have happened this way."

"Stop beating yourself up about it," Blake said, then looked at Robert. "What about the dead man?"

"Not much except New Orleans Missing Persons has a report of a homeless fellow who stopped showing up at a soup kitchen in late February."

"Those people keep track of who comes in?" asked Laura.

"They know the regulars. This fellow was a tall guy—the only one who fits so far. Nothing checked out in Memphis, Mobile, Birmingham, or Baton Rouge. Toxicology reported that there weren't any drugs present in the dead man's system, legal or otherwise. Looks like he was a drinker, not a doper," Robert shrugged. "And he didn't take care of himself."

"Could definitely be a homeless person," Laura said.

"So let me tell you what I know about Wexler," Blake suggested. "He wasn't in the Navy or any of the other armed services, at least not under that name. Social Security told me his number was issued in Mississippi when he was in college. Their computer says he was born in Summers, Arkansas, on February 22, 1942, parents were Eli and Georgia Wexler. But there wasn't any such person born that day. And no social security numbers were issued for Eli or Georgia Wexler in Arkansas."

"Does social security have an actual document from when he got a card?" Laura asked.

"Yes, but it's in Baltimore and it'll take several days to get a photocopy of it. I've got a friend on the Arkansas Patrol who's going to do some more checking on birth records and families from Summers."

"What about his fingerprints?"

Blake shook his head. "Nothing. Department of Defense didn't keep fingerprints from that far back. We do know that Wexler was the person who signed the signature cards at the Georgia Guaranty National Bank when the fake business account was opened. The GBI handwriting analyst confirmed that today. Wexler was withdrawing that money in big chunks—$9,950 in cash—over a million in eight years." This last number elicited a little whistle from Robert.

"Which brings us to what Wexler was doing in the days before the wreck," Blake concluded.

Robert waved his finger to take over. "I spent part of yesterday talking to the owner of the Islander, the hotel in Roatan. He wasn't going to be helpful until he heard the story. The only interesting thing was that Wexler shaved his head while he was there, part of a bet in an all-night card game he lost. Everyone watched him do it. They were a little looped at the time."

"What sort of place is this?"

"Small. Ten rooms in five small cabins and a main building that has the dining room and a big sitting room. Brent's group takes it over completely for the last week in February. The same group has been gathering for years."

Robert continued, "Then he went into Tegucigalpa and bought a hairpiece the next day. But he didn't wear it, seemed to enjoy the new look."

"I don't think it was cheap, either," Everett interjected. "I suspect he spent three hundred or so. Can't be exact because I'm not certain about the exchange rate."

Blake and Robert looked at Everett, amazed with this tidbit. "You get that from the credit card data?"

Everett nodded. "I started with the most recent bills first. All credit cards, bank transactions, business expenses. Julia St. Clair has been terrific."

He passed out several sheets to each person. "These list everything in reverse date order, from the most recent backward. From left to right, the source, the date, the amount, the location, the item if I knew it, and a comment field."

"What's this gas purchase after the 1st?"

"Farm pickup truck—Chevron card. Mrs. Wexler said she found the card in the truck and took it, along with the receipts, when she went out there in mid March. It looks like all the Chevron purchases from that card were for the pickup."

"How do you know that?"

"The wad of receipts she gave me account for all the purchases on the last few bills. They were behind the visor with the card."

"Who signed them?"

"Trey signed most, but Wexler signed some too. I've put a T or a W in the comment field depending," Everett said.

The room grew quiet as they studied Everett's data.

"You can see that the last day, he paid his bill at the hotel in Roatan, paid for his Roatan rental car, went to a restaurant in the airport called the Catfish Corner, and ate or drank."

"What's all this cash?"

"Advances at automatic teller machines. He withdrew the daily maximum on the bank account and both his credit cards."

"I thought he was going out to dinner with a client?"

"I figure that's what the restaurant bill was."

"They ate at the airport? In New Orleans?" Robert asked,

skeptical.

"Maybe whoever he was meeting was going somewhere," Everett responded.

"Did he put gas in his car for the drive north?" Jimmie asked.

"No, not using a credit card. He had plenty of cash and could easily have paid for it, though."

"Something's wrong. That car gets twenty miles to the gallon, tops, and it has a sixteen gallon tank. Without putting in more gas, he'd have been nearly empty when the wreck occurred, even if he started out with a full tank. He had to get gas on the way up."

"And it probably wasn't full. The last time he got gas for the Mercedes was February 25th," Everett pointed out.

"Go back to this cash on March 5th. What else do you know?" Blake asked.

"It was cash. What more is there to say?"

"Can you find out what time he withdrew it?"

"I can try," Everett said.

"Check on it, will ya?" Blake asked.

Everett nodded, circling that item on his sheet and making a note.

"And tell me more about that Chevron bill."

"Here's the printout of just that account." Everett handed out more papers.

Blake murmured the litany. "Trey bought gas on February 26th, in Hammond, Louisiana. Trey bought more gas on the 28th—a lot of gas, in fact, in Saragossa."

"Yeah, over thirty-three gallons."

"How big is the tank on the truck?"

"Twenty, twenty-five tops."

"And he bought more than a tank full? What kind of gas did he buy for it?"

"It's a standard truck," Robert interjected. "Saw it the other night when I was out there. Takes regular."

"But he bought ten gallons more than his tank could hold." Everett said.

"He might have bought extra stuff and they just put down

more gas," Blake suggested.

Everett shook his head. "Nope. This station always item-izes. He probably filled up gas cans or a second car."

Jimmie spoke up. "So, our man flies into New Orleans from Honduras, drives north, kills some guy, fakes his death, pours some extra gasoline on the wreck to make it burn, and disap-pears. Or..."

"Or, he had help," Blake said. "I think we need to know when he ate in the restaurant and when he withdrew that money."

"And who the dead guy is, don't forget about that," Robert added.

■ ■ ■ ■

"You're on speaker phone, Kramer," Blake said. "Robert's in here with me."

"Hey, boss," Master Sergeant Kramer Jennings said to Robert.

"Evenin' Kramer," Robert answered.

"What's going on?" Blake said, impatient.

"He's at home doing whatever he does at night," Kramer said with an unmistakable hint of disgust in his voice. "He left the office, stopped at the grocery store for a couple of bags of something, and drove through Northwoods."

"Past the Wexler house?"

"Yes sir."

"What cars could you see?"

"Hers was out front, but Julia's was in the garage with the doors closed. He made three passes. Almost saw me."

"Then?"

"Went to Second Creek."

"What are your plans now?"

"I'm gonna get a few hours sleep and be out here when he heads in tomorrow."

"You need some relief?"

"Not yet. I'll tell ya."

"You're a good man." Blake said.

■ ■ ▨ ▨

Laura logged on the Internet. No mail. She hit "New Message" and began typing.

NAOMI:

HAVE YOU EVER DISTRUSTED JOHN? I MEAN, HAVE YOU EVER THOUGHT HE HASN'T BEEN TRUTHFUL WITH YOU? ABOUT SOMETHING IMPORTANT?

THAT NEVER HAPPENED BETWEEN SEMMES AND ME. I THINK HIS WORST LIE (THOUGH HOW WOULD I KNOW) WAS NOT FESSING UP ON EXACTLY HOW MUCH HE LOST AT POKER.

I DON'T KNOW WHAT HAS HAPPENED EXACTLY, AND I'M SUFFICIENTLY PARA-NOID THAT I CAN'T TELL YOU THE GORY BACKGROUND DETAILS. BUT MY PROBLEM WITH VIC IS THAT I THINK HE MAY HAVE BEEN KEEPING SOMETHING FROM ME AND BY DOING THAT, HE'S PUT ME IN JEOPARDY. HE'S LET ME OPEN A PANDORA'S BOX. AND I DON'T KNOW WHAT TO THINK. THIS IS ALL VERY CONFUSING BECAUSE UP UNTIL A FEW HOURS AGO, I WAS FANTASIZING ABOUT MAKING LOVE TO HIM.

PLEASE DON'T MENTION THIS TO JOHN. I DON'T WANT TO BE ACCUSED OF "LEAKING" THINGS TO THE POLLSTERS, THAT WOULD REALLY SCREW THINGS UP.

LAURA

# Seventeen

The door closed, leaving Holden Bowser alone with the Governor and Vic. He'd just come from a conference committee meeting where the Patrol's appropriation had passed out without any changes to the Senate version. The most recent head count showed only two dissenting votes, so as soon as it got on the House calendar, it would pass and be sent to the Governor.

"It looks like we'll send you the Patrol appropriation with the pay raise included within a couple of days," Bowser said. "Please promise me you'll sign it."

"Haven't made up my mind. Might be a good opportunity to use the line item veto," Carver growled back. "Just like y'all did on my capital improvement bill? Why wasn't the Ole Miss project in there?"

"The House didn't want to show favoritism to one university. It was either add in projects for all the other schools or hold that one out. We didn't have the money for another slew of projects."

"But you've got money for the pay raise?"

Bowser's growing impatience was obvious. He inched forward on his chair, ready to stand. "Pardon my candor, Governor, but you're a fool if you veto. The pay raise is limited to state troopers and fully funded with a portion of the new revenue created for the crime bill, so no other program money is touched. I don't understand your hesitation."

"I would rather have used that money for the other programs I presented than for a pay raise that singles out one group. It's fundamentally unfair."

"It's not unfair—troopers are different. Just like teachers are different. And it didn't gut the crime bill. Frankly, we might not have passed any of the criminal reforms if the bill hadn't been paired down."

"So I'm supposed to be grateful?" Carver glared at Bowser. "This torpedoes next year's budget all to hell—we'll have to have an equivalently large raise for everyone else."

"At least, you held it off this long," Bowser said. "Besides, the smart money says it probably won't be your problem."

Carver softened instantly. "What have you heard?"

"That you've got that Senate seat walkin' away."

"It's only that easy when you run unopposed," said Carver.

"Well, I doubt you'll be worrying about next year's budget. Let that be our problem. Just sign the bill."

"You know as well as I do that it'll be over if I veto. There won't be enough votes to override."

Bowser tapped the edge of Carver's desk with his index finger. "I'm well aware of that. But be a hero like the *Wall Street Journal* says you are."

Vic waited for Bowser to leave before speaking. "For God's sake, sign the bill as soon as it gets here. Get this out of the way, end all the game playing, and start racking up your own points. It will look good in your crime-fighting portfolio."

"If my whole agenda had passed, I might have," Carver said. "But what do I say to Harry Curlett and all the other people who were depending on me for those contracts?? They could have funded that Ole Miss project but they didn't. They spent it on a pay raise that's fundamentally unfair."

"Curlett and the rest will understand. Besides, there's plenty of work for them to bid for—that bill is a damn gravy train."

Carver ignored his argument. "I might not be quite so intractable if Owen hadn't started pressuring me with this business about Brent, God rest his soul."

"His soul isn't resting—that's the point. And she didn't start out looking for a way to pressure you. If you don't sign the bill right away, you'll lose everything you stand to gain as an advocate for better police and tougher crime fighting."

"I will not be pussy-whipped," Carver replied.

"I think you're damn lucky the press hasn't picked up on this squabble."

■ ■ ■ ■

When Robert signaled he wouldn't be long finishing up his phone conversation, Blake closed the door and moved the stack of case files from the armchair to the floor so he could pull up close to the desk.

"For a man so careful about his appearance," Blake muttered.

"Not now," Robert said, shaking his head. "This is Rankin. He's at New Orleans airport. One Delta ticket agent remembers seeing someone like Wexler but can't tell him when. She's been working the evening shift for the past three months so it had to be after 5:00 P.M. but she can't remember any details."

"Which composite did she recognize?"

"The one with glasses and hair."

"Did he take a plane somewhere?"

"She doesn't remember anything."

"Tell him to work the gate agents, the restaurant, the shops and..." Blake paused, thinking, "and check the cabbies."

Robert nodded, relaying instructions to Rankin and hanging up.

"Is he going to see that guy at the soup kitchen about the dead man?" Blake asked.

"He's having lunch with him."

"Hope he eats somewhere else."

"Don't worry, Rankin will look out for his stomach."

"Everett reported in," Blake said. "The bank says Wexler withdrew cash from his account at 9:38 P.M. on the 5th. They're working on the credit card withdrawals now, but that's a different company and it may take time."

"If he left New Orleans by 10 P.M., he could have been in Saragossa by one in the morning," Robert mused.

"What doesn't make sense is him hanging out at the airport."

"Particularly since that ATM isn't near the front."

"Where is it?"

"On the Delta concourse. Rankin checked it."

"Where's Turner now?"

"Downstairs. Came in bright and early."

"What about the wife? Ever find her?" Blake asked.

"She's remarried, living in Memphis. I left a message on her machine."

"Maybe we should have someone from Batesville go by there."

"I want to talk to her myself if we find her."

"We don't have time for that."

"I'm gonna make time."

Blake thought a minute. "When was the last surprise inspection for your people?"

"I've never done a surprise. You were the only jerk who ever ordered that."

"Well, today would be a good day. Keep Trey busy and get a look in his trunk. And get his current mileage. We need to look at all those mileage reports for the last couple of months to see if we can tie anything down."

Robert nodded.

"Get someone else to handle it if you go to Memphis," Blake said as headed to the door. "I'm going to pay a visit to the hunting camp."

■ ■ ■ ■

Sarah rang the doorbell at 10:30 P.M. Grace was on the phone with the credit card company trying to find out about the cash withdrawals and Julia St. Clair answered it.

"Good morning, Mrs. Carver," Julia said. "Please come in."

"Julia, what are you doing here?"

"Ahh..." she faltered a moment, "I'm staying with Mrs. Wexler for a few days."

"Is there some trouble? She hasn't returned my calls. I've left at least three messages."

"Well, we don't know for certain," said Julia, obviously hesitating.

"Please let me talk with her."

"She's on the phone right now. Would you like some coffee?"

Sarah looked over Julia's shoulder down the hall toward the kitchen. "Yes. I can get it myself."

"I'll let her know you're here." Sarah followed Julia through the house to the kitchen, then Julia disappeared into Grace's office.

An open box of glazed donuts was on the kitchen island, something Grace never allowed herself, and two Styrofoam cups half full of coffee were nearby. The coffee maker was keeping a full pot warm. Sarah got out a mug, poured the coffee and opened the huge stainless steel door of the refrigerator for milk only to find it crammed with take-out boxes and Chinese food cartons. She turned away empty handed when she heard the sharp sound of heels on the tile floor.

"Sarah, I'm sorry I haven't called. It's been hectic," Grace said, approaching and giving her a quick hug.

"What's going on?"

"Didn't Gibbs tell you?"

"Tell me what?"

"Brent's not dead."

Shock kept Sarah silent.

"They don't know where he is. We've been trying to figure it out since Saturday. I can't begin to tell you what all this means."

"Lord, Grace, how can I help?"

"At this point, there's nothing you can do. We've been going over everything I can think of, looking for a needle in a haystack. He's just vanished."

"But who was in the car?"

"We don't know that."

A telephone rang in the office, and a moment later, Everett appeared. "Excuse me, Mrs. Wexler, the bank is calling back on the cellular."

"Stay here, Sarah. I'll just be a moment."

"Let me get out of your way, Grace, but..." Sarah looked at her, pained by her helplessness, "promise me you'll keep in touch."

"I'll try."

■ ■ ■ ■

Trey was finishing paper work on his most recent chop-shop case.

"Hustle up, Turner." Kramer was holding the door open as the other investigators filed out of the workroom for the inspection.

"Let me give this to Nima. I'll be right down," Trey shouted, moving toward the records room.

Trey noticed Kramer hesitate and it pissed him off. "What's the big deal? I'll be right there."

"Just don't be late."

Nima wasn't at her desk, in fact no one was in the records room, so he dropped his draft report in the overflowing in-box, then jogged down the long row of file cabinets to Everett's file drawers. His papers were neatly organized, as usual, and on top was a printout that listed Wexler, Inc. contracts from the Western District dated the previous day.

"Shit. That little worm won't give up." Trey slammed the drawer shut and flew out of the records room, taking the stairs to the first floor rather than wait for the elevator.

■ ■ ■ ■

Grace and Everett sat on opposite sides of the big desk, both punching financial information into their respective computers.

"Would have been nice if your husband had kept computerized records," Everett observed.

"At one time, he did," Grace said without even looking up.

Julia perked up from her chair where she sat surrounded by copies of checks and bills. "What do you mean, at one time?"

"I know all the campaign stuff was on some computer because those were the only kinds of records that I found. Gave all that stuff to Gibbs."

Everett had stopped working. "Where's his computer?"

"It's a laptop, in the closet," Grace said, jerking her thumb back as Everett got up from his seat. "But there's nothing on it. Only games. That was one of the first places I checked."

"Have you done anything except look at the files?"

"Only thing I did after I discovered there weren't any business files on it was to play a few rounds of Hearts and Minesweeper," Grace said. She cleared enough space at the end of the table to set up the system.

Everett plugged the laptop into the power strip. "Maybe we can recover whatever he erased—if he ever stored anything on it." He watched the screen for the system information. "I can't imagine anyone would have this big a hard drive just to play games."

■ ■ ■ ■

A gate sealed off the lane to Trey's house, so Blake left his car on the side of the road a few hundred feet past and walked back, carefully stepping through an old barbed wire fence to enter the property. Once out of the brush and trees, he followed the lane as it curved around, avoiding deep muddy tracks at a low spot. A huge live oak spread its long moss-dripping limbs over the circular part of the drive near the house. He could see spotlights positioned in all the trees, enough to chase away even the darkest night, if necessary.

Everything—the house, the sheds, the barn—was locked up tight and every blind was drawn. It was quiet, except for the birds constantly twittering in their safety just beyond the clearing.

No dogs, thank God.

Blake didn't want to take a chance breaking in, so he surveyed the place making notes on a file card, scouting locations to position the men. This was the woods, there were plenty of possibilities.

The Red Crown Road twisted and turned into the hardwood forest, and Blake kept up a good pace, noting the trails and lesser roads to the sides, judging distances by the time it took him to walk. The woods were spectacular—the dogwoods had been late blooming and a few white petals still graced their branches. The canopy above was filling in with the rich green of a sub-tropical climate, a fresh smell permeated everything. It was no wonder Turner and Wexler had spent so much time here.

Not knowing how far the road went, Blake turned back after fifteen minutes. After one more turn around the house, he drove around the edge of the property on the county road. He turned into the only lane passable for an automobile that he could find leading into the hunt club land from the other side, one as wide as the lane to Trey's house. It climbed a fairly steep hill and an eighth of a mile in, it was gated and locked. Blake parked and got out, stooping to get under the gate. Not more than a hundred yards farther, at the edge of a construction clearing, he found the Red Crown Hunting Club's sign-in board, with a map drawn on an aerial photograph, outlining all the roads, trails, stands, and food plots.

Turner's three hundred acres were clearly marked off-limits to the hunt club, and although the map didn't specify that the road was gated at Trey's property line, Blake assumed it was, as careful as Trey seemed to be. He must have almost reached it on his walk from the other direction.

■ ■ ■ ■

State Patrol Lieutenant Carl Rankin had talked to everyone at the New Orleans airport who would give him the time of day. In the late morning, he headed to the I. J. Riley Center, a food kitchen and shelter for homeless citizens, housed in an abandoned fire station. He stepped politely through the throng of diners, mostly men, dressed in multiple layers of tattered clothing. A young woman was serving food.

"Is Mr. Tomasetti here today?"

The woman motioned with her head toward the back, never breaking her rhythm with the spoon, the stew, and the molded plastic tray. "Go around the kitchen and keep going down the hall. Last door if he's in."

Nat Tomaselli was in, but only just. His suit coat was on, barely encircling his girth, and he was putting papers in a small satchel when Rankin knocked.

"Mr. Tomasetti?"

"Selli, not setti. Tomaselli," Nat said impatiently.

Rankin looked down at a white filing card. "I'm sorry. Nima wrote this pretty quickly." He reached in his jacket pocket and pulled out a card, offering it to Nat in one practiced move. "Carl Rankin, Mississippi State Patrol. I called this morning, and they said you'd be able to talk for a moment about Myron DeLaureal."

"I'm heading out for a meeting with several businessmen. The city has decided it wants this building back for fire department offices. What do you need?" Nat said.

"Let me drive you, we can talk on the way."

Nat looked him over carefully. "Fine. You'd probably be safer than a cab."

They left by the back door, walking single file through the alley to the street. Rankin stepped ahead, pointing the way toward his car when they reached the sidewalk. "Do you have time for lunch?"

Nat smiled. "Do I look like I miss many meals?" he said, patting his immense tummy.

"Then let me take you. Your choice."

"Acme Oyster Bar," Nat said without hesitation.

Fond memories of fresh oysters tickled Rankin's throat. "A man after my own heart. Is there somewhere to park near there?"

"If we don't find something on the street, I know the guy at a hotel lot that'll slip us in."

Nat told Rankin nearly everything he knew about Myron before their platters of oysters arrived. Since the time he'd filed the report with New Orleans Police Department Missing Persons, one of the other regulars at the Center thought he'd found Myron's few belongings scattered under the crawl space below a highway overpass, but it was hard to be certain.

"It took weeks to track down his mother," said Nat, proud of his bit of sleuthing. "But once I found out who she was, the rest came easily."

"Can I ask why you did this?"

Nat busied himself with his oysters, not answering immediately. "I don't think that really matters to you. Let's leave it like this—I owed him a lot."

"Fine."

They slipped into the silence of satisfied diners.

"The family was pretty well off," Nat said after polishing off half his plateful. "At least if the mausoleum is a measure. Myron has a space, bought and paid for in the 70s by his sister when she was making her own arrangements."

"Sounds like they didn't trust him to handle it himself."

"Maybe. Myron never told me how he got to drifting. Never even hinted."

"And no one else is alive?"

"There's one other brother. The sister paid for his spot, too. He was the oldest, would be in his sixties if he's still living, but there's no trace of him in New Orleans."

Satiated, they both pushed their plates, now piled with empty shells, toward the center of the table.

"You have time for coffee?"

Nat extended a thick arm and wrist to look at his watch. "I'd better get on."

"Let me drive you."

"No, I need to walk off lunch," Nat said, patting his tummy, "and get ready for dinner."

Rankin signaled the waitress for the check.

Nat stood and swung on his suit coat. "You know, I'm honestly surprised that anyone followed up on my report. Never happened before."

"Your guy was tall and we were looking for a tall man. Set him off from all the others. If he'd been average size, there would have been too many to trace."

"What'll you do now?"

"My boss'll decide. But if they want to pursue it, there's a test they can do on the mother to see whether Myron is related."

"But she's been dead for years."

"Doesn't matter. There's still something they can do: DNA from her teeth can be matched to her children's."

"Weird."

"Science."

"And if it's him?"

"We'll send the remains down here to be buried."

"Who'll pay for everything?"

"I think we'll be able to handle that. But we've got a long way to go. Need a court order to get the mother exhumed and all that rigmarole."

"Will you keep me informed?"

"Certainly. You've got my card?"

Nat checked his jacket pocket and pulled it out. "Right here." He pulled out his billfold and placed it inside.

On the street, they walked to Rankin's car.

"Keep in touch," Nat said. "Preciate lunch."

Rankin nodded. "My pleasure, I assure you. Maybe we'll do it again if this thing goes forward."

"I'd like that."

"Thanks for your help."

■ ■ ■ ■

Robert made it to Cordova, a suburb of Memphis, in record

time, even for State Patrol speed. He arrived at a relatively new tract home, six minutes before his appointment with Seddon McWillie, formerly Seddon Turner. There were muffled sounds of a child's frightened cries coming from the back of the house, and instead of going to the front door, he opened the side fence and rushed around to find the sliding doors to an indoor swimming pool open and the screams continuing unabated. Two women were in the pool with a little girl, one hovering just out of the child's sight.

"One more fall-in and you can play," said an athletic, dark-haired woman in her forties, closer to the child, and oblivious to the wailing. "Swim to the side, Jessica, swim to the side."

She looked up for only a moment to see Robert, who had stepped into the pool area. Then she turned back and pulled the screaming child from her perch on the edge of the pool down into the water. The child thrashed her way around toward the side, her little hand grasping to hold on to something. As soon as the little girl's mouth cleared the water, she let out another scream. Her mother moved quickly to her side, screaming almost as loudly, "You did it, Sweetie, you did it."

The instructor's voice broke through all the excitement and sobbing. "You did so good. Miss Seddon loves you. Why don't you play around with Mommy for a few minutes."

The woman pulled her own lithe body out of the water, and immediately wrapped a towel about herself as she approached Robert. "Hope it didn't scare you. The first lesson is always the worst." She stretched a wet hand toward him then wiped it again on her towel. "I'm Seddon McWillie."

"Robert Stone, ma'am," he said, pulling his card out of his wallet and handing it to her. She held it by the edge trying not to get it wet. "That was my last lesson for the day. If you give me just a moment, I'll get dressed and we can talk."

She said a few final words to the mother and child about the next day's lesson. Then she led the way across a river of beach towels, showed Robert to the living room, and disappeared into the back of the house. The furniture was well-worn but comfortable—a long sofa with plenty of pillows, two large recliners, one next to a bookshelf crammed with paperbacks and magazines, and the other directed toward a big-screen television, which stood in the middle of all the other electronic equipment on the far wall. Two large photographs of older couples were on one wall, and opposite them was a color portrait of a happy family with a slightly younger Seddon in the center surrounded by a man, two teenaged girls with bright eyes and smiles, and one younger snaggle-toothed boy. The coffee table was littered with personal checks, daily schedules, and lists of names—the paperwork of a swimming lesson business.

Seddon was wearing blue jeans and a sweater when she returned, her hair combed straight back from her forehead and clipped in a barrette. "Can I get you something?"

Robert shook his head. "No, thanks. I appreciate your talking with me, Mrs. McWillie."

"Call me Seddon. Wish I could say I remembered you, but I don't. Those days with the Patrol faded long ago."

"I didn't come on until the late Seventies."

"That's right," her eyes lighting with the memory. "I never did understand how the Patrol thought it could operate around here without any black troopers."

"Neither did we, I assure you."

"This must be important if you couldn't settle for a phone call."

"I need to know everything I can learn about your first husband, Trey Turner."

"Is Trey in trouble?"

"We don't know—maybe, maybe not."

"What kind?"

"A man he worked for has disappeared under very strange circumstances. We're trying to figure out what happened."

"So what do you want from me?"

"No one knows much about Trey, he keeps to himself. We thought you might help us."

"I'll tell you what I can, which isn't much. I haven't laid eyes on him in years."

"What kind of a relationship has he had with his children?"

"None. Hasn't seen them since the day we moved out. Which was fine with me, actually. I met my second husband shortly after the divorce, and the children have grown up thinking of him as their father. But I'll say this for Trey: After the first few months, he was never late with his child support. And he paid half their college expenses, without so much as my asking. My oldest daughter graduated from Memphis State last year in nursing, and my youngest's a sophomore at the University of Tennessee now."

"Can you tell me why you left him?"

"For starters, I woke up one morning to see his .357 magnum pointed at my face."

Robert nodded. "That would do it for me."

"It wasn't loaded, but he had a camera ready. An instant later when the flash went off, I nearly died of a heart attack. He said he'd always wanted to photograph someone in that situation and I was his first subject."

"Was that the only reason you left?"

Seddon stared straight at him, not blinking. "He was cruel. Beat the living daylights out of me once. I couldn't risk having him go after the girls, so I left."

"Did he try and get you to come back?"

"No, not really."

"So what kind of man was he? How would you describe him?"

"Macho. All he wanted to do was hunt and kill, hunt and kill. Didn't pay any attention to us."

"What was his childhood like?"

"You mean, did he torture animals or something? I don't know. His mother ruled with an iron hand, but once he was grown, she didn't have much to do with him, truth be known. In fact, she only came to see her first grandchild, my daughter Jenni, once. Never saw my younger girl, Lissa. I do know that his father left them when he was fairly young. He adored his father, though he was scared of him—I think he was very, very strict. Trey thought his mother had caused his dad to leave, and hated her for that. Wish I knew why I ever married him."

"Why did you?"

"I wanted out, to get away from my own parents. He was strong, I thought he'd take care of me. I was young and I didn't have the courage to be on my own, but I wanted to get out of there. We used to talk all the time about how terrible our mothers were. I guess that's what we had in common, hating our mothers. Plus, he was the best-looking thing that ever came my way."

"Do you know anything about what he's been doing since you left him?"

"Only that the check arrives like clockwork. He must have had a great side job because I know the patrol doesn't pay good enough for him to send the kids to college like he has."

"He worked for a man named Brent Wexler."

"Never mentioned it, but then again, we haven't talked but five times in seventeen years. Do you think he had something to do with the disappearance?"

"Maybe."

"Come on, you can tell me. You didn't drive all the way up here for nothing. And I'm surely not going to mention it to anyone."

Robert bit his lip, hesitating. "He may have been involved in the murder of an unidentified man."

"Well, if what you want to know is, could he have done it, the answer's 'yes.' I don't know anyone with colder blood than Trey. Death was nothing to him—animals, people, didn't matter. Never saw him cry, never saw him show much sympathy. He was always on the alert, always practicing that Patrol karate stuff."

"What karate stuff?"

"You know, all that self-protection action, hand slices, and chops on the neck." She mockingly shot her hand out from her chest. "Trey even practiced while he was riding up and down the highway. Practically had to have the seat replaced in our personal car, he wore it out so."

Seddon grew quiet and Robert waited for her to continue. "Know what I'm glad about?"

Robert shook his head.

"I'm glad the Lord gave me a short memory. I haven't thought about this stuff in years and I'll forget it a minute after you're gone."

■ ■ ■ ■

Before Laura was completely out of the elevator from her afternoon meetings at the Capitol, the fifth floor receptionist stepped quickly from around her desk and handed Laura her call sheet.

"The Governor is waiting for you, Commissioner."

With a deep breath, she hustled down the hall, too preoccupied to even look at her calls. Gibbs Carver had never visited her before. Sandy Quinn sat in a chair outside her door, jumping up when he saw her coming and throwing his hands out, exasperated.

"Good afternoon, Sandy," she said, slowing down.

Sandy's eyes shot toward her office. "Commissioner," was all he said, nodding as a weak smile spread across his face. Anything else Carver would have heard.

She braced herself as she entered her office. Carver was standing at the window looking at the Museum construction in the park across the interstate. Without even turning toward her, he said, "Very nice office, Laura. I bet you enjoy it here."

"The Patrol's always done things on a grand scale, Governor."

"So I've noticed." He moved toward a brown leather chair in front of her desk. "May I?"

"Of course, can I get you some coffee?"

"No thanks, I don't plan to be here long. What I came for was to find out what's going on with Grace Wexler. My wife said she's surrounded by patrolmen in her own home. I want to know why. You should have informed me each step of the way."

"She needs protection, sir."

"From what or should I say, whom?"

"We don't know that yet. As I explained on Sunday, two

people are dead, Wexler has disappeared, and a lot of money is missing. Grace's sitting on top of all the records that provide any clues at all."

"Grace?" Carver shot back. "When did you get to be such a good friend?"

"Excuse me," Laura said quickly, "Mrs. Wexler. Until we know the whole story, I don't think she should be alone."

"I want this wrapped up, Commissioner."

"Governor, with all due respect, we've done a better than decent job of keeping this quiet. My people need time."

"I don't want Mrs. Wexler harassed, and I don't want this to drag out."

"We're not harassing her, sir. She's been very cooperative and I think she appreciates having company, particularly with the burglary incident. But I can't perform miracles. Whoever's behind this didn't want to be found and was smart enough to cover his tracks well. That's put us at a disadvantage right off the bat. If you want me to review what we know, I can go over it."

She doubted he would. And she was right.

Carver stood to leave abruptly. "Do your best," he brusquely admonished her. "I've got a lot at stake and so do you."

If Carver was expecting an obedient silence from Laura, she had no intention of cooperating. She met the Governor's glare. "Is this some sort of quid pro quo, sir?"

"Have a good day, Ms. Owen," Carver said, his tone icy.

Once Carver was out the door, Laura punched in Blake's number and started looking down her call sheet.

"Coleman."

"Come on down if you can. The Governor just left."

"Carver was here?"

"That's right."

"I'll be right there. I've got a few things to tell you, too."

A minute later, Blake closed her door behind him. "Robert is interviewing Trey's former wife. He'll report back later today. And the handwriting analyst confirmed that the check was endorsed by Carver, unless it was written by a high-quality signature machine. Sometimes those can't be distinguished."

"Wish I'd known that ten minutes ago. Carver was such a prick."

"What did he want?"

"To trade the pay raise for Wexler, if I read the tea leaves correctly."

"What'd you say?"

"In my dreams, I said 'Go to hell.' In fact, I didn't say anything. He walked out before I could respond."

■ ■ ▨ ■

Brent hadn't been able to resist taking a spin through downtown Jackson. He drove past the Governor's Mansion, the Capitol and then on to his office. The parking lot of Wexler, Inc. was empty except for Leb Bailey's car and a couple of others sporting Alabama tags.

He drove on to Saragossa to get there before sundown, praying Grace hadn't rented the place to someone else. He let himself in the lower gate where the cow barns were and left the car, hidden from the road, and approached the house. Brent didn't realize how much he'd missed the familiar view from his porch until he was walking up the hill and turned to watch the sky as it slowly, imperceptibly broke into evening color.

The Alps might be majestic, but this was where he belonged.

He was too old to be wandering around the world.

No one was living at the house. He could see furniture piled in the center of the living room, covered with cloths as someone redecorated. The furniture on the porches hadn't been changed and unless Grace had sold the place lock, stock, and barrel, she was the one having the work done. The extra keys for this house as well as Trey's were still in the key rock he'd hidden in the garden, but they no longer fit the door. Besides, as vigilant as Grace had been about using the alarm on the Northwoods house, he suspected she would have installed one out here, first thing.

He walked around the pond and up to the fields, breathing in the comforting smell of recently mown grass. When Trey's house came into view, he was careful to stay close to the trees, out of sight as much as possible. It looked empty, the curtains gone from the windows, the porch chairless, no cars out front. In the dim evening light, he peered in the windows, and finding no hint of occupancy, tried the key. It still worked.

The house was bare and clean, pristine in fact, but empty long enough for dust to collect on the countertops. Brent checked the range and found the electricity still connected. He could sleep there and have heat, something the porch at the main house couldn't supply. He took off across the field to his car, and drove cautiously along the tree line, and parked in the barn, out of sight.

■ ■ ■ ■

Will Owen was testing his new bicycle headlight in the driveway when Robert and Blake arrived. "Are those new wheels, man?" Robert asked, leaning out the driver's window.

"Yes, sir. I got it for my birthday and my mom brought the headlight home with her tonight."

"We heard about the water balloon war," Robert said.

"It was awesome."

"Bet you can go faster than ever on that."

"Wanna see?"

"Sure," Robert said. "Let me pull up all the way."

As the two men got out of the car, Laura appeared from the side of the house. The beam of Will's light could be seen coming toward them, shifting from side to side as he pumped the pedals for more speed. He did a modified spin stop a few feet from them to a round of applause.

"Very impressive, very impressive." Blake stepped closer to get a full view of the bike.

"How about some light out here, Will?" suggested Laura.

"Keep it dark, Momma. That's why I have a headlight."

"All right. We're going in to talk and I'll turn the lights on when it's time for you to come in. Bath night, remember?"

"Ahh, Momma."

"Bath *night*?" Robert asked, amazed. "Will, I had to have a bath *every* night. Don't mess with a good deal, man."

"Okay, okay," Will said, momentarily defeated, "I'll see you later," and raced off.

"So where do we stand?" Laura asked the moment they turned toward the house.

"We've got everything but evidence," Blake said.

"I want to bring him in and talk to him," Robert pushed.

"And I think the jig would be up if we did that," Blake replied. "We've got nothing but ten extra gallons of gasoline and a passion for karate."

She opened the door from the patio into the main room which, except for the chairs and sofa in front of the fireplace, looked like a combination toy store and pet shop. Ranger, fenced in the kitchen, began yipping when she saw the new faces. The long dining table was covered with at least nine thousand Legos in various stages of construction, but Laura ignored it all.

"Beer?" she said as they headed to the sofa and easy chairs.

"Better not."

"Doesn't it bother you that Turner's walking around with a badge and a gun?" Laura inquired.

"Not if we keep an eye on him, no. This guy isn't impulsive."

"What are you planning?" Laura inquired.

"At least one more day before we bring him in to talk. It's his birthday tomorrow, and Robert here, as his boss, is going to take him to the Sizzler for lunch. Then Jimmie's gonna walk in with a couple of others and join him and they're gonna talk about Brent's torched car, and give him the day off. Then we'll see what he does."

"When did you come up with this idea?" Robert asked.

"Watching Will's light on the driveway," Blake responded. "That little light of his told me exactly where he was and when he was wobbling. It's time to give Turner something to think about and see what he does."

"Won't that be a little obvious?" Laura asked.

"Not really. The Sizzler's the usual place for celebrations, and Jimmie eats there all the time. Besides, if Trey caught on, his reaction might be interesting."

"Hmmm." Laura looked at Robert. "Hear anything about the dead guy?"

"Doc says there are some DNA tests we could do on the New Orleans woman to determine if she's related, but we'd have to exhume her body. It'll take a court order for that."

"What about you?" Blake asked her. "Ready to talk to the Governor tomorrow?"

"I'm starting with Vic, and depending how that goes, I may never have to mention the topic to Carver. Not directly, at least."

■ ■ ■ ■

While Will was looking at books in bed, Laura checked her e-mail. One message and four unsolicited invitations to experience cyberporn.

There ought to be a law.

LAURA:

IT LOOKS REAL SIMPLE FROM HERE: GIVE VIC THE BENEFIT OF THE DOUBT. I SAY THIS BECAUSE, THOUGH I HAVEN'T BEEN AROUND HIM LATELY, IN LAW SCHOOL HE HAD STRONGER CONVICTIONS AND PRINCIPLES THAN ANYBODY I KNEW. EXCEPT YOU MAYBE. I CAN'T BELIEVE HE'S FUNDAMENTALLY CHANGED.

IF HE'S INVOLVED IN SOMETHING WRONG, IT CERTAINLY ISN'T INTENTIONAL. AND IF IT IS INTENTIONAL, THERE WILL BE A DAMN GOOD REASON FOR IT. I JUST KNOW THAT IN MY HEART.

LET ME HEAR FROM YOU,

NAOMI

■ ■ ■ ■

From the front, it didn't appear to Brent that anything had changed at the Northwoods house except the season. Flowers and plants were blooming everywhere, and what he couldn't see, he could smell. Brent parked near the pond at a turn-in where it wasn't uncommon for cars to be and walked quickly back, slipping into the patio area.

His room wasn't a bedroom anymore—it looked more like an office, ablaze with lights. A man was sitting at a portable computer to one side typing, and a tall woman who was wearing a shoulder holster and looked vaguely familiar, was leaning against the jamb of the open French doors, her back to Brent. Grace was typing at another computer.

The shoulder holster and their intense activity at this late hour was alarming. He approached close enough to make out a few of the woman's words, racking his brain for why she was familiar to him.

"June 7, deposit $1150. June 21 deposit $2300. July 12 withdrawal $9000."

The woman's deep voice rang the bell, and Brent remembered Julia St. Clair from the second inaugural events when Sarah had needed a female bodyguard in evening dress. The State Patrol was at Grace's house going over financial records.

It was only a matter of time.

He crept back to his car, wondering whether to leave right then or find Trey.

He'd better find Trey, deal with him, and get out.

■ ■ ■ ■

"Blake, it's your phone," Sally said, shaking him awake.

"Huh?" Blake looked around the dark room, still lost in deep sleep.

"Your phone, it's ringing."

"I'm sorry," he said, picking up the handset. "Coleman."

"Blake, this is Kramer. Hope I didn't wake Sally."

"No, no, she's still asleep but hold on, let me switch phones." He pushed down the hold button.

"Sorry, Dear."

A gentle snore was all he heard. His swung his feet to the

floor and moved stiffly toward the kitchen.

"What's up?"

"Just put him to bed. He left the office, did the Wendy's drive-thru on High Street, then backtracked to Northwoods. Mrs. Wexler's and Julia's cars were both in the garage. He made a couple of passes, then went to Alta Woods."

"Alta Woods?"

"That residential section over near Terry Road and the interstate."

"North or south of Interstate 20?"

"South. They've got a real nice park over there."

"I know the place. What did he do?"

"He parked and watched 604 Little Street for a few minutes. No one was home and the carport was empty. Then he let himself in and cased the place, I assume. He came back out and waited until a car came in around midnight. He watched for a while and then left."

"Could you see the driver?"

"No, I was too far away."

"What did Trey do?"

"He watched some more, then he left."

"Any idea who lives there?"

"The guy backs his car in, if you can believe it, so I couldn't see the tag."

"I'll get Nima on it in the morning. Give me that number again."

# EIGHTEEN

Brent watched the sun rise from the front porch of the main house. He cursed himself for not buying a pot so he could brew the coffee he'd bought, but mostly he cursed the stupidity that had taken all this away from him.

When the sun was high enough for him to feel some of its warmth, Brent returned to Trey's little house to pack up and get on the road before whoever was working there arrived. Coffee would have to wait.

At Hazlehurst, he took a slight detour and headed northwest on a stretch of road that crossed Turkey Creek. Reed Morgan had promised him that contract when he'd delivered the four new suits in February. The job was underway, but Triple-A's equipment was on site, not Wexler's.

Slimy bastard, didn't even bother to make good on done deals.

It was after nine when he reached Second Creek. He pulled into the west end of the Red Crown Road and tried his key, certain it would work since there hadn't been any reason to change those locks. A few hundred yards further in on the left, was a sign-in station with a map tacked up. It showed a large area in the northwest corner, including the camp house, blocked off and marked "Turner - Off Limits." Below it was a notice that the hunting lodge was available for members' use from Friday noon through Sunday sundown until the end of turkey season.

Brent estimated Trey's land to be about three hundred acres more or less and the Red Crown Road, which ran all the way to the house, split Trey's parcel in two. He drove on though the road was almost too rough for his rental car. There were several large muddy areas—general maintenance was definitely slipping. A little deeper into the tract than he expected, a locked bar gate and a hastily constructed barbed wire fence closed off the remainder of the road from the hunt club land. When he saw the well-worn lock, Brent tried the standard combination that he and Trey had always used at the farm—the street number for Wexler's offices—and it worked. He drove far enough in that his car couldn't been seen from the hunt club land, locked it up, and walked the rest of the way.

■ ■ ■ ■

Nima stuck her head around the door to see who was in Robert's office and found Kramer with him.

"604 Little Street is owned by Christian E. Passage," Nima said.

"Could that be our Everett?" Robert said.

"I believe so."

■ ■ ■ ■

Laura and Blake left a meeting at the Attorney General's office on an anti-drug initiative as soon as they could. Blake's beeper had gone off three times during their hour-long session.

"Who paged you?"

"Robert, Eddie Williams, and Jimmie. Robert added the emergency signal, so he's who I called."

"And?"

"Trey's watching both Grace and Everett Passage."

"What?"

"That's who lives at the house in South Jackson. Robert had just hung up talking with Everett and told him to stay at Grace's for the time being. St. Clair's been alerted."

"You think Trey found out that Everett's working on Morgan?" Laura asked. "Or does Trey know Everett's working at Grace's?"

"Got to be the Transportation Department stuff. I've had someone on his tail since the day Everett started at her place, and Trey hasn't been by there when Everett's car wasn't hidden in the garage. I doubt he knows where Everett's working. He's probably trying to find out."

"Damn, I hope Trey trips up soon," said Laura. "I don't know if I can stand this much longer."

"The credit card companies called in," Blake added. "Wexler made two withdrawals, one at 10:16 P.M. and the other at 11:42 P.M., both from the same machine in the airport. That last withdrawal would make it very difficult to get to Saragossa in time to set up the wreck."

"Did any planes leave after that?"

"We're checking them," said Blake. "I gotta get going— there's too much to do at headquarters. Good luck with Regis."

"For once, I don't need luck," Laura replied, her voice more upbeat than it had been in several days.

"Yes, you do," Blake chided. "Don't ever take anything for granted."

Laura crossed High Street to the Capitol, its parking lot still bursting at the seams as the legislative session staggered to its end. Vic had said he'd be around all morning, though where exactly he wasn't certain. She took a seat in the waiting area and silently practiced the choicest lines from her speech, knowing she probably wouldn't have the courage to deliver half, if any, of them.

"Come on in," Vic said quietly behind her.

She hadn't heard him slip out the door from the governor's

secretary's office. As gaily as possible, she chirped, "There you are, I didn't hear you."

Vic waited until she'd caught up with him and gently took her arm. "How's Will doing?"

"Great. Buddy ball practice is in full swing," Laura said, sinking into an arm chair. The season's about to begin."

"Is it coach pitch or are they using the machine?"

"Coach pitch and thank God, Will has a nice coach. Doesn't get all serious and yell at them. I couldn't ask for better."

Vic took the chair next to hers rather than sitting behind his desk. "When do they play?" he asked.

"He's got a game tomorrow at 7:00 P.M. and then the next one is Monday at 5:30."

"Could I join the cheering section one night?"

"Of course," said Laura, completely surprised. She'd assumed that after all the bitterness in the past few conversations, their relationship was over. "He'd be delighted."

Vic only waited six seconds before he changed the subject. "What's happening on Wexler?"

"Didn't the Governor bring you up to date?" Laura said sarcastically.

"I heard, and I'm sorry."

"It wasn't pleasant."

"So I gathered."

"I didn't ask for any of this...." Laura said.

"I know...."

"I'm doing the best job I can."

"You don't need to tell..."

"And I've had enough of his patronizing crap, goddamn it," Laura added.

"Don't waste words sugar-coating it."

She raised her hands to halt her own harangue. "This isn't your fault, and there isn't anything you can say, so I'll be a big girl and drop it."

"Thank you," said Vic, his own voice was quieter, too. "Now, what can you tell me about Wexler?"

"The news today is he was converting a lot of money to cash.

Where it went, we still don't know."

"Money from the public relations firm?" Vic asked.

"That and what looks like a campaign account. We checked with Dede Kilgore, since he was the accountant for the campaign, and he had no record of that particular account."

"Why are you calling it a campaign account?"

"The checks going in were made out to Brent Wexler, Brent Wexler PAC, Gibbs Carver, Gibbs Carver for Governor, Carver Exploratory Fund."

"This is news to me." Vic stood up and moved behind his desk. "I'm a signatory on all the official ones."

Laura kept her eyes on Vic's face. "Let's quit kidding around, I'm tired of games."

"I'm serious," he said. His surprise seemed genuine. "Brent had his own way of doing things—he and Carver talked constantly, and I wasn't party to half of it. I don't know about another bank account, nor has there ever been a PAC by that name."

"Look at these spreadsheets." Laura laid a computer printout on the desk. "Over ten years, eight hundred thousand and change went in, most of it came out as cash around the time of the primaries or the general elections, always under the currency reporting threshold."

"Most?"

She nodded. "Most, but not all. A couple of times there were checks, but there were also several withdrawals at other times of the year, all in amounts of $9,950." She leaned over, pointing to a separate column of four-figure numbers. "Here, here, and here, for instance."

Laura straightened up to watch him again. "Keep going down that column. It's totaled on the last page."

"I know nothing of this," Vic protested as his finger raced down the figures.

"Wasn't Wexler the one who always came up with the GOTV money?"

"Yes, but it was reported. I've got boxes of check copies and contribution forms. Sooner or later it all came through me."

"Show me where you reported this one." Laura dropped a copy of a corporate check made out to Gibbs Carver for $10,000.

"We couldn't accept this. It's from a corporation."

"Well, Wexler did, and the Governor endorsed it." She flipped the copy over for Vic to see Carver's signature.

"This can't be his..."

"I had it analyzed by a handwriting expert," Laura replied before Vic could say more.

"You did what?"

"I had this and several other checks with Gibbs Carver endorsements analyzed. Every endorsement except this one was in Wexler's handwriting. But don't worry, it was done under the guise of a theft case."

"What are you accusing Carver of?" Vic demanded.

"He signed it, Vic. Though it wasn't made out to a campaign fund, it found its way into one. I assume the Governor didn't pay income taxes on it as a salary or a dividend, did he?"

"Well, I don't know anything about it."

"Are you suggesting I should take this up with Carver?"

"No, for God's sake."

The anguish in Vic's voice was so clear, Laura relented. "If it makes you feel any better, Carver didn't write the words 'for deposit only.' Wexler did."

"Who knows about this?"

"Only me and Blake Coleman," Laura said. "Mrs. Wexler knows about the account, and she ordered all the backup but she never saw the actual checks. The bank delivered all of it yesterday, and I picked them up before she had a chance to see them. She seemed completely satisfied with my explanation that we didn't have to worry about it since it was campaign stuff. She said she'd given all the campaign records to Carver some weeks ago."

"That's right. He's got it all at the Mansion."

Laura stayed silent, letting it sink in.

"Where do we go from here?" Vic asked quietly, folding up the papers and putting them to the side.

"Maybe we don't have to go anywhere," Laura added quietly. "This is what I think—you tell me if I'm wrong. Brent handled all this questionable money for the campaign himself. He didn't tell you. Maybe he told Carver, maybe he didn't. Maybe he claimed it all came from him. From the disclosure statements, he contributed into the six figures to the campaign."

Vic said nothing. He just stared back at Laura's quick blue eyes.

"But he kept a little for himself. In fact, if my assumptions are correct about the withdrawals at times when there wasn't a primary or a general election, he kept a lot for himself. About $175,000." A certain confidence returned to her voice. "Those odd withdrawals were for the same amount as his withdrawals from the fake public relations firm account—$9,950. The banks never had to report it. My guess is he was putting that money somewhere else but leaving no trail. What he stole, if I'm right, far exceeds the total of illegal corporate contributions that he deposited."

She watched Vic as he watched her. They were treading on the thinnest of ice and she knew he recognized their danger.

"Failure to report contributions is a misdemeanor, chargeable to the person who failed to report, in this case Wexler, as the campaign finance chairman. Frankly, that's the least of my worries about him."

Vic still said nothing, so she continued.

"The only check that really bothers me is the one the Governor endorsed, but I can't be certain where Carver thought that check was going since Wexler was the one who wrote the words 'For deposit only.' I don't have to tell you, I don't like being in this position. Not one iota. Here I sit, his alleged Top Cop. I go along and don't say anything about this and I'm no better than any of these jerks I've investigated over the past five years. I don't go along and I throw away everything—everything Carver's done, everything you've done, everything I've done—for something that most likely will end up being nothing. And, if I don't pursue this today, but sometime down the road it comes out, the fact that I hid something will be worse than what I hid. There are no good choices for me. None."

Vic nodded in agreement but said nothing. His silence confirmed every bit of her analysis.

"I think the Governor ought to know what I found. But I'm not going to pursue it. If Carver goes down, I'd go down, and everything good he's started would grind to a halt unfinished— all over one questionable contribution handled by a person I now know is a thief and probably a murderer." Laura paused, moving her eyes to look squarely at Vic. "But I want something in return."

"Are you blackmailing him?" Vic asked.

Laura shook her head. "Blackmail's the wrong term. That supposes I want something I'm not entitled to. I want your word and his that this will never happen again as long as I'm associated with him. And if there's something I've missed, that I or anyone else might possibly stumble on some day, I want it corrected before that happens so I don't waste any more time on something like this."

"That's all?"

"I would also appreciate a level playing field and a decent attitude."

"You've got my word," Vic said solemnly. "And you'll have his."

She looked down at her watch and started collecting her papers to leave. "I've got to get back," she said. "I'd prefer not to ever talk about this with him."

"I understand," Vic responded. "Keep me posted?"

"Sure thing."

"And send me the ball game schedule?"

"It'll make Will's day," Laura said, softening.

Before she had closed the door behind her, Vic called out again. "Thank you for the way you've handled this."

"You owe me," Laura said. "Big time."

Once he was alone, Vic opened the file drawer in his credenza and drew out a thick folder of computer spreadsheets. He checked the total from one of the reports and compared it to the spreadsheet Laura had prepared from Brent's bank account, his anger mounting with every passing second.

Quietly, he slipped in the door to Carver's office. From Carver's expression, he could see that his appearance was opportune—the Governor needed to be rescued from a particularly troublesome senator who was rambling on about fish and game officers working in his district.

In a pause while the senator caught his breath, Carver spoke up. "Ahh, Vic, there you are."

The senator turned, scowling at Vic for stealing the stage from him.

"I must run, Senator," Carver said, as evenly as possible. "You'll have to excuse me. I'll look into that matter, I can assure you."

They both stood. "Well, I hope so, Gibbs. It's important to me and to your supporters up there."

"I understand."

When the door closed, Gibbs looked at Vic. "God, he's insufferable."

"Laura Owen's been by this morning," Vic said, not wasting a moment.

"And what did she have to report?" Carver asked curtly.

"All the details on that bank account of Brent's that Grace discovered. Laura's the only one who's seen the checks—she persuaded Grace that it was a standard campaign account and took all the documents into her own possession."

Carver stood there, silent.

"She's got everything. Even a corporate check you endorsed."

Gibbs sank into his chair.

"But guess what else," Vic said, anger mounting in his voice and demeanor. "Brent kept some of the money for himself."

"What?"

Vic nodded, slowly, staring all the while at Carver.

"How much?"

"About $250,000 I think. I'm comparing my tallies to Laura's spreadsheets of all the activity in the account. That amount assumes every dollar Brent collected was deposited. He could have kept even more."

"Does Laura know that too?"

"She's no dummy, Gibbs. She figured out his scheme but her estimate of what he took is a little low. She thinks he only took $175,000."

"What's she going to do?"

"Nothing."

"Nothing?" asked Carver.

"The way she figures it, the campaign violation is a misdemeanor and Brent's the one chargeable with it. Since it looks as if Brent skimmed more than the total of the illegal contributions, that's theft, but it's Brent's theft."

"Are you sure she's not going to move on this?"

"Yes sir, I am," Vic said confidently. "She's taking a big risk. But she wanted my word—and yours—that nothing like this would ever happen again. She wants any other problems—ones she doesn't know about—corrected."

Carver shook his head. "This is amazing."

"And, she'd appreciate, I'm quoting, a level playing field and a decent attitude."

"What does she mean by that?"

Vic didn't answer but looked at his papers, avoiding Carver's glance.

"I guess I should sign the Patrol's appropriation."

"Including the pay raise," Vic said.

"You trust her?"

Vic was nearly trembling with rage. "You're asking me if I trust Laura Owen when I have just discovered that your friend Brent Wexler stole God knows how much money and operated a secret campaign account that no one ever told me about? What did you two take me for, a complete fool?"

"Now I never knew about this business," Carver insisted, rising from his chair and approaching Vic.

Vic waited until they were facing one another, then said, "Never knew about the account or that he was stealing from it?"

"I never knew exactly how he handled things and I certainly

didn't know he was keeping the money for himself. Should I talk to her about this?" Carver asked, plaintively.

"No, she'd rather not. I'll handle it," said Vic, turning toward his office, the disgust clear on his face.

"I'm sorry," Carver said, reaching out for him. "I guess I should have asked Brent more questions but I knew I wouldn't like the answers, so I just kept my mouth shut."

Vic spun back. "Apologies are nice, but this puts me in a helluva spot. I've got to think about this one."

"We've got a campaign to run. You can't go South on me now."

Vic kept walking toward his door. Carver called out, "She's a decent sort, like you always said."

"You bet she is and you should tell her that someday," Vic replied. "Maybe not too soon, but someday."

As he pulled his door open, he turned back, "Give me some time, Gibbs. I won't leave you in suspense for long." He saw how shocked the Governor was, exactly the intended effect. He doubted Carver had ever considered the possibility that he would quit. Vic closed the door without another word.

■ ■ ■ ■

"Happy Birthday to you, you belong in the zoo," several investigators sang, their voices off-key and out of sync as they approached Trey with an open box of donuts, a thick emergency candle stuck down through the centers of a stack of two. Trey barely smiled, uncomfortable with the attention.

Robert came up behind them and peered over at their offering. "You guys went all out."

Trey tried to hand the box to Nima. "You make a wish," Trey said.

"No, no. Bad luck if you don't do it," Nima said, pushing it back to him.

Trey reluctantly puffed out the candle.

The ceremony over, it was Robert's turn. "How about lunch today, Turner? On me."

Trey started to protest but Robert's gaze ended it. "Sure. Thanks."

"Meet me at my car at 11:30."

"Okay, Colonel."

■ ■ ■ ■

Out at the Training Academy, away from headquarters, Carl Rankin and two other members of the State Patrol tactical team were testing the encrypted portable radios with Eddie Williams when Blake arrived with maps of the hunting camp and Trey's property. The doors to Peregrine, the State Patrol's special operations van, were open wide. Eddie was inside testing reception. Unlike most details of this sort where troopers were pumped up to get a bad guy, this small assembly was somber.

"I hate that we're doing this," Blake said, handing out the maps.

The three nodded, clearly uneasy, glancing at each other, but avoiding Blake. Rankin finally spoke. "Better us taking him than the FBI or someone else, I figure."

"This is reconnaissance," Blake said, looking each one in the eye, "not a take-down unless something happens."

They all nodded again.

"Turner lives here," Blake said pointing to a square on the map he'd drawn. "There's a locked gate here and another one on the other end of this road. It's the Red Crown Road and it's private. From the map I saw at the sign-in here, I'm assuming it's passable because it's a good road on either end. If I had to bet, Trey's put a gate here," he pointed to the boundary of Trey's land.

"I walked part of it yesterday but I didn't get to the gate from this direction and I didn't have time to explore much from the other," Blake continued. "The land around the house is his and as long as we stay on it, there shouldn't be any chance of other hunters coming through. I understand he's got the boundary clearly marked and in some places, mostly on the eastern side, it's fenced. That's what Mrs. Wexler heard he was doing on the weekends."

"And what are we supposed to do?" Rankin asked.

"Robert's carrying him to lunch and he's going to give him the afternoon off. We don't know that he's going to go home afterward, but we think he will. Kramer and I will be tailing him from the time he leaves headquarters, following the bird-dog on his car. I want you on the ground, ready to watch him when he gets there. Just watch him. There's plenty of cover.

"I think one person should be here," Blake said, indicating a spot on the map, "another here, and the last one here. Eddie's going to stay in the van on the radio, parked somewhere down the road, in range, but probably past the east boundary with Oak Den, the adjoining piece of property.

"When he's getting close, I'll signal you. I'll be coming in from the hunt club side on foot."

■ ■ ■ ■

Brent walked quietly toward Trey's house not knowing who he'd find there. When he reached the edge of the clearing, he stopped, obscured by the blackberry canes, and watched. There was no sign of activity.

He slipped onto the back porch, gently closing the screen door at the top of the steps, and listening. The only noise was intermittent squawks from Trey's scanner somewhere in the back of the house, probably the kitchen. The shades in what had always been Trey's room were drawn. He felt under the front-room air conditioner for the spare key, opened the door, and replaced the key before stepping inside.

Not much had changed. Trey had installed a hasp on his bedroom door and secured it with another of the beaten up com-bination locks from the farm. Brent unlocked it and entered. The extra bed had been moved out. What had been Trey's din-ing table at the farm was in front of one of the two windows that opened onto the porch, set up as a desk and work area. He'd moved the industrial shelving from the Saragossa barn and placed it against the other wall with all his electronic equipment, a television, and VCR. Everything was neatly and efficiently arranged. His considerable collection of video tapes was stacked on the bottom shelf.

The rest of the place was the bunkhouse it had always been except for the addition of a few pieces of furniture from Trey's Saragossa house here and there. A new set of antlers was mounted in the dining room. Brent brewed himself a cup of strong coffee and sat at the kitchen table trying to decide whether he should alert Trey that he was back. He doubted Trey would have left the scanner on if he'd been going out of town. He picked up the phone and dialed Jackson.

"Investigations," a deep voice answered.

"Trey Turner, please."

"He left for lunch a while back and I think he's got the afternoon off," the man said. "Can I take a message?"

"No, I'll try later."

■ ■ ■ ■

Brent's burnt-up Mercedes was on the slide-back wrecker, parked outside the shop as Trey came down the front steps. He stared at it while he opened the front door to Robert's car, his concentration momentarily broken by the noisy chatter of Nima and the other analysts coming out behind him.

Nima pulled open Robert's back door. "Can three of us go with you?"

"I'm not paying for all of y'all, now," Robert said.

"All we want is a ride, Robert, don't get all hot and bothered," Nima chided.

"Turner, let's go," Robert called out.

Trey ducked his head in the car, a distant, disturbed look still on his face.

"You okay?" Robert asked.

"Yeah, sure," Trey said, distracted.

■ ■ ■ ■

"May I join you?" Jimmie asked Robert when he arrived at the

Sizzler.

"Of course, Anderson. We're celebrating Turner's birth-day."

"Congratulations. I won't ask how old you are."

"Let's leave it at too old," Trey said. "And for the record, I'm not celebrating. The Colonel and everyone else is, not me."

"I was thinking about you this morning, actually," Jimmie said.

Trey looked up from cutting his T-bone steak. "Hope it was good."

"I'm going to use Wexler's Mercedes as part of the accident reconstruction course we're doing at the academy for sheriffs and police departments. I had it hauled in this morning."

Trey looked long and hard at Jimmie. "I saw that car on the wrecker but I didn't recognize it."

"Who would? Did you ever see it after the accident?"

Trey shook his head, keeping his eyes down.

"I did the measurements the other day. Wexler was doing nearly fifty when he hit that tree," Jimmie said.

"Is it still going to be at the shop when we get through?"

"Probably. Want to have a look?"

"Sure."

■ ■ ■ ■

In the gun case in the hall, Brent's Smith & Wesson .357 was still in its place on the rack. He loaded it with hollow point bullets from the boxes of ammunition in the bottom. He looked through the knives on the top shelf and picked out one of his own, sharpened it on a whetstone, and put it in a sheath that he attached to his belt. Then he took a crossbow down from the wall and placed it on the floor with an arrow pointing toward Trey's room.

In the dining room, he pulled down the rack of antlers, fairly certain it was the buck he and Trey had killed in the ravine, and left it on Trey's bed. Then he locked all the doors and left the house as quickly and quietly as he had come.

Trey would know he was out there.

■ ■ ■ ■

Eddie Williams drove Peregrine past Trey's Second Creek driveway and pulled over. The back doors opened and the three troopers slipped out and disappeared into the woods. He drove to the Oak Den boundary road, pulled in around a curve and climbed in the back of the van. When the equipment warmed up, he tested it with each trooper, making notes on their positions.

■ ■ ■ ■

Kramer and Blake had trouble keeping up with Trey without being obvious. After he'd inspected Brent's wreck, he roared out of headquarters and turned north not south, disappearing in the Lakeland Boulevard traffic.

Blake sat in the passenger seat in camouflage clothes with the bird-dog monitor on his lap. "Nice to have someone else to operate that thing," said Kramer. "As fast as he's going I would have had a hard time handling it myself and staying on the road."

"Looks like he's going to Mrs. Wexler's," said Blake, picking up his cellular phone and dialing Grace's.

"St. Clair."

"Coleman here. Keep a lookout for Turner's maroon Bonneville. I think he's headed your way."

"Will do."

"What cars are in the driveway?"

"The Volvo. Mine and Everett's are in the garage."

"Is the garage door closed?"

"Supposed to be."

"Check for me," Blake said, watching the blip on the screen. It was heading right for the house.

Julia raced through the kitchen to the back door only to find it open to view from the street. She jammed the automatic door opener switch and the door was rattling down as Trey's red Bonneville passed by.

"Damn, we must have left it up when we took out the trash," she said. "It was closing as he passed by."

"He's turned around and he's coming back. Where's Everett?"

"Right here."

"Mrs. Wexler?"

"Upstairs."

"Send him upstairs, too," Blake ordered. "Turner's slowed down."

"Hold on," Julia said. "Everett?" she called out, as she moved to a window in the dining room. "Get upstairs with Grace."

From the first window, Julia could see the hood of Trey's car, but not him. She moved cautiously into view at the second window. Though she wasn't certain, it looked as though he had binoculars trained on the house.

"Everett!" she yelled again.

Everett appeared at the door.

"Get upstairs as quickly as possible. And stay away from the windows."

He started to move into the dining room.

"No," she shouted. "Go through the hall." Julia looked back at Trey's car. He did have binoculars, she was certain of it.

Then suddenly, he shot forward, and passed the house.

Julia raced back to the phone. "I think he's leaving the neighborhood."

"We're just a block away," Blake said. "And here he comes."

"Glad to hear that," Julia answered, relieved.

"Keep this line open, Julia."

"You bet."

■ ■ ■ ■

The smell of cool cypress rushed up to Trey as he unlocked the front door. It took the usual two second for his eyes to adjust to the dimmer light of the long dark hallway, and he'd stepped on the end of a crossbow before he'd seen it. Trey drew out the compact 9mm semi-automatic Glock from his shoulder holster, and moved quickly down the hallway.

His room was locked. He dialed in the combination, swung the hasp free, and cautiously pushed the door open. It was undisturbed except for the antlers sitting in the middle of his bed. Trey checked all the other rooms as he passed them, and opened the tall gun case near the front door.

Brent's revolver and a knife were missing. He was certain they'd been there when he opened the case last.

He looked back at the crossbow, so carefully aimed at his room.

No one else but Brent had the combination to those locks.

Brent was back. Waiting in the ravine.

■ ■ ■ ■

Once Trey was in his house, Blake and Kramer drove along the western boundary of the hunt club and turned onto the Red Crown Road. At the top of the hill, a navy blue pickup truck came through the gate.

"Go on up," Blake said. "I want to talk to this guy."

By the time they reached him, the man had already locked the hunt club gate and was getting back in his truck. Blake jumped out. "Just a minute, please."

The man looked up at Blake in his camouflaged clothing. "This is a private club. Sorry."

"I'm not here to hunt. Lookin' for Red Crown Road. I was told a house on it was for rent."

"This is Red Crown Road, but the only house is on the other end. You can't drive through. Private land."

"Does it go all the way?"

"It does, but there's another gate about two thirds of the way back. Even so, it's shorter and easier to go around on the county road. This here's hardly a straight shot." The man pointed back down the gravel road. "Go down there, turn left, then your first left again, and go about three miles. It'll be on your left. But I don't believe the house is for rent."

"Does Trey Turner live there?"

"Sure does."

"Then that's the house. Told me he had a room."

"Oh, now a room might be different. I thought you said a house."

"My mistake. Turner said he was looking for someone who could help out with a hunting club."

"That'd be Trey. He runs our club."

"You've been hunting today?"

"Only turkeys are in season, but I don't hunt much anyway—I take photographs. It was just too pretty to stay in my office this afternoon."

"This is a big place, isn't it?"

"Nearly three thousand acres. Well, twenty-seven hundred now. Plenty of room enough for everyone to have a separate favorite spot."

"Well, let me get on. Thanks for the directions."

"What'd you say your name was?"

"Bill Johnson," Blake answered without hesitation. "And you?"

"Bennett Gilliam."

"Are you the head of the club?"

"No, that's my father. How'd you know that?"

"Trey said some nice things about your father. Told me he was a good guy to work with."

"'Preciate that," Gilliam responded, moving toward his truck.

■ ■ ■ ■

Trey changed into camouflage pants, a bullet-proof vest, hunting jacket, and deerskin moccasins. He locked up the room and the house and slipped out the back door with his knife and gun, heading for the ravine, alert and wary. For several yards, he watched the path carefully, then concentrated on the land to the southwest of the Red Crown Road.

■ ■ ■ ■

Blake hustled back to Kramer. "It goes through he said, but it's a long, twisted road."

"Whatcha wanna do?"

"Let's look like we're leaving and going around by the county road. Then we'll come back in."

The portable crackled and Rankin's hushed voice came on. "B-87 to Peregrine."

"Peregrine," Eddie answered.

"Turner left his house, walking in on Red Crown Road," Rankin whispered. "I'm following him."

"This is A-1," Blake said. "Be careful. We're going to come on in from the other direction."

"10-4," Rankin said.

"Can you pick a padlock?" Blake asked Kramer.

"No problem," Kramer replied, reaching over behind the seat for a pair of bolt cutters. He snapped them a couple of times. "Piece of cake."

At the sign-in board, Blake checked to make certain no one else was in the area around Trey's property. Gilliam was the only one who'd checked in all day and he's been in King's Bottom, an area in the opposite direction from Trey's three hundred acres.

"B-87, A-1," Rankin said.

"Go ahead."

"I lost him."

"Where do you think he went?"

"South from the road, I think."

"Have any estimate of how far in your are?"

"Maybe half a mile."

"Okay. Take cover and keep a lookout," Blake commanded.

"10-4."

■ ■ ■ ■

Brent watched from his perch in a huge magnolia as Trey approached the ravine. He didn't head south down the path and enter the narrow pass but stayed on the rim, periodically moving stealthily to the edge to peer down.

So much for a warm welcome home.

When Trey was twenty-five yards away, Brent eased himself out of the magnolia and followed.

■ ■ ■ ■

They reached Trey's low-slung gate.

"Should I use the bolt cutters again?" Kramer asked.

"I'm not sure. We don't know where he is." Blake pulled out the map he'd sketched. Trey's land was diamond shaped in the northwest corner of the tract, and Red Crown Road was diagonal, splitting Trey's section in half. "From what Rankin said, he's in this area. I think the car would make too much noise. Let's go a ways on foot. It can't be much more than three miles to Trey's house as the crow flies."

"The crow hasn't been laying out the road, so far."

After the curve to the left came a curve to the right, and there, blocking the lane, was a white Ford Taurus with Georgia tags, splattered with dry mud.

"What have we here?"

All the doors were locked, but there was a newspaper on the passenger front seat and sticking out from underneath it was a map with Hertz logos. Blake inspected the front windshield. There was a current Georgia inspection sticker and a Hartsfield International Airport decal.

"A-1, Peregrine," Blake whispered into the radio.

"Go ahead."

"Check out a Hertz rental car, Georgia tag, David-Charles-Boy-7-2-3, DeKalb County, white Ford Taurus."

"10-4."

"I'm going back for my lock picks," said Kramer, turning to leave.

"And I'm headed in the rest of the way."

■ ■ ■ ■

Where should I look next? Trey wondered. He's out here somewhere.

Moving slowly, Trey absorbed everything he could about his surroundings. How had he missed Brent?

A twig broke behind him. Trey didn't turn around or slow down.

Brent's been here, all along, hiding somewhere, waiting. And now he's behind me.

Goddamn! That bastard's here to kill me. I saved his ass, but now I know too much. I did too good a job, I'm the only person who could destroy him.

Well, two can play that game.

Trey picked up his pace to get out of sight.

■ ■ ■ ■

Spring, deep in the woods, was more beautiful than anything he'd seen in years. Nothing Sally had ever planted in their yard could compare.

The terrain had leveled off. Up ahead Blake could see that it sloped slightly downhill. He started in at a slow jog, looking for the rhythm that long ago had taken him mile after mile on the track at the academy or through the roads of his neighborhood. But after seventy or eighty yards, he slowed to a walk, winded. It was another fifty yards before he could start up again, slower than before.

Damn, time is critical.

Blake pushed himself as far as he could, counting his paces, adding two more every time he started a running sequence.

■ ■ ■ ■

Brent passed an old beech tree on his left, its big groups of new leaves shooting out from the tips of every branch. He'd temporarily lost sight of Trey.

He must be moving very quickly, Brent thought.

He took a few more steps and stopped.

Trey had heard that twig. He knows I'm following him.

Brent spun around, retraced his steps, and darted toward the south opening of the ravine, his heart pounding so fast he could barely hear anything else.

Whoever said man makes the best quarry in a hunt was sure as hell right.

■ ■ ■ ■

Blake was relishing the fine feeling the forest gave him, when his radio crackled again.

"A-1, I can see you," Rankin whispered into his radio. "I'm on the left at the big oak tree."

Blake looked carefully in the foliage and finally spotted Rankin sitting with his back against the base of a wide post oak. If he hadn't known Rankin was there, he would have passed right by him.

"That's more exercise than I've had in years," Blake whispered as he sat down next to Rankin.

"I'm sorry I lost him," Rankin apologized. "He moved very fast and very quietly. I haven't seen or heard anything except animals since then."

■ ■ ■ ■

Trey had circled around to watch for Brent coming along his trail. But he didn't appear.

Where had he stopped? He moved down the hill and climbed the beech tree, scanning wildly in all directions.

■ ■ ■ ■

Blake and Carl Rankin sat in silence a while, Blake greatly

relieved to get a rest.

"Whose car do you think that was?" Rankin asked.

"No idea."

"What's your plan?"

"By rights," Blake said, "we have no business being here. So I guess we sit tight, and if he comes out, watch him."

"For how long?"

"As long as it takes."

"You sure he's the one?"

"If instinct is the best lead, yes, 'cuz I don't have shit otherwise."

■ ■ ■ ■

Trey wouldn't go to the west rim again, Brent thought. He knows I know he did that. If he stays out of the ravine, he'll be on the other rim.

Certain Trey couldn't be ahead of him, Brent hugged the wall of the ravine until he reached the cane thicket. There he could take cover, but still see anyone coming toward him from either end. Now he had an unobstructed view of the western rim. Only a portion of the eastern rim immediately behind him was obscured. His cover gave him a few moments to think, but he pulled out his gun, just in case.

■ ■ ■ ■

"B-14, A-1," Kramer called over the radio.

"Go ahead," Blake answered.

"I'm in the car. It's rented by some guy named Bob Wheeler. There's a US passport, says he's from Atlanta, and a half-used round trip ticket from Geneva to Atlanta and back. I don't have my photo of Wexler with me but it could be him. Shaved head, no eyebrows, thick glasses. Date of birth 8-22-42. A checkbook with a New York City P.O. address, and a Swiss checkbook with a Swiss address. Nothing else."

"B-Boy, A-1," Robert called.

"When did you get here?"

"Just a few minutes ago," Robert said. "I'm at the house. That birth date is the same year Wexler was born. And Bob Wheeler's initials are BW just like Brent Wexler."

"Yup," Blake said. "Is the warrant for Wexler ready yet?"

"The paperwork's done but we've been holding it."

"Then add both aliases and get it out here as fast as possible. I think the time has come."

"I'll call Jackson," Robert responded. "We'll need a fingerprint check on the car."

"I'll stay here and nose around some more," Kramer added.

"Good," said Blake.

"A-2, A-1," Jimmie Anderson said. "I'm in my car. There are three plus me working the roads in case anyone comes out."

■ ■ ■ ■

Trey slithered out to the edge of the ravine and pushed a clod of dirt down, watching for movement. Brent's bald head swiveled at the noise. Stupid bastard, Trey thought. I taught you better than that.

Brent had raised himself to a crouch when Trey leaped into the ravine and landed in front of him with a grunt. Brent fell back, letting his gun slip to his side.

"Almost didn't recognize your bald head."

Brent started to get up, but Trey showed no sign of welcoming him. "I had to come back, just like you said. I've missed this place, I've missed you." His voice was the same old Brent, easy and friendly, but with a touch of tension.

"You never should have left," Trey responded, his voice dry and bland. He unzipped his pockets and stuffed his hands inside. "Wish I'd known you were coming, I'd have brought some more food home for supper."

"We could hunt. There's plenty to eat here."

"Lost my taste for it," Trey said.

"I don't believe that for a second," Brent said. Trey watched as Brent began moving his hand, millimeter by millimeter, toward his gun. "Why'd you kill Morgan?"

"They didn't stop auditing like he told you they would, and I couldn't run the risk of having him talk and exposing you."

"But what about Grace?" Brent asked.

"What do you mean?"

"The burglary. I saw the news story."

"You were here?"

"No."

"It wasn't me."

"Then why are there two troopers at her house?"

"One trooper and an accountant, actually. I just found out today that he was over there. He's the one who was investigating Morgan."

"And now he's at Grace's? They must have figured it out."

Trey didn't comment. "How'd you get here?"

"Drove. Came in the Red Crown Road from the south. Parked just inside your gate."

"Then let's get out of here. No one followed me home, but if they're on to you, I doubt we have much time."

"On to me? I'm not the one who's been killing people. We don't have any time at all, Trey, it's over. We might as well go hunting."

"You may want to hunt, but I wanna get the hell out of here."

Neither said anything for a moment. Brent nearly had the gun in his hand but Trey knew he'd need time to aim and fire.

"Come on, Brent. Let's go," Trey urged. He turned away, then swung back. Brent was taking aim when Trey fired through his jacket pocket.

■ ■ ■ ■

A shot rang out, echoing through the woods so loud it must have come from a large caliber weapon. As both Blake and Rankin looked toward the forest in front of them, they heard a second shot, equally loud, from nearly the same direction. How far exactly was hard to judge in the woods.

They stood up and stepped into the road, listening for something more. There was nothing.

"Peregrine, A-1," Eddie called for Blake.

"Did you hear that?" Blake asked.

"A little to the southeast."

"It was directly in front of us, deep in the woods. We're facing southwest, I think."

"B-14, A-1. I heard it too," Kramer whispered.

"Where was it?" Blake asked.

"Directly west of me, if I'm not turned around."

"B-Boy, you there?"

"Go ahead," Robert answered.

"Time to go in," said Blake. "Round up the men we have on standby."

■ ■ ■ ■

Trey dragged his bloody leg toward Brent's unmoving body and searched the right pocket of Brent's pants for the keys. Then he shoved Brent's body over and took his wallet.

He pulled off Brent's jacket, and using his knife, ripped off the sleeves, tying them together to bandage his leg. Every movement was so exhausting that by the time he'd tightened the cloth around his upper thigh, he had to lie back to gather strength.

Steeling himself, he rose with excruciating pain and headed east to Brent's car.

# NINETEEN

When the Nicholson County sheriff pulled in, Robert stepped out of Peregrine to greet him.

"Sheriff, I was about to call you," Robert said politely as he approached Olier "Slick" Worn's door.

"What do you mean having the county covered up with troopers and no one lets me know?" the sheriff bellowed as he stood up to his full 6'4" height. His huge gut made him seem larger than life to most citizens. Slick Worn had been sheriff for twenty-five years, and as long as he could walk and talk, he'd remain the sheriff. And he never let the State Patrol forget who was the boss in his county.

"You wouldn't have wanted anything to do with it, Slick, so I didn't bother you."

"What's so damn important?"

"We heard shots from the woods. Trey Turner and a man who's been missing for a couple of months are in there."

"You got awful damn good ears to hear that way up in Jackson."

"No, we were on the road coming out here when it happened."

"Convenient. What else haven't you told me?"

"Nothing. It's Patrol business, Slick, let us handle it."

"You're in my county. It's my business, too," said Slick, stabbing his huge finger in the air to punctuate his point.

Jimmie Anderson pulled up behind them and Robert motioned for him. He got out quickly. No one could call Slick progressive—he'd hired a couple of black deputies, but only out of political necessity, so having to deal with Robert on an equal footing probably rankled him considerably. Robert hoped Jimmie's fortuitous presence could lighten up the situation.

"Hey, Slick, how's it been going?" Jimmie called out.

Slick turned. Jimmie, hustling, was a step away from the sheriff. "Must be one helluva problem to have all the brass here. Is Coleman around, too?"

Robert jerked his thumb back at the woods, nodding, as four patrol cars pulled in and parked on the grass. Six troopers piled out and headed their way.

"You about to search for them?" Slick asked.

"Soon as we get everyone here," Robert replied.

A smirk covered Slick's broad jowls. "Would you like someone who knows the terrain to come along?"

"The warrant's on the way, but we don't have it yet. This is just a walk in the woods, maybe a rescue mission."

Slick paused a moment. "Been on a few of those. I'm game."

"Glad to have you along," Robert said. "Just wanted you to know the score."

"Been hunting these woods since I was a kid."

"Sure could use your knowledge."

"Where are you lookin'?"

"Southwest from Red Crown Road," Robert said.

"There's a ravine down there in the bottom," Slick warned. "You gotta be careful 'cuz it drops off kinda sudden-like."

"We'll let you lead."

"Need more men?" asked Slick asked Robert.

"Got any?" asked Robert, relieved that Slick had calmed

down. Involving him in the plans had been the charm.

"Four or five."

"We'll take 'em all if you can spare 'em."

"Well, hell, what're y'all waiting for?"

■ ■ ■ ■

Robert and Slick gathered the twenty men together. "We're gonna load up, four to a car and drive part way in. There's one unit already in there at the spot where Coleman wants us to start. We'll form a line heading southwest. We're looking for two men and both could be armed. One is Master Sergeant Trey Turner, who most of you know, a criminal investigator and a damn good woodsman from what I hear. He's in camouflage clothing. The other is Brent Wexler, we believe, a tall guy, bald. We don't know what he's wearing." Robert turned, motioning to the sheriff, with the bullhorn he was holding. "The sheriff here knows the territory pretty well. Slick, tell us about the terrain, will you?"

Slick stepped forward, a serious look settling across his huge face. "There's a ravine straight ahead, fairly far in, and it's deep. It runs on an angle to the road, so the people farthest in will hit the edge first. It's getting dark quickly so watch yourselves."

Robert moved to the center again. "If you've got your low-band portable, W-William will be talking from the helicopter, letting us know what he can see on the infrared in front of the line. Coleman will be on the farthest south, Slick will be in the center, and I'll be on the north."

■ ■ ■ ■

Trey was twenty yards from Brent's car when he heard the bullhorn. He knelt down close to the tree, the pain in his leg searing though his body as he crouched.

"Trey Turner, this is Robert Stone. I've got twenty men here, heading in to find you. Give us some signal where you are."

Someone got out of Brent's rental car but he couldn't see the man's face clearly enough. When Robert stopped talking, a gun discharged behind him.

Trey looked back toward the ravine.

■ ■ ■ ■

Kramer keyed his mike. "A-1, B-14."

"Go ahead," Blake answered.

"I'm still at the car but unless you tell me different, I'll head in from here."

"Got a flashlight?"

"Yes."

Robert called out again over the bullhorn. "Turner, we heard you. I assume you're hurt. Fire one more round."

There was no response.

"A-2 here," Jimmie Anderson radioed. "I'm going to head in the Red Crown Road from the south."

"Good idea," said Blake.

■ ■ ■ ■

The pilot radioed that he'd seen a single motionless hot spot about a hundred yards ahead of them. Moments later, the men at the northernmost end of the search line hit the edge of the ravine, almost tumbling headlong into it.

"Keep going along the edge," Slick hollered. "It'll slope down. There's an entrance that can't be far."

Robert halted everyone else where they were on the rim until Slick could lead the group around and down into the bottom.

"Here's the bald guy," a deputy shouted. "He's alive but barely. Get a gurney."

Blake watched the chopper sweep by him. "A-1, W-William," Blake said to the pilot.

"Go ahead, Colonel."

"This one is Wexler, I think," Blake said. "Turner's still out there."

"Peregrine, A-1," Eddie called. "The Med Center helicopter is on the way out here."

"10-4."

"Coleman," Slick yelled. "I think the other guy must be bleeding pretty bad."

"Can you follow the trail?"

"Not in the dark. We need the dogs."

■ ■ ■ ■

Trey had struggled up and braced himself against a huge red oak. He could hear the man coming toward him. If he had to kill him, it had to be quietly. No shots.

He pulled his knife from its sheath, dropping his hand to his side so the blade wouldn't catch any light.

The helicopter was heading west toward the main road, directly away from his location.

"Turner," Robert called out again over the bullhorn. "We've found Wexler and we know you've been wounded. Give us a signal if you can."

The man's flashlight played on the ground directly beside him. Trey took a deep breath, carefully raising his knife, ready. He recognized Kramer when he passed by, moving fairly quickly and making enough noise that he didn't notice Trey.

Trey exhaled. His entire leg was soaked with blood, but the car was so close that he pushed off from the tree and moved as quickly as he could. The knife was still in his hand as he half dragged his leg the final twenty feet. Barely conscious, he stepped on a dead branch, and the crack was loud enough to make Kramer turn around.

Kramer's flashlight was a target. Trey dropped the knife, jammed his hand in his pocket, and squeezed the trigger of his gun.

■ ■ ■ ■

"W-William," Blake radioed the helicopter pilot when he heard the gunshot. "Turn back east. Turner just responded to Robert's call with a signal shot."

■ ■ ■ ■

Trey made it to the car. "Jesus," he groaned, as he hauled his leg in. He barely had the strength to crank the engine. He put the car in reverse and backed toward the gate as fast as he could.

■ ■ ■ ■

Kramer's car was still at the gate and Jimmie Anderson pulled up behind it. The helicopter was roaring overhead, its searchlights beaming directly down.

"A-1, W-William. We've got a hot spot right below us."

Jimmie keyed his mike. "This is A-2. I'm right near there. It's only thirty yards from the gate. Bring the ambulance in this direction."

Jimmie hopped the fence just as the rental car barreled around the corner, swerving in a high-speed reverse. He leaped to the side, tumbling out of the way. Jimmie's hand was on his holster before he stopped rolling.

The car rammed into the gate, and the driver hit his head on the windshield when he was thrown forward at the impact.

Jimmie stayed low to the ground, trying to see the driver.

As the helicopter searchlight scanned the area where Jimmie lay in wait, there was enough light to identify Turner. Then the searchlight beam caught his gun.

Trey fired almost immediately through the right passenger window, shattering the glass, and kicking up dirt inches from Jimmie.

Jimmie fired back, aiming for the only target he had, Trey's face.

■ ■ ■ ■

The Medical Center's helicopter landed moments after Brent's gurney reached the house.

"Can you wait for the other men?" Blake asked the pilot.

"I can only take two," said the pilot, deferring to the trauma care technician who'd flown down with him.

"This guy may not make it if we wait any longer," the medic said.

"Then let's go on," Blake said. "The Patrol chopper can get the other two."

They lifted Brent's gurney into the chopper, locking it into place.

"Can I go along?" Blake asked the pilot.

"Sure," said the pilot. "Climb in."

Blake signaled to Robert that he was going. After the helicopter lifted off, he keyed his mike. "B-boy. Make sure they get all the details on Turner's wounds."

Blake hung near Wexler all the way, hoping the IV fluids would revive him enough to mumble something. But Brent hardly moved, his pulse steadily weakening. Blake stayed with him on the race through the corridors as medical personnel gathered around and began their work. He turned back only because the operating room doors were shut in his face.

The Medical Center chopper had barely cleared the hospital pad when the Patrol helicopter landed with Trey, Kramer, and Robert. Kramer wasn't in grave danger, although the shot had punctured his lung and he'd lost a fair amount of blood. Trey's vital signs were at best unsteady.

Two separate trauma teams were waiting at the door for them. Robert stayed with Trey to talk to the surgeon. Jimmie had made a mess of Trey's face but missed his brain. The surgeon shook his head. "I don't know if we can save him, but we'll try our best," he said to Robert.

"Make sure we know the angle of the entrance wound on the leg, please," Robert asked.

"He may lose the leg entirely or even die, and you're worried about the angle?"

"There's more at stake here than just the leg, I assure you," Robert replied.

# TWENTY

Vic was still at his office in the Capitol when Laura called.

"Wexler's dead. This time for sure. He and Trey Turner shot each other. Turner wounded another trooper and almost got a third."

"Will they make it?

"The trooper is doing fine, but Turner's barely hanging on. He's headed for surgery. I'll call when I know more."

"Please."

"I trust you'll let the Governor know?" Laura said.

"Right away," Vic answered. " Has Grace heard the news?"

"Robert Stone is talking to her now."

■ ■ ■ ■

Grace, Everett, and Julia, too tired to go through any more financial records, were sitting tight, as ordered, watching an old James Bond movie, the best of the videos dropped off by a trooper Julia had sweet-talked into making a run for her. Robert called Grace from outside the pathology suite where the

Medical Examiner was doing Brent's autopsy. Grace heard his brief description of what had happened in Second Creek and handed the phone to Julia.

She looked at Everett. "Trey and Brent shot each other. Brent's dead, and Trey's almost dead."

"I'm sorry Mrs. Wexler," Everett said.

"I'm just glad it's over."

Everett had learned an awful lot in the previous seventy hours about how Brent Wexler operated and just how loveless Grace's life had been. "This may sound pretty crass, but I think your life insurance worries are solved."

Grace brightened, "You're right."

"So can all this work stop?"

"Don't pack up yet," Julia said as she hung up. "Robert says they may need it for the murder charges against Trey if he lives. We'll talk about it tomorrow. But you two are out of danger."

"For now," Everett said quietly.

Grace smiled. "That's good enough for me."

■ ■ ■ ■

Doc Hershel looked up from Brent's lacerated corpse when Robert returned to the hospital pathology suite.

"This guy was shot by someone standing in front and slightly above him," Hershel said. "He was sitting on the ground, with his legs pulled up."

"You're sure?"

"Fairly certain." Hershel crouched down to demonstrate what the angles showed him. "The bullet glanced by the knee cap, then entered the chest."

"Did the surgeon send you the documentation on the entrance wound angle on the shooter?" Robert asked.

"Didn't need to. Gave me the whole leg. He...," said Hershel, pointing to Brent, "raised his gun no more than twelve inches off the ground and shot upward to get the leg the way he did. I'd say our dead man keeled over from where he was sitting but had enough strength to get off one final round."

"And not the other way around?"

"Theoretically, anything is possible. But if the dead guy shot first, he shot from the ground, then pulled his leg up in front of him while our one-legged man was still standing up tall and shot him back. Unlikely, but possible."

■ ■ ■ ■

Sarah Carver called. "Are you okay?"

"I'm fine," said Grace, sitting up straighter in her bed. "I'm just reading."

"You need some company?"

"No. I've got a pot of chamomile tea, a good book, and warm covers. This is all I need tonight."

"In bed already?"

"Yes. Julia and Everett left a little while ago."

"What's in store?"

"I've got to bury him again—sometime tomorrow."

"I'll come with you."

"Thanks, I'd appreciate it."

"How about I arrange for dinner and a video," Sarah suggested.

"Sounds great," Grace answered. "I'm not quite up to going out in public."

■ ■ ■ ■

Trey was hanging on, minus his left leg. He must have turned his face away from the shattering glass just as Jimmie fired because the bullet entered above the lower jaw, destroying the zygomatic arch and his sinuses. Trey could survive that wound, though the right side of his face wouldn't be much to look at without very expensive plastic surgery. But he'd lost so much blood from the leg wound, he was still in substantial danger. He didn't regain consciousness for hours, so Blake and Robert waited most of the night outside the intensive care ward. When Trey finally regained consciousness, an enormous nurse blocked their path as they started through the door to talk to him.

"Only one person can go in," she said.

"Ma'am, I need a witness," Blake said with matching determination. "I've got to read this man his rights."

She looked from one to the other. Robert flashed his most appeasing smile. "Then only one person does the talking."

"Fine," Blake answered and pushed inside the room.

Trey's head was wrapped in bandages and from the covers, it was obvious that one leg was missing. Robert stood next to Blake as he leaned over, rattling through the Miranda warnings flawlessly. Blake hadn't given them in years, but he knew them better than the alphabet.

"What happened out there?" Blake asked.

"Wexler ambushed me," Trey said. His voice had a strange nasal quality. "He shot first, I shot back in self-defense."

"Why?"

"I know too much."

"About what?"

"About him and Reed Morgan."

"You saying he killed Morgan?"

"Probably. He had a reason to. Wexler had been paying him off for years and the IRS was after Morgan."

"What do you know about Wexler's wreck?"

"Nothin'. Didn't have anything to do with it."

"Why'd you shoot your way out?"

Trey didn't answer.

The humorless nurse bustled back in. "That's enough for now."

Blake nodded, and looked back at the faceless body. "We'll get your statement later."

Trey didn't move. The nurse cleared her throat impatiently and Robert and Blake left.

"What a performer," Blake said, walking stiffly down the hospital corridor, tired but now angry. "We gotta get that sorry bastard."

"It's not going to be easy. I'll send Rankin back to New

Orleans in the morning," Robert said. "With a name and a better photo, he maybe can find someone who saw Wexler. Maybe he stayed at a motel somewhere."

"Let's hope the teller machine had a camera and the banks still have the film from those withdrawals. How's Kramer doing?"

"Fine, " Robert answered. "But feeling real stupid that he wasn't wearing his vest."

■ ■ ■ ■

"Good morning, ladies," Laura said to the two switchboard operators stationed in the lobby of headquarters.

"Good morning, Commissioner," one said, smiling broadly. The other, in the middle of handling a phone call, just nodded. Laura punched the elevator button and the door opened instantly.

"Have a good day, Commissioner," one called out as the door closed.

Six troopers got on at the second floor where the Jackson District had its troop offices, each one either nodding or mumbling, "Good morning." Every face turned quickly away from Laura as the big men squeezed in the elevator, trapping Laura in the front corner near the control panel.

"Five, please, ma'am."

"Do y'all have a meeting in the conference room or something?" Laura asked as the doors closed.

"Yes, ma'am," one officer said, nodding his head respectfully.

When the doors opened, the men pushed back to let her exit first. The fifth floor reception area was filled with troopers—a sea of blue and gray uniforms, broad smiles on every face, most of them holding up copies of the morning paper with the headline, "Troopers Get Pay Raise." The applause began immediately, stunning Laura. Her cheeks flushed with deep color as she looked from face to face. A lieutenant stepped forward, his hand up for silence and the applause halted.

"On behalf of all the troopers, we want to thank you for everything you've done, getting us this raise. We know it wasn't easy."

Laura struggled for words. "It wasn't my doing really, it was your efforts that saved the day." Every eye was on her, waiting for her to say more, but this sort of impromptu speaking wasn't her forté. "But I must say, this is one helluva way to start the day. Thank you," Laura said, feeling a little more comfortable. "Thank you very much."

Stepping up to the closest group of troopers, to shake their hands, she said, "Don't blow it all in one night."

■ ■ ■ ■

The meeting area in the back corner of the cavernous first floor of headquarters started filling up with reporters, cameramen, and equipment shortly after ten o'clock. In front of the two rows of folding chairs, Laura stood at a podium so loaded with microphones that there was nowhere to place her papers. While cameramen did color checks, Laura made idle chitchat with a young reporter in the front row whose daughter was in Will's first grade class.

The State Patrol Public Affairs Director paced at the back, waiting anxiously for WTBS, the one TV station that hadn't shown up. Their reporter was Tim Cropley, a young man who was particularly hostile toward Laura, and who would demand that the entire show be repeated if they started without him. When Cropley finally came hustling around the corner and took a seat, the Public Affairs Director signaled Laura to start.

Laura tapped on one of the microphones to get everyone's attention. "Good morning."

There was a murmur in reply, and everyone in the room settled down. The camera lights came on.

"Late yesterday evening, Master Sergeant Trey Turner of the Mississippi State Patrol was apprehended in connection with the death of Brent Wexler, who was shot on Turner's land near Second Creek. He was also wanted in connection with the assault on fellow officers Master Sergeant Kramer Jennings and Lieutenant Colonel Jimmie Anderson. Turner died an hour ago from his wounds. The evidence from the scene and the autopsy confirm that Turner and Wexler shot each other, but we believe Mr. Turner shot first."

"If you recall, it was thought that Mr. Wexler had died in a car wreck, which was discovered on March 6th of this year. No autopsy was performed at the time because several personal items identified the driver, and the location of the wreck was consistent with Mr. Wexler's announced plans. The identity of the body in that car is still undetermined, but we have reason to believe that tests will establish it was a homeless man from New Orleans."

"Do you know his name?"

"We're verifying it now, and until we do, we won't release it."

"Commissioner, why did Turner kill Wexler?" asked the young woman in the front row.

"We don't know and may never know his reasons, but we've established that Wexler paid Turner substantial sums over the last fifteen years."

"Why?" the reporter pushed.

"As I said, we don't know those details."

A question came from the left of the room. "How did you learn about the New Orleans man?"

"Six days ago the body from the car wreck was exhumed and autopsied. We determined that it was not Wexler. Our inquiries with missing persons bureaus in the area led us to one particular person. He's the only one so far who fits the description of the man who died, and he's been missing since shortly before the accident."

"Wasn't Wexler the Governor's chief fund-raiser?" asked Tim Cropley from WTBS.

"Yes."

"Does this involve the Governor?" Cropley continued.

"Not in any way," Laura replied. Seeing that Cropley wasn't satisfied, Laura changed the topic. "In the late Seventies, we believe Wexler and Morgan defrauded the state on highway construction contracts."

There was a hush throughout the room, then a burst of hands and questions.

"So Reed Morgan didn't commit suicide?" asked the young woman in the front.

"Once again, we don't have that answer at this time but there are still questions about his death. It appears..." Laura emphasized the last word, "that Wexler was out of the country when Morgan died."

"So Turner knew about Wexler and Morgan?" Cropley asked.

"Yes."

"And he blackmailed him?" Cropley continued.

"That's one theory."

"How much money did Turner extort?"

"Extortion may not be the right word, but it's safe to say Wexler paid Turner well into six figures."

"How much did Wexler and Morgan steal?"

"Because the records are incomplete or missing, we may never know exactly what happened, but it looks like many thousands of dollars extra were paid on several contracts."

Vic listened from the back of the room as the questions went on for thirty minutes, never focusing again on the Governor. He slipped out before any of the news people saw him and returned to the Mansion.

■ ■ ■ ■

Shortly after lunch, a delivery truck arrived at headquarters with an enormous arrangement of fresh spring flowers for Laura. The card read, "Masterful. I owe you, very big time."

■ ■ ■ ■

The sun wouldn't set for a couple of hours but since Will was going to his baseball game with his friend and teammate, Sam,

Laura decided she deserved a quiet cocktail hour. She took a beer from her office refrigerator and disappeared up the stairwell. At the top, she pulled back the heavy fire door, its hinges stiff from infrequent use, reminding herself once again to bring in some oil so it wouldn't squeal when she opened it.

In the darkness, she fumbled for the light switch which controlled the single bulb hanging in the middle of the mechanical room. In the glare, she made her way around the big machines to the other side where a crude cinder block step had been fashioned beneath the door to the roof, a jerry-rig Laura was certain OSHA wouldn't approve.

Sitting with her back against the warm bricks of the west wall, the low buildings of the Medical Center complex spread out before her on the land adjoining the department's property. It certainly wasn't Big Sky country, nor was it the rooftop of the Washington Hotel in D.C., but she had a nearly uninterrupted view of the western horizon. The best part was that no one else knew about it, or if they did, they didn't relish the view because no one had ever disturbed her up there.

■ ■ ■ ■

Robert and Blake were at the front door of headquarters when they saw Laura's car still parked in her spot. The rest of the lot was nearly empty. "Where could she be?" Robert asked.

Blake looked to the western sky, filled with billowy clouds. "Did you check the conference room?"

"I did," Robert answered.

"Then I've got one other idea. I usually wouldn't interrupt, but she deserves to hear some good news."

When the metal door onto the roof pushed open, Laura hid her beer until she saw who it was.

"How'd y'all find me?" she asked Blake and Robert.

"This pilot told me he'd seen you scooting around the corner one time when he was landing," Blake answered.

She toasted them with her beer can. "There's more in my

refrigerator. Hi- and lo-octane."

"Were you expecting company?"

"Best to be prepared."

"Well, I don't mind if I do," Blake said. "Can I bring you one, Robert?"

"Please. Lo-test."

Robert settled down next to her, his back against the wall. "Come here often?"

"Whenever I can but not nearly often enough. If you like this, you ought to see the sunrises."

"I catch quite a few but from a little closer to the ground," Robert said. "I usually start my run about daybreak."

A huge crane moved around the steel skeleton of the addition to the hospital. They were almost too tired to chat.

"Can I ask you a question?" asked Laura.

"Sure."

"How have you stood this for so long?"

"It was easier when I was just an investigator," Robert replied. "I took my orders, followed leads, wrote reports, got the bad guys. I didn't deal with the politics. That stuff can wear a guy out pretty quick."

Blake reappeared with the beers and took a seat on the other side of Laura. He raised his in a toast. "To all that ends well."

"Too bad we won't know what really happened."

"We know something for certain: Rankin found the hotel in New Orleans where Wexler stayed the night of the wreck. He didn't check in until midnight and ordered room service at one in the morning. He couldn't have set it up."

"But you can't prove Turner did, can you?"

"If we had the time, maybe," said Blake. "I'll be interested in what they find in Switzerland. How much money did Everett think Wexler had stolen?"

"A couple million, or so," Laura said.

Robert sighed. "The rich get richer."

"At least Mrs. Wexler's in the clear—she surely didn't deserve any of this."

"What about the IRS?" Blake asked.

"I talked to her accountant this afternoon," said Laura. "Taxes will take a big chunk out of the total, but there'll still be plenty left, at least by any normal person's standards."

Two jets crossed the sky leaving crisscrossing contrails. "I'm sorry I sort of sacrificed the Patrol this morning," she said.

"You didn't."

"Sure I did. I laid it all off on Turner and that might not be true."

"We don't have proof of anything else either," said Blake. "Turner's wagon was already loaded, we just piled a little more on."

Robert added, "It won't hurt the patrol. There's always a bad apple here or there. No big deal."

"Besides, the Governor's announcement that he qualified for the Senate race has taken the spot light off of us. Did you know that was going to happen?"

"Yes," Laura admitted. "I wish I could have said something but Vic told me in confidence several weeks ago."

"What if Carver wins?"

"Adios, mis amigos."

"Maybe not," Blake said. "The Lieutenant Governor likes the job you're doing."

"How do you know that?"

"I had to interview him, remember? He asked a lot of questions about you and said some real positive things."

"Really?"

"Scout's honor," Blake said.

Laura took another sip of beer. "That's nice to know. Maybe I'll sleep a little better."

"You know, speaking of sleeping better, Turner's lucky he died," Robert interjected. "Parchman Penitentiary would have been bad—rough on a one-legged former cop with half a face."

"My God, what a gruesome thought," Laura said, shaking her head in disgust.

"But the Governor ended up grateful," Blake raised his beer in another toast. "Saw the flowers."

She clicked his can with her own and swung to do the same

with Robert's. "Did you steam open the card?"

"We have our sources in the floral trade. They did come from the Mansion, didn't they?"

"They could have been from Vic," she said.

"Could have," Blake said. "But he's the man's man, so what's the difference?"

"There's a lot of difference," Laura said, softly.

Blake and Robert exchanged a quick glance over her head, their eyebrows raising in unison.

"How long do you think Carver's warm and fuzzy feelings about me will last?" Laura asked.

"I don't think he'll forget them any time soon," said Blake.

"I suspect tonight he's glad he's got such..." Robert paused to choose his word, "'competent' people in charge."

"Well, he'd better not forget," said Laura gruffly, "'cuz I'd hate to have to remind him."

She polished off her beer and got to her feet. "Well, gentlemen, I hate to drink and run but Will's got a ball game tonight."

Neither Blake nor Robert made a move to leave.

"Don't hesitate to help yourself to another."

"Thanks," they said in unison. Then Robert added, "We kind of like this spot."

"Just give me credit for finding it. And don't tell anyone else."

■ ■ ■ ■

Laura stood at the fence on the third base line, watching Will's game. It was a perfect night at the ball field. Cool enough that the mosquitos weren't a problem, but not chilly. And the sky was phenomenal. The billowy clouds had been transformed into orange and reddish puffs with a purply underside. She felt blessed to have had two knock-your-socks-off sunsets in one week.

Will's team had a terrific infield and some very good batters. As a result, the Bobcats often racked up the maximum six runs per inning and usually stopped the other team from getting on base. But tonight, it was a cliffhanger.

"What's the score?"

Laura spun around to see Vic surveying the play.

"Top of the sixth, nine to nine, two outs, two strikes, Will's playing third base."

The coach eased a ball across the plate and the batter drilled a grounder. Will moved to his left, formed a perfect alligator's mouth with his open right hand above his gloved left hand, fielded the ball, threw straight across to first base, and the runner was out by two steps. The parents went nuts.

"Nice toss," Vic called out as Will returned to his position. He gave him a thumb's up sign and Will smiled. "I certainly picked the right moment to arrive," Vic said to Laura.

"I'll say. Thanks for coming."

Another batter was up. He swung at the first pitch and sent a high soft one right for the short stop. The inning was over.

"This is our last at bat," Laura said. She pointed toward the darkening sky. "This early in the season, it's a race to get finished while they can still see to play."

The first batter went to first on a fly ball the third baseman dropped. Then Will stepped up to the plate.

"Go Will," Laura yelled. "He hates batting," she told Vic.

"Probably nerves more than anything."

Will hit the first pitch, a line drive past the second baseman. The runner was safe at second and Will was on first.

"That wasn't bad," Vic said, clapping. "Great hit," he called out.

"I know but he thinks he needs to knock it out of the park like his friend Sam."

"Maybe I can take him to the batting cages."

"He d like that," Laura said, her eyes were trained on the plate. "That's Sam up to bat now. They all call him Grand Slam Sam."

"And what about you?" Vic asked.

Out of the corner of her eye, Laura could tell Vic was looking at her, not the game.

"Would you like that?" he asked.

At that moment, Sam knocked the ball into the fence for an in-the-park homer. The kids went crazy, all the parents were screaming and clapping, and Will trotted home from first with the easy gait of a pro. He beamed at Vic and Laura as he passed.

She looked at Vic. He was watching her so earnestly, so expectantly, that she felt herself blush. "Yes. I'd like that."

ABOUT THE AUTHOR

Louisa Dixon was born in Stamford, Connecticut and is a summa cum laude graduate of Ohio State University and Creighton University School of Law. She has held two federal judicial clerkships, worked as Assistant Solicitor for the Department of Energy, and was the Commissioner of Public Safety for the State of Mississippi from 1988 to 1992—the first woman in the U.S. to head a state law enforcement agency. She now lives in Jackson, Mississippi with her husband and ten-year-old son where she is at work on her third novel.